Hector Berlioz, Eleanor Holmes, Rachel Holmes Scott Russell

Autobiography of Hector Berlioz

Vol. 1

Hector Berlioz, Eleanor Holmes, Rachel Holmes Scott Russell

Autobiography of Hector Berlioz
Vol. 1

ISBN/EAN: 9783337349059

Printed in Europe, USA, Canada, Australia, Japan

Cover: Foto ©Raphael Reischuk / pixelio.de

More available books at **www.hansebooks.com**

UTOBIOGRAPHY

OF

HECTOR BERLIOZ,

MEMBER OF THE INSTITUTE OF FRANCE,

FROM 1803 TO 1865.

COMPRISING

HIS TRAVELS IN ITALY, GERMANY, RUSSIA,
AND ENGLAND.

TRANSLATED BY

RACHEL (SCOTT RUSSELL) HOLMES,
AND
ELEANOR HOLMES.

IN TWO VOLUMES.

VOL. I.

LONDON:
MACMILLAN AND CO.
1884.

Life's but a walking shadow ; a poor player,
That struts and frets his hour upon the stage,
And then is heard no more : it is a tale
Told by an idiot, full of sound and fury,
Signifying nothing.

SHAKESPEARE (*Macbeth*).

AUTHOR'S PREFACE.

THE notices of my life which have from time to time appeared are so crowded with errors and inaccuracies as at length to suggest to me that I myself should record those portions of my agitated and laborious career which may be interesting to the lovers of art. Such a retrospective study will afford me the opportunity of giving my opinion on the difficulties which at present beset the career of a composer, and of tendering some useful advice to my brethren.

Portions of my travels have been already included in a book published many years ago, which also contained some fragments of criticism; but this is now out of print.[1]

I have been often urged to rearrange and complete these rough notes; and if at length I yield to the request it is not from any misconception of the value of such work. I have no belief that the public at large cares at all what I may do, or feel, or think. But a certain number of musical artists and amateurs have shown some curiosity on the subject, and it is certainly better to tell them the truth than to allow them to believe what is wrong. I have not the least wish either *to appear before God book in hand as the best of men,* or to

---

[1] " Voyage musical en Allemagne et en Italie. Etudes sur Beethoven, Gluck, et Weber. Mélanges et Nouvelles. Par Hector Berlioz. Paris: Jules Labitte, Libraire-Editeur, No. 3, Quai Voltaire. 1844." 2 vols. 8vo.

write " *Confessions.* " I shall say only what I choose to say; and if the reader refuses me his absolution he must be of a severely orthodox turn, as I have none but venial sins to confess.

But time presses, and I must conclude. Republicanism is at this moment passing like a vast roller over the face of the Continent. Musical art, which has been long dying, is now dead, and will soon be buried, or thrown on the dust-heap. For me France and Germany exist no longer. Russia is too remote, I can never go there again. England, since my first visit, has shown me much noble and cordial hospitality. But with the first shocks of that earthquake which has overturned so many European thrones, England became the centre for streams of terrified artists, arriving from all points of the compass, like frightened sea-birds before a storm. How long will the metropolis of Great Britain be able to maintain so many refugees? Will not their mournful accents be drowned by the acclamations of the neighbouring nations, as each sovereign people is crowned? Nay! how long will the English themselves resist the contagion? *Jam proximus ardet Ucalegon!* who knows what resort may be left to me before a few months are over? There is no longer any certain subsistence for myself and my family. Every minute is precious, and before long I may have to imitate the stoical resignation of the Indians of Niagara, who, finding their best efforts against the current useless, measure with steady glance the short distance which separates them from the edge, and disappear over the cataract into the abyss beneath, with a song in their mouths.

H. B.

London, *March 21st*, 1848.

CONTENTS.

CHAPTER VI.

CHAPTER VII.

CHAPTER VIII.

CHAPTER IX.

CHAPTER X.

CHAPTER XI.

CHAPTER XII.

CHAPTER XIII.

CHAPTER XIV.

CHAPTER XV.

CHAPTER XVI.

CHAPTER XVII.

CHAPTER XVIII.

CHAPTER XIX.

CHAPTER XX.

CHAPTER XXI.

CONTENTS.

CHAPTER XXII.

CHAPTER XXXI.

CHAPTER XXXII.

CHAPTER XXXIII.

CHAPTER XXXIV.

CHAPTER XXXV.

CHAPTER XXXVI.

CHAPTER XXXVII.

CHAPTER XXXVIII.

CHAPTER XXXIX.

CHAPTER XL.

CHAPTER XLI.

CHAPTER XLII.

CHAPTER XLIII.

CHAPTER XLIV.

CHAPTER XLV.

CHAPTER XLVI.

CHAPTER XLVII.

CHAPTER XLVIII.

CHAPTER XLIX.

CHAPTER L.

CONTENTS.

CHAPTER LI.

MEMOIRS OF HECTOR BERLIOZ.

CHAPTER I.

[LONDON, *March* 21*st*, 1848.]

I WAS born on the 11th of December, 1803, at La Côte St. André, a very small town in France, situated in the department of the Isère, between Vienne, Grenoble, and Lyons. During the months which preceded my birth, my mother never dreamt, as Virgil's did, that she was about to bring forth a branch of laurel. However painful to my *amour propre* this confession may be, I ought to add that neither did she imagine, like Olympias, the mother of Alexander, that she bore within her a fiery brand. Strange, I admit, but true. I came into the world quite naturally, unheralded by any of the sign which, in poetic ages, preceded the advent of remarkable personages.

La Côte St. André is built, as its name indicates, on the slope of a hill, overlooking a rich, golden, fertile plain, the silence of which has an unspeakable, dreamy majesty, intensified by the chain of mountains bounding it on the east and west. Behind these again rise, in the distance, the gigantic snow-capped peaks of the Alps.

I need scarcely state that I was brought up as a member of the Holy Catholic and Apostolic Church of Rome. Since she has ceased to inculcate the burning of heretics, her creeds are charming. I held them happily for seven years; and, though we quarrelled long ago, I still retain the tenderest recollections of that form of religious belief. Indeed, I feel such sympathy for it that had I had the misfortune to be born in the midst of one of those ponderous schisms evolved by Luther or Calvin, my first rush of poetical enthusiasm would have driven me straight into the arms of the beautiful Roman faith. I made my first communion on the same day as my eldest sister, and in the Convent of the Ursulines, where she was being brought up. It is probably owing to this curious circumstance that I retain so tender a recollection of that religious ceremony. The almoner came to fetch me at six o'clock, and I felt deeply stirred as we crossed the threshold of the church. It was a bright spring morning, the wind was murmuring softly in the poplars, and the air was full of a subtle fragrance. Kneeling in the midst of a multitude of white-robed maidens we awaited the solemn moment, and, when the priest advanced and began to intone the service, all our thoughts were fixed on God. I was rudely awakened by the priest summoning me to take precedence of all those fair young girls, and go up to the altar first. Blushing at this act of discourtesy, I went up to receive the sacrament. As I did so, the choir burst forth into the eucharistic hymn. At the sound of those fresh young voices I was overwhelmed with a sudden rush of mystic passionate emotion. A new world of love and feeling was revealed to me, more glorious by far than the heaven of which I had heard so much; and, strange proof of the power of true expression and the magical influence of real feeling, I found out ten years afterwards that the melody which has been so ingeniously married to sacred words and introduced into a religious ceremony was Nina's song, *Quand le bien-aimé reviendra*! What joy filled my young soul, dear d'Alayrac! And yet your ungrateful country has almost forgotten your name.[1]

This was my first musical experience, and in this manner I became religious; so religious that I attended mass every day and the communion every Sunday; and my weekly confession to the director of my conscience was, "My father, *I have done nothing;*" to which the worthy man always replied, "Go on, my child, as you have begun;" and so I did for several years.

---

[1] [Nicholas d'Alayrac, a once favourite French composer of operas, born 1753, died 1809. *Nina* (1786) was one of his masterpieces.]

CHAPTER II.

My father, Louis Berlioz, was a doctor. It is not for me to
estimate his abilities; but I may say that he inspired great
confidence both in our own and in the neighbouring towns.
He was keenly sensitive to the responsibilities of his profession, and believed that in the practice of so dangerous
and difficult an art as medicine, it behoved him to devote
every spare moment to mastering it, since the life of his
fellow-creatures was dependent on his skill. He was a
credit to his profession, which he regarded more as an opportunity for doing good to the poor than as a means of
emolument to himself. In 1810 my father gained the
prize offered by the medical society of Montpellier for an
essay on " Chronic Diseases." It was published in Paris,
and several celebrated physicians appropriated his ideas
without acknowledgment. My father was aware of this,
and it astonished him; but he always said, "What matter,
so long as truth triumphs?" He is too old to practise
now, and passes his time in reading and meditation.

He is a free-thinker—that is to say, he has no prejudices, social, political, or religious; but he promised my
mother so solemnly to do nothing to unsettle the faith
which she regarded as indispensable to my salvation, that
he sometimes even heard me my catechism. I confess

that I am quite incapable of acting with such loyalty or philosophic indifference towards my own son. My father has an incurable internal disease, which has often brought him to death's door. He eats scarcely anything, and only keeps himself alive by constant and ever-increasing doses of opium. Once, years ago, he was so maddened by pain that he took thirty-two grains at a dose. "I don't mind telling you," he said to me afterwards, "it was not to cure myself that I took it." Instead of killing him, however, so large a dose relieved him instantly of his pain.

At ten years old I was sent to a small school on the hill to learn Latin; but my father soon took me away again and taught me himself. My poor father! What a patient, unwearied, careful, clever teacher of languages, literature, history, and geography he was! He even taught me music, as we shall see presently.

What love is necessary to carry out such a task, and how few fathers there are who could and would do it! Still I cannot but think that a home education has in many respects fewer advantages than that of a public school. Children are thrown almost exclusively into the society of relations, servants, and a few chosen companions, instead of being inured to the rough contact of their fellows; they are utterly ignorant of the world and of the realities of life; and I know perfectly well that at twenty-five I was still an awkward, ignorant child.

For a long time my father could not give me a taste for the classics, and I hated having to learn even a few lines of Horace and Virgil by heart every day. It was an immense mental effort, and I found it impossible to keep my mind fixed on my task. On the other hand, I spent hours in studying maps, and in mastering the complicated contours of the islands, capes, and straits of the southern seas and the Indian Archipelago, pondering on the aspect of those remote regions, their vegetation, their inhabitants, and their scenery, and longing intensely to see them. It was the beginning of my love of travel and adventure.

My father often said of me that, though I knew the name of every one of the Sandwich Islands, Moluccas, or Philippines, and the Straits of Torres, Timor, Java, and Borneo, I did not know how many departments there were in France. My interest in foreign countries, especially those in the other hemisphere, was whetted by reading all the books of travel, both ancient and modern, which I could lay hands on at home; and, had I chanced to live in a seaport town, I should certainly have run away to sea. My son has inherited my tastes. He is now in the navy, and I trust that he may distinguish himself in his profession.

Further acquaintance with La Fontaine and Virgil, however, caused my sea-dreams to pale before the beauties of poetry. The epic passion of the Latin poet first kindled my smouldering imagination. How often have I felt my heart throb and my voice quiver and break when construing the fourth book of the *Æneid* to my father! . . . One day I was intensely affected by the sound of my own voice uttering the translation of the line:

At regina gravi jamdudum saucia cura.

I struggled on bravely till I came to the crisis, where Dido expires on her funeral pile, with the gifts and weapons of her betrayer heaped round her, and the familiar couch bathed in her blood. But when I came to the despairing cries of the dying queen, " thrice rising on her elbow, thrice falling back," and had to describe her wounds, and the anguish of her heart rent with its fatal passion; the cries of her distracted sister and nurse, and all the details of her death of torture, which moved even the gods to pity—my lips quivered, I could scarcely stammer out the words; and when I reached the line:

Quæsivit cœlo lucem, ingemuitque reperta,

the sublime vision of Dido, "seeking light from heaven, and moaning as she found it," overwhelmed me, and I broke down utterly.

With kind tact my father rose and shut the book, saying, "That will do, my boy, I am tired." I was intensely grateful to him for taking no notice of my emotion, and rushed away to vent my Virgilian grief in solitude.

CHAPTER III.

Meylan—My Uncle—The Pink Shoes—The Hamadryad of Saint
Eynard—Love at Twelve Years of Age.

I WAS twelve years old before the magic of music was
revealed to me; but earlier than that I had experienced
the pangs of that great passion which Virgil depicts
with so much power. It came about in this wise. My
maternal grandfather, who bore the same name as Walter
Scott's hero, Marmion, had a country house at Meylan,
three miles from Grenoble, near the frontier of Savoy.
The village and the neighbouring. hamlets, with the
Isère valley winding below them, and the mountains of
Dauphiné rising beyond, form one of the loveliest views
I have ever beheld. My mother and sisters and I used to
pay my grandfather a·visit at the end of the summer, and
were sometimes joined there by my uncle, Felix Marmion.
He was then deep in the brilliant vortex of the great
Emperor, and came among · us perfumed with gunpowder, and bearing on his person tangible traces of the
battlefield. One time it was a bullet-wound in his foot,
another time a splendid sabre-cut across his cheek, and then
again a mere lance-thrust which 'needed healing. Our
young cavalry adjutant never doubted that the Emperor's
throne was as immovable as Mont Blanc; he was intoxi-
cated with glory, and would gladly have laid down his
life for his hero; he was a joyous, gallant, accomplished

young fellow, who played the violin admirably, and sang opéra-comique music to perfection.

Above Meylan, and close under the steep wall of the mountain, lies a little white villa buried in gardens and vineyards, with a far-reaching outlook over the valley of the Isère; it is surrounded by rocky hills and woods; behind it rises the bold mass of the great St. Eynard rock; close by is a ruined tower, and it looks as if it were made to be the scene of a romance. This villa belonged to a Madame Gautier, who used to spend the summer there with two nieces, the younger of whom was called Estelle. The name of itself would have attracted me because of its association with Florian's idyl (*Estelle et Némorin*), which I had discovered in my father's library and devoured in secret. The real Estelle was a tall, slight girl of eighteen, with splendid shining eyes, a mass of hair which might have waved on the casque of Achilles, and the feet—I will not say of a Spaniard, but of a thoroughbred Parisian—clad in a pair of pink shoes! You laugh? Well, I had never seen a pair of pink shoes before! I have forgotten the colour of her hair (I think it was black); but whenever I think of her I see a vision of large brilliant eyes and equally brilliant pink shoes.

The moment I set eyes on her I felt an electric shock; in fact, I fell in love with her, desperately, hopelessly. I had no wishes, no hopes, I had no idea what was the matter with me, but I suffered acutely and spent my nights in sleepless anguish. In the daytime I crept away like a wounded bird and hid myself in the maize-fields and the orchards. I was haunted by Love's ghostly companion, Jealousy, and suffered tortures when any man approached my idol; and it makes me shudder even now when I recall the ring of my uncle's spurs as he danced with her.

The spectacle of so young a child overwhelmed with a feeling so far beyond his years, seemed to afford all our neighbours the keenest amusement. Estelle was the first to discern my feelings, and she was, I am sure, more amused than anyone. One evening there was a large party at my aunt's; prisoner's base was proposed, and the guests were divided into two parties, the men choosing their companions. I was purposely called up first, but I dared not choose, and stood motionless with downcast eyes and beating heart, while they all laughed at me. At last, Estelle took me by the hand and said, "Well, then I will choose. I take Mr. Hector!" Alas! the cruel girl, too, was laughing at me, as she stood looking down on me in her beauty. . . .

No, time itself is powerless . . . no after-loves can blot out the first. . . . I was but thirteen when I ceased to see her . . . I was thirty when, on my return from Italy, I caught sight of St. Eynard in the distance, the little white villa and the old tower, through a mist of tears . . . I still loved her. . . . I heard that she was . . . married . . . and all the rest of it . . . and even that did not cure me. My mother used often to tease me about my childish love, and one day played me a trick which was scarcely kind. A few days after my return from Rome, she handed me a letter, which she said she had been asked to deliver to a lady who was to pass through, in the Vienne diligence, in about an hour's time. "Go to the coach office, and, while they are changing the horses, ask for Mdme. F., and give her the letter. It is seventeen years since you saw her, but I am sure if you look at her carefully you will recognise her." . . . I had no suspicion of what awaited me, and when the coach drew up I went to the door and asked for Mdme. F. "It is I," said a voice, which I at once recognised with a throb of pain. Estelle! Estelle! still beautiful, Estelle, the nymph, the hamadryad of St. Eynard and the wooded hills of Meylan! It is indeed she, with her magnificent hair and her winning smile; but ah! where are the little pink shoes? She took the letter. Did she recognise me? Who can tell? The coach drove off, and I returned quivering with excitement to my mother, who, on seeing my face, said, "Ah, I see, Némorin has not forgotten his Estelle!" *His* Estelle! cruel mother!

CHAPTER IV.

When I stated that love and music had been revealed to me at twelve years old, I should rather have said "composition," because my father had already taught me to read music at sight and to play two instruments. I had discovered a flageolet hidden away in a drawer, and made the most futile efforts to pick out the popular air of *Malbrouk* upon it. My father, annoyed at this tiresome tootling, begged me to lay aside the instrument until he could find time to teach me how to play the heroic strain I had selected, less discordantly. He did so ; and I showed such aptitude that in two days I was able to perform my *Malbrouk* tune to the assembled family.

Does not this clearly prove my instinctive feeling for the great capabilities of wind instruments ? . . . What thoroughbred biographer would fail to draw the inevitable conclusion from such an incident ? . . . This induced my father to teach me to read music ; he initiated me into its first principles, and gave me a clear idea of musical signs and their meaning. He then explained the mechanism of the flute, and taught me to play it by means of Devienne's method, and I worked so hard that in seven months I could play fairly well.

My father then combined with some other families of the Côte to get a master from Lyons, and the services of the second violin of the Théâtre des Celestins were secured. He played the clarinet also; and the promise of a certain number of pupils, and of a fixed salary as conductor of the bands of the regiment, and of the Garde Nationale, tempted him to come and settle in our Philistine town and be the pioneer of musical culture among us. His name was Imbert, and he gave me two lessons every day; I had a pretty soprano voice, and soon became a fearless reader and a fair singer, and could play Drouet's most complicated concertos on the flute. I had struck up a friendship with my master's son, who was a little my senior, and an accomplished cornet player. One morning, when I was going to Meylan, he came to see me. "You were going away without saying good-bye. I may never see you again." I marvelled at the strange solemnity of his leave-taking; but the delight of being at Meylan, and the radiant *Stella montis*, soon drove all other thoughts away. What sad tidings greeted my return! Young Imbert had hung himself in the house while his parents were out, and no motive for his suicide has ever been discovered.

I had discovered Rameau's treatise on harmony, annotated and simplified by D'Alembert, among some old books, and spent sleepless nights in fruitless efforts to unravel its mysteries. I have since discovered that, in order to grasp the author's meaning, the student must not only have completely mastered the theory of chords, but must also have deeply studied the subject of experimental physics, on which the system is based. It is, therefore, a treatise for experts only.

Still, I was longing to compose. I arranged duets and

trios with impossible basses and more impossible chords ; but by dint of listening to Pleyel's quartets, as played by our students on Sundays, and studying Catel's treatise on harmony, I at last obtained some insight into the mystery of the formation and sequences of harmony. I instantly wrote a *pot-pourri* in six parts on a collection of Italian airs which I possessed. The harmony seemed tolerable, and I undertook to compose a quintet for flute and strings, which was performed by three friends, my master, and myself.

My triumph was great ; but my father did not seem to share in the general enthusiasm. Two months later another quintet was produced. My father was like many people who think they can judge of a quartet by hearing the first violin part, and asked me to play him over the flute part beforehand. I did so, and at a particular passage he called out, "Bravo ! that *is* music !" But this quintet, which was much more elaborate than the first, was also much more difficult, our amateurs were unable to cope with it, and the alto and bass blundered about most hopelessly.

As I was twelve and a half years old at this time, it is evident that the biographers who have asserted that I did not know my notes when I was twenty, are curiously mistaken. I burnt the two quintets some years later, but it is a remarkable fact that long afterwards, when composing my first orchestral work in Paris, the phrase my father approved of came back to me, and I embodied it in my new composition. It is the melody in B minor, introduced by the first violins soon after the beginning of the *allegro* in the overture of the *Francs Juges*.

Shortly after his son's sad and mysterious death poor Imbert returned to Lyons, where I think he died. He was soon replaced at the Côte by a far more talented man named Dorant.   Dorant was an Alsatian from Colmar, and could play almost every instrument, though he excelled on the clarinet, double-bass, violin, and guitar.   He taught my elder sister, who had a good voice but absolutely no musical gift, to play the guitar. She is fond of music, but has never been able to read or make out even the simplest air.   I took lessons with her, until one day Dorant, who was an honest man and a true artist, suddenly said to my father, "Sir, I cannot go on teaching your son to play the guitar!"   "Why?   Has he annoyed you? or is he so lazy that he won't learn?"   "Neither; but it is useless to go on teaching him when he already plays as well as I do myself."

I was thus a past-master on those potent and perfect instruments, the flageolet, the flute, and the guitar.   Does not this fortuitous choice look like the instinctive action of nature urging me towards the most powerful orchestral effects and the Michael Angelesque in music? . . . The flute, the guitar, and the flageolet—these are the only instruments I play, but they seem to me by no means contemptible.   By-the-bye, I can also play the drum.

My father did not wish me to learn the piano, otherwise I should doubtless have swelled the ranks of the innumerable army of famous pianists.

He had no intention of making an artist of me; and I dare say he thought that if I learnt the piano I should devote myself to it, and become more absorbed in music than he wished or intended me to be.   I have often felt the want of this accomplishment, and it might have been of the greatest use to me; but when I consider the appalling number of miserable musical platitudes to which the piano has given birth, which would never have seen the light had their authors been confined to pen and paper, I feel grateful to the happy chance which forced me to compose in silence, and has thus delivered me from the tyranny of the fingers, so dangerous to thought, and from the fascination which the sound of a common air always exercises on a composer. Many amateurs have pitied me for this deprivation, but that does not affect me much.

My youthful compositions all bore the stamp of deep melancholy ; most of my melodies were in minor keys ; and though I knew this to be a defect, I could not help it. My thoughts seemed to be veiled in crape ; they had all been tinged by the Mcylan love affair. During this state of mind I was always reading Florian's *Estelle*, and, as a matter of course, ended by setting some of the songs in that feeble pastoral to music.

I composed a very sad one to some words which expressed my despair at leaving the· woods and the spots which had been "honorés par les pas, éclairés par les yeux,"[1] and, I might add, by the pink shoes of my cruel fair one. And as I sit here in London, absorbed in business of importance, harrowed with anxiety, raging against the absurd obstacles which pursue me even here, a faint ray of sunshine recalls the sickly words to my mind. Here is the first verse :

> Je vais donc quitter pour jamais
> Mon doux pays, ma douce amie,
> Loin d'eux je vais traîner ma vie
> Dans les pleurs et dans les regrets !
> Fleuve dont j'ai vue l'eau limpide,
> Pour réfléchir ses doux attraits,
> Suspendre sa course rapide,
> Je vais vous quitter pour jamais.

---

[1] La Fontaine, "Les Deux Pigeons."

The song was burnt, with the sextet and the quintets, before I went to Paris; but when I undertook to write my *Symphonie Fantastique*, in 1829, the melody came back to me, and, as it seemed to express the overwhelming grief of a young heart in the pangs of a hopeless passion, I adopted it. It is the air for the violins at the opening of the *largo* in the first part of the work—*Reveries, Passions;* I put it in just as it was.

While engaged in these experiments, and absorbed in reading, geography, religion, and the storms and calms of my first love affair, the time approached for me to choose a career. My father intended me to follow his profession, which he considered the finest in the world; and had told me so long before. I had often expressed my views on the subject most emphatically, and he thoroughly disapproved of them. I had as yet no very definite ideas; but I felt a strong presentiment that I was not intended to spend my life at the bedsides of sick people in hospitals, or in dissecting-rooms, and was firmly determined to resist all attempts to make a doctor of me. About this time I read the lives of Gluck and Haydn in the *Biographie Universel*, and they excited me immensely. "What a glorious existence!" I said to myself, as I thought of their careers; "what an art, and what happiness to be able to live for it!" An apparently trifling incident strengthened my bent in this direction, and opened up to me new and undreamt-of regions in the realms of music.

I had never seen a full score. The only pieces of music I knew were *solfeggios* accompanied by a figured bass, solos for the flute, or bits of operas with pianoforte accompaniment. One day, however, I found a sheet of paper with twenty-five staves upon it. I realised in a moment the wondrous instrumental and vocal combinations to which they might give rise, and I cried out, "What an orchestral work one might write on that!" From this moment the musical fermentation in my head went on increasing, and my distaste for medicine redoubled. But I was far too much afraid of my parents to venture to impart my wild dreams to them, and one day my father suddenly determined to use my love of music as a lever for removing what he called a "childish aversion," and by one masterstroke to embark me at once on the study of medicine.

In order to familiarise me with the things I was soon to have constantly before my eyes, he spread out in his study Munro's enormous treatise on anatomy, with life-size illustrations of the structure of the body.

"This is the work you are to study," he said to me. "I do not suppose you will persist in your prejudice against medicine, for it is unreasonable and wholly unfounded, and if you promise to work earnestly at anatomy, I will get you a beautiful flute, with all the new keys, from Lyons."

I had long coveted such an instrument, and what could I say? . . . The earnestness of the proposal, the mingled respect and fear with which, in spite of all his kindness, my father inspired me, and the promised reward, were too much for me. I stammered out a faint Yes, fled into my room, and threw myself on my bed overwhelmed with grief.

Become a doctor, study anatomy, dissect, and witness horrible operations, instead of throwing myself heart and soul into the glorious and beautiful art of music? Forsake the empyrean for the dreary realities of earth? the immortal angels of poetry and love and their inspired songs for filthy hospitals, dreadful medical students, hideous corpses, the shrieks of patients, and the groans of the dying? . . . Such a state of things was the utter reversal of the natural conditions of my life; horrible and impossible. Yet it came to pass.

My anatomical studies were undertaken in company with my cousin A. Robert, since become a great Paris doctor, who was also to be my father's pupil. Unfortunately, Robert played the violin very well, and was one of my performers in the quintets, so that we spent more time in music than in anatomy. But he worked so hard at home that he always knew his demonstrations much better than I did. This called forth severe rebukes and even fierce bursts of anger from my father. Still, partly by my own efforts, partly by coercion, with the aid of prepared skeletons, I at last learnt in a kind of way all my father could teach me about anatomy; and at nineteen, encouraged by my fellow-student, I decided to go with him to Paris, and there enter upon my medical studies in earnest.

10th April, 1848.—Here I pause for a moment before beginning the story of my Parisian life, and of the bitter war against men, ideas, and things which I waged almost from the moment I arrived there, and have carried on ever since. The reader will grant me breathing-time. Besides, the demonstration of the two hundred thousand Chartists is to take place to-day, and perhaps in a few hours England will be as unsettled as the rest of Europe, and even this shelter be denied me. I am going out to watch the course of events.

8 P.M.—Well, the Chartists are a good type of revolutionist. Everything went off well. The cannons, those

powerful speakers whose penetrating logic is so irresistibly convincing to the masses, were in the chair. But they had no opportunity of making their voices heard; their mere presence was enough to convince everyone of the inexpediency of a revolution, and the Chartists dispersed in perfect order.

Excellent creatures! About as fit to carry out an insurrection as the Italians are to write a symphony! The Irish are probably just the same, as O'Connell well knew when he said, " Agitate, agitate, but don't act."

12th July.—I have found it impossible to go on with my memoirs during the last three months. I am just going back to the unhappy country which is still called France, and which is, after all, my native land. I am going to see how an artist can live there, and how long it will take him to die amidst the ruins which have crushed and buried the flower of art. Farewell, England! . . .

France, 16th July, 1848.—Here I am back again! Paris has buried her dead. The paving-stones from the barricades are laid down in their places, only, perhaps, to be up again to-morrow.

The moment I arrived I rushed off to the Faubourg St. Antoine. What a sight! what hideous ruins! Even the genius of Liberty on the top of the column of the Bastille has a bullet through her body. The fallen trees, the crumbling houses, the squares, the streets, the quays, seem still quivering with the murderous struggle! . . . Fancy thinking of Art at such a period of wild folly and bloodshed! . . . All the theatres closed; all the artists ruined; all teachers are idle, all pupils have fled; poor pianists play sonatas in the squares; historical painters sweep the streets; architects are mixing mortar on the public works. . . . . . The Assembly has just voted considerable sums towards the opening of the theatres, and in aid of the unfortunate artists. But how inadequate this to meet the wants, especially of musicians!   Some of the first violins at the Opéra only had thirty-six pounds a year, and barely eked out their means of livelihood by giving lessons. They could not possibly have saved much; and now that their pupils are gone, what is to become of the poor creatures? They will not be transported (although for the most part their only chance of gaining a livelihood would be in places like America, India, or Sydney), for it would cost the Government too dear; to get a free passage one must deserve it, but all our artists fought against the insurgents, and charged the barricades. . . .

Is not this horrible confusion of justice and injustice, of good and evil, truth and falsehood, in which words seem perverted from their original meaning, enough to drive one mad? . . .

I may as well go on with my autobiography, I have nothing better to do; and in recalling the past may forget the present.

CHAPTER V.

WHEN I arrived in Paris with my fellow-student,
Robert, I gave myself up entirely to preparation for the
career which had been forced upon me, and faithfully
kept the promise given to my father at parting. But
I was sorely tried when Robert announced one morning
that he had bought a *subject* (a corpse), and asked me to
accompany him to the dissecting-room at the Hospital de
la Pitié. When I entered that fearful human charnel-
house, littered with fragments of limbs, and saw the
ghastly faces and cloven heads, the bloody cesspool in
which we stood, with its reeking atmosphere, the swarms
of sparrows fighting for scraps, and the rats in the corners
gnawing bleeding vertebræ, such a feeling of horror
possessed me that I leapt out of the window, and fled
home as though Death and all his hideous crew were
at my heels. It was twenty-four hours before I recovered
from the shock of this first impression, utterly refusing
to hear the words anatomy, dissection, or medicine, and
firmly resolved to die rather than enter the career which
had been forced upon me.

Robert wasted much eloquence in combating my disgust
and demonstrating the absurdity of my plans. But he

finally induced me to make another effort, and I consented to return to the hospital, and face the dread scene once more. How strange! I now merely felt cold disgust at the sight of the same things which had before filled me with such horror; I had become as callous to the revolting scene as a veteran soldier. It was all over. I even found some pleasure in rummaging in the gaping breast of an unfortunate corpse for the lungs, with which to feed the winged inhabitants of that charming place.

"Well done!" cried Robert, laughing; "you are growing quite humane! Aux petits des oiseaux tu donnes la pâture."

"Et ma bonté s'étend sur toute la nature," I retorted, casting a shoulder-blade to a great rat who was staring at me with famished eyes. And so I went on with my course of anatomy, stoically, if not enthusiastically. I was strongly attracted by Professor Amusat, who seemed possessed by the same passion for medicine that I felt for music, and was an artist in anatomy. The fame of this bold scientific explorer has spread all over Europe, and his discoveries have aroused the wonder and opposition of the learned world. Day and night are not long enough for his researches, and, although exhausted by his labours, he pursues his dangerous way with dogged determination. All his traits are those of a man of genius: I often see him, and I love him.

I afterwards found complete compensation in the classes of Thénard and Gay-Lussac, the professors of chemistry and physics in the Jardin des Plantes, and in a course of literature in which Andrieux captivated his audience by his subtle simplicity, and in which I took ever-increasing interest. I was thus in a fair way to swell the ranks of the medical students, and might have added another name to the long list of bad doctors but for a visit I paid to the Opéra. There I saw *Les Danaïdes*, by Salieri. The gorgeous splendour of the spectacle, the rich fulness of the orchestra and the chorus, the wonderful voice and pathetic charm of Madame Branchu, Dérivis' rugged power, the air of Hypermnestre, in which I seemed to trace the features of Gluck's style, according to the ideal I had formed from some fragments of his *Orphée* in my father's library—while the crashing bacchanal and the voluptuously dreamy dance-music added by Spontini to the score of his countryman, filled me with excitement and enthusiasm. I was like a lad with the inborn instincts of a sailor, who, never having seen anything but fishing-boats on a lake, suddenly finds himself transported to a three-decker in mid-ocean. Not a wink did I sleep the night after that performance, and my anatomy lesson the next morning suffered in proportion. I sang the air of Danaüs, *Jouissez du destin propice*, while sawing away at the skull of my "subject;" and when Robert, irritated by my constantly humming *Descends dans le sein d'Amphitrite*, when I should have been reading a chapter of Bichat, cried, "Do attend to your work; we are not getting on at all, our subject will be spoiled in three days; eighteen francs wasted. You must really be sensible!" I retorted by singing the hymn of Nemesis, *Divinité de sang avide!* and the scalpel fell from his hands.

I went to the Opéra again the following week, and saw Méhul's *Stratonice*, and Persuis's ballet of *Nina*. I admired the overture to *Stratonice* very much, and also the air for Séleucus, *Versez tous vos chagrins*, and the quartet in the conference; but as a whole the work seemed to me cold. I was, however, delighted with the ballet, and greatly touched by hearing the hymn which my sister's companions had sung at the Convent of the Ursulines, on the day of my first communion, played on the *cor anglais* by Vogt, during Mademoiselle Bigottini's harrowing pantomime. It was the song, *Quand le bien-aimé reviendra*. The man next me, who was humming the words, told me the name of the opera and the author from whom Persuis had borrowed the tune, and thus I learnt that it was taken from d'Alayrac's *Nina*.

However great may have been the power of the singer who created the part of Nina,[1] I find it difficult to believe that that song as sung by her could ever have made as true and touching an effect as the combination of Vogt's instrument and Bigottini's acting produced on me.

In spite of these temptations, and the hours I spent every evening in meditating on the melancholy contrast between my tastes and my studies, I persisted in this distracted life for some time longer without either making much progress in my medical studies, or sensibly increasing my musical knowledge. I had given my promise and I kept it. But when I learnt that the library of the Conservatoire, with its wonderful wealth of manuscripts, was open to the public, I could not resist the longing to become better acquainted with Gluck's works, for which I had an instinctive love, and which were not then being played at the Opéra. Once I entered that sanctuary I never quitted it. It was the death-blow to my medical career, and the dissecting-room was finally abandoned.

I was so completely absorbed by my love of music that, with all my admiration for Gay-Lussac and the fascina-

____
[1] Madame Dugazon.

tions of the experimental electricity which I had begun to study with him, I never went near him again.

I read and re-read Gluck's scores, copied them, learnt them by heart, in my enthusiasm forgot either to eat, drink, or sleep; simply raved about them. One day, after weary waiting, I at last succeeded in hearing the *Iphigénie en Tauride*, and I vowed as I left the Opéra that I would be a musician come what might, despite father, mother, uncles, aunts, grandparents, and friends. I actually wrote off on the spot and told my father how irresistibly strong my bent was, and besought him not to oppose it needlessly. He answered me by gentle arguments, assuring me I should soon see the folly of my ways, and quit the pursuit of a chimera to follow in the beaten track of a regular profession. But my father was wrong. The more he argued the more my determination was confirmed, and the correspondence became more angry and threatening on his side and hotter and hotter on mine, until it culminated in a perfect fury of passion.

CHAPTER VI

I become one of Lesueur's Pupils—His Kindness—The Chapel
Royal.

WHILE this bitter controversy was raging I had been
busy writing, and had composed among other things a
cantata with full orchestral accompaniments on Mille-
voye's *Le Cheval Arabe.*

One of Lesueur's pupils, Gerono, whom I used often to
meet at the Conservatoire library, suggested that I should
try and obtain admission to his master's composition class,
and offered to introduce me to him. I was delighted at
the idea, and went to M. Lesueur one morning, armed
with the score of my cantata and a canon for three voices,
which I regarded as an appropriate selection for this
solemn occasion. Lesueur was kind enough to read
through the first of these crude efforts carefully. He
returned it to me with the remark: "There is a great
deal of power and dramatic feeling in your work, but you
don't know yet how to write, and your harmony is one
mass of blunders. Gerono will teach you the principles
of harmony, and when you have mastered them suffi
ciently to follow me, I shall be glad to receive you as a
pupil." Gerono willingly accepted the task thus confided
to him, and in a few weeks had indoctrinated me
into the whole system of Lesueur's theory of the production and succession of chords, which is based on Rameau's

system, and on his speculations on the vibrations of a
string. I inferred at once from the manner in which
Gerono laid down these principles that it was no use
disputing their value, for they constituted an article of
religion in Lesueur's school, to be accepted with unques-
tioning faith. Such is the force of example, however,
that I soon became one of Lesueur's most ardent followers.
I am by no means ungrateful to the excellent and worthy
master who guided my first tottering steps so kindly, and
remained my warm friend to his life's end. But what
precious hours I wasted—first, in studying his antediluvian
theories, then in practising them, and, finally, in unlearn-
ing them, and beginning all over again at the beginning!
And now, when I come across one of his scores, I involuntarily put it aside with the same sort of instinctive
impulse with which one avoids the portrait of a lost
friend. I had so admired those little oratorios of Lesueur's
at the Chapel Royal, and was so grieved when I found
my admiration failing! I feel so old and worn-out and
disenchanted, as I recall the distant days when I used
to go every Sunday to the Tuileries to listen to them.
How few of the celebrated artists I met there are alive
now! What struggles and trials and troubles lie between
us! Those were the days of vast enthusiasms, great
musical passions, long dreams, unspeakable joys! . . .
When I entered the orchestra at the Chapel Royal,
Lesueur used to employ the interval before the service
began in explaining the plan and purpose of the music to
me. Some knowledge of the composer's intention was
indeed necessary, for it had rarely any connection with
the words of the service. Lesueur wrote a vast number
of masses, and had also a particular affection for the
beautiful stories of the Old Testament, such as Naomi,

Ruth and Boaz, Rachel, Deborah, etc. . . . ; these he rendered with so much truth of colouring that in listening to them, one forgot the thinness of their musical fabric, his persistent imitation of the airs, duets, and trios of the old Italian school, and the childish feebleness of the instrumentation. Lesueur owes more of the development of his special talent to the Bible than anything else, except, perhaps, MacPherson's poem (which he persisted in attributing to Ossian). I shared his tastes, and my imagination was possessed by the East—the calm of its vast deserts, the grandeur of its great ruins, its historic past, and its wonderful legends.

The *Ite missa est* was followed by King Charles X.'s withdrawal, to a grotesque flourish of an enormous drum and a fife, in 5-time, worthy of the barbaric ages which had given it birth; and after this my master used often to take me for a long walk. Those were days of precious counsels and of curious confidences. For my encouragement Lesueur used to tell me strange stories of his youth, of his first beginnings as conductor at Dijon, his admission to the Sainte Chapelle, his competition for the conductorship of the school at Notre Dame; of Méhul's enmity; the ill-treatment he met with from the *rapins* of the Conservatoire; the many cabals against his opera, *La Caverne*, and Cherubini's noble conduct on the occasion; the friendship of Paisiello, who preceded him at the imperial chapel; the intoxicating favours lavished by Napoleon on the author of *Les Bardes*,[1] and the great man's historical *mots* on the sub-

---

[1] *Ossian, ou les Bardes*, was Lesueur's masterpiece. The inscription engraved inside the gold casket which Lesueur received after the first performance of the opera is: "The Emperor Napoleon to the Author of *Les Bardes*."

ject of the work. My master told me what difficulties
he had in getting his first opera performed; his anxiety
the first night it was played; the sadness and lassi-
tude which followed its success; his desire to try his
chance again; his completion of the opera *Télémaque*
in three months; Madame Scio's proud beauty when
she appeared as Diana at the chase, and her irresistible impetuosity as Calypso. Then we had long
arguments about his theory of fundamental bass and
modulation, for he allowed me to argue with him when
alone, and I sometimes abused this privilege. When
we had exhausted musical topics, we discussed philosophy and religion, and on these subjects we generally
differed. But there were some things about which
we were both enthusiastic, and on which we were always
certain to agree—Gluck, Virgil, and Napoleon. After
these long talks by the Seine, or in the shady gardens of
the Tuileries, I used to leave him, that he might indulge
in the long, silent reveries which had become a necessity
to him.

CHAPTER VII.

SOME months after I had been admitted into Lesueur's special class (I had not yet got into the Conservatoire) I took it into my head to write an opera, and ventured to ask M. Andrieux, the able professor with whom I had studied literature, for a book. I don't know what I said to him, but here is his answer:

"Your letter interested me keenly. Your love for your glorious art is the guarantee of your success; I wish you may achieve it with all my heart. I should be only too glad if I could contribute towards it; but I am too old for the work you propose; my ideas and studies all lie in another direction; and you would call me a savage if you knew how long it is since I have set foot in the Opera-house, or the Feydeau. I am sixty-four, and it would therefore ill become me to write love-poems; and in the matter of music, I am afraid a requiem is all that now concerns me. I am sorry you were not born thirty or forty years earlier, or I thirty or forty later—then we could have worked together. You will, I am sure, accept these excellent excuses and my kindest and most affectionate regards.

"ANDRIEUX."

"17th June, 1823."

He was his own messenger, and we had a long talk.
When we parted he said, "In my youth, I too was a
passionate lover of music, and raved first about Piccini . . .
and then about Gluck."

Somewhat damped by my failure to secure the co-
operation of a literary celebrity, I had recourse to Gerono,
who dabbled in poetry. I asked him (please admire my
ingenuousness) to dramatise Florian's *Estelle*. He did so,
and I set his *poem* to music. Fortunately no one ever
heard a note of this offspring of my Meylan memories.
Impotent past! My music was as feeble as Gerono's
text. This wishy-washy composition was followed by
a gloomy work taken from Saurin's drama, *Beverley; ou,
le Joueur*.[1] I was delighted with this blustering fragment, written for a bass voice, with orchestral accompaniment, and I wished to have it sung by Dérivis, for
whom it seemed to me peculiarly adapted. The difficulty was to discover a suitable occasion for its performance, and I fancied I had found one when I saw
that *Athalie* was to be performed, with Gossec's choruses,
at the Théâtre Français, for Talma's benefit. As there
is to be a chorus, thought I, there must be an orchestra; and as my scena is an easy one, Dérivis will
certainly sing it if Talma puts it in his programme. I
will go to Talma.—But the idea of addressing the great
tragedian and of facing Nero awed me. As I neared the
house my heart began to beat in the most deadly manner;
at the sight of the door I tremble, and pause irresolute
on the threshold. Dare I go in? . . . Shall I give up
the idea? Twice I raise my hand to ring the bell, twice
I let it fall. . . . I blush scarlet, there is a singing in my
ears; I feel dizzy and faint. My fear masters me. I

[1] [Known in England as *The Gamester*.]

turn, or rather rush, away as fast as my legs can carry me. Who can understand this? Only a half-civilised young enthusiast such as I was then.[1]

Soon afterwards, M. Masson, the conductor at the church of Saint Roch, asked me to write a mass for the Innocents' Day, the feast-day of the choir-children. We were to have a hundred picked musicians in the orchestra, and a still larger choir, with a month for practice. The copies were to be made gratis by the Saint Roch choir-children, etc. etc. I set to work heart and soul at my mass, which is a bad copy of Lesueur's style, with the same casual inequality of colour.

Like most masters, Lesueur, when he had looked over the score, praised those passages in which his manner was most faithfully reproduced. As soon as it was finished I gave my MS. to M. Masson, who handed it over to the pupils to copy and study. He swore by all his gods that the performance should be grand and perfect. We only wanted a good conductor, as neither he nor I was accustomed to direct such a body of performers. Valentino was at that time the leader at the Opéra, and was anxious to obtain the leadership of the Chapel Royal. It was therefore very unlikely he would refuse my master, who was superintendent of the chapel.[2] He accordingly acceded to Lesueur's request, and promised to help us, although he evidently felt no confidence in the executive I had at my disposal. On the day of our full rehearsal, our *great choral and instrumental forces* resolved themselves into a choir of twenty singers, consisting of fifteen tenors and five basses, twelve children, nine violins,

---

[1] [It was a close counterpart to Schubert's interview with Beethoven. See *Dictionary of Music*, iii. 336.]

[2] The superintendents were present when their works were performed, but did not conduct in person.

a viola, a hautboy, a horn, and a bassoon. Imagine my despair at having to introduce Valentino, the celebrated conductor of one of the first orchestras in the world, to such a phalanx of musicians ! . . . " Never fear," persisted Masson, "they will all be here at the performance to-morrow. Let us begin." Valentino took up his baton with a resigned air, tapped his desk, and began ; but he was obliged to stop almost immediately, because of the endless mistakes in the copies, in which flats and sharps were missing on all sides ; a pause of ten bars left out in one place, and thirty bars in another. It is a miserable hash ; I suffer the torments of the damned ; and at last am forced to resign my long-treasured hope of hearing one of my works performed by a large orchestra.

But the lesson was not lost. The little I had heard of my composition had shown me its principal defects, and I resolved to rewrite almost the whole work. Valentino strengthened me in my resolution by promising to help me when the time came for my revenge ; and I set to work at once. In the meanwhile, however, my parents had heard of my failure, and seized the occasion to point out the futility of my hopes and the absurdity of my supposed vocation.

When the new score was ready, mindful of my recent painful experience, I set to work myself (as I could not afford to pay anyone else to do it) to copy, double, triple, and quadruple the parts ; and in three months they were ready. But I found myself much in the same position as Robinson Crusoe, with the canoe which he was unable to launch. I had absolutely no hope of getting it performed. I was not such a fool as to trust to M. Masson's *musical forces* again. As I knew none of the artists I wanted personally, I could not ask them to perform ; and, finally, as regarded the Chapel Royal, my master had told me once and for all that the thing was impossible.[1] It was then that my friend Humbert Ferrand, about whom I shall have more to say presently, conceived the bold idea of my addressing myself to M. de Chateaubriand, as the only man likely to grant such a request, and asking him to enable me to get up a performance of my mass by lending me twelve hundred francs. Here is his answer:

"Paris, 31st December, 1824.

" You ask me for twelve hundred francs. Sir, I would send them to you if I had them. I cannot assist you as regards the ministry.[2] I sympathise most truly in your troubles. I love art, and I honour artists; but genius often owes its triumphs to its failures. . The day you succeed all else will be forgotten. Accept my deep regrets; they are very real.

" CHATEAUBRIAND."

[1] I did not then know why. If Lesueur had proposed that the whole choir of the Chapel Royal should transport itself to Saint Roch to perform a work by one of his pupils, the proposal would have been regarded as quite natural. But he was probably afraid that some of my fellow-students would claim the same privilege, which would have led to all sorts of complications.

[2] I must have also asked M. de Chateaubriand for an introduction to the powers of the day. When one asks an inch one may as well ask an ell.

CHAPTER VIII.

I WAS greatly discouraged, and found myself wholly
unable to give any satisfactory answer to the letters
which poured in from home, and threatened to withdraw
the small allowance that enabled me to live in Paris.
Luckily for me, I met a clever young amateur at the Opéra
one night when Piccini's *Dido* was being played. He was
of a generous, ardent nature, and had been an indignant
spectator of the collapse at Saint Roch. He was a
member of an aristocratic family in the Faubourg St.
Germain, and was then well off, but afterwards lost all
his money, married a second-rate singer, who had been
educated at the Conservatoire, against the wish of his
mother ; she went on the stage, and he became an actor,
and accompanied her through France and Italy. When
his *prima donna* deserted him, he returned to Paris, and
supported himself there by teaching. I have since been
enabled to give him some assistance in the *Débats* ; but I
deeply regret having done so, little, for the service he
rendered me had a great influence on my career, and I
shall never forget it. His name was Augustin de Pons.
Last year he was barely able to support himself by his
lessons. What his fate has been since the February

Revolution, which must have deprived him of all his pupils, I shudder to think!

When we met in the green-room of the Opéra, he called out to me in his stentorian voice, "What news of the mass? Is it rewritten yet? and when is it to be performed in real earnest?" "Goodness knows! it is rewritten and copied, but how am I to get it performed?" "How? why, by paying for it. How much do you want? Let us see. Will twelve hundred francs do it? or fifteen hundred—or two thousand? I will lend it to you?" "Pray lower your voice, I beseech you! If you mean what you say, I shall be only too glad to accept your offer, and twelve hundred francs will be enough." "All right. Come to me to-morrow, and we will settle it. We must engage the chorus from the Opéra, and a strong orchestra. Valentino must be satisfied, we must be satisfied, and by heaven it shall succeed!"

And it did succeed. My mass was conducted by Valentino, and splendidly performed before a crowded audience at Saint Roch. The papers praised it, and thus, thanks to Pons, I succeeded in obtaining a public performance of a work of my own, the difficulty and importance of which in Paris every composer knows.

The mass was performed again long afterwards (in 1827) in the church of St. Eustache, on the day of the great outbreak in the Rue St. Denis. This time the orchestra and chorus of the Odéon had offered me their services gratuitously, I ventured to conduct them myself, and got through it pretty well, in spite of some blunders caused by my excitement. But how little I then dreamed of the qualities necessary to produce a good conductor! Precision, versatility, passion, sensitiveness and coolness combined, together with an indefinable subtle instinct !   How much time, practice, and thought have I spent in acquiring even a few of these !   We often mourn over the paucity of good singers; good conductors are rarer still, and in most cases are of far greater importance to a composer.[1]

This second performance convinced me of the inferiority of my mass, and, reserving the *Resurrexit*,[2] which seemed to me better than the rest, I burnt it, in company with *Beverley* (for which my enthusiasm had cooled), the opera *Estella*, and a Latin oratorio, *The Passage of the Red Sea*, which I had just completed.   After an impartial criticism, I ruthlessly condemned it also to a place in this *auto-da-fé*.

A strange coincidence !   Last night, after writing the above, I went to the Opéra Comique.   There I met a musician who greeted me with these words : "When did you return from London ?"   "Some weeks ago."   "Well; how about Pons ? . . . Have you heard ?"   "No; what ?"   "He poisoned himself last month."   "Good God !"   "Yes; he said that he was weary of life; but I fear the truth of the matter is that he could not live.   The Revolution had dispersed his pupils, and the sale of his furniture did not produce enough even to pay his rent."   Poor creature !   Poor forsaken artists !   What a republic of beggars and pickpockets !

"*Horrible! horrible! most horrible!*" and now the *Morning Post* brings me details of the death of the unfortunate Prince Lichnowsky, vilely assassinated at the gates of Frankfort by those brutes of German peasants, worthy rivals of our June heroes !   They stabbed him all over with knives, hacked him to pieces with scythes, tore

---

[1] [For an excellent account of the joys and sorrows of a conductor see the letter to Liszt in chapter liv.]

[2] I destroyed it afterwards.

him limb from limb! riddled him with bullets, *but so as
not to kill him!* and then stripped him and left him lying
by the roadside! . . . He lived for five hours, and died
without a murmur! Noble, clever, brave, enthusiastic
Lichnowsky! I knew him well in Paris, and met him in
Berlin last year on my return from Russia. It was just
at the beginning of his successes as a speaker. Filthy
dregs of humanity! a hundred times more stupidly brutal
in your revolutionary outbreaks and antics than the
baboons and orang-outangs of Borneo! . . .

CHAPTER IX.

Now that I had made some progress in the study of harmony, Lesueur wished me to have a recognised position as one of his pupils in the Conservatoire. He spoke to Cherubini, who was then director, and I was admitted. Fortunately no one suggested that I should be introduced to the terrible author of *Medée*, for the previous year I had put him into one of his white-heat furies by opposing him in a matter which I shall now narrate, and which he probably had not forgotten.

No sooner was Cherubini appointed director, after the death of Perne, than he at once set to work to signalise his accession to power by the introduction of all sorts of restrictions in the internal economy of the school, which had not, up to that time, been organised on exactly puritan principles. In order to prevent the intermingling of the two sexes, except in the presence of the professors, he issued an order that the men were to enter by the door in the Faubourg Poissonnière, and the women by that in the Rue Bergère; the two being at opposite ends of the building.

Wholly ignorant of this moral decree, I betook myself one morning to the library, entering as usual by the Rue Bergère, the female door, and was making my way to the

library, when I found myself suddenly confronted by a
servant, who stopped me in the middle of the courtyard,
and ordered me to go back and return to the very same spot
by the other entrance.   I thought this so absurd that I
sent the liveried Argus about his business, and went on
my way.   The rascal, hoping to find favour in the eyes
of his new master by emulating his severity, ran off to
report the circumstance.   I had forgotten all about it,
and was absorbed in *Alceste*, when Cherubini entered the
reading-room, his face more cadaverous, his hair more
dishevelled, his eyes more wicked, and his step firmer
than ever.   He and my accuser made their way round
the table, examining several unconscious students, until
the servant stopped in front of me and cried, "Here he
is!"   Cherubini was in such a passion that he could
not utter a word.   "Ah! ah, ah, ah!" he cried at last,
his Italian accent comically intensified in his anger,
"and so you are the man who, who, who dares to
come in by the door by which I forbid you to enter?"
"I was not aware, sir, of your order, and another time I
will obey it."   "Another time! another time!   What—
what—what are you doing here?"   "As you see, sir,
I am studying Gluck's scores."   "And what—what—
what—are Gluck's scores to you? and who allows you to
—to—to enter the library?"   "Sir! (I was getting
angry) Gluck's music is the grandest I know, and I need
no one's permission to come here to study.   The Conservatoire library is open to the public from 10 till 3,
and I have a right to use it."   "The—the—the right?"
"Yes, sir."   "I—I forbid you to come here!"   "Nevertheless, I shall return."   "What—what—what is your
name?" he cried, trembling with passion.   I was, by this
time, white with anger too.   "Sir, perhaps you may hear

my name some day . . . but you will not hear it now!"
"Sei—sei—seize him, Hottin" (that was the servant's
name), "seize him, and—and—take him away to
prison!" Then, to the astonishment of everyone, master
and servant pursued me round the table, knocking over
stools and reading-desks in the vain effort to catch me, until
at last I escaped, calling out as I vanished: "You shall
neither have me nor my name, and I shall soon come
back and study Gluck's scores again!"

This was my first interview with Cherubini. I do not
know whether he remembered it when I was presented to
him officially. But it is curious that, twelve years afterwards, I should have been appointed, against his wish,
to the charge of the library out of which he tried to
turn me. As regards Hottin, he is now porter to the
orchestra, devoted to me, and a most zealous partisan of my
music; he used even to declare, before Cherubini died,
that I was the only man who could take his place at the
Conservatoire. M. Auber apparently thought otherwise.
I could tell many more stories about Cherubini, from
which it might be seen that though he gave me some
bitter pills to swallow, he had to accept some unpalatable
draughts in return from me.

CHAPTER X.

THE partial success of my mass had for a time silenced the
distressing opposition of my family; but, unfortunately,
it was soon reawakened.

I had entered as a competitor in the annual musical
examination at the Conservatoire. For this there was a
preliminary examination, which I unfortunately failed to
pass. The moment my father heard of this he peremp-
torily informed me that he would withdraw my allowance
if I remained in Paris. My kind master at once wrote,
begging him to reconsider his decision, and assuring him
that there could be no question as to my future, inasmuch
as *I exhaled music at every pore.* Unfortunately, the
religious principles which he invoked to support his argument in favour of my being allowed to fulfil my vocation,
were the most unlucky he could have selected. My
father's reply was stiff, rough, and almost rude, and
offended and pained Lesueur on his most sensitive points.
It began: "Sir,—I am an unbeliever!" and the rest may
be imagined.

I had a dim hope that, by resigning myself for a time
and pleading my own cause, I might yet prevail, and I
therefore returned to the Côte.

I met with a chilling reception, and was left for some days to my own reflections. Then my parents called upon me to choose some other profession, since I did not choose to be a doctor. I replied that my sole desire was to be a musician, and that I could not believe they would refuse to let me return and pursue my career at Paris.

"You may as well make up your mind on that score," replied my father, "for you shall never go back."

From that moment I lapsed into almost complete silence, barely answering when spoken to, scarcely eating, wandering about the woods, or else shutting myself up in my room. To tell the truth, I had no plans; my mind seemed paralysed by the ferment in my brain and the constraint which controlled me. I had not even strength to be angry, I was perishing for want of air. One morning early I was awakened by my father.

"Get up," he said, "and, when you are dressed, come into my study, I want to speak to you."

I obeyed, without any presentiment of what was coming. My father was grave rather than angry; but, nevertheless, I stood expecting another attack, when these words fell on my startled ears :

"After several sleepless nights I have made up my mind. You shall go to Paris and study music ; but only for a time. If after several trials you fail, you will, I am sure, acknowledge that I have done what was right, and you will choose some other career. You know what I think of second-rate poets ; second-rate artists are no better, and it would be a deep and lasting sorrow to me to see you numbered among the useless members of society."

My father was, it may be remarked, far less intolerant of second-rate doctors, who are not only more numerous than bad poets or artists, but are also actively instead of passively dangerous. It is always so even among clever men; they use the most powerful arguments in combating the prejudices of their neighbours, wholly unconscious that their weapons can be turned with deadly effect against their own most cherished opinions. I threw myself into my father's arms, and promised all he asked. "Seeing how radically your mother's ideas and mine differ on this subject," he continued, "I have thought it better, in order to avoid painful scenes, not to inform her of my determination; and I wish you to keep it secret and to start for Paris without telling her." The first day, therefore, I was most careful to keep my own counsel; but it was impossible to conceal this sudden and extraordinary change, from silent, morose sadness to delirious and exuberant joy, from my sisters. Nancy, the eldest, besought me so constantly to reveal the cause to her, that I did so, with many injunctions not to tell. She succeeded just as well as I had done; and in a short time the whole household, all our friends, and finally my mother, were informed of it.

In order to understand what follows, it is necessary to realise that, in addition to her religious prejudices, my mother held strong opinions with regard to all arts connected with the stage, opinions unfortunately shared by many people in France even in our own day. She looked upon all actors, actresses, singers, musicians, poets, and composers as abominable creatures excommunicated by the Church, and therefore predestined to eternal damnation.[1] *À propos* to this, an aunt of mine—she now

---

[1] [Actors were so treated by the Gallican Church up to a comparatively recent period. "In France," says Mr. Lecky (*History of Rationalism*, vol. ii. p. 347), "the sacraments were denied to actors

loves me very dearly, I hope, and even esteems me—whose head was full of my mother's strange *liberal* ideas, one day made the following astounding remark. We had been arguing, and I said, "To hear you speak, dear aunt, one would think you would be ashamed to own Racine as a member of the family?" "Ah, my dear, *respectability* before everything !" Lesueur was convulsed with laughter when I repeated this story to him in Paris. As he could only conceive of such a speech emanating from a mind verging on second childhood, whenever he was in a good humour he used to ask after Racine's enemy, *my old aunt*, although she was then young and as beautiful as an angel.

So, when my mother got wind of what was happening, her whole soul was roused to anger. She was convinced that, in adopting music as a career (at that time music and the theatre were inseparably connected in the minds of Frenchmen), I was pursuing a path which leads to discredit in this world and damnation in the next. The moment I saw her face I knew that she knew, and tried to avoid her until the moment of my departure. But I had scarcely found a hiding-place when she discovered me, and, with flashing eyes and excited gestures, exclaimed : "Your father has been weak enough to allow you to return to Paris, and to encourage your wild, wicked plans ; but I will not have this guilt on my soul, and, once for all, I forbid your departure." "Mother !" "Yes, I forbid it, and I beseech you not to

who refused to repudiate their profession, and their burial was the burial of a dog. Among these was the beautiful and gifted Adrienne Lecouvreur. . . . She was buried in a field by the side of the Seine. . . . Molière was the object of especial denunciation, and it was with extreme difficulty that permission could be obtained to bury him in consecrated ground."]

persist in your folly, Hector. See; I, your mother, kneel to you, and beg you humbly to renounce it." "Good heavens, mother; do not kneel to me! Rise, I entreat you!" "No; I will kneel." After a moment's pause: "Wretched boy! you refuse? Can you stand unmoved, with your mother kneeling at your feet? Well, then, go! Go and wallow in the filth of Paris, sully your name, and kill your father and me with sorrow and shame! I will not re-enter the house till you have left it. You are my son no longer. I curse you!"

It is almost incredible that bigotry, backed up by even the most fanatical provincial contempt for the life of an artist, could have led to such a scene between so tender a mother and so grateful and respectful a son. It is possible that the recollection of this painful, unnatural, horrible scene, which I can never forget, has inspired me with my deep hatred for those stupid doctrines which, having their origin in the Middle Ages, are so common in France even in the present day.

The trial was not yet over. My mother had vanished; she had taken shelter in a country house, called Le Chuzeau, near the Côte, which belonged to us. When the hour for my departure had arrived, my father wished me to make a last effort to induce her to bid me good-bye, and retract her cruel words. We arrived at Le Chuzeau with my two sisters. My mother was reading, under a tree in the orchard. When she saw us, she rose and fled. We waited for a long time; we followed her; my father called her; my sisters and I stood there crying. All in vain; I had to leave without bidding her good-bye, without a word or a look, and with her curse on my head.

CHAPTER XI.

WHEN I was back in Paris and had resumed my music with Lesueur, my first object was to repay Pons the money he had lent me. The debt weighed upon me, and I did not see my way to paying it off out of my monthly allowance of one hundred and twenty francs. I was fortunate enough to get some pupils, to whom I taught singing, the flute, and the guitar; and the money I thus obtained, with what I saved out of my allowance, enabled me to pay back my kind creditor six hundred francs in a few months. You may wonder how I managed to save anything out of my small allowance, and this is how I did it. I took a cheap little room on the fifth storey, in the Cité, at the corner of the Rue de Harlay and the Quai des Orfèvres, and, instead of dining at a restaurant as before, I restricted myself to a frugal meal which only cost me fourpence, and usually consisted of dry bread, and raisins, prunes, or dates.

As it was summer-time I used to buy my delicacies at a neighbouring grocer's, and carry them to the little terrace on the Pont Neuf, at the foot of the statue of Henry IV. There I ate my frugal meal, without a thought of the *poule au pot* which the good king desired all his peasants to have for their Sunday dinner, watching the sun's course towards Mount Valerien, revelling in the shining waters of the river as it flowed beneath me, my mind full of Moore's beautiful poems, of which I was then reading a translation. Unfortunately Pons, in distress at the privations I was obliged to incur, which, as we were intimate, it was impossible to conceal from him, and being also probably in urgent need of the money, wrote to my father, telling him the whole story, and asking for the remaining six hundred francs. The step was disastrous. My father had bitterly repented of his kindness. I had been five months in Paris; my position was apparently unchanged, and my musical career seemed to be at a standstill. He imagined, no doubt, that by that time I should have obtained the *grand prix* at the Conservatoire, have composed an opera in three acts, which would have been performed with unprecedented success, received the Legion of Honour, a pension from Government, etc. etc. Instead of this, he was dunned for a debt! It was a heavy blow, and it rebounded on me. He paid Pons, and told me that, if I did not renounce the pursuit of my musical chimera, he would give me no assistance, and would leave me to provide for myself. But I had my pupils, I did not want much to live on, and my debt was paid. So I at once made up my mind to remain. As a matter of fact, I was working very hard at music. Cherubini, whose love of routine was all-pervading, knew that I had not been through the usual Conservatoire course before I entered Lesueur's class, and he therefore put me into Reicha's counterpoint and fugue class, which precedes composition in the hierarchy of studies. I was thus working with both masters at the same time. Besides this I had struck up a friendship with a clever, warm-hearted young fellow whom I am still proud to number among my friends, Humbert Ferrand. He had written the book of an opera for me, the *Francs Juges*, and I was setting it to music with intense enthusiasm. The poem was afterwards refused by the Royal Academy[1] of Music, and my music was consigned to a limbo from which it has never emerged. The overture only has been played. I have used some of its best ideas in subsequent compositions, and the remainder will either be treated in the same way or burnt. Ferrand had also written a grand scena, with choruses, on the Greek Revolution, a subject of which all men's minds were at that time full, and this I had set to music, without much interruption to my work of the *Francs Juges*. It was through this work, every page of which was redolent with traces of Spontini's powerful influence, that I first became acquainted with the hard egotism which one encounters in almost all celebrated artists, but of which I had no previous knowledge, and which showed me how little a young composer has to hope for from them.

Rodolphe Kreutzer was the conductor-in-chief of the music at the Opéra. The season for the concerts of sacred music which take place in Passion Week, and are given in the Opera-house, was drawing near. The decision as to whether my scena should be performed lay with him. I went to him myself about it. He had been prepared for my visit by a letter from M. de Larochefoucauld, the Superintendent of Fine Arts, who had been induced to write to him about me by one of the secretaries, a friend of Ferrand's. Besides this, Lesueur had recommended me to him most warmly; so there was good ground for

---

[1] [The official name of the Grand Opéra of Paris.]

hope. This, alas! was soon dispelled. I was received by Kreutzer, the great artist, the author of *The Death of Abel* (a fine work, on which I had written the most enthusiastic panegyric a few months before)—Kreutzer, whom, because I admired him, I had always pictured as kindly and genial, like my master—received with contemptuous rudeness. He barely returned my salutation, and, without looking at me, threw these words at me over his shoulder: "My good fellow" (he did not even know me), "we cannot perform new pieces at these concerts of sacred music. We have not time to get them up; Lesueur is well aware of this." I left him with a heavy heart. On the following Sunday, Lesueur and Kreutzer had an explanation at the Chapel Royal, where the latter played the violin. When pressed by my master, he answered, without attempting to conceal his annoyance: "Good heavens! what would become of us if we were to help on the young fellows like that?" He was frank enough, at any rate.

CHAPTER XII.

BUT winter was approaching. In my eagerness to finish
my opera I had somewhat neglected my pupils. A raw,
cold, damp atmosphere had replaced the sunny warmth
of my dining-hall on the Pont Neuf, which was no
longer a fitting spot for my luxurious feasts. I needed
firewood and warmer clothes. Where was the money for
these necessaries to come from? My lessons at a franc
each were wholly insufficient for my needs, and even
they seemed likely to fail me. Should I return to my
father, contrite and vanquished, or die of hunger? These
were my alternatives. The mere notion aroused such an
indomitable determination never to yield, as to inspire
me with new energy for the struggle; and I resolved to
do anything—even quit Paris, if necessary—rather than
return meekly to vegetate on the Côte. My old passion
for travel came to the aid of my music, and I determined
to apply to the agents for foreign theatres, and try for an
engagement as first or second flute in an orchestra in New
York, Mexico, Sydney, or Calcutta. I would have gone
to China, and become a sailor, filibuster, buccaneer, or
savage, sooner than own myself defeated. Such is my
nature. It is as futile and dangerous to thwart my

will, when I am resolved on anything, as it is to try and prevent gunpowder from exploding by compressing it.

Fortunately my efforts to obtain employment abroad failed, and I was at my wits' end, when I suddenly heard that the Théâtre des Nouveautés was about to open, and that vaudevilles and a certain class of opéra comique would be played there. I rushed off to the manager and applied for a place as flute-player in the orchestra. There was no vacancy. I then tried for the chorus; that was full too. Death and fury ! . . . However, the manager took down my address, promising to let me know if they enlarged their chorus. The hope was a very slight one ; but it buoyed me up for some days, until I received a letter saying that I might compete for the appointment. The examination of the candidates was to take place in the Freemasons' Hall in the Rue de Grenelle St. Honoré. I went there, and found five or six poor devils like myself, awaiting the advent of their judges with keen anxiety. Among them were a weaver, a blacksmith, an actor who had been dismissed from a small theatre on the boulevards, and a chorister from St. Eustache. Bass voices were wanted, and my voice was at the outside a passable baritone ; but I hoped our examiner would not be too particular.

It was the manager himself. He entered, followed by a musician called Michel, who still plays in the Vaudeville orchestra. There was neither piano nor pianist; Michel's violin was to be our accompaniment. The trial began. My rivals sing as best they can the song they have carefully learnt. When my turn comes the colossal manager, whose name oddly enough is St. Léger, asks me what I have brought.

"Brought ? Nothing."

"Nothing? Then what do you mean to sing?"

"Anything you like. Is there nothing here? No *solfège*, no score, no book of exercises?"

"No; we have none of these. And besides," added the manager contemptuously, "I don't suppose you can read at sight?"

"Pardon me, I can; anything you like to give me."

"Ah, that is another matter! But as we have no music of any sort; don't you know any popular song by heart?"

"Yes; I know the *Danaïdes, Stratonice, La Vestale, Cortez, Œdipe,* the two *Iphigénies, Orphée, Armide. . . .*"

"That will do. What a prodigious memory! Well, come now, as you are so learned, sing the song *Elle m'a prodigué,* from Sacchini's *Œdipe.*"

"Certainly."

"Can you accompany him, Michel?"

"Of course; only unfortunately I forget what key it is in."

"In E flat. Shall I sing the recitative?"

"By all means; let us hear the recitative."

The accompanist played a chord in E flat, and I began:

Antigone me reste ; Antigone est ma fille, etc.

The other competitors cast despairing glances at one another as the glorious melody rolled forth; evidently conscious that, although I was neither a Pischek nor a Lablache, they had sung like crows in comparison; and, to use a piece of theatrical slang, I saw by a little signal from the big manager that they were *enfoncés jusqu'au troisième dessous.* The next morning I received the official notification of my appointment. I had beaten the weaver, the blacksmith, the actor, and even the chorister from St. Eustache, and was to enter upon my duties at once at fifty francs a month.

So behold me, on my way to become an accursed dramatic composer, sunk to the level of a chorus-singer in a second-rate theatre, despised and excommunicated to the innermost core of my being. I could not help admiring the success which had crowned my parents' efforts to save me from the pit of destruction.

Blessings never come singly. I had scarcely achieved this brilliant success when the sky rained down two pupils upon me; and I also made the acquaintance of a compatriot, Antoine Charbonnel, who was studying chemistry. He wanted to live in the Quartier Latin, to be near his classes, and wished, like me, to practise a Spartan economy. No sooner had we calculated the amount of our joint fortunes than, parodying the words of Walter, in *La Vie d'un Joueur*, we both cried out : " Ah ! tu n'as pas d'argent; eh bien, mon cher, il faut nous associer ! "

We took two little rooms in the Rue de la Harpe. Antoine, who was accustomed to furnaces and retorts, undertook the duties of head cook, and used me as a mere scullion. Every morning we sallied forth to buy our own provisions at the market, which I carried home in the most unblushing way, to my companion's disgust, under my arm. And, oh, chemical proprieties ! we actually once had words on the subject.

So we lived like two princes—in exile—on thirty francs a month each. I had not known such luxury since I arrived in Paris. I was actually extravagant; I bought a piano[1]—and such a piano ! I hung framed pictures

---

[1] It cost me one hundred and ten francs. I have said already that I could not play the piano; but still I like to hear one, and

of my musical deities on the walls, and presented myself
with a copy of Moore's *Loves of the Angels*. Antoine,
who was as clever as a monkey with his fingers (which is
a very poor simile, for monkeys can only destroy), spent
his spare moments in manufacturing all sorts of orna-
mental and useful trifles. He made us each a pair of
well-conditioned clogs out of some of our firewood ; and
in order to vary the sameness of our frugal repast,
contrived a net and a decoy bird, with which, when the
spring came, he caught quails in the plain of Montrouge.
The funniest part of it all was that, in spite of my
periodical absence in the evening (the Théâtre des Nouveautés was open every night), Antoine never found out
during all the time we lived together that I had the
misfortune to belong to the stage—for I was not proud
enough of my position as a chorus-singer to boast of it.
While at the theatre I was supposed to be giving
lessons in a remote part of Paris. · My pride was on a
par with his ! I could not bear to let my companion
know how I gained my living, and he blushed scarlet and
could scarcely bear to be seen with me in the streets when
I was carrying the bread earned by my honest labour.
But to tell the truth, and in justice to myself, I must
acknowledge that my reticence did not arise from foolish
pride. In spite of my parents' severity and their desertion of me, I would not for the world have caused
them the anguish (which to them with their ideas would
have been intense) of knowing what I had done ; and

occasionally to crash out some chords on it. I like also to have
musical instruments in the room with me ; and if I were rich, I would
always have by me, while I worked, a concert grand piano, two or
three of Erard's harps, some of Sax's trumpets, and a collection of
Stradivarius violins and violoncellos.

indeed there was no reason for doing so. I was, therefore, doubly careful lest by any indiscretion on my part my secret should be revealed to them, and I kept my own counsel. And so, like Antoine Charbonnel himself, they were only informed of my dramatic career, seven or eight years after it had come to an end, through the biographical notices of me which appeared in various papers.

CHAPTER XIII.

First Composition for the Orchestra—Studies at the Opéra—
Lesueur and Reicha.

It was at this period that I wrote my first great instrumental work, the overture to the *Francs Juges*, soon afterwards followed by *Waverley*. I was at that time so ignorant of the mechanism of some of the instruments, that, after I had written the trombone solo in the key of D flat, I feared it might be too difficult to play. I took it to the trombone-player at the Opéra. He examined it, and reassured me by saying: "The key of D flat is, as it happens, one of those best suited to this particular instrument, and you may count on the passage producing a grand effect."

I was delighted at this, and was so absorbed in thinking of it that I walked home as in a dream, without looking where I went, and sprained my ankle in consequence. I get a pain in my foot now when I hear that piece. Perhaps it gives others a pain in their heads.

Neither of my masters taught me anything about instrumentation. Lesueur's ideas on the subject were most limited. Reicha understood the qualities of wind instruments; but I don't think he had any real conception of grouping them in larger or smaller bodies. Besides, his department was counterpoint and fugue, and he had nothing to do with this branch of music, which is not, even now, represented in the Conservatoire. Before my engagement at the Théâtre des Nouveautés, I had become acquainted with a friend of Gardel, the celebrated ballet-master. Thanks to the pit-tickets he gave me, I was always able to go to the Opéra. I used to take the score of the piece with me, and read it during the performance. By this means I grew to understand the handling of an orchestra, and recognise the accent and tone of the instruments, even though I could not grasp their mechanism or their power.

By a careful comparison of the means used with the effects produced, I perceived the subtle connection which subsists between musical expression and the special art of instrumentation; but no one ever pointed this out to me. It was by studying the methods of the three modern masters, Beethoven, Weber, and Spontini; by an impartial examination of the regular forms of instrumentation, and of *unusual* forms and combinations; partly by listening to artists, and getting them to make experiments for me on their instruments, and partly by instinct, that I acquired the knowledge I possess. Reicha's lessons in counterpoint were singularly lucid; he did, in a short time, teach me a great deal, without waste of words; and, unlike most masters, he generally explained to his pupils the meaning of the rules he wished them to obey.

Reicha was neither an empiric nor a conservative. He believed in progress in certain departments of art; and his respect for the fathers of harmony had not degenerated into fetish-worship. Hence his perpetual discussions with Cherubini. The latter pushed his idolatry for musical authority so far as to submit his own judgment to it, as when he says in his *Treatise on Counterpoint*: "This arrangement of harmony seems to me preferable to the other; but the old masters thought otherwise, *and we must obey them.*" In his compositions, however, Reicha followed the routine he despised. I once asked him to tell me what he thought of whole fugues composed on the word *Amen*, or on *Kyrie Eleison*, with which the masses and requiems of the greatest composers are infested. "Oh," cried he quickly, "it is barbarous." "Then, sir, why do you write them?" "Ah! because all the world does." *Miseria!*

Lesueur was more logical in this respect. Those monstrous fugues, which imitate the shouts of a crowd of drunkards, and seem like a parody on the sacred texts, he regarded as remnants of a barbaric age; he never wrote them himself, and the occasional fugues which are found in his sacred compositions have nothing in common with such grotesque abominations. On the contrary, one of his fugues, which opens with the words *Quis enarrabit cœlorum gloriam?* is a masterpiece of dignified style and scientific harmony; and, what is more, it is a masterpiece of expression, to which the fugued form is here conducive. When, after the exposition of the *subject* (broad and beautiful) in the dominant, the *answer* comes dashing in in the tonic with a repetition of the words *Quis enarrabit*, it seems as if the one part of the choir, fired with the enthusiasm of the other, rushed off in its turn to sing with redoubled joy of the glories of the firmament. And then how the brilliant instrumentation floods the voices with gladness! With what power the basses are heard through the tracery of the violins, which shine like stars in the higher registers of the orchestra. What a thrilling *stretto* on the pedal! This fugue in its glorious beauty is justified by the meaning of the words, and wholly worthy of them!

It is the work of a musician who is inspired by his subject, and of an artist who understands his art ! But as for the fugues of which I spoke to Reicha, *low tavern fugues*, I could cite numbers signed by masters far greater than Lesueur ; but in writing them simply because it was customary to do so, those masters, be they who they may, turned their talent to base uses, and are guilty of an unpardonable outrage against musical expression.[1]

Before he came to Paris, Reicha had been a fellow-student of Beethoven's at Bonn.[2] I do not think they ever cared much for one another. Reicha was very proud of his mathematical attainments. "It is by the study of mathematics," he once said to us, in one of his lessons, "that I have succeeded in achieving a complete mastery over my ideas ; by this means I have subdued and tempered my imagination, which used to overpower me ; and, now that it is controlled by reason and reflection, it has doubled its power." I don't know whether Reicha's theory is as true as he thought, or whether his musical faculties were really much strengthened by his study of exact science. It is possible that to it he owed his taste for abstract combinations and clever tricks in music, and the actual charm he used to find in solving some of those difficult propositions which really divert art from its true path, by concealing the high end towards which it should

[1] [One of the cleverest things in Berlioz's *Faust* is his imitation of one of the orthodox fugues which he criticises above with so much energy. Had he taken the trouble he might have found the same qualities that he so justly praises in Lesueur's chorus in many another fugue of Handel, Mozart, Leo, and others of the old composers.]

[2] [Not a "fellow-student." They were both members of the Elector's band, where Beethoven played the viola and Reicha the flute, while Reicha's uncle was conductor of the band. Beethoven was much attached to young Reicha.]

evermore be tending. On the other hand, this love of
numbers probably marred much of his work by robbing
it of its harmonious or melodious expression—that is to
say, of its pure music; and what it gained by its laborious
combinations, conquest of difficulties, and strange effects,
was more calculated to affect the eye than the ear.
However, Reicha regarded neither praise nor blame; he
seemed to care for nothing but the success of the young
artists at the Conservatoire over whose studies he presided, and whom he taught with all possible care and
attention. He grew fond of me at length; but at first I
observed that my asking him the why and wherefore
of all the rules annoyed him: he could not tell me the
reason of some of them—because they had none. His
quintets for wind instruments were the fashion for a time
in Paris. They are interesting, but very cold. On the
other hand, I remember hearing a magnificent duet, full
of fire and passion, in his opera, *Sappho*, which was played
several times.

CHAPTER XIV.

Competition at the Conservatoire—My Cantata declared unplayable—Adoration for Gluck and Spontini—Arrival of Rossini—The Dilettanti—Fury—M. Ingres.

THE period of the Conservatoire examinations had come round; I went up again and was admitted. We were given a scena to write for full orchestra, on the subject of the death of Orpheus.

I think my piece was not devoid of merit; but the mediocre pianist (it will be seen presently how extraordinary the organisation of these competitions was) who had to play the orchestral accompaniments on the piano, was unable to get through the *Bacchanale*, whereupon the musical section of the Conservatoire, consisting of Cherubini, Paër, Lesueur, Berton, Boïeldieu, and Catel, pronounced my work unplayable, and thereby excluded me from the competition.

I had already seen how musicians, in their selfish dread of competition, discourage young artists; I now realised how the ridiculous tyranny of the Academy strangles them. Kreutzer denied me an opportunity of success which was of immense importance to me; the academicians, by carrying out an absurd rule to the letter, robbed me of my chance of winning a prize which, though not brilliant in itself, would have encouraged me; whereas his rebuff overwhelmed me with rage and dumb despair.

I had got ten days' leave from the Théâtre des Nouveautés, in order to attend the competition; when the time had expired I had to resume my fetters. But just then I became seriously ill, and was nearly carried off by an attack of quinsy. Antoine, who was running after *grisettes*, left me alone all day and almost all night. I had no servant and no nurse. I think I should certainly have died one night if I had not, in a paroxysm of agony, made a desperate cut at the abscess in the back of my throat, which was choking me, and lanced it. This unscientific operation saved my life. I was almost well again when my father, who was probably vanquished by my persistence, and must have felt some anxiety as to my means of livelihood, restored my allowance. Thanks to this unexpected act of paternal tenderness I was able to give up my situation as chorus-singer—no slight advantage; for, apart from the overpowering physical fatigue of the work, I was utterly sick of the wretched music to which I was obliged to listen, and which would infallibly have brought on an attack of cholera, or driven me into an asylum. Any true musician who knows the music of these little vaudeville operas, and of the larger vaudevilles which ape real operas, will realise what I went through.

I was now free to revel in my evenings at the Opéra, which I had been obliged to give up on account of my dreary work at the Théâtre des Nouveautés, and to plunge entirely into the study and culture of grand dramatic music. The only other serious music I had ever heard was at the concerts in the Opera-house, where the execution was so poor and thin as to awaken no enthusiasm in me. I had, therefore, never paid much attention to purely instrumental music. The symphonies of Haydn and

Mozart (which are, speaking generally, of an essentially *domestic* character), played by a feeble orchestra on far too large a stage, and with very bad acoustic arrangements, produced about as much effect as if they had been performed on the plain of Grenelle; and sounded confused, poor, meagre. I had looked through two of Beethoven's symphonies and had heard an *andante*[1] played, which made me feel dimly that he was a great luminary, but a luminary only faintly discernible through dark clouds. Weber's masterpieces had not then seen the light, and his name was wholly unknown. As to Rossini and the rage for him which possessed the fashionable Parisian world, it aroused my passionate indignation, all the more because the new school was looked upon as rivalling that of Gluck and Spontini. I could conceive of nothing more grand, sublime, or true than the works of those great composers; and Rossini's melodious cynicism, his contempt for the traditions of dramatic expression, his perpetual repetition of one kind of cadence, his eternal petty *crescendo*, and his crashing big drums, exasperated me to such a degree as to blind me to the dazzling qualities of his genius and the real beauties of the *Barbiere*, with its delicate instrumentation and *no* big drum. I used often to speculate on the possibility of undermining the Théâtre Italien, so as to blow it and its Rossini-worshippers into space. And when I met one of those hated *dilettanti*, I used to mutter to myself as I eyed him with Shylockian glance, "Would that I might impale thee on a red-hot stake, thou scoundrel!" I must confess

---

[1] [Doubtless the slow movement of the Seventh Symphony, which Berlioz elsewhere tells us was for long the only orchestral movement of Beethoven that would go down at Paris, and which is known to have been introduced into the Second Symphony in its performance at the Paris Concerts to make the latter work float.]

that time has not tempered the violence of my feelings,
or caused me to change the strong views I hold on this
subject. Not that I now desire to impale anyone *on
a red-hot stake*, or that I would blow up the Théâtre
Italien, even if the powder were laid and the match ready
to my hand; but I echo Ingres' words with all my heart
and soul when I hear him speak of some of Rossini's
music as " the work of an underbred man." [1]

[1] M. Ingres and I are not alone in our opinion of several of
Rossini's great Italian operas. But this does not prevent the
illustrious author of the *Martyr of St. Symphorien* from regarding
me as a vile musician, a monster, a brigand, and an Antichrist.
However, I forgive him most heartily, because of his admiration
for Gluck. Is enthusiasm the opposite of love? it makes us love
those who love what we love, even when they hate us.

CHAPTER XV.

My evenings at the Opéra were solemn occasions, for which I generally prepared myself by serious study and examination of the works which I was to see performed. The fanatical admiration of myself and some of my companions in the pit for our favourite composers was only equalled by an intense detestation of the others. The Jupiter of our Olympus was Gluck; and not even the most ardent musician of the present day can conceive of the intensity with which we worshipped our idol. But if some of my friends were faithful to our musical creed, I may say without vanity that I was its priest. When I saw any wavering in their devotion I sought to rekindle it by addresses worthy of the St. Simonians. I dragged them off to the Opéra, and even went so far as to buy tickets for them myself, which I pretended had been given to me by someone belonging to the theatre.

After having thus succeeded in getting my man into the theatre when one of Gluck's masterpieces was to be played, I placed him on a seat in the pit, conjuring him not to change his place, seeing that others were not equally good for hearing, and that I had tried every one. Here you were too near the horns, there you could not hear them; on the right the trombones were too loud, on the left the echo from the stage-boxes produced a disagreeable effect; nearer to the stage you were too close to the orchestra, and the voices were drowned; higher up you were too far from the stage, and the words were inaudible, or you could not see the faces of the actors; the instrumentation of this work was best appreciated from such a place, the chorus from another; in one act the scene was laid in a sacred forest, which was so vast that the sound was lost in most parts of the theatre, therefore it was necessary to go nearer; in another, which represented the interior of a palace, and was what is called, in the language of the theatre, a *salon fermé*, the force of the sound being doubled by this seemingly trifling change, it became advisable to move to the back of the pit, from whence the voices would seem to blend in more complete harmony.

When I had instructed my neophytes thus far, I asked them if they were familiar with the piece they had come to hear. If they were not, I produced the libretto, and spent the time before the rising of the curtain in making them read it, interpolating such remarks as I imagined would facilitate their apprehension of the composer's meaning. We always came early so that we might get good places, hear the first notes of the overture, and indulge in the delight of anticipating a great pleasure one is certain to enjoy. One of our treats was to watch the empty orchestra, which seemed at first like a stringless piano, fill gradually with music and musicians. First there was the attendant who put the parts on the desks. That was always an anxious moment; some accident might have happened, another piece might have been substituted, and instead of one of Gluck's masterpieces we might have some *Rossignol*, or *Prétendus*, or *Caravane du Caire*, or *Panurge*, or *Devin du Village*, or *Lasthénie*, or other thin, sickly piece, more or less dreary and poor—for we regarded them all with the same sovereign contempt.

The name of the opera inscribed in huge letters on the double-bass parts nearest to the pit either relieved or confirmed our fears. In the latter case we rushed out of the place, swearing like a trooper who has got water instead of brandy, anathematising alike the author and the piece, the manager who palmed it off on the public, and the Government which sanctioned its performance. Poor Rousseau who valued his score of the *Devin du Village* as highly as the masterpieces of eloquence which have made him immortal, who thought he had utterly eclipsed Rameau, and even the trio of *Les Parques*,[1] by the little songs, little roulades, little rondos, little solos, little pastorals, and all the little drolleries of which his little interlude is made up; to whom the Holbachians so grudged this musical achievement, and who was so worried about it; he who was so often accused of not being the real author; he whose music was sung by everyone in France, from Jéliotte and Mdlle. Fel[2] to Louis XV., who was never tired of singing, *J'ai perdu mon serviteur*, more out of tune than any of his subjects; he whose music was in fact a most complete success in every possible sense —what would poor Rousseau have said if he could have heard our curses? How could he dream that his precious opera, which was received with such enthusiasm, would one day suddenly disappear and be obliterated under a huge peruke thrown at Colette's feet by some

---

[1] A once celebrated and very remarkable piece from an opera by Rameau, *Hippolyte et Aricie*.

[2] The actor and actress at the Opéra who created the parts of Colin and Colette in the *Devin*.

insolent scoffer?   Oddly enough I was present at the
last performance of the *Devin;*[1] and therefore many
people have laid the *scene of the peruke* to my charge,
but I protest mine innocence.   Besides, I recollect feeling
quite as much indignation as amusement at so grotesque
a piece of irreverence, and cannot make up my mind
whether I could have perpetrated it.

But imagine Gluck—Gluck himself—going so far as
to write and print, some fifty years ago, *à propos* of this
wretched *Devin,* in a perfectly serious letter addressed
to Queen Marie Antoinette, such words as these:
"*France, which has so little to boast of in the way of
music, has, however, produced some remarkable compositions, among which may be cited M. Rousseau's Devin
du Village.*"   Who would have credited Gluck with
such a sense of humour?   By this one sentence he has
borne away the palm for facetious perfidy from the
Italians themselves.

But to return to my narrative.   When we saw, by
the title-page of the orchestral parts, that no change
had been made in the opera, I went on with my
lecture, singing the principal passages, explaining the
instrumental procedure to which certain effects were due,
and so enlisting the sympathy and enthusiasm of the
members of our little club beforehand.   Our excitement
caused a good deal of surprise among our neighbours
in the pit, for the most part good country folks, whose
expectations, being keenly excited by my preliminary
perorations, were generally much more disappointed
than amused by the reality.   I then named each per-
former as he entered the orchestra, introducing him
with a running commentary on his habits and powers.

---

[1] It was never given at the Opéra after that memorable evening.

"There's Baillot. *He* does not reserve himself for the ballets, like the other violins; *he* does not consider it a disgrace to play Gluck's accompaniments; he will play a passage on the fourth string presently; and you will hear it through all the rest of the orchestra.

"That fat, red fellow yonder is the double bass, Father Chénié. He is a robust old fellow, in spite of his years; a host in himself, and worth four of the others. You may be sure his part will be played as the author wrote it; he does not belong to the school of simplifiers.

"The conductor ought to keep an eye on Guillon, the flute-player, who is just coming in. He takes the strangest liberties with Gluck. For the religious march in *Alceste*, for example, the composer has written a low part for the flutes, so as to obtain the special effect of its deep tones. Guillon does not approve of this; he must take the lead; he *will* be heard; and so what does he do but play his part an octave higher, destroying the author's effect, and turning an ingenious idea into a common one."

The three taps which announced that the opera was about to begin put an end to our critical review of the orchestral notables. We sat with beating hearts, silently awaiting the signal from Kreutzer or Valentino. When the overture had begun it was criminal to speak, beat time, or hum a bar; if anyone did so, we at once made use of the well-known saying, "Confound those musicians who prevent me from hearing this gentleman!"

As I was intimately acquainted with every note of the score, the performers, if they were wise, played it as it was written. I would have died rather than allow the slightest interference with the old masters to pass unnoticed. I had no notion of biding my time and protesting in writing against such a crime—oh dear no!—I apostrophised the delinquents then and there in my loudest voice, and I can testify that no form of criticism goes so straight home as that. For example, I once remarked that in the *Iphigénie en Tauride* cymbals had been put into the first dance of the Scythians, in B minor, where Gluck had only strings; and that in Orestes' grand recitative, in the third act, the trombone parts, which, in the score, are so exquisitely adapted to the situation, had been left out altogether. The next time the opera was played I was resolved that if these errors were repeated I would show them up. Accordingly, when the Scythian ballet began I lay in wait for my cymbals; they came in just as they done before. . . . Boiling with anger, I nevertheless contained myself until the piece was finished, and then, seizing the occasion of the momentary lull which preceded the next piece, I shouted out with all my might, " There are no cymbals there ; who has dared to correct Gluck ? " [1]

The hubbub may be imagined. The public, who are not very sharp-sighted in matters connected with art, and to whom changes in an author's work are matters of complete indifference, could not understand what made the young lunatic in the pit so angry. But it was worse in the third act, where the trombones in Orestes' monologue were suppressed, just as I feared they would be ; and the same voice was heard shouting out, " Not a sign of a trombone ; it is intolerable ! "

The astonishment of both orchestra and audience

---

[1] There are no cymbals except in the Scythian chorus, *Les dieux apaisent leur courroux.* The character of the ballet being quite different, it is of course differently instrumented.

was only equalled by Valentino's perfectly legitimate indignation. I learnt afterwards that the unfortunate trombones were only carrying out a distinct order[1] to omit that particular passage, which stands in their parts exactly as it does in the score.

As to the cymbals, which Gluck has introduced so happily in the first Scythian chorus, I do not know who took upon himself to import them into the dance, thus falsifying the colour and marring the sinister silence of that weird ballet. But I know that in all subsequent performances order was restored; the cymbals were silent, the trombones were heard; and I listened content, muttering through my teeth, "All right."

Soon afterwards De Pons, who was just as rabid as I, and who objected to the suppression of Sacchini's dance-music in the first act of *Œdipe à Colonne*, suggested to me that we should put an end to the interminable solos for horn and violoncello which had been inserted in their stead. Could I refuse my help in so just a cause? The means we had employed in the case of the *Iphigénie* were equally successful in that of the *Œdipus*; and the result of a few well-timed words from the pit was the permanent withdrawal of the objectionable airs.

Only once, however, did we succeed in carrying the public with us. It had been announced in the bills that Baillot would play the violin solo in the ballet in *Nina.* The evening arrived, and, either because he was indisposed, or for some other reason, he did not perform, and the managers deemed it sufficient to acquaint the public with the fact by means of a minute piece of paper pasted on the theatre door, and seen by no one. The

[1] So much the worse for whoever issued the order.

greater part of the spectators, therefore, expected to hear the great violinist.

Even Mdlle. Bigottini's pathetic pantomime, when she comes to her senses in the arms of her father and her lover, failed to make us forget Baillot. The scene was almost over. "So far good," said I, loud enough to be heard, "but where is the violin solo?" "That is true," said one of the public; "it looks as if they were going to leave it out. Baillot, Baillot! the violin solo!"

The pit took fire at once; and then a thing which I had never seen at the Opéra happened. The entire house rose and loudly demanded that the programme should be carried out.

The curtain fell in the midst of this hubbub. The uproar redoubled; the musicians fled; the angry public dashed into the orchestra, overturning chairs and music-desks, and smashing the drums. In vain did I cry: "Gentlemen, gentlemen, don't smash the instruments! What vandalism! Don't you see that you are destroying Father Chénié's beautiful double-bass, with its infernal tone?" My words fell unheeded, and the rioters never rested till they had overturned the whole orchestra and smashed I don't know how many seats and instruments.

This was the seamy side of the active criticism we exercised so despotically at the Opéra. Its good side was our enthusiasm when all went well. Then you should have seen with what a frenzy of applause we greeted the passages which no one else noticed —a fine bass, a happy modulation, a right accent in a recitative, an expressive note by a hautbois, etc. The public took us for *claqueurs* out of work, whereas the real chief of the *claque*, who was only too well aware of the true state of affairs, and whose cunning combinations were deranged by our thunders of applause, looked as furious as Neptune when he uttered his *Quos ego.* Then when Mdme. Branchu excelled herself there were calls and stampings of feet such as are never heard in these days, even in the Conservatoire—the only place in France in which true musical enthusiasm is still to be found.

The most curious scene of this sort that I remember took place one evening when *Œdipe* was being played. Though Sacchini held a far lower place in our esteem than Gluck, we nevertheless admired him greatly. I had dragged one of my friends,[1] who cared for nothing but artillery, but of whom I was nevertheless determined to make a musical proselyte, to the Opéra. To my disgust, my friend was but moderately affected by the sufferings of Antigone and her father, so after the first act I gave him up as hopeless, and went to a seat in front, where I should not be disturbed by his insensibility. As though to throw his coldness into further relief, however, chance had placed on his right hand a spectator who was as emotional as he was the reverse. I soon became aware of this. Dérivis had made a great hit in his fine recitative :

> Mon fils? tu ne l'es plus!
> Va! ma haine est trop forte!

Absorbed though I was by the beauty and truly antique character of the scene, I could not help overhearing the dialogue which was going on behind, between my man, quietly peeling an orange, and his unknown neighbour, who was evidently suffering from the most intense emotion.

---

[1] Leon de Boissieux, my fellow-student at the little school on the Côte. He figured for a time in the *Illustrations du Billard de Paris.*

"Good God, sir, be calm."

"No, it is too much; it is overwhelming!—it is terrible!"

"But, sir, you are wrong to give way like this. You will be ill."

"No; let me be. . . . Oh!"

"Sir, come sir, cheer up! After all *it is only a play.* Will you have a piece of this orange?"

"Ah! how sublime!"

"It is Maltese!"

"What heavenly music!"

"Do not refuse."

"What music!"

"Yes; it is pretty."

During this discordant discourse we had got to the fine trio, *O doux moments,* which follows the scene of reconciliation; I was deeply affected by the penetrating sweetness of the simple melody, and, hiding my face in my hands, was weeping silently. Scarcely was the trio ended when I felt myself raised from my seat by two powerful arms which clasped me like a vice; they belonged to the unknown enthusiast, who, perceiving that I alone of all his neighbours shared his feelings, and unable any longer to control his emotion, was embracing me with wild enthusiasm, exclaiming convulsively, *"Sac-r-r-re Dieu, monsieur,* how beautiful it is!" Without expressing any surprise, and turning my face all blurred with tears towards him, I said, "Sir, are you a musician?" . . . "No! but I could not love music more if I were." "What matter? shake hands; you are a right good fellow."

And thereupon, regardless of the jeers of the spectators who had formed a circle round us, and of the astounded look of my orange-eating friend, we whispered to each other our names and professions.　He was an engineer! a mathematician!　In what strange soils can keen susceptibility thrive!　His name was Le Tessier.　I never saw him again.

CHAPTER XVI.

Weber at the Odéon — Castilblaze — Mozart — Lachnith —
"Adapters" — "Despair and die!"

WHILE thus absorbed in my musical studies, and while
my fever for Gluck and Spontini, and my aversion for
the Rossinian forms and doctrines were alike at their
height, Weber appeared on the scene. The *Freyschütz*
was given at the Odéon, not in its own beautiful form,
but a distorted, disfigured, vulgar "adaptation" under
the title of *Robin des Bois*. The orchestra, which
was a young one, was excellent, and the chorus fair, but
the singers were atrocious. One of them, Mdme. Pouilly,
who played the part of Agatha (rechristened Annette
by the translator), possessed a fair amount of execution,
but nothing else, the result being that the part, being
sung without intelligence, passion, or fervour, was
virtually annihilated. She sang the grand air in the
second act with as much feeling as if it had been one of
Bordogni's exercises, and it was not until long afterwards
that I discovered what a mine of beauty it contains.

The first performance was greeted with a storm of
laughter and hisses; but, on the second night, the waltz
and the huntsmen's chorus, which had excited attention
at first, created such a sensation that they saved the rest
of the work, and it drew full houses every night. Then,
the bridesmaids' chorus, and Agatha's prayer (cut in

half), became popular. Then, by degrees, the public became aware of a certain *racy charm* in the overture, and Max's song was allowed to be not *wholly wanting in dramatic feeling.* Lastly, the devilries in the Wolf's Glen were tolerated as *comic.* All Paris flocked to see so *whimsical* a piece; the Odéon throve on the proceeds; and M. Castilblaze received over a hundred thousand francs for mutilating a masterpiece.

Prejudiced, as I was, by my exclusive and intolerant idolatry for the old classics, I was nevertheless over-whelmed with surprise and delight at Weber's music. Even in its mutilated form, I was positively intoxi-cated by its delicious freshness, and its wild, subtle fragrance. To a man sated by the staid solemnity of the tragic muse, the rapid action of this wood-nymph, her gracious brusqueries, her dreamy poses, her pure maidenly love, her innocent smile, and her sadness, brought a torrent of new feelings and emotions. I forsook the Opéra for the Odéon, and, as I had a pass to the orchestra, I soon knew the *Freyschütz* (as there given) by heart.

The composer himself at this time paid his first and only visit to Paris on his way to London, where he was to witness the failure of one of his greatest works, and die. How I longed to see him! How my heart beat as I followed him about on the evening of the revival of Spontini's *Olympie*, shortly before he left for London! He was ill, but he wanted to see it. In the morning, Lesueur said to me: "Weber has just been here, and, if you had come five minutes sooner, you would have heard him play me whole acts of our French operas; he knows them all." Entering a music-shop, a few hours later, I heard: "Do you know who has just been sitting there?" "Who?" "Weber!" When

I reached the Opéra, I heard whispers on all sides, " Weber has just passed through ; he crossed the hall, and is in the first row of boxes." I was in despair at not being able to find him. But all my efforts were vain ; no one could point him out to me. He was the inverse of Shakespeare's apparitions, in that, being visible to all, he was invisible to me alone. And so I missed making his acquaintance, because I dared not write to him, and knew no one who could have introduced me.

If men of genius only knew what love their works inspire ! If they only realised with what an intense, concentrated devotion some hearts yearn towards them, how they would rejoice to receive and surround themselves with such kindred spirits, and how such worship would console them for the bitter envy, petty hatred, and careless indifference which they meet with elsewhere !

In spite of his popularity, the stupendous success of the *Freyschütz*, and his consciousness of power, Weber would probably have appreciated such silent, sincere adoration more than anyone. He had written beautiful things which had been coldly received by artists and critics alike. His last opera, *Euryanthe*, had only obtained a moderate success ; and he could not but feel anxious as to the fate of *Oberon*, for he must have known it to be a work which could only be truly appreciated by an audience of poets and thinkers. Even Beethoven, the king of kings, had long misunderstood him, so it is easy to realise how, at times, he lost faith in himself, and how it was that the failure of *Oberon* killed him.[1]

The striking contrast between the fate of this glorious

---

[1] [It was not the non-success of *Oberon* that killed Weber, but a disease of long standing, aggravated no doubt by his exertions over

work and that of its eldest brother, the *Freyschütz*, is not due to any defects in the favourite of fortune; it is neither vulgar nor petty in form, it owes its brilliancy to no sham effects, to nothing turgid or exaggerated in its expression; in neither the one nor the other has the composer ever yielded one iota to the petty requirements of fashion, or the more imperious demands of the artist. He was as simply true, as fearlessly original, as independent of precedent, as regardless of the public, and as determined not to truckle to them, in the *Freyschütz* as in *Oberon*. But the former is full of poetry, passion, and contrast. The supernatural element introduces strange and sudden effects. The melody, harmony, and rhythm alike, thunder, burn, and illumine; everything combines to fetter attention. The characters also, are taken from daily life, and appeal strongly to the general sympathy; the depiction of their feelings and their manners calls for a less exalted form of music, and this simpler melody being worked up with exquisite skill, has a peculiar fascination even for minds which are wont to disdain melodious trifles; while by their very enrichment they become, to the popular mind, the perfect ideal of art, and marvels of originality.

In *Oberon*, on the other hand, while human passion also plays a considerable part, the supernatural element is supreme; but it is the supernatural in a calm, fresh, graceful form. Instead of monsters and terrible apparitions, we have choruses of spirits of the air, sylphs, fairies, and water-nymphs. And the language of this gentle people—a language entirely their own—which

the production of the opera. Even before he quitted Germany for England his frequent expression was, " Whether I go or stay, in a year I shall be a dead man." See Benedict's " Weber," p. 111.]

owes its chief charm to its harmonies (its melodies being capriciously vague, with a strange veiled rhythm difficult to follow), is almost unintelligible to the general public, and is only to be fully appreciated by those who have studied it deeply, and possess, moreover, the gift of a vivid imagination. This exquisite poetry is, no doubt, better suited to the dreamy German temperament than to ours; I fear that, having studied it as a curiosity, we should soon weary of it.[1] This was proved in 1828, when a company came over from Carlsbad to perform at the Théâtre Favart. There are only two short verses in the mermaids' chorus, the soft cadence of which is a beautiful rendering of pure, perfect happiness. But after a few bars of this softly monotonous rhythm, the interest of the public flagged. At the end of the first verse a murmur arose in the theatre, the end of the chorus was barely audible, and it was cut out altogether at the next performance.

When Weber saw what a hash Castilblaze had made of his *Freyschütz*, he was very angry, and his just indignation found vent in a letter which he published before leaving Paris. Castilblaze had the audacity to reply that it was very ungrateful of M. Weber to reproach the man who had popularised his music in France, and that it was *entirely* owing to the modifications of which the author complained that *Robin des Bois* had succeeded!

The wretch! . . . and to think that a miserable sailor is punished with forty lashes for the least act of insubordination! . . .

---

[1] The truth of this statement has been controverted by the performance of *Oberon* at the Théâtre Lyrique (1857), and the sensation it created. It was a complete success, and proves that the Parisian public has made notable progress in music.

It was some years before this that, in order to ensure the success of Mozart's *Magic Flute*, the manager of the Opéra produced that marvellous travestie of it, *Les Mystères d'Isis*,[1] the libretto of which is a mystery as yet unveiled by no one. When he had manipulated the text to his liking, our intelligent manager sent for a *German* composer to help him patch up the music. The German proved equal to the occasion. He stuck a few bars on the end of the overture (the overture of the *Magic Flute*!), turned part of a soprano chorus[2] into a bass song, adding a few bars of his own; transplanted the wind instruments from one scene to another; changed the air and altered the instrumentation of the accompaniment in Sarastro's glorious song; manufactured a song out of the slaves' chorus, *O cara armonia;* and converted a duet into a trio. Not satisfied with the *Magic Flute*, this cormorant must next lay hands on *Titus* and *Don Juan*. The song, *Quel charme à mes esprits rappelle*, is taken from *Titus*, but only the *andante* is there, for the *allegro*, with which it ends, does not seem to have pleased our *uomo capace;* so he decreed a violent divorce, and, in its stead, put in a patchwork of his own, interspersed with scraps of Mozart. No one would dream of the base uses to which our friend put the celebrated *Fin ch' han dal vino*, that vivid outburst of libertinism in which Don Juan's whole character is epitomised. He turned it into a trio for a bass and two sopranos, with the following sweetly sentimental lines:

Heureux délire !
Mon cœur soupir
Que mon sort diffère du sien !
Quel plaisir est égal au mien !

---

[1] [Parodied in Paris at the moment as *Les Misères d'ici*.]

[2] The chorus, *Per voi risplendi il giorno*.

> Crois ton amie,
> C'est pour la vie
> Que mon sort va s'unir au tien.
> O douce ivresse
> De la tendresse !
> Ma main te presse,
> Dieu ! quel grand bien !

When this wretched hotch-potch was ready it was dubbed *The Mysteries of Isis*, was played in that form, and printed and published in full score with the name of that profane idiot Lachnith[1] (which I publish that it may be perpetuated with that of Castilblaze) actually bracketed with Mozart's on the title-page.

In this wise, two beggars in filthy rags came masquerading before the public in the rich robes of the kings of harmony ; and, in this sordid fashion, two men of genius, disguised as monkeys, decked in flimsy tinsel, mutilated and deformed, were presented to the French people, by their tormentors, as Mozart and Weber !

And the public was deceived, for no one came forward to punish the miscreants or give them the lie.

Alas ! how little the public recks of such crimes, even when it is cognizant of them ! In Germany and England, as well as in France, such adaptation (which means profanation and spoliation) of masterpieces by the veriest nobodies is tolerated.

Theoretically it is recognised as an axiom that when any alteration in a great work is required it should be made by the very greatest artists only ; that, in fact, correction should come from above, never from below. Practically what takes place every day is the exact opposite. Mozart was murdered by Lachnith ; Weber, by

---

[1] And not Lachnitz ; there should be no errors in the spelling of the names of great men.

Castilblaze; Gluck, Grétry, Mozart, Rossini, Beethoven, and Vogel were all mutilated by Castilblaze;[1] Beethoven saw his symphonies corrected by Fétis,[2] Kreutzer, and Habeneck; Molière and Corneille were hacked about by the obscure familiars of the Théâtre Français; in England, adaptations of Shakespeare by Cibber and others are still played. It does not look as if the corrections came from above, but rather from below, and very perpendicularly below too.

It is futile to assert that, in botching masterpieces, these adapters have sometimes made lucky hits; no exceptions can condone such abominable desecration. No, no, no; a thousand times, no; musicians, poets, prose-writers, actors, artists, conductors of the third, second, or even of the first order, have no right to meddle with Beethoven or Shakespeare, or to bestow their *scientific* or *æsthetic* alms on them.

No, no, no; a hundred thousand times, no. No man, be he who he may, has any right to compel any other man, be he who he may, to wear a mask not his own; to speak in tones not his own; to take a shape not his own; to become a puppet, subject to his will; or to be galvanised after he is dead. If he was not a great man, let him lie. If he was a great man, let his equals—nay, even his superiors—respect him; and let his inferiors bow down humbly before him.

No doubt Garrick invented the *dénouement* of *Romeo and Juliet*, which is the most touching thing ever played, and substituted it for the one Shakespeare wrote, which is less effective. But, on the other hand, what wretched

---

[1] There is scarcely a work by any of these masters which he has not botched to his fancy; he must surely be mad.

[2] I will show how. (See chapter xliv.)

rogue perpetrated the ending to *King Lear* which is often played instead of the scene Shakespeare wrote, and put those coarse tirades into Cordelia's mouth, expressing passions so foreign to her gentle, noble nature?   And how *Richard the Third* was distorted!   And the *Tempest*; were not a crowd of additional passages thrust into it? And *Hamlet* and *Romeo*?   Such is the result of Garrick's experiment!   Everybody wanted to try his hand at improving Shakespeare![1]

And to return to music.   At the last *concerts spirituels* at the Opéra, Kreutzer cut out ever so many passages from one of Beethoven's symphonies,[2] and Habeneck profited by his example to suppress some of the instruments in another.

[1] [This is too true as to England.   *The Barber of Seville* is thus announced in the bill of Covent Garden, October 13th, 1818 : "A comic opera in two acts, called *The Barber of Seville* (founded on the opera of that name), in which will be introduced part of Rossini's and Paesiello's celebrated music from *Il Barbiere di Siviglia*.   The overture and new music composed, and the whole adapted to the English stage, by *Mr. Bishop*."

On February 28th, 1819, we find that " *The Marriage of Figaro* has been long in rehearsal, and will be produced " (at Covent Garden) " early in the week after next.   The music selected chiefly from Mozart's operas."

Eight years later, Mozart's *Entführung* was produced in the same disgusting fashion, also at Covent Garden : "November 29th, 1827, will be performed a new grand opera, called *The Seraglio*.   The music arranged and adapted from Mozart's celebrated opera, with additional airs, etc., composed by Mr. Kramer."

Cenerentola, again, was thus presented : " *Cinderella ; or, The Fairy and the Little Glass Slipper*.   The music composed by Rossini, containing selections from his operas of *Cenerentola*, *Armida*, *Maometto Secondo*, and *Guillaume Tell*.   The whole arranged and adapted to the English stage by Mr. Rophino Lacy."

[2] The Second Symphony in D major.   For the last twenty years the Symphony in C minor has been played at the Conservatoire without the double basses at the beginning of the *scherzo*, because Habeneck cut them out.   He thinks they don't sound well! Improving Beethoven!

And does not one hear strange big drum, ophicleide, and trombone parts in London which Mr. Costa has stuck into the scores of *Don Giovanni*, the *Nozze di Figaro*, and the *Barbier de Séville*? And if conductors are permitted to suppress or add instruments to such works as these, who shall prohibit violin- or horn-players, or a whole host of petty musicians, from following their example? And what is to restrain translators, editors, or even copyists, engravers, and printers from doing the same thing?[1]

Does not this lead to the utter ruin and destruction of all Art? And is it not the bounden duty of those who love Art and glory in her beauty to guard the liberty of the human mind, and to prosecute the culprit who violates its unwritten laws, and denounce him with all possible wrath, crying: "Your crime is ridiculous. Despair! Your stupidity is culpable. Die! Be thou rejected, derided, accursed of men. Despair and die!"

----

[1] And they do it too.

CHAPTER XVII.

Prejudice against Operas with Italian Words—The Influence produced by this Feeling on my Appreciation of some of Mozart's Works.

I HAVE stated that when I went up for my first examination at the Conservatoire I was wholly absorbed in the study of dramatic music of the grand school; I should have said of lyrical tragedy, and it was owing to this cause that my admiration for Mozart was so lukewarm. Only Gluck and Spontini could excite me. And this was one reason for my coolness with regard to the author of *Don Juan*. *Don Juan* and *Figaro* were the two of Mozart's works oftenest played in Paris; but they were always given in Italian, by Italians, at the Italian Opera; and that alone was sufficient to prejudice me against them. Their great defect in my eyes was that they seemed to belong to the ultramontane school. Another and more legitimate objection was a passage in the part of Donna Anna which shocked me greatly, where Mozart has inserted a wretched exercise which is a perfect blot on his brilliant work. It occurs in the *allegro* of the soprano song in the second act, *Non mi dir*, a song of intense sadness, in which all the poetry of love finds vent in lamentation and tears, and which is yet made to wind up with such a ridiculous, discordant phrase, that one wonders how the same man could have written both. Donna Anna seems suddenly to have dried her tears and broken out into coarse buffoonery. The words of this passage are, *Forse un giorno il cielo ancora sentira-a-a-a-* (here comes the incredible feature in execrable taste) *pietà di me.* A truly singular form of expression for a noble, outraged woman, the *hope that heaven will one day have pity on her!* . . . I found it difficult to forgive Mozart for this enormity. Now I feel that I would shed my blood if I could thereby erase that shameful page and others of the same kind which disfigure some of his work.[1]

I therefore received his dramatic doctrines with distrust, and my enthusiasm fell to just one degree above freezing point. Still I felt the warmest admiration for the religious grandeur of the *Magic Flute;* though I had only heard it in its travestied form as *The Mysteries of Isis,* and it was not until long afterwards that I was able to compare the original score in the Conservatoire library with the wretched French *pot-pourri* played at the Opéra.

As I first heard the works of this great composer under such disadvantageous circumstances, it was only many years later that I was able to appreciate their charm and sweet perfection. The wonderful beauty of his quartets and quintets, and of some of his sonatas, first converted me to the worship of this angelic genius, whose brightness was slightly dimmed by intercourse with Italians and contrapuntal pedagogues.

---

[1] Even the epithet "shameful" scarcely seems to me strong enough to blast this passage. Mozart has there committed one of the most flagrant crimes recorded in the history of art against passion, feeling, good taste, and good sense.

CHAPTER XVIII.

I HAVE now come to the grand drama of my life; but I
shall not relate all its painful details. It is enough
to say that an English company came over to perform
Shakespeare's plays, then entirely unknown in France,
at the Odéon. I was present at the first performance
of *Hamlet*, and there, in the part of Ophelia, I saw
Miss Smithson, whom I married five years afterwards. I
can only compare the effect produced by her wonderful
talent, or rather her dramatic genius, on my imagination
and heart, with the convulsion produced on my mind by
the work of the great poet whom she interpreted. It is
impossible to say more.

This sudden and unexpected revelation of Shakespeare
overwhelmed me. The lightning-flash of his genius revealed the whole heaven of art to me, illuminating its
remotest depths in a single flash. I recognised the
meaning of real grandeur, real beauty, and real dramatic
truth, and I also realised the utter absurdity of the ideas
circulated by Voltaire, in France, about Shakespeare:

> Ce singe de génie
> Chez l'homme, en mission, par le diable envoyé,

and the pitiful pettiness of our old poetic school, the offspring of pedagogues and *Frères ignorantins.*

But the shock was too great, and it was a long while before I recovered from it. I became possessed by an intense, overpowering sense of sadness, that in my then sickly, nervous state produced a mental condition adequately to describe which would take a great physiologist. I could not sleep, I lost my spirits, my favourite studies became distasteful to me, and I spent my time wandering aimlessly about Paris and its environs. During that long period of suffering, I can only recall four occasions on which I slept, and then it was the heavy, death-like sleep produced by complete physical exhaustion. These were one night when I had thrown myself down on some sheaves in a field near Ville-Juif; one day in a meadow in the neighbourhood of Sceaux; once on the snow on the banks of the frozen Seine, near Neuilly; and, lastly, on a table in the Café du Cardinal at the corner of the Boulevard des Italiens and the Rue Richelieu, where I slept for five hours, to the terror of the *garçons,* who thought I was dead and were afraid to come near me.

It was on my return from one of these wanderings, in which I must have seemed like one seeking his soul, that my eyes fell on *Moore's Irish Melodies,* lying open on my table at the song beginning, "When he who adores thee." I seized my pen, and then and there wrote the music to that heartrending farewell, which is published at the end of my collection of songs, *Irlande,* under the title of *Elégie.* This is the only occasion on which I have been able to vent any strong feeling in music while still under its influence. And I think that I have rarely reached such intense truth of musical expression, combined with so much realistic power of harmony.

The song is immensely difficult both to sing and to accompany, and takes two accomplished artists[1] to render it adequately; above all, a singer gifted with a sympathetic voice and intense power of feeling to enable him to express the deep, tender, passionate despair Moore must have experienced when he wrote the words, and which I felt when I married them to music. It would give me intense pain to hear that song feebly sung. In order to avoid such a trial, I have never, in all the twenty years since it was written, asked anyone to sing it to me. Alizard once saw it in my room, and tried it over without accompaniment, transposing it (into B) to suit his bass voice, and this upset me so completely that I was obliged to beg him to stop. He appreciated the song; I saw that he would sing it perfectly, and so I determined to arrange the accompaniment for an orchestra. But I then considered that works of this nature are not suited for the ear of the concert-public, and that to expose them to careless criticism would be sacrilege; so I stopped short, and burnt what I had done.

As good luck would have it, the French prose translation of Moore's poetry is so good that I was able, afterwards, to adapt the original words to my music. If this elegy ever becomes known in England and Germany, it may possibly find some few admirers among those who have known what grief is. But it would be incomprehensible to a Frenchman, and simple insanity to an Italian.

When I left the theatre after seeing *Hamlet*, I was so

---

[1] If Pischek could play his own accompaniment, that would realise my ideal of a performance of the song.

appalled at what I had experienced, that I determined never again to expose myself to the fire of Shakespeare's genius.

The next day *Romeo and Juliet* was announced. . . . I had a pass to the orchestra of the Odéon, but so afraid was I that the doorkeeper might have had orders to suspend the free-list, that, the moment I saw the advertisement, I rushed off to the ticket-office to buy a stall and secure a seat at any cost. From that moment my fate was sealed. After the harrowing sufferings, the tearful love, the bitter irony, the black meditations, the heartrending sorrows, the madness, the tears, mourning, catastrophes, and malign fortune of Hamlet—the dark clouds and icy winds of Denmark—the change was too great to the hot sunshine and balmy nights of Italy—to the love, quick as thought, burning as lava, imperious, irresistible, illimitably pure and beautiful as the smile of an angel; the raging revenge, heartbreaking embraces, and desperate struggles between love and death. And so, at the end of the third act, scarcely able to breathe, stifled with a feeling as though an iron hand held my heart in its grip, I cried out, "Ah, I am lost!" I must add that I did not then know a syllable of English, that I only dimly discerned Shakespeare through the misty medium of Letourneur's translation, and had no conception of the exquisite poetry in which his wonderful creations were clothed. Nor indeed am I much better off even now. It is far more difficult for a Frenchman to sound the deeps of Shakespeare's style, than it is for an Englishman to appreciate the subtlety and originality of Molière or La Fontaine. Our two poets are rich continents, Shakespeare is an entire world. But the play of the actors, and especially of the actress, the succession of scenes, the action, and the tones of voice, penetrated me with the Shakespearian ideas and passions, as our poor, pale translations never could have done. It was stated last winter in an article in the *Illustrated London News*, that after seeing Miss Smithson in *Juliet*, I cried out, "I will marry that woman! and will write my greatest symphony on that play!" I did both; but I never said anything of the kind. My biographer has endowed me with a vaster ambition than I possessed. This narrative will show what strange circumstances brought about a result which I was too completely overwhelmed even to dream of at the time.

The success of Shakespeare in Paris, which was in great measure due to the enthusiastic support of the new school of literature, led by Victor Hugo, Alexandre Dumas, and Alfred de Vigny, was, however, surpassed by that of Miss Smithson. No actress in France ever touched, stirred, and excited the public as she did; no one ever received such glorious eulogies from the French press as were published in her honour.

After these two performances of *Hamlet* and *Romeo*, I had no difficulty in keeping away from the English theatre; more experiences of that kind would have killed me; I shrank from them as one shrinks from physical pain; and the mere thought of such a trial made me shudder.

I had spent some months in the kind of hopeless stupor of which I have only faintly indicated the nature and the cause, dreaming ceaselessly of Shakespeare, and the fair Ophelia of whom all Paris raved, and contrasting her splendid career and my own miserable obscurity, when all at once I rose up and determined that the light of my obscure name should flash up even to her, where she stood. And so I resolved to do what no composer had ever ventured

to do in France. I resolved to give a great concert in the
Conservatoire, in which only my own works should be
played. "I will show her," I said, "*that I also am an
artist.*" To achieve this, three things were necessary—
copies of my music, the room, and the performers.

The moment my mind was made up, I set to work to
copy out the parts of the pieces I had selected, and this
took me sixteen hours a day.

My programme included the overtures of *Waverley* and
the *Francs Juges;* a song and trio, with chorus, from
the *Francs Juges;* a *Scène héroïque Grecque;* and my
cantata, *La Mort d'Orphée*, which the jury of the Institute
had pronounced unplayable.

While copying *indefatigably* I managed by rigid economy
to add a few hundred francs to my former savings, and
with these I proposed to pay my chorus. With regard to
the orchestra, I was certain of obtaining the gratuitous
services of that of the Odéon, and of portions of those of
the Opéra, and of the Théâtre des Nouveautés. The
chief difficulty was, as is always the case in Paris, the
room. In order to get the use of the hall of the Conservatoire, which was the only perfectly satisfactory one, it
was necessary to obtain the sanction of the Superintendent
of Fine Arts, M. Sosthènes de Larochefoucault, and the
consent of Cherubini.

M. Larochefoucault at once granted my request ; but
the moment I spoke of my plan to Cherubini he burst
into a passion.

"You want to give a concert?" he began, with his
usual courtesy.

"Yes, sir."

"You will have to obtain the sanction of the Superintendent of Fine Arts."

“ I have got it.”

“ M. de Larossefoucault consents ?”

“ Yes, sir.”

“ But—but—but, *I* don’t ; a—a—a—and I object to your having the room.”

“ But, sir, you have no right to refuse ; because the Conservatoire has nothing to do with it at present, and it is not in use during the next fortnight.”

“ But I tell you that I don’t want you to give this concert. Everybody is in the country, and you won’t make any money.”

“ I don’t want to make any. I only want to be known.”

“ There is no necessity for your being known. Besides, you will want money for your expenses. Have you any ?”

“ Yes, sir.”

“ Ah ! And wha—wha—what music are you going to play at this concert ?”

“ Two overtures, part of an opera, and my cantata on *La Mort d’Orphée.*”

“ That competition-cantata that I would not have? It is bad ; it—it—it—cannot be played.”

“ So you thought, sir ; but I am very glad to have an opportunity of judging for myself. . . . If a bad pianist could not play it there is no reason why a good orchestra should not.”

“ So you want to—to—to—insult the Academy ?”

“ No, sir ; I only want to try an experiment. If, as is probably the case, the Academy was right in pronouncing my cantata unplayable, it is quite evident that it won’t be played. If, on the other hand, the Academy was mistaken, you have only to say that I took its advice and corrected my piece.”

" You can only give your concert on a Sunday."

" It shall be on a Sunday."

" But Sunday is the only holiday for the attendants of the Conservatoire ; and surely you don't want to kill these poor creatures, to—to—to—kill them with work ?"

" You must be joking, sir ; these poor creatures, for whom you feel such pity, are only too delighted to have the opportunity of making some money, and you would do them a great injury if you deprived them of the means of doing so."

" I won't have it, I won't ! and I shall write to the superintendent and ask him to withdraw his sanction." [1]

" You are very kind, sir ; but M. de Larochefoucault will not break his promise. Besides, I shall write to him myself and send him an accurate account of our conversation. He will then understand your reasons and mine."

And I did send it just as it is given here. I heard some years afterwards from one of the secretaries of the Fine Art Department that the superintendent had laughed over it till he cried. Cherubini's consideration for the poor Conservatoire attendants, whom I wanted to *kill with work* by my concert, struck him as peculiarly touching ; and so he replied at once, as anyone with any common sense must have done, renewing his authorisation and adding these words, for which I shall always feel grateful to him : " I advise you to show this letter to M. Cherubini, who has received the necessary *orders* with regard to you." The moment I receive this official document I rush off to the Conservatoire and hand it to the director, asking him to read it. Cherubini takes the paper, reads it carefully,

---

[1] [These dialogues lose half their drollery in translation, owing to the impossibility of representing Cherubini's Italian pronunciation of French, which is conveyed in the original.]

re-reads it, turns first pale and then green, and hands it back to me without a word.

That was the first dose he received from me in return for the mortification I endured when he turned me out of the library after our first interview.

I left him with a kind of feeling of satisfaction, muttering to myself, in irreverent imitation of his soft tones: "Come, sir, it is only a tiny dose, swallow it quietly; and gently, gently, please! It will not be the last, my man, if you do not let me alone!"

CHAPTER XIX.

A futile Concert—A Conductor who cannot conduct—A Chorus
which cannot sing.

HAVING got my orchestra and chorus together, and forced
a concession of the hall from the *burbero Direttore*, I had
still to provide myself with solo-singers and a conductor.
As I was afraid to conduct myself, Bloc, the leader
of the Odéon orchestra, kindly undertook to do so;
Dupréz, who had only just left Choron's class, and was
quite unknown, consented to sing the song from the
Francs Juges, and Alexis Dupont was determined, in
spite of his illness, to make another attempt at *La Mort
d'Orphée*, for which he had already tried to obtain a hearing from the jury of the Conservatoire. For the soprano
and bass parts of the trio from the *Francs Juges* I was
obliged to get two singers from the Opéra who had neither
voices nor talent.

The rehearsal shared the fate of all gratuitous performances; a great many players were absent at the beginning,
and they nearly all vanished before the end.

Still, the song, the cantata, and the two overtures
went fairly well; that of the *Francs Juges* was warmly
applauded by the orchestra, and a still greater sensation was produced by the finale of the cantata.

In this piece I made the wind instruments repeat
the air of Orpheus' hymn to Love, in accordance with the

unexpressed but palpable meaning of the words after the *bacchanale*, the orchestra accompanying it with a vague, dreamy, rushing sound like the faint murmur of the river as it bears along the pale head of the murdered poet, while a dying voice from time to time utters the despairing cry re-echoed from the river-banks : "Eurydice ! Eurydice !   Unfortunate Eurydice ! "

I had these five lines from the *Georgics* in my mind :

> Tum quoque, marmoreâ caput a cervice revulsum
> Gurgite quum medio portans Oeagrius Hebrus,
> Volveret, Eurydicen, vox ipsa et frigida lingua.
> Ah ! miseram Eurydicen, animâ fugiente vocabat ;
> Eurydicen ! toto referebant flumine ripæ.

The strange sadness of this musical picture, the poetical meaning of which was sure to be missed by three-fourths of an ordinary uneducated audience, sent a shiver through the whole orchestra, and was received with a storm of applause.   I am sorry now that I destroyed the score ; I ought to have kept it for the sake of its last pages.   With the exception of the *bacchanale*,[1] which the orchestra rendered with splendid fury, the rest of the cantata did not go well.   Dupont was so hoarse that he could scarcely sing his upper notes at all, and warned me not to count upon him for the performance.

So, to my great disgust, I was unable to insert the scena—which I had entitled in the programme, "*La Mort d'Orphée, the scena which was voted unplayable by the Academy of Fine Arts, and was played on the . . . May*, 1828."   And no doubt Cherubini, ignoring the true reason of its withdrawal, maintained that the orchestra had endorsed his verdict.

---

[1] The piece in which the Conservatoire pianist broke down.

During the rehearsal of this unlucky cantata, I noticed how incapable conductors, unaccustomed to lead great operas, are of following the capricious time of recitative. At the Odéon, Bloc only conducted operas interspersed with dialogue, and so, when he came to the recitative after Orpheus' first song, which is interspersed with concerted orchestral passages, he always failed to bring in the instruments at the right moment. Seeing this, an antique amateur, who was present at the rehearsal, made the remark: "Ah, talk to me of the old Italian cantatas! That is music which does not tax a conductor; it leads itself." "Yes," I retorted, "like old donkeys, which find their way home alone." That was how I made friends.

However, the cantata was replaced by the *Resurrexit* from my mass, which was well known to both chorus and orchestra, and the concert took place. The overtures and the *Resurrexit* were well received and applauded; and the song was well rendered by Dupréz, whose voice was at that time gentle and soft. It was an invocation to sleep. But the trio and chorus were pitifully sung, and *without chorus*, for they failed to come in at the right time, and prudently kept silence till the end. The public did not appreciate the Greek scene, which requires a large chorus to produce a proper effect. It was never performed again, and I destroyed it.

Still, the concert did me some good; first, by introducing me to the artists and the public, which, in spite of Cherubini's opinion to the contrary, was necessary; and then, in bringing me face to face with the enormous difficulties which beset a composer when he undertakes the performance of his own works, and showing me what a task I had before me. It is scarcely necessary to add that the receipts barely covered the expenses of lights, advertisements, the *droit des pauvres*, and my priceless chorus, with their judicious gift of silence.

The concert was warmly praised by some of the papers. Fétis (who afterwards . . .), Fétis himself—spoke most flatteringly of me in a drawing-room, as a man whose appearance before the public was a great event.

Would the tidings of my success reach Miss Smithson, in the intoxicating whirl of her own triumphs? Alas! I learnt afterwards that, absorbed in her own brilliant career, she never even heard of my name, my struggles, my concert, or my success!

CHAPTER XX.

It sometimes happens that in the life of an artist one
thunderclap follows another as swiftly as it does in those
great storms in the physical world, where the clouds,
charged with the electric fluid, seem literally to sport with
the thunder, while they hurl it to and fro as if exulting
in the effect they produce.

I had scarcely recovered from the visions of Shakespeare and Weber when I beheld Beethoven's giant form
looming above the horizon. The shock was almost as
great as that I received from Shakespeare, and a new
world of music was revealed to me by the musician, just
as a new universe of poetry had been opened to me by
the poet.

A society for the performance of orchestral works had
been organised at the Conservatoire, under the leadership
of Habeneck. We must not allow the defects and short-
comings of this able and enthusiastic conductor with
regard to the great master whom he worshipped, to
blind us to his good intentions, his undoubted ability,
or the fact that to him alone is due the glorious success
of Beethoven's works in Paris. It is to his ceaseless
exertions that the great society, the Société des Concerts,

which has attained world-wide celebrity, owes its existence. He had to inspire other musicians with his own enthusiasm, and he found that their indifference turned to active opposition when they saw what a vista of unremunerative labour opened before them, and when they realised the ceaseless rehearsals which were necessary to secure a satisfactory performance of a class of music which was then chiefly noted for its eccentricity and its difficulty.

Not the least of Habeneck's obstacles lay in the silent opposition, ill-concealed dislike, and ironical coldness of the French and Italian composers, who were but ill-pleased to see an altar erected to a German, whose works they deemed monstrosities, and regarded as fraught with danger to themselves and their school. What abominable nonsense I have heard them talk about these marvels of learning and inspiration!

My master, Lesueur, a thoroughly honest man, without malice or jealousy, but a devoted adherent of certain musical dogmas, which I call stupid prejudices, made a characteristic remark to me about Beethoven's music. A rumour of the sensation which the performance of Beethoven's symphonies, at the first series of the Conservatoire concerts, had produced on the Parisian musical world, reached him even in his retirement. His surprise was great, for, in common with most of his fellow-academicians, he regarded instrumental music as a respectable, but distinctly inferior, branch of the art, and believed that Haydn and Mozart had achieved all that could be looked for in that direction.

Like Berton, who regarded the whole of the modern German school with contemptuous pity; like Boïeldieu, who did not know what to make of it, and expressed the most

childish surprise at any combination of harmonies outside
the three chords with which he had trifled all his life;
like Cherubini, who dissembled his bile, not daring to vent
it on the master whose success exasperated him, and
sapped the foundations of all his pet theories; like
Paër, who, with Italian astuteness, went about dissemi-
nating stories about Beethoven, with whom he professed
himself acquainted—stories which were always more or
less discreditable to the great man and advantageous to
himself; like Catel, who had quarrelled with music and
was entirely devoted to his roses; like Kreutzer even,
who shared Berton's contemptuous disdain for everything
German;—like all these masters, Lesueur remained obstinately silent and resolutely deaf, and persistently absented
himself from the Conservatoire concerts, in the face of
the fever of enthusiasm with which he saw that all artists
in general, and I myself in particular, were possessed.
Had he gone he would have been obliged to come to some
conclusion about Beethoven, and to give expression to that
conclusion; he would have been a reluctant witness of the
wild enthusiasm which his works had aroused; and this
was just what Lesueur dreaded, though he did not acknowledge it even to himself. I left him no peace, however,
and insisted so strongly on the necessity for his understanding and appreciating an event of such importance
as the introduction of this new style and these colossal
forms, that he reluctantly yielded, and allowed himself
to be taken to the Conservatoire on a day on which
Beethoven's Symphony in C minor was to be performed.
He wished to listen to it undisturbed; so he sent me
away, and seated himself among strangers in one of the
lower boxes. When it was over I went down to find
out what effect the marvellous work had produced on him.

I met him striding up and down the passage with flushed cheeks. "Well, dear master?" ... "Hush! I want air; I must go outside. It is incredible, wonderful! It stirred and affected and disturbed me to such a degree, that when I came out of the box and tried to put on my hat I could not find my own head! Do not speak to me till to-morrow." ...

I was victorious! The next day I rushed off to his house, and we at once fell to talking of the masterpiece which had stirred us so deeply. He allowed me to run on for some time, assenting in a constrained manner to my enthusiastic eulogies. It was easy to see that I was talking to a quite different being to the man of the day before, and that the subject was painful to him. But I persisted until Lesueur, after again admitting how deeply the symphony had affected him, shook his head with a curious smile, and said, "All the same, such music ought not to be written." To which I replied, "Don't be afraid, dear master, there will never be too much of it."

Poor human nature! ... poor master! ... His words, which men are evermore uttering under one form or another, express obstinacy, regret, envy, and dread of the unknown, and an implicit confession of impotency. To say, "Such music ought not to be written," after having felt its power and beauty, is tacitly to acknowledge that you will not produce such because you could not if you would.

Haydn had already said much the same thing of Beethoven, of whom he always spoke obstinately as *a great pianist*.[1]

---

[1] [This is more than doubtful. Haydn and Beethoven were antagonistic in many respects, but there is no trace of any expression of

Grétry gave utterance to some equally inappropriate criticisms regarding Mozart, who had, he said, *placed the statue on the orchestra and the pedestal on the stage.*

Handel said *his cook was a better musician than Gluck.*[1]

Rossini, speaking of Weber's music, says *that it gives him the colic.*

But the aversion of Handel and Rossini for Gluck and Weber is, I think, due to a different cause. It is impossible for two men of stomach to understand two men of heart. The feeling of bitter hatred, on the other hand, displayed against Spontini by the whole French school and the greater part of the Italian musicians, is certainly caused by the wretched, contemptible, complex feeling to which I adverted above, and which has been scourged so ruthlessly by La Fontaine in his fable of the fox and the sour grapes.

The persistency with which Lesueur strove against the evidence of his own senses gave the death-blow to my wavering faith in the doctrines with which he had striven to imbue me; I at once forsook the beaten track and took my way over wood and meadow, mountain and valley. But I hid my defection as well as I could, and Lesueur only became aware of it long afterwards, when

---

the kind given in the text. Even if Haydn had said what is attributed to him, it need not have been in depreciation; for Beethoven *was* a great pianist, the greatest in Vienna *at the time* when he and Haydn were there together; and Haydn had ceased to go to public performances before Beethoven became known as a great orchestral writer.]

[1] [This is always misunderstood. Handel said nothing of the kind. He said: "Gluck knows no more counterpoint than my cook, Waltz." Counterpoint was never Gluck's *forte*, and the sting of the comparison with the cook is very much reduced when it is recollected that Waltz was a musician, and a very good singer, and took the part of Polyphemus in *Acis and Galatea*.]

he heard some of the new compositions I had taken care not to show him.

I shall return to the subject of the Society's concerts and Habeneck when I come to the period of my intercourse with that clever, unsatisfactory, capricious conductor.

CHAPTER XXI

Fatality—I become a Critic.

I must here mention the circumstances by which I became involved in the complications of musical criticism. Messrs. Humbert Ferrand, Cazalés, and De Carné, names well known in the world of politics, had just started a periodical review as an organ for their religious and monarchical opinions. It was called the *Révue Européenne*, and they wanted to complete their staff.

Humbert Ferrand asked me to undertake the musical critiques; but I told him I could not write, that my style would be abominable, and that, in fact, I could not. "You are mistaken," he replied; "I have read your letters, and you will soon acquire the requisite knack; besides, we will look over your articles before they are printed, and point out anything which needs correction. Come and see De Carné, and he will tell you the terms of your agreement."

I was immensely attracted by the idea of wielding such a weapon in the defence of beauty, and the destruction of what I deemed unbeautiful, and the opportunity of adding slightly to my limited resources was very welcome. So I went with Ferrand to Carné's, and it was all arranged.

I never feel much confidence in myself until I have

proved my power; but on this occasion my natural diffidence was increased by the recollection of a former unsuccessful excursion into the field of musical polemics. It was in this wise. I had been wrought into a condition of absolute fury by the blasphemies which the Rossinian papers were uttering against Gluck, Spontini, and the entire school of feeling and common sense, by their exaggerated laudations of Rossini and his sensual system of music, and by the hopeless absurdity of the reasoning by which they endeavoured to demonstrate that the only end of music, dramatic or other, is to charm the ear, and in no wise to give expression to feeling or passion, together with a great deal of arrogant nonsense uttered by men ignorant of the very A B C of music.

One day, after reading the ramblings of one of these lunatics, I was seized with a sudden impulse to answer them. I wanted a respectable organ, so I wrote to M. Michaud, the editor and proprietor of the *Quotidienne*, which was then a popular paper. I explained my wish, my object, and my opinions, and promised to hit fair as well as hard. My letter, which was half jest, half earnest, pleased him, and his reply was favourable. My proposal was accepted, and my first article eagerly looked for. "Ah, wretches!" I cried, leaping with joy, "I have got you." I was mistaken; I had got no one— nothing. My inexperience in the art of writing, in the usages of the world, and the etiquette of journalism, coupled with the intensity of my musical feelings, culminated in a regular *fiasco*. The article I took to M. Michaud was not only badly conceived and worse written, but it exceeded all bounds, even of polemics. M. Michaud listened, and, shocked at my audacity, he said: "It is all true, but you smash everybody's windows; I could not insert such an article in the *Révue Quotidienne*." I went away, promising to alter it; but I was too lazy, and too much disgusted at the idea of so many precautions, and so I left it alone.

When I talk of my laziness, it only applies to the writing of prose. I have often sat up all night over my scores, and have spent eight hours at a time labouring at instrumentation, without once changing my position; but it is an effort to me to write prose, and about the tenth line or so I get up, walk about the room, look out into the street, take up a book, and strive by any means to overcome the weariness and fatigue which instantly overpower me. I have to return to the charge eight or ten times before I can finish an article for the *Journal des Débats*, and it takes me quite two days to write one, even when I like the subject, and am interested by it. And then, what erasures, and what scrawls! You should see my first copy. Musical composition comes naturally to me, and is a delight; but prose-writing is a labour. Nevertheless, incited and encouraged by Ferrand, I wrote several laudatory articles on Gluck, Spontini, and Beethoven; after touching them up according to some hints of M. de Carné's, they were printed and well received; and I began to understand the difficulties of this dangerous task, which has since played so deplorable and important a part in my life. My readers will see how impossible it was for me to avoid this, and in how many ways it has influenced my career as an artist in France and elsewhere.

CHAPTER XXII.

The Competition for Musical Composition—The Constitution of the
Académie des Beaux Arts—I gain the Second Prize.

It was in the month of June, in the year 1828, that I presented myself for the third time at the competition of the Institute. I was haunted by my Shakespearian passion, which had been painfully intensified by the effect produced on me by Beethoven; and was at that time a dreamy, savage creature, silent to the verge of dumbness, disorderly in my attire, as great a burden to my friends as to myself, and my only occupation the occasional production of a small article on music. I succeeded in obtaining the second prize.

The privileges it bestows are: a laureate crown and a gold medal of no great worth—both publicly bestowed, a free pass to all the opera-houses, and many chances of obtaining the first prize at the next examination.

The first prize confers much higher privileges. It secures the artist a yearly pension of three thousand francs (£120) for five years, on condition of his spending the first two in the French Academy at Rome, and the third in travelling through Germany. The remainder is paid him in Paris, where he does his best to make himself known and to keep the wolf from the door.

I will now give a *résumé* of what I wrote in various

papers, fifteen or sixteen years ago, regarding the curious way in which these examinations are organised.

The intention of the Government, in establishing the Prix de Rome, was, first, to bring forward year by year the most promising among the young French composers; secondly, to enable them, by means of a pension, to devote themselves entirely for five years to the study of music. These being the objects in view, we shall now consider what means were, until lately, taken to secure them.

Things are somewhat better now, but only slightly.[1]

To most readers the facts I am about to relate may seem strange and improbable; but, as I obtained both the second and first prizes at the Conservatoire, I shall merely state what I saw myself and knew to be true. My success enables me to speak my mind quite unreservedly, without any fear that what I utter from pure love of my art, and from my innermost conviction, will be attributed to the bitterness of wounded vanity.

Cherubini, who is the most academic of academicians, and, therefore, the most susceptible to my remarks, has already reproached me with "striking my nurse," the Academy. Had I failed in obtaining the prize, he could not have taxed me with ingratitude; but he and others would have declared that I was avenging my own defeat. So that there is apparently no way in which I can approach this sacred topic. Yet I do approach it, and I intend, moreover, to treat it as I would any other topic.

According to the rules, all Frenchmen or naturalised Frenchmen were and are eligible for competition. When

---

[1] They are completely altered now. The Emperor has just suppressed that section in the Conservatoire rules, and the Académie des Beaux Arts no longer awards the prize for Musical Composition (1865).

the date of the competition had been fixed, the candidates entered their names at the *secrétariat* of the Institute. They underwent a preparatory examination called *concours préliminaire*, the object of which was to designate the five or six most advanced pupils.

The subject for the great competition was to be a lyrical scena, for one or two voices and orchestra ; and, in order to show that they possessed the requisite feeling for melody and dramatic expression, and also a sufficient knowledge of instrumentation, to produce such a work, the candidates were called upon to write *a vocal fugue*. They were given a day to do this, and *each fugue was to be signed*. On the following day the members of the musical section of the Institute assembled, looked through the fugues, and made their choice, which was not altogether impartial, seeing that a certain number of them bore the signatures of their own pupils.

Then when the votes had been registered and the competitors designated, the latter were called in to hear the words they were to set, and to enter their "boxes." The permanent secretary of the Academy then dictated the words of a classic poem which usually began thus :

"Déjà l'aurore aux doigts de rose." Or :
"Déjà le jour naissant ranime la nature." Or :
"Déjà d'un doux éclat l'horizon se colore." Or :
"Déjà du blond Phœbus le char brillant s'avance." Or :
"Déjà de pourpre et d'or les monts lointains se parent." Etc. etc.

The candidates were then shut up, with some such luminous poem and a piano, in separate rooms called "boxes" until their score was finished. At eleven and at six the jailer unlocked the doors and the prisoners met for their meals ; but they were forbidden to leave the building. All papers, letters, clothes, or books, sent from the outside world were carefully examined, to guard against the least chance of external assistance. But they were allowed to receive visitors from six to eight in the evening, and even to invite guests to festive dinners, where there was no limit to the communications, verbal or otherwise, which might pass between one bottle of champagne and another. Twenty-two days was the period allowed for the completion of the work, and those who finished before that time were allowed to go away, after they had handed up their manuscript, *numbered and signed*.

When all the scores were ready the lyric Areopagus reassembled, their numbers being strengthened by the addition of two members from the other sections of the Institute : a sculptor and a painter, or an engraver and an architect, or a sculptor and an engraver, or an architect and a painter, or even two engravers, two architects, or two painters. The important thing was that they should not be musicians. They had votes, and were to pass judgment on an art of which they were wholly ignorant. The scenas were gone through one after another, and, though written for orchestra, they were accompanied on the piano. . . . And this is still the case.

Can anyone conceive the absurdity of trying to judge of the merits of an orchestral work thus mutilated? The piano can give an idea of an orchestral work to anyone who has already heard it played by an orchestra, because memory supplies what is lacking and recalls the full performance. But, in the present state of music, it is utterly impossible to give any adequate idea of a new work in that way. Music such as Sacchini's *Œdipe*, or any work of that school, in which there is no instrumentation, loses

very little by being heard on the piano. But with any
modern music—that is supposing, of course, the composer
has availed himself of the means now at his disposal—it
is quite another matter. Take the Communion march
from Cherubini's mass *du Sacre*, for example. What
would become of those wonderful prolonged notes of the
wind instruments which fill you with rapt mystic ecstasy?
or of those delicious interlacings of flutes and clarinets to
which almost the whole effect is due? They disappear
completely, because the piano can neither hold nor swell
a note. Try to accompany Agamemnon's song in Gluck's
Iphigenia with the piano! In the passage,

> J'entends retentir dans mon sein,
> Le cri plaintif de la nature,

there is a most masterly and touching solo for the hautbois,
which, when played on the piano, sounds like a meaningless bell, instead of a plaintive wail. In this way the
ideas, the thoughts, the inspiration are either marred or
destroyed. It is unnecessary to mention the great
orchestral effects which are lost on the piano ; the piquant
exchanges between the wind and string instruments ; the
sharp contrasts of colour between the brass and wood
instruments ; the mysterious and gorgeous effects of the
instruments à percussion when employed *piano ;* of their
enormous power when employed *forte ;* of the striking
effects which are achieved by the separation of the
groups of instruments, or a hundred other details.
The injustice and absurdity of the whole thing is self-
evident. By destroying the instrumental effects the
piano at once reduces all composers to the same level,
and places the clever, profound, ingenious instrumentalist
on the same platform with an ignorant dunce, who

knows nothing of that branch of his art. The dunce may have put trombones for clarinets, ophicleides for bassoons; may have committed the most outrageous blunders, and not know even the compass of the various instruments; while the work of the other may be a masterpiece of ingenious instrumentation—and yet on the piano it will be impossible to distinguish the difference. The piano is a guillotine, and severs the head of noble or of churl with the same impartial indifference.

To continue: when the pieces have been performed in this manner then comes the ballot (I speak in the present tense, as this still remains unchanged), and then the prize is awarded. Do you think it is all over? Not at all. Ten days afterwards all the sections of the Académie des Beaux Arts assemble for the final decision. This imposing jury of thirty-five members is made up of painters, sculptors, architects, engravers, etchers, not excluding even the six musicians. These six members are to some extent able to supplement the inadequacy of the pianoforte accompaniment by looking over the scores; but that resource is not available for the other academicians, to whom music is a sealed book.

When the performers—that is, the singers and the pianoforte-player—have gone through all the compositions, the fatal urn is handed round, the votes are counted, and the choice of the musical section, made a week earlier, is either confirmed, modified, or upset by the majority. In this way, then, the prize for music is adjudged, by men who are not musicians, and who have not even had a chance of hearing a proper performance of the compositions, on which, by an absurd rule, they are required to pass judgment.

It is only fair to add that, if painters and engravers

have to decide musical questions, musicians are, in their
turn, summoned to award prizes for painting, engraving,
etc.; all prizes, for all branches of art, being adjudged in
precisely the manner described—by a collective jury of
all the art sections of the Academy. I must, however,
confess that, if I were a member of that august body, I
should find it very difficult to state my grounds for
awarding a prize for painting or engraving, and should
testify my perfect impartiality by drawing lots.

On the solemn day when the prizes are distributed, the
cantata thus chosen by painters, sculptors, and engravers
is adequately performed. It is somewhat late in the day,
and it would probably have been better to summon the
orchestra before pronouncing the verdict. It seems rather
a waste of money to have this tardy performance at all,
as the decision is beyond recall; but the Academy is
curious; it really wishes to *hear* the work to which it has
adjudged the prize. What more natural?

CHAPTER XXIII

The Academy Porter—His Revelations.

In my day there was an old porter at the Institute whose indignation at all this procedure was very funny. It was his duty to shut us up in our boxes during the competition, to open our doors morning and evening, and to watch over our intercourse with visitors during play-hours. He also acted as usher to the academicians, and was therefore present at all the private and public sittings, where he had made some curious observations.

He had gone out as a cabin-boy, at the age of sixteen, on board a frigate, and visited the East Indian islands; and was the only one of the crew who survived the pestilential fevers of Java.

I never weary of listening to travellers' tales of distant lands; their digressions never tire me, and I follow them into all the endless intricacies of every minute episode; so, when the narrator loses himself in a digression, strikes his forehead, and cries, "Good heavens! where was I?" I am always able to put him on the right track, and give him the name and date he wants, and then he says, "Ah, yes, that was it." So old Pingard and I were great friends, and he liked me because I enjoyed talking to him about Batavia, the Celebes, Amboyna, Coromandel, Borneo, and Sumatra, and because I was very curious about the Java women, whose love is fatal to Europeans. I rose greatly in his esteem one day by speaking of Volney, as "that excellent simple creature, Count de Volney, who always wore blue stockings;" and his enthusiasm knew no bounds when I asked him if he had known the celebrated traveller, Levaillant.

"M. Levaillant! M. Levaillant!" he cried, delighted; "know him? I should rather think so. Look here: one day, when I was walking up and down the quay at the Cape of Good Hope, whistling—I was waiting for a little negress who had given me an assignation on the shore, because, between you and me, there were reasons why she could not come to my house. I will tell you . . ."

"Never mind that, you were going to tell me about Levaillant."

"To be sure. Well, one day when I was walking about whistling at the Cape of Good Hope, a big, sunburnt man with a bushy beard stopped and turned round; he had evidently heard me whistling in French, and that was how he recognised me. 'I say, my boy, are you French?' 'I should rather think so,' I said. 'I come from Givet, in the Ardennes, Méhul's[1] part of the country.' 'Ah! You're a Frenchman?' 'Yes.' 'Ah!' And he turned away. It was M. Levaillant. So now you see I do know him!"

Thus it will be seen that old Pingard was my friend, and he showed his confidence in me by telling me things he would not have dared to reveal to anyone else. I remember a very animated conversation we had the day that I received the second prize. That year the subject

---

[1] Méhul belonged to Givet, but I doubt his having done so at the time Pingard pretends to have mentioned his name to Levaillant.

wo were to set to music was taken from Tasso—the faithful and unhappy Herminia disguising herself in Clorinda's armour, and being thus able to leave Jerusalem and go to nurse Tancred.

In these academic cantatas there were always three songs—first, the rising of the inevitable dawn; then the first recitative and the first song; then the second recitative and the second song; and then the third recitative and the third song, all for the same person.   In the middle of the third song came these words :

> Dieu des chrétiens, toi que j'ignore,
> Toi que j'outrageais autrefois,
> Aujourd'hui mon respect t'implore,
> Daigne écouter ma faible voix.

I was audacious enough to think that although the last piece was marked *agitato*, yet, this verse being a prayer, the Queen of Antioch could hardly move the God of the Christians with melodramatic cries to the accompaniment of an excited orchestra.   So I turned it into a prayer, and that *andante* was certainly the best part of my cantata.

When I reached the Academy on the night of the final decision, to learn my fate, and see whether, in the eyes of the painters, sculptors, and engravers, I was a bad musician or a good one, I met Pingard on the stairs.

"Well," I ask, "who has got it?"

"Ah! You, Berlioz.   That's right.   I was looking for you."

"What have I got?   Tell me quickly.   The first prize, the second, honourable mention, or nothing?"

"Oh, look here!   I am quite upset.   Just think, you only missed the first prize by two votes."

"This is the first I have heard of it."

"But I tell you it is so ! . . . You have got the second prize, that's good; but you only missed the first by two votes. Oh ! *look here.* I *am* sorry, for, you see, though I am neither a painter, an architect, nor an engraver, and so know nothing about music, still your *Dieu des chrétiens* brought a great lump into my throat. And, by Jove! *look here*, if I had met you then I would . . . I would have stood you *a small cup of coffee!*"

"Thanks, thanks, Pingard, you are very kind. You understand it all; you have good taste. By-the-bye, have you not been on the Coromandel coast ?"

"I should think so.   Why ? "

"And Java ? "

"Yes ; but——"

"And Sumatra ? "

"Yes."

"Borneo ? "

"Yes."

"You knew Levaillant *well ? "*

"I should think so, as well as I know myself."

"You have often spoken to Volney ? "

"The Count de Volney who had blue stockings ? "

"Yes—well, you know, Pingard, you are a good judge of music."

"I don't quite understand."

"It is not necessary that you should; only if anyone should by any chance say to you, 'What right have you to judge between one composer and another ? Are you a painter, engraver, architect, or sculptor ?' you must say, 'No ; I am a sailor, a traveller, a friend of Levaillant and of Volney.' That is enough. Ah ! by-the-way, how about the meeting ?"

"Oh ! *look here*, don't talk to me of that; it is always

the same thing. If I had thirty children I should take precious good care not to make one an artist. You see I know all about it. You can't conceive what a confounded job it all is. . . . For instance, they give away and even sell their votes to one another. Listen : once, at a competition for painting, I heard M. Lethière ask M. Cherubini to give him his vote for one of his pupils. 'We are such old friends,' he said, 'that you cannot refuse. Besides, my pupil is clever, and his picture is very good.' 'No, no, no, I will not, I will not,' returns the other; 'your nephew promised my wife an album she wanted, and he has not even drawn her a tree. I will not vote for him.' 'Ah, you are wrong,' said M. Lethière ; 'I give you my votes and you will not give me yours!' 'No, I will not.' 'Then I will do the album for you myself—I cannot say more than that.' 'Ah ! that is another matter. What is your pupil's name? I always forget; give me his christian-name too, and the name of the picture, so that there may be no mistake. I will write it all down.' 'Pingard !' 'Sir !' 'Bring a sheet of paper and a pencil.' 'Here, sir.' . . . They retire into the embrasure of a window, write down something, and then, as they part, I hear the musician say, 'All right, he shall have my vote.' Well, isn't that abominable ? And if one of my sons were a competitor, and I did that sort of thing, wouldn't they discharge me on the spot ?"

"Come, now, Pingard, don't get excited, but tell me what happened to-day."

"I have told you : you got the second prize, and you only lost the first by two votes. When M. Dupont had finished singing your cantata, they brought the *hurn*.[1] A

---

[1] Good old Pingard persisted in calling the ballot-box by this name.

musician near me was whispering to an architect, and saying : 'Look here, that fellow will never do anything; don't vote for him, he is a hopeless subject. He admires nothing but that atrocious Beethoven : we shall never get him back into the right path.' 'Do you think so?' said the architect. 'Still' . . . 'Oh, I am sure of it; you have only to ask our great Cherubini. I daresay you will take his opinion; he will tell you that the young man is mad—he has got Beethoven on the brain.'

"I beg your pardon," said Pingard, interrupting his story, "but who is this Beethoven? He does not belong to the Academy, and yet everyone is talking about him."

"No; he is not a member of the Academy. He is a German. Go on."

"Ah, well, it was soon over. When I handed the *hurn* to the architect I noticed that he voted for No. 4 instead of for you. Suddenly one of the musicians stood up and said : 'Gentlemen, before we go farther, I wish to point out to you that the orchestration of the second part of the work we have just heard is very remarkable, and must be very effective; but, of course, the pianoforte score gives no idea of it. . It is well you should know this.' 'What on earth are you talking about?' retorts another musician; 'your pupil has not followed the programme, and has written *two* songs *agitato* instead of *one*, and in the middle he has stuck in a wholly superfluous prayer. We cannot have the rules broken in this way, we must make an example of him.' 'Oh, this is too bad! What does the secretary say?' 'I think our friend is a little severe, and that we may pardon the young man's mistake. But it would be as well to let the jury understand what are the merits of the composition which cannot be rendered on the pianoforte.' 'It is all a mistake,' breaks in Cherubini, 'these orchestral effects do not exist, it is a regular hotch-potch, and would sound detestable in the orchestra.'   'There, now you hear,' cry the painters, sculptors, engravers, and architects; 'we can only go by what we hear ourselves; and, besides, if you are not agreed——' . . .   'Ah, yes.' 'Ah, no.' 'But, good heavens!' 'Well, what now?'   'I tell you that——' 'Oh, come now!'

"Well, they were all talking at once, and as they got tired of that, M. Regnault and two others declined to vote and went away. Then the votes in the *hurn* were counted, and you missed the first prize by two votes, and so you got the second."

"Thank you, my good Pingard. Now, tell me, do they manage things like that at the academy at the Cape of Good Hope?"

"Oh, come now; that is too much of a good thing. An academy at the Cape! A Hottentot institution! You know quite well that there is none."

"Really? And have the Indians at Coromandel not got one either?"

"No."

"Nor the Malays?"

"Of course not."

"How sad for the Orientals."

"Oh, they don't care."

"What barbarians."

And I left the old porter, thinking what a good thing it would be to send the Academy to Borneo to civilise it. I had a complete project in my mind which I thought of laying before the academicians in the hope of getting them to go off to the Cape, like Pingard. But we Westerns are such egotists that I had soon forgotten all about the poor Hottentots and the unfortunate Malays who have got no academy, and never gave them another thought. I got the first prize the following year. Good old Pingard, unfortunately, died in the interval; which was a great pity; for I am sure if he had heard the Burning of Sardanapalus's Palace in my piece he would have stood me a *large* cup of coffee.

CHAPTER XXIV

Miss Smithson again—A Benefit—Cruel Fate.

AFTER the examination, and the distribution of prizes which followed it, I relapsed into the state of dreary inaction that had become my normal condition. I was still the same obscure planet revolving unnoticed round my shining luminary! . . . so brilliant then, yet doomed to so dark an eclipse. My beautiful Estelle, the *Stella montis*, my *Stella matutina*, had so paled before my brilliant sun, that I never dreamed she could shine for me again. . . . Though studiously avoiding the English theatre, and turning away my eyes whenever they encountered Miss Smithson's portrait, I continued to write to her—without ever receiving a line in reply. My letters frightened instead of pleasing her, and she gave her maid stringent orders not to take in any more of them. The season was nearly over, it was rumoured that the *troupe* was to make a tour through Holland, and Miss Smithson's last appearances were announced. I felt that it would be madness to go and see her play Juliet or Ophelia again, so I steadily kept away. But when I saw that Miss Smithson and Abbot were to play two acts of *Romeo and Juliet* at Huet's benefit, at the Opéra Comique, I suddenly resolved that my name should figure beside that of the great actress on the playbill. I hoped in this way to attract her attention, and, possessed with this childish idea, I rushed off to see the manager of the Opéra Comique, and to get him to play one of my overtures at Huet's benefit. As the conductor saw no objection, the manager agreed. When I went to the theatre for my rehearsal the actors were finishing theirs; I came in just as the poor distracted Romeo carries Juliet off in his arms. As my eyes fell on the group I gave a loud cry and rushed out of the theatre, wildly wringing my hands. Juliet had seen and heard me. . . . I had frightened her, and she asked the men who were with her to watch me, *as she did not like the look of my eyes.*

When I returned an hour afterwards the stage was empty, the orchestra were in their places, and my overture was rehearsed. I sat as in a dream, without hearing a note; but when the applause with which the musicians received it roused me, I hoped that the public might like it, too, and that their enthusiasm might kindle Miss Smithson's. What madness! Is it not incredible that anyone could be so ignorant of the ways of the world?

Even if the overture to the *Freyschütz* or the *Magic Flute* were played on a benefit night in France, no one would listen to it. It is a mere prelude to the rising of the curtain, and even if it were differently received, there is nothing in the feeble performance of an isolated overture, by a small theatrical orchestra, to provoke enthusiasm. Besides, the great actors who play for a benefit generally arrive at the eleventh hour, and are, naturally, preoccupied with their own performance. They have barely time to dress, and are not found waiting about behind the scenes, listening to chance overtures. It had never occurred to me that, even if my overture had been received with acclamations, and loudly encored, it would have passed unnoticed by Miss Smithson, who would be full of her part, and absorbed in the details of dressing. And supposing, even, that she had heard it; what then? She would have asked what the applause meant, and her maid would have replied, "It is nothing, madame; they are going to play the overture again." Let us go farther, and suppose she had heard the composer's name; would that have changed indifference into love?

My overture was well played and fairly applauded, but not encored, and Miss Smithson never heard of it. She left the following day, after winning fresh laurels in her favourite part. By the purest accident (she never could believe this), I had taken a lodging at No. 96, Rue Richelieu, almost opposite her own, at the corner of the Rue Neuve Saint Marc. After lying prostrate on my bed until three in the afternoon, I rose mechanically, and, as usual, went to the window to look out into the street. By one of those gratuitous, cruel freaks of fate, it happened that, just at that moment, Miss Smithson left her house, stepped into her carriage, and drove away. . . .

No words can describe what I suffered; even Shakespeare has never painted the horrible gnawing at the heart, the sense of utter desolation, the worthlessness of life, the torture of one's throbbing pulses, and the wild confusion of one's mind, the disgust of life, and the impossibility of suicide. But the great poet has numbered such cries of suffering among the most terrible features of life.

I had left off composing; my mind was paralysed as my passion grew. I could only—suffer.

K

CHAPTER XXV.

WHEN June came round again, I once more entered the
academic lists. My success was generally predicted, and
it was even rumoured that the members of the Institute
themselves had said I was sure to obtain the first prize.
It was a great advantage to me that I had already secured
a second prize, whereas my competitors were altogether
unknown; and, as I felt pretty confident of my success,
I resolved on a course of action which subsequent
events proved to be suicidal. As the academicians had
virtually decided that I was to have the prize, I thought
it unnecessary to cramp myself by writing the kind of
music I had written the previous year, in order to suit
their special prejudices; and I resolved to let myself go,
and write something perfectly original, after my own
heart. "I will be a true artist," I said, "and write a
real cantata."

The subject was Cleopatra after the Battle of Actium.
The Queen of Egypt poisons herself by means of an asp,
and dies in convulsions. But before committing the fatal
act she invokes the shades of the Pharaohs, and questions
them in dread awe as to what hope there is that so disso-
lute and wicked a woman shall obtain admission to the

giant tombs in which lie buried the sovereigns distinguished for their valour and virtue.

It was a grand idea to be expressed in music. I had often set Juliet's wonderful monologue: "But if, when I am laid into the tomb," in imagination, and it expresses the same feeling of dread which the French poet has put into Cleopatra's prayer. But I stupidly put Juliet's words as a heading to my score, and that in itself would have condemned it irrevocably in the eyes of such Voltairean academicians as my judges.

My task was therefore a congenial one, and I composed a piece, large in treatment, with rhythm of striking originality, with enharmonic harmony of a solemn sonority, and a melody dramatically developed in a long-drawn *crescendo*. I used it just as it was, afterwards, for the chorus (in octaves and unisons) entitled *Chœur d'Ombres*, in my lyrical drama, *Lélio*.

I have heard it performed at my concerts in Germany, and I know the effect it produces, and also know, although I have forgotten what the rest of the cantata was like, that this piece of itself should have secured me the first prize. The jury, however, decided not to award any first prize that year rather than encourage a young composer who *manifested such tendencies*. The day following this decision I met Boïeldieu on the boulevard. I give the conversation just as it took place, for it was so curious that I remember every word. When he saw me he cried out:

"My dear boy, what *have* you done? You had the prize in your hand, and have deliberately thrown it away."

"I assure you, sir, I did my best."

"That is just it. You ought not to have done your best; your best is too good. How could I approve of such music, when soothing music is, above all others, the music I like ? "

" It seems to me rather difficult to write soothing music for an Egyptian queen who has poisoned herself and is dying a most painful death in the agonies of remorse."

" Oh ! I know you are sure to have plenty of excuses, but that makes no difference ; it is always possible to be graceful."

" Yes, I know the gladiators learnt how to die gracefully ; but Cleopatra was not so clever, it was not in her line ; and besides, she did not die in public."

" Now you are exaggerating ; we don't want her to sing a country dance. But what need was there to drag such extraordinary harmonies into her prayer ? I am not strong in harmony myself, and I must confess that I could make nothing of those other-world chords of yours."

I bowed silently, for how could I venture upon the patent retort, " Am I to blame because your knowledge of harmony is limited ? "

And then he continued, " Why introduce a rhythm into your accompaniment, the like of which no one ever heard before ? "

" I was not aware, sir, that in composing music it was desirable to avoid unusual forms if they were otherwise applicable, and you were lucky enough to light upon them."

" But, my dear fellow, it took all the skill and power of Madame Dabadia to get through your music ; and yet she is an accomplished musician."

" I certainly was not aware that music was intended to be sung without skill or power."

" Ah, well, you are sure to have the last word, so good-bye ; you can benefit by this lesson next year. Come and see me before then and have a chat, and I will argue it out with you, but like a *chevalier français.*" And he walked off delighted at having *made a hit*, as actors say.   In order to appreciate the point, which was worthy of d'Ellcviou,[1] it is necessary to understand that Boïeldieu's parting shaft was a quotation from one of his own works[2] in which the two words in italics occur.

In this quaint conversation, Boïeldieu was merely expressing the ideas about music current in France at that time.   What the Paris public wanted was soothing music, slightly dramatic in tone, but simple and colourless, with no unusual harmonies, unwonted rhythms, strange forms, or unexpected effects; whatever the subject might be it must be so set as to make no unusual demands on the attention or talents of either audience or actors.   Music was to them simply a pleasing, tasteful art, and they liked the music suited for evening dress, neither too exciting nor too dreamy, but joyous, troubadour, *chevalier français*—Parisian music.

Some years ago they wanted something different, and not much better; now they don't know what they want —or rather, they want nothing.

What could the Almighty have been thinking of when he set me down *in this pleasant land of France?* And yet I am fond of this strange country of mine, when I can forget art and dismiss our absurd political outbursts. What spendthrifts we are (in words)!   How we laugh, and how we amuse ourselves, at times!   How we tear the universe and its Creator to rags with our pretty white teeth and our polished pink nails!   How our wit sparkles!   How we play upon words!   How royally and republicanly we *swagger!*   This last is the least amusing thing about us.

---

[1] A celebrated actor from the Opéra Comique, who was the type of a gallant French cavalier of the time of the Empire.

[2] *Jean de Paris.*

CHAPTER XXVI.

I read Goethe's *Faust* for the first time —*Symphonie Fantastique*—
Fruitless endeavours to get it performed.

ANOTHER of the most remarkable events of my life was
the deep and wonderful impression made on my mind by
Goethe's *Faust*, which I read the first time in a French
translation by Gerard de Norval. I was fascinated by it
instantly, and always carried it about with me, reading it
anywhere and everywhere—at dinner, in the theatre, even
in the streets. The translation was in prose, with some
fragments of songs. I yielded to the temptation of
setting these; and no sooner was this difficult task ended
than I was foolish enough to have them printed—at my
own expense, without having even heard a note of them.
They were published in Paris under the title of *Huit
Scènes de Faust*, and a copy fell into the hands of Marx,
the celebrated Berlin critic and theorist, who wrote me
a very kind letter about it. This unexpected encouragement, coming as it did from Germany, gave me the
greatest pleasure; but it did not blind me to the many
and grave defects of the work, which was incomplete
and badly written. It had, however, some good points,
which I retained and developed in quite a new form
in my legend, *La Damnation de Faust*.

As soon as I became convinced of its worthlessness I

withdrew the work from circulation, and destroyed all the copies I could lay hands on.

I remember that a piece of music for six voices, called a *Concert des Sylphes*, was performed at my first concert. It was sung by six pupils of the Conservatoire, produced no effect, and was pronounced meaningless, vague, colourless, and *wholly devoid of melody*. Eighteen years later this very piece, with some slight alterations in the instrumentation and modulations, achieved European celebrity. It was encored whenever it was given, either in St. Petersburg, Moscow, Berlin, London, or Paris, and is now declared to be perfectly intelligible and deliciously melodious. It is true that it is now always sung by a chorus, for as I was unable to find six good solo-singers I took twenty-four chorus-singers, and the piece became popular at once. The form, colour, and effect are now tripled, and also clearly defined. A good many pieces of this kind are spoiled by the weakness of the singers, which would stand out vividly and powerfully if performed by a sufficient number of well trained chorus-singers. Where one ordinary voice fails hopelessly, fifty ordinary voices may ensure a brilliant success. A soulless singer paralyses the most powerful effects of the best composer, and renders them ridiculous; whereas the average warmth of feeling which always resides in a really musical multitude is sufficient for a proper interpretation; and the work thus rendered is appreciated and applauded, instead of being stifled by the want of power in the interpreter.

It was immediately after this, my first effort at setting *Faust*, and while I was yet strongly under the influence of Goethe's poem, that I wrote my *Symphonie Fantastique*. Some portions cost me great labour, while others

were composed with incredible ease. For instance, I
laboured for three weeks over the *Adagio* (*Scène aux
Champs*), which always affects the public so keenly—and
myself too, for that matter—and three times gave it up as
hopeless. *La Marche au Supplice*, on the other hand,
was written in one night. Still, I kept on adding
finishing touches to both numbers, and to the whole work,
for several years.

The Théâtre des Nouveautés had been playing *opéras
comiques* for some time, and had a fair orchestra, conducted by Bloc. He advised me to ask the directors
to perform my symphony, and to help me to get up a
concert for that purpose. They agreed, because the
strange programme of the work struck their fancy, and
seemed to them calculated to excite the curiosity of the
public. As I wanted a really great performance, I invited
eighty other musicians, which, added to Bloc's orchestra,
gave us altogether one hundred and thirty performers.
There was, of course, no accommodation for such numbers
—neither seats nor even music-desks. With the calm-
ness of people who have not realised the extent of a
difficulty, the managers replied to all my demands by
assuring me that all would be well, and that their scene-
shifter might be relied on. But on the day of rehearsal,
when my hundred and thirty musicians were assembled,
there was no room for them. The little orchestra below
had barely space for the violins, and there was an uproar
on the stage which would have maddened a much more
equable temper than mine. There was a call for desks,
and the carpenters hastily clutched anything which might
serve the purpose; the scene-shifter went about swearing
at his flies and wings; on one side there were cries for
chairs, on another for candles; the double-basses wanted

strings; there was no room for the drums, etc. etc. The porter was hopelessly bewildered. Bloc and I did the work of four, sixteen, thirty-two men; but all in vain; order could not be evolved from such chaos, and it turned into a regular rout—a musical Passage of the Beresina.

Still, in spite of the confusion, Bloc was determined to try two numbers, so as to give the directors "some idea of the symphony;" we went through the *Bal* and the *Marche au Supplice* as well as we could with such a disorderly orchestra, and the latter created a perfect *furore* amongst the players. Nevertheless, the concert did not take place; the directors were daunted by the disturbance, and withdrew from the enterprise. *They had not realised that a symphony necessitated such elaborate preparations.* And thus my plan fell to the ground for want of a few stools and desks. . . . Since then I have taken the utmost pains about the *matériel* of my concerts, having fully realised the disasters which ensue from neglect of details.

CHAPTER XXVII

Fantasia on *The Tempest*—Its performance at the Opéra.

GÉRARD was at this time conductor of the Théâtre Italien. In order to console me for my mishap, he advised me to compose something shorter than my *Symphonie Fantastique*, and undertook to have it properly performed at his theatre. I therefore set to work to write a *fantaisie dramatique*, with chorus, on Shakespeare's *Tempest*. The moment Gérard saw it he cried out: "This is on much too large a scale; we cannot perform a work of this kind at the Théâtre Italien. It can only be done at the Opéra." I instantly rushed off to offer it to M. Lubbert, the director of the Académie Royale de Musique. To my great surprise he agreed to insert it in the programme of a concert in aid of the Artists' Benevolent Society. He had heard my name in connection with my first concert at the Conservatoire, and he trusted me so entirely that, without even looking through the score, he gave me his word, and kept it nobly. He is a *rara avis* among directors. As soon as the parts were copied out, the choruses were taken in hand at the Opéra. There were no hitches; the full rehearsal went off brilliantly, and Fétis, who supported me with might and main, was present and expressed the greatest interest both in the work and in its author. But, with my usual luck, a tremendous storm, such as had not

been known for fifty years, broke over Paris shortly
before the hour of performance! There was a regular
waterspout, the streets were flooded and turned into
rivers and lakes, and all traffic was suspended, so that,
during the first half of the performance, while my *Tempest*
(accursed tempest!) was being played, the Opera-house
was all but empty. The audience consisted of some two
or three hundred people, at most—including the performers—and I might be said to have given a regular
kick in the air.

CHAPTER XXVIII.

A violent Distraction—Everything fair in Love.

These musical enterprises were not my only sources of excitement. The German pianoforte-player and composer II., with whom I had formed an intimacy since his arrival in Paris, was desperately in love with a young lady, who has since become celebrated through her talents and her adventures. II., who was the confidant of my great Shakespearian passion, and was deeply distressed by my sufferings, had very imprudently confided the story to Mdlle. M., telling her at the same time that he had never heard of such a case of infatuation. "I should never be jealous of *him*," he said one day; "I know that he would never fall in love with you."

The effect of this idiotic speech on the mind of a Parisian may be imagined. She became possessed with the idea of proving to her platonic and too-confiding admirer the error of which he had been guilty.

I had been asked, that summer, by Mdme. d'Aubri, the superintendent of a girls' school, to give guitar lessons to her pupils. I accepted the offer, and, oddly enough, my name still figures in the prospectus as professor of that noble instrument. Mdlle. M. gave pianoforte lessons in the same school; she rallied me on my doleful looks, and told me *there was someone in the world who took the deepest interest in me.* She also spoke to me about H., who, she said, was very fond of her, but it would never come to anything.

One day I received a letter from her, in which, under pretext of speaking to me about H., she made an appointment with me for the following morning. As luck would have it, I forgot all about her; which, if it had not been purely accidental on my part, would have been the most subtly diplomatic course I could have adopted. My cool indifference completed the work of conquest, and after playing the part of Joseph for a few days, I yielded, and threw myself, with all the ardour of youth, into this *liaison* with a young and beautiful girl, striving to forget my past sorrows in a new passion. If I were to narrate all the strange and romantic details of this little episode, my readers would probably be highly diverted; but as I am not penning my confessions, it will be sufficient to say that I ran through the whole gamut of passion in my intercourse with Mdlle. M. I told everything to poor H., who wept bitterly; but as he could not but acknowledge that he had only himself to blame, he made the best of it, and acquitted me of treachery, bade me farewell with a convulsive clasp of the hand, wished me joy of my good-fortune, and fled to Frankfort.[1] I have always admired his conduct under such trying circumstances. The narrative of my Italian journey will show how dramatically this episode ended, and how nearly Mdlle. M. was to giving tragic confirmation to the truth of the proverb, “It is dangerous to play with edged tools.”

[1] [For a somewhat different version of this, see Hiller's *Künstlerleben*.]

CHAPTER XXIX.

Fourth Competition at the Conservatoire—I obtain the Prize—The
Revolution of July—The Taking of Babylon—*La Marseillaise*—
Rouget de Lisle.

THE annual competition took place on the 15th July,
a little later than usual. I went up for the fifth time,
fully determined never to try again if I failed. It was
in the year 1830. I was just finishing my cantata when
the Revolution broke out.

> Et lorsqu'un lourd soleil chauffait les grandes dalles
> Des ponts et de nos quais déserts,
> Que les cloches hurlaient, que la grêle des balles
> Sifflait et pleuvait par les airs ;
> Que dans Paris entier, comme la mer qui monte,
> Le peuple soulevé grondait,
> Et qu'au lugubre accent des vieux canons de fonte
> La Marseillaise répondait.[1]

A number of families had taken shelter in the Palais
de l'Institut, and it looked strangely transformed—
with long-barrelled muskets protruding from the barred
doors, and its façade riddled with bullets, the air filled
with the shrieks of women, and, in the lulls between the
discharges of musketry, the shrill twitter of the swallows.
I hurriedly dashed off the last pages of my cantata to
the tune of the dry thud of the bullets as they struck
close to my windows or on the walls of my room; and on

[1] *Iambes* d'Auguste Barbier.

the 24th I was free to loaf about Paris with the *sainte canaille*,[1] and my pistol in my pocket, till the next day.

I shall never forget the aspect of Paris during those memorable days—the wild bravado of the street arabs, the enthusiasm of the men, the frenzy of the women, the mournful resignation of the Swiss and Royal Guards, the curious pride which the workmen exhibited in not pillaging Paris though they were masters of the situation, the astounding stories told by young fellows of their exploits, in which the real bravery of the deed was lost in the sense of the ridiculous aroused by the manner in which it was told; as, for instance, when they described the storming of the cavalry barracks of the Rue de Babylone—in which considerable loss had been incurred—with a gaiety worthy of Alexander's veterans, as "the capture of Babylon "—an abbreviation forced on them by the length of the real name. With what pompous prolongation of the "o" the name of " Babylon" was pronounced! . . . Oh Parisians, what buffoons you are! Great, if you will, but still buffoons! . . .

No words can give any idea of the music, the songs, and the hoarse voices which rang through the streets!

And yet it was only a few days after this harmonious revolution that I received a most extraordinary musical impression, or shock. I was crossing the Palais Royal, when I heard a tune which I seemed to recognise, issuing from among a crowd of people. As I drew nearer I perceived that ten or twelve young fellows were singing a war-song of my own, the words of which, translated from one of *Moore's Irish Melodies*,[2] happened exactly to

---

[1] " Sacred rabble," an expression of Auguste Barbier's.

[2] *Chant Guerrier* (Op. 2); from Moore's " Forget not our wounded companions, who stood."

suit the situation. Delighted at the discovery, and little
used to that kind of success, I enter the circle of
singers, and ask to be allowed to join. I am admitted,
and a superfluous bass is interpolated into the chorus.
I did not, of course, betray my identity; but I remember
having a warm discussion with the leader as to the
time in which he was taking my song. Luckily I
recover his good graces by singing my part in Béranger's
Vieux Drapeau, which he had set to music, and which
we next performed, quite correctly. During the *entr'actes*
of this improvised concert three National Guards, whose
duty it was to keep the crowd off the singers, went round,
shako in hand, to make a collection for those who had
been wounded during the Three Days. The Parisians,
struck by the quaintness of the idea, contributed libe-
rally, and there was a perfect hailstorm of five-franc pieces,
which our music alone could hardly have charmed from
the pockets of their owners. As the audience went
on increasing it became more and more difficult to keep
the necessary space clear for the performers, and an
armed force soon became impotent to control the curious
crowd. We find great difficulty in escaping; the crowd
streams after us; and at last, when we reach the Galerie
Colbert, leading to the Rue Vivienne, we are hunted out
like bears at a fair, surrounded on all sides, and more
songs demanded of us. The wife of a draper, over whose
shop there is a semicircular glazed gallery, suggests that
we should go up, and pour down our torrents of harmony
on our ardent admirers from thence, without fear of
being crushed to death. We agree, and begin with the
Marseillaise. The noisy crowd at our feet is hushed
at once. The air is as still as it is in the Piazza of St.
Peter's when the Pope pronounces the blessing, *urbi et*

orbi, from the pontifical balcony. At the end of the second verse, still the same silence. At the end of the third again, not a sound. This was not at all what I wanted. When I beheld that vast concourse I suddenly remembered that I had just arranged Rouget de Lisle's song for full orchestra and double chorus, and had put in the margin: *For all who have voices, hearts, and blood in their veins.* "Ah!" I said to myself, "that is what we want." So I was greatly disappointed at this persistent silence, and at the end of the fourth verse, unable to contain myself, I shouted, "Why on earth don't you sing?" Then the people roared out, *"Aux armes, citoyens!"* with the precision and power of a trained chorus. You must remember that the gallery which opened into the Rue Vivienne was crowded, so was the one opening into the Rue Neuve des Petits Champs, so was the area in the middle; and also that these four or five thousand voices came reverberating back in the enclosed space, from the closed shops below, the glass frames above, and the pavement beneath their feet. You must not forget either that the singers, men, women, and children, were hot from the combat of the previous day, and you can imagine the effect produced by their thundering refrain. . . . I can only say that I actually fell prostrate in the midst of our little band, who stood completely dumbfounded by the explosion like birds after a peal of thunder.

I have just said that I had arranged *La Marseillaise* for a double chorus and full orchestra. I dedicated it to the author of the immortal song, and received the following letter, which I have carefully kept, in reply:

"Choisy-le-Roi, 20 Dec., 1830.

"We are strangers, Monsieur Berlioz; are we to become friends? Your head seems to be a volcano in a perpetual state of eruption; there was a straw fire in mine which is burnt out, and has left a little smouldering smoke. But the wealth of your volcano and the poverty of my smoke combined may yet produce something. So I have two proposals to make to you. But we must see and know each other first. If you like the idea, tell me what day I can see you; or come to breakfast or dine with me at Choisy. You won't get much; but you are a poet, and the country air will be the best sauce for you. I should have endeavoured to make your acquaintance sooner, and thank you for the honour you have done a certain poor little creature in clothing her with your brilliant imagination. But I am merely a lame hermit who rarely visits your great city, and spends three quarters and a half of the time he is there in doing what he does not want to do. May I hope that you will not reject my humble offer, but will in some way or another enable me to thank you personally, and to express to you the pleasure with which I, like all true lovers of art, welcome your daring genius?

" ROUGET DE LISLE."

I heard afterwards that Rouget de Lisle—who, by-the-bye, has written a great many fine songs beside the *Marseillaise*—had a manuscript opera, founded on *Othello*, which he wanted to show me. But as I had to leave Paris the day after I received his letter, I told him I must postpone seeing him until after my return. The poor fellow died in the interval, 'and I never met him.

When peace was restored after a fashion, and Lafayette had presented Louis Philippe to the people as the best of all possible republics—when, in fact, the play was played out and the social machine was set going again—the Académie des Beaux Arts resumed its functions.

Our cantatas were played, on the piano of course, before the two Areopagi, whose working I have already explained. And as my piece (since burned) proved my conversion to the established faith, they at last, at last, at last, awarded me the first prize. I had suffered keenly the year before at not getting it, and did not feel much elated when Pradier the sculptor came to look for me in the library, where I stood awaiting my fate, and said cordially, with a warm shake of the hand, "You have got the prize!" Seeing him so glad and me so indifferent, you would have thought he was the laureate and I the academician. But I soon felt all the advantages of my position. I could not, with my sense of the manner in which the whole thing was managed, feel much pride in my success, but it set an official seal on my powers which would undoubtedly gratify my parents, and it gave me a pension of a thousand crowns and free admission to the theatres; it was a diploma, a certificate of my ability, and it secured me independence, nay, wealth, for five years to come.

CHAPTER XXX.

Two months afterwards the prizes were distributed, and
the successful cantata was performed. The ceremony was
precisely the same then that it is now. Year by year
the same musicians play pieces which are almost always
the same, and the prizes, which are awarded with the
same amount of discrimination, are bestowed with the
same solemnities. Every year, on the same day, at the
same hour, the same academician standing on the same
step of the same staircase, repeats the same sentence
to the successful candidate. The day is the 1st of
October, the hour four in the afternoon, the step the
third ; everyone knows who the academician is, and here
is the sentence :

"Now, young man, *macte animo ;* you are going on a
delightful journey . . . the classic home of the Fine Arts
. . . the country of Pergolesi and Piccini . . . inspired
by those blue skies . . . you will return with some
splendid work . . . the world is at your feet."

In honour of the great event the academicians don
their green embroidered uniforms ; they are radiant,
almost dazzling. They are about to crown a painter,

sculptor, architect, engraver, and musician. There is great joy in the abode of the muses.

What am I saying? . . . it sounds like poetry. To tell the truth I was not thinking of the Academy at all, but of some lines of Victor Hugo's, which, for some reason or another, came into my head:

> Aigle qu'ils devaient suivre, aigle de notre armée,
> Dont la plume sanglante en cent lieux est semée,
> Dont le tonnerre, un soir, s'éteignit dans les flots;
> Toi qui les a couvés dans l'aire maternelle
> Regarde et sois contente, et crie et bats de l'aile,
> Mère, tes aiglons sont éclos !

To return to our laureates, some of whom, by-the-way, are more like La Fontaine's "surly little monsters," the owls, than young eagles, but who are all impartially beloved by the Academy.

On the first Saturday in October their radiant mother "flaps her wings," and the successful cantata is fully performed. An *entire* orchestra is brought together, complete in all its parts. There are stringed instruments, two flutes, two hautboys, two clarinets. (To tell the truth this important section has only been completed recently. When the *grand prix* rose above my horizon, there was only one clarinet and a half, for the old man who had played the first clarinet from time immemorial, having but one tooth left, was only able to produce about half the notes from his asthmatic instrument.) There are four horns, three trombones, and even so modern an instrument as the cornet-à-piston. Do you call that nothing? It is all true. The Academy is completely transformed; it is off its head; it is guilty of actual extravagance. The maternal bird is pleased; "she screams and flaps her wings;" her owlets (I mean eaglets) are hatched at last.　We are all at our posts, and the conductor raises his baton.

The sun rises ; violoncello solo, slightly *crescendo*.

The little birds awake ; flute solo, violin *tremolo*.

The little brooks murmur ; second violin *solo*.

The little lambs bleat ; hautboy *solo*.

And as the *crescendo* increases, it comes to pass that by the time the little birds, little streams, and little lambs have each had their say it must be at least midday.　Then comes the recitative :

Already dawning day . . . etc. . . . .

Then follow the first song, the second recitative, the second song, the third recitative, and the third song, which generally kills the hero and revives the audience. The perpetual secretary then gives out the name of the author in sonorous tones, grasping the wreath of artificial laurels with which to crown the victor's brow in one hand and the real gold medal (which will enable him to pay his bills before he leaves Rome—it is worth a hundred and sixty francs, I know this for certain) in the other.

The laureate rises :

Son front nouveau tondu, symbole de candeur,
Rougit, en approchant, d'une honnête pudeur.

He embraces the life-secretary (slight applause).　He sees his august master standing close by ; pupil and master embrace ; as it is right they should (more applause). The laureate's parents are on a bench behind the academicians, shedding silent tears of joy ; he vaults over the intervening benches, crushes the toes of one man, treads on the coat of another, and casts himself into the arms of his sobbing parents, which is quite natural.

But, instead of applauding, the public is beginning to smile. On the right of this touching group stands a young girl, making desperate signs to the hero of the hour; he dashes towards her, tearing a lady's gauze dress to shreds in his haste, and crushing in a dandy's hat; she is his cousin, and he clasps her waist in his arms. He sometimes even kisses his cousin's neighbour (much laughter). Another woman, standing in a dim, remote corner, makes signals, which the hero is careful not to observe. But he flies to embrace his sweetheart—his betrothed, who is to share his good-fortune. He is careless of other women in his anxiety to reach her; knocks one down, gets caught in the footstool of another, and comes down with a heavy fall; he renounces his purpose, and returns to his seat humiliated and bathed in perspiration (loud applause and roars of laughter). How delightful! how charming! That is the crowning moment of the academical *séance*, and I know a great many people who go there on purpose to enjoy it. I bear the jesters no ill-will, for it happened that in my case there was neither father nor mother, cousin, *fiancée*, master nor mistress to embrace. . . . My master was ill, my parents absent or angry, and my mistress. . . . So I merely embraced the secretary, and as for my blushes, they were hidden beneath a shock of red hair, which, combined with certain other peculiarities, placed me undeniably in the category of owls.

Besides, I was in anything but an embarrassed mood that day; I don't think I ever was in such a passion in my life, and this was the reason of it. The subject of the cantata was *The Last Night of Sardanapalus.* The poem closes at the point where Sardanapalus, feeling himself vanquished, calls for his prettiest slaves, and mounts his

funeral pyre with them. I had at first intended to write
a sort of symphony, descriptive of the conflagration,
the shrieks of the women, the defiant words of the
proud voluptuary in the midst of the devouring flames,
and the crash of the falling palace. But when I recollected
how limited were the means at my disposal I refrained.
A glance at the orchestral *finale* would have caused
the academicians to condemn the whole piece; and, played
on the piano, it would have sounded perfectly unintelligible. So I bided my time, and when I had secured
the prize, and knew that my work would be performed
by a full orchestra, I wrote my conflagration scene.

It produced such an effect when rehearsed that some
of the academicians, quite taken by surprise, came up
and congratulated me, unaware of the trap into which
they had fallen. The hall was full of artists and amateurs, curious to hear the work of the youth of whom
such strange tales were told. Many of them too had
heard such glowing reports of the sensation produced
by the conflagration scene at rehearsal that an unusual
amount of interest was excited.

Before the concert began, I placed myself, score in
hand, beside Grasset, the ex-conductor of the Théâtre
Italien, for I had my misgivings as to his powers. Mdme.
Malibran, whose curiosity had been aroused by the reports
of the rehearsal, could not find a seat in the hall, so
we got a stool for her between the two double-basses. I
have never seen her since.

The *decrescendo* begins.

(The cantata opens with the words, " Night has already
drawn her veil across the day," so that I had to describe
a sunset instead of the usual dawn, which looks as if I

had been predestined to take life and the Academy against the grain from the beginning.)

The cantata proceeds in due course. Sardanapalus hears of his defeat, resolves on death, sends for his women; the conflagration begins. Those who were present at the rehearsal whisper to their neighbours, " Now the crash is coming; it is wonderful—astounding !"

A hundred thousand curses on musicians who do not count their bars ! In the score, the horns give the cue to the drums, the drums to the cymbals, the cymbals to the big-drum, and the first sound of the big-drum brings in the final explosion. But the d——d horns make no sign, the drums are afraid to break the silence, and the cymbals and big-drum naturally follow their leaders ; nothing is heard ! nothing ! ! ! And all the time the violins and basses carry on their impotent *tremolo*, and there is no explosion, no conflagration—or, at least, nothing but its embers ; and so we have an absurd failure instead of a crashing success. *Ridiculus mus!*   No one who has not been through a similar experience can conceive what a fury I was in ! With a cry of horror, I flung my score right across the middle of the orchestra, dashing down the music-desks. Mdme. Malibran started back as though a shell had burst at her feet. There was a general uproar at once in the orchestra, among the scandalised academicians, the mystified musicians, and the enraged friends of the composer. This was the most disastrous of all my musical catastrophes; would that it had been also the last !

CHAPTER XXXI.

In spite of the urgent representations I addressed to the
Minister of the Interior to induce him to excuse me
from the Italian journey, which as laureate I had to
undertake, I was obliged to prepare for going to Rome.

I did not want to leave Paris without having a satisfactory performance of *Sardanapalus*, the finale of which
had previously been so marred. So I got up another
concert at the Conservatoire, in which the prize cantata
was to figure next to the *Symphonie Fantastique*. The
latter had not yet been heard, Habeneck undertook to
conduct, and all the performers were good enough to offer
me their services gratuitously for the third time, for
which I cannot sufficiently thank them.

On the day before the concert I received a visit from
Liszt, whom I had never yet seen. I spoke to him of
Goethe's *Faust*, which he was obliged to confess he had
not read, but about which he soon became as enthusiastic as myself. We were strongly attracted to one
another, and our friendship has increased in warmth and
depth ever since. He was present at the concert, and
excited general attention by his applause and enthusiasm.

The performance was by no means perfect, as two

rehearsals are wholly insufficient for so complicated a work; but it went well enough for its principal features to be appreciated. *Le Bal, La Marche au Supplice,* and *Le Sabbat* created a great sensation; the march especially carried the audience by storm. The *Scène aux Champs* fell flat; but it was very different in those days to what it is now. I made up my mind on the spot to re-write it. Hiller, who was in Paris at the time, gave me some admirable hints, by which I hope I profited.

The cantata was well performed; the conflagration took place, the great crash followed, and the success was perfect. Some days later articles appeared in the newspapers fiercely attacking or passionately praising my music. But instead of pointing out, as they might easily have done, the palpable defects in both works (defects which it took me years of work to eradicate from my symphony), my hostile critics fell foul of me for my absurd ideas (which were not mine at all), the crudeness of certain modulations (which did not exist), my systematic contempt for certain fundamental rules of art (which I had religiously obeyed), and my neglect of certain musical forms (which were the only ones employed in the very passages cited to the contrary)! On the other hand I am bound to confess that my partisans have often credited me with aims of which I was wholly unconscious, and which were utterly absurd. The amount of nonsense, folly, and rubbish, the extravagant theories and ridiculous systems which the critics of the French press have perpetrated on my behalf pass all belief. Only two or three writers have discussed me with intelligent self-restraint. It is not easy, even nowadays, to find critics who possess the requisite knowledge, imagination, feeling, and impartiality to pass a sound judgment on my works, and to appreciate my aims and the tendency of my mind. They certainly did not exist when I began my career; and the few and imperfect performances of my works would necessarily have left much to their imaginations.

I was far better understood and appreciated in Paris by the young men who possessed some musical training, and what we may call the sixth, or artistic, sense, than by the prosy, puffed-up, pretentious, ignorant clique of critics. I became a regular bugbear to the composers whose landmarks I so ruthlessly removed, and my un-disguised contempt for certain scholastic articles of faith goaded them to exasperation. God knows that there is nothing on earth so ruthless and violent as such fanaticism.

Cherubini's indignation at this storm of heterodoxy, and the sensation it awakened, may be imagined. His followers had informed him of the effect produced by the last rehearsal of the "abominable" symphony; on the day of performance he passed the door of the concert-room as the audience was trooping in, and someone stopped him and said, "Are you not coming to hear Berlioz's new work?" "*Ze* n'ai pas besoin d'aller savoir comment *il né faut pas faire!*" ("I don't want to be taught *how not to write!*") he retorted, with the air of a cat forcibly choking down a dose of mustard. When the concert turned out a success he looked like the cat *after* its dose of mustard; he was speechless, and could only sneeze. Then, after some days, he sent for me. "Are you going to Italy?" "Yes, sir." "Your studies are at an end, and your name will be struck off the books of the Conservatoire. *Mais il me semble qué, qué, qué, vous deviez venir me faire une visite. On—on—on—on—*

né sort pas d'ici comme d'une écurie!" . . . I was on
the point of retorting, "Why not, since we are treated
like horses?" but I was wise enough to refrain, and
assured our amiable director that I should certainly pay
him a farewell visit and thank him for his kindness.

So, much against my will, I was forced to go to
Rome, and there forget good old Cherubini's gracious
encouragement, the rusty lance-thrusts of the *chevalier
français* Boïeldieu, the grotesque disquisitions of my
newspaper critics, the enthusiasm of my friends, and the
invectives of my enemies, the whole musical world and
even music itself, at my leisure. No doubt the objects
of the Institute were, on the whole, good, and it is not
for me to judge how far the intentions of the founders
have been carried out as regards the careers of painters,
sculptors, engravers, and architects; but as regards musicians, the Italian journey is, to say the least of it,
useless for their special study, though the artistic
treasures, scenery, and associations of the country may
assist in developing their imaginations. This will be
clearly proved by a truthful account of the life led by
French artists in Rome.

Before starting, the five or six new laureates assemble
to make arrangements for the journey. A *vetturino* undertakes to convoy the cargo (they generally travel together)
to Italy in a huge chariot, into which they are thrust,
for all the world like a batch of country folk going to a
fair. As they never change horses, it takes a long time
to traverse France, cross the Alps, and reach Rome; but
the tediousness of the journey is doubtless beguiled by
the countless incidents certain to befall a cartload of
light-hearted young fellows. I cannot, however, speak

from personal experience, for I was detained in Paris until the middle of January, and after spending some weeks at the Côte St. André with my parents—who were proud of my success and received me most warmly—I bent my steps towards Italy, feeling lonely and somewhat sad.

CHAPTER XXXII.

Marseilles to Leghorn—Storm—Leghorn to Rome—The Académie
de France in Rome.

THERE was no inducement to cross the Alps at that time
of year, so I determined to go round by Marseilles. It
was my first sight of the sea. I spent some time in
looking for a tolerably clean vessel going to Leghorn; but
saw nothing but wretched little ships, with evil-smelling
cargoes of wood and oil, or stinking bones for the manu-
facture of bone-black, and not a hole or corner on board
in which a man could sleep, no shelter, and no food.
I was to provide my own victuals, and sleep in a filthy
little hole with four sailors, with faces like bull-dogs,
and more than doubtful honesty, for my sole companions. I refused the tempting offer, and spent some
idle days wandering about the rocks near Notre Dame
de la Garde, which is a very pleasant way of killing
time. At last I heard of a Scandinavian brig, which was
on the point of sailing for Leghorn. Some nice-look-
ing young fellows, whom I met at La Cannebière, told
me they were going in her, and that we should be fairly
comfortable if we arranged to mess together. The captain
would have nothing to do with our commissariat, so we
had to look after it ourselves. We laid in a stock of provisions for a week, which was more than enough, as the
crossing only took three or four days in fair weather.

One's first journey on the Mediterranean is a delightful experience, if the weather is fine and one has no dread of sea-sickness. I congratulated myself on my fortunate exemption from the malady by which my fellow-passengers were prostrated during the first two days of our voyage. Our dinners on deck, as we sailed along the Sardinian coast in the brilliant sunshine, were delightful. My fellow-passengers, who were all Italians, told endless stories, most of them wholly incredible, but very interesting. One had fought in the Greek War of Independence, and had known Canaris intimately. We pestered him with questions about the revolutionary hero whose glory seemed to have burned itself out as quickly as the flame of his own fire-ships. A Venetian, an underbred fellow, who spoke abominable French, averred that he had commanded Lord Byron's corvette during the poet's adventurous excursions in the Adriatic and the Grecian Archipelago. He gave us a minute description of the brilliant uniform Lord Byron had insisted on his wearing, and the orgies in which they indulged; and his modesty did not prevent him from repeating the praises which the illustrious traveller had bestowed on his courage. During a storm, Byron invited the captain to play *écarté* with him in his cabin; and the latter deserted his post and accepted the invitation. While they were playing, the ship gave a lurch, which upset both table and players.

"Pick up the cards, and go on!" cried Byron.

"With pleasure, my lord."

"You are a brave fellow, captain."

I dare say there is not a word of truth in all this; but the gold-laced uniform and the game of *écarté* savour strongly of the author of *Lara*. Besides, the narrator was

not clever enough to have invented the local colouring of
his stories, and, in my case, I was too much pleased to
find myself with a man who had possibly shared *Childe
Harold's Pilgrimage*, to question his veracity.

Meanwhile, our progress was slow; we were becalmed
in sight of Nice for three days; and though we drifted
along about three miles every evening, with the light
breeze which sprang up after sunset, a counter-current
always carried us back again during the night. Every
morning, when I went on deck, I asked the sailors what
the town on the shore was, and always got the same
answer: "*E Nizza, signore. Ancora Nizza. E sempre
Nizza.*" I began to think the lovely city must possess
magnetic power, and that, though she did not draw out
our iron bolts and screws one by one, as the sailors say the
North Pole does, she yet held us spell-bound to the spot.
But I was disabused by a raging north wind, which rushed
down upon us from the Alps like an avalanche. Eager
to avail himself of such a chance, the captain put up
every rag of sail. Thus caught on the flank, the vessel
leaned over horribly, which alarmed me a good deal; but
I soon became used to that angle of inclination. Towards
evening, however, as we were making for the Gulf of
Spezzia, the *tramontana* blew with such violence that
the sailors themselves began to quake, seeing that no sail
was taken in. It was a regular hurricane, which I shall
some day describe in fine academical language. I clung
to an iron bar on deck, watching the wonderful scene
with a beating heart, while the Venetian hero kept a
strict eye on the captain of the ship, who was steer-
ing, exclaiming now and again, "What madness! what
obstinacy! The fool will drown us all. . . . Fifteen
sails set in such a wind!" The captain paid no heed,

but stood to the helm, when suddenly an awful gust caught him and threw him down, and the ship heeled right over on her side. It was a terrible moment. Our poor captain lay rolling about among the casks which the shock had sent flying about in all directions, while the Venetian pounced on the helm and assumed temporary command of the ship, an illegal act which was warranted by the circumstances, and accepted by the sailors, who had given themselves up for lost, and were calling upon the Madonna to save them. " What do you want with the Madonna, you fools? Up with you to the top-sails, every man jack of you !" The men swarmed up the rigging, and, in a few seconds, the principal sails were furled, the ship slowly righted herself, more sail was taken in, and we were saved.

We reached Leghorn the following day, with one ragged sail, all the remainder having been torn to shreds by the wind. Some hours later, while sitting in the Hôtel Aquila Nera, the sailors came in a body to see us, not, as we at first supposed, with a view to *bakshecsh*, but simply to congratulate us on our escape. The poor fellows barely earned their miserable rations of salt cod and ship's biscuit, but we could not get them to accept any money, and had even the greatest difficulty in inducing them to share our breakfast. Such delicacy of feeling deserves to be recorded, especially in Italy, where it is unusually rare.

During the journey, my companions had confided to me that they were on their way to join the insurrection against the Duke of Modena. They were very enthu-siastic, and evidently believed that the hour for the liberation of Italy had struck. Once Modena was in their hands, the whole of Tuscany would rise, and they would march on Rome at once; France would step forward and help the good cause, etc., etc. Alas! two of them were captured by the police on their way to Florence, and sent to prison, where they may be languishing still. I heard afterwards that the others had distinguished themselves in the ranks of the patriots at Modena and Bologna, but that they had subsequently shared the fate of brave Menotti. Thus ended their dreams of liberty.

After bidding one another what we little thought would be an eternal farewell, I began to prepare for my journey to Rome. The time was a most unfavourable one, and, as a Frenchman coming from Paris, I had the greatest difficulty in getting into the Papal States. The officials refused to *viser* my passport, as the Academy students were suspected of having fomented the insurrection of the Piazza Colonna, and the Pope by no means desired an increase of the little revolutionary colony. I wrote to our director, M. Horace Vernet, who, after reiterated applications, succeeded in obtaining the necessary permission from Cardinal Benedetti.

I happened, oddly enough, to have left Paris alone, and to be the only Frenchman on board the brig, and now the *vetturino* could find no other passenger going to Rome, so that I arrived there all by myself. I had picked up two volumes of the Empress Josephine's Memoirs at a bookstall in Siena, which helped me to pass the long hours in that crawling coach. My Jehu could not speak a word of French, and my Italian was limited to such phrases as "*Fa molto caldo*," "*Provi quando lo pranzo?*" so that our conversation could scarcely be called interesting. The country was not particularly picturesque, and the utter absence of anything approaching to comfort in the towns through which we passed, increased my irritation at the absurd decree which had forced this visit to Italy upon me. At last we arrived at a little cluster of houses called La Storta, and the *vetturino*, who was pouring out some wine for himself, remarked casually, "*Ecco Roma, signore!*" pointing carelessly over his shoulder to the dome of St. Peter's. No words can express what I felt when I turned and saw the Eternal City lying before me in the centre of that great barren plain. . . . It seemed unutterably grand, poetical, sublime; the imposing grandeur of the Piazza del Popolo through which you enter the city on the road from France, deepened my religious awe, and I awoke as from a dream, when the horses, whose sluggishness I had ceased to revile, stopped in front of a noble palace. It was the Académie.

The Villa Medici, in which the students and the director of the Académie de France live, was built in 1557, by Annibale Lippi, Michael Angelo adding a wing and some ornaments; it stands on the side of the Monte Pincio, overlooking the city, on one of the finest sites in the world. On the right lies the Pincian Way, the Champs Élysées of Rome, which is thronged every evening with carriages, equestrians, and pedestrians, defiling in a never-ending stream along the magnificent plateau. They disperse at the stroke of seven like a swarm of flies in the wind, for the Romans have an invincible, almost superstitious, dread of *l'aria cattiva*, and if you see a group of pedestrians lingering to admire the gorgeous glow of the sunset behind Monte Mario, you may feel certain that such rash loiterers are strangers. To the left of the villa the Pincian Way leads into the little piazza of the Trinita del Monte, with an obelisk in the centre, from which a great marble staircase leads down the hill to the Piazza d'Ispagna.

On the opposite side the palace looks out over beautiful gardens laid out in Le Nôtre's style, as all orthodox academy gardens ought to be. It contains a small wood of laurel and oaks, placed on a raised terrace, and running up to the ramparts of Rome on one side, and the French convent of the Ursulines on the other.

In front of the palace, in the middle of the waste lands of the Villa Borghese, stands the dreary, desolate house in which Raphael lived, and beyond it the horizon is bounded by a circle of umbrella-pines, peopled by a swarm of black crows, which enhance the gloom of the scene.

This is an accurate description of the splendid quarters in which the French Government lodges its artists during their sojourn in Rome. The director's apartments are sumptuous, and an ambassador might envy them ; but the pupils' rooms are small, inconvenient, and very badly furnished. A quartermaster in the Popincourt Barracks, at Paris, is better off in this respect than I was in the Palace of the Accademia di Francia. Most of the studios are in the gardens ; the others are scattered about the interior of the palace, and some are built out on a raised balcony overlooking the garden of the Ursuline Convent, with the Sabine Hills, Monte Cavo, and Hannibal's Camp in the distance. The library contains a fair collection of classical works, but absolutely no modern books. It is open to the students till three, and is a great resource for those who have nothing to do ; for it is only fair to say that they enjoy the most complete liberty, and, beyond sending a picture, drawing, engraving, or piece of music once a year to the Académie at Paris, nothing is required of them ; they may work as much or as little as they choose. The director's duties are confined to seeing that the rules of the establishment are not infringed; he exercises no sort of control over the students' work. This is inevitable, for no one man could by any possibility superintend five branches of art, since he cannot excel in all, and his criticisms on those he had not mastered would, of course, be perfectly worthless.

CHAPTER XXXIII

THE *Ave Maria* had just sounded when I alighted at the door of the Academy, and, as it was dinner-time, I made at once for the dining-hall, where I was told that all the students were assembled. As my coming had been so long delayed they had given up expecting me, and my sudden appearance was greeted with deafening shouts from the noisy group seated at the well-furnished table.

"Oh, Berlioz, Berlioz! That head; those locks; that nose! Oh, I say, Jalay, your nose *is* put out of joint now."

"And as for you, what is your hair to his?"

"Great gods, what a mop!"

"Hullo, Berlioz! Don't you remember me? Have you forgotten our meeting at the Conservatoire, and your confounded drums, which would not set Sardanapalus' pyre alight? What a rage he was in; but, by Jove! he had a right to be! Don't you remember me?"

"Of course I remember you; but your name?"

"It's Signol."

"Rossignol, you mean!"

"What an atrocious pun!"

"Ridiculous!"

"Let him sit down."

"Who, the pun?"

"No ; Berlioz."

"Here, Fleury, bring some punch ; . . . the very best; that will be better than the atrocities of this punster."

"At last our section is completed."

"I say, Montfort,[1] here is your colleague. Embrace him."

"Let us embrace."

"They shall not embrace !"

"They shall !"

"They shall not !"

"Yes !"

"No !"

"Oh, I declare, while they are making this noise you are gobbling up the macaroni.   Please leave me some."

"Let us all embrace him, and there will be an end of all this."

"End ?   Why, it's only the beginning.   Here is the punch ; don't drink your wine."

"No more wine for us !"

"Down with the wine !"

"Here go the bottles.   Look out, Fleury !"

Crash ! bang !

"Gentlemen—gentlemen ! Spare the glasses ! You will want them for the punch ; for I don't suppose you will care to drink it out of small glasses."

"Small glasses—never !"

"Well done, Fleury ! You were just in time."

Fleury is the factotum of the establishment ; a capital fellow, who deserves the confidence the director has in

[1] The laureate who had gone to Rome before me. As no prize was awarded in 1829, the Academy awarded two in 1830, and Montfort obtained the lesser one, which entitled him to the pension for four years.

him. He has waited on the boarders for years, and is so used to scenes like the present that he watches them unmoved, and his cool demeanour is a charming contrast to the uproar around him. When I had recovered from the shock of my reception, and had time to look about me, I noticed that the dining-hall was a very strange-looking place, and that one wall was decorated with life-size portraits of about fifty former students—a sort of nightmare of frescoes of the most monstrous grotesqueness. Unfortunately want of space has prevented the continuation of the portrait gallery down to the present time.

In the evening, after I had paid my respects to M. Vernet, I joined my companions at the celebrated Café Greco,[1] which was their usual place of resort. It is a miserable hole—dirty, dark, and damp; and it is impossible to understand why all the artists in Rome should flock there. Its only advantages are its proximity to the Piazza di Spagna and the Lepre Restaurant, which is opposite. You pass your time there in smoking execrable cigars and drinking worse coffee, served on wretched little wooden tables the size of a hat, and as greasy and filthy as the walls of this delectable resort. Nevertheless, the Café Greco is so much frequented by foreign artists that most of them have their letters sent there, and fresh arrivals know they are sure to meet all their countrymen collected there.

The next day I met Felix Mendelssohn, who had been some weeks in Rome. I will describe our meeting and the incidents to which it gave rise in my account of my first visit to Germany (chapter lv.).

---

[1] [For the Café Greco, and also for Horace Vernet, see Mendelssohn's Letters. Berlioz and Montfort are also alluded to by Mendelssohn in no sparing terms in his letter of March 29, 1831.]

CHAPTER XXXIV.

It took me a long time to get used to this novel kind of
existence, and I had something on my mind which prevented me from taking any interest either in surrounding
objects or in the society into which I was thus suddenly
thrown. I expected to find letters from Paris waiting
for me, and for the next three weeks I watched for them
with ever-increasing anxiety.

Unable any longer to control my desire to fathom the
reason of this mysterious silence, I determined to return
to Paris at once, despite M. Horace Vernet's friendly
remonstrances, and his warning that he would be obliged
to strike my name off the Academy lists if I persisted
in my rash resolve. On my way back I was detained for
a week in Florence by an attack of quinsy, which confined me to my bed. While there I made the acquaintance of the Danish architect, Schlick, a capital fellow,
who is thought very highly of by connoisseurs. During
my illness I reconstructed the *Scène du Bal*, in my
Symphonie Fantastique, and made the existing addition
to the *coda*. It was almost finished when I was allowed
out for the first time, and I at once proceeded to the
post-office for my letters. The packet which was handed

to me contained a letter the tenor of which was inconceivably painful to a man of my years and temperament. I was beside myself with passion, and shed tears from sheer rage; but I made up my mind on the spot what to do. My duty was clear. I must at once proceed to Paris, and kill two guilty women and an innocent man.[1] After that, it would, of course, be incumbent on me to commit suicide. I arranged all the details on the spot. Knowing me as they did, my reappearance in Paris would be looked for. . . . A complete disguise and the greatest precautions were therefore necessary; and I rushed off to Schlick, to whom I had already confided my story.

"Good God! what is the matter?" he cried, when he saw my white face.

"Look and see," I said, handing him the letter.

"This is horrible!" he replied, when he had read it; "what are you going to do?"

I knew that, if I told him my plan, he would try to dissuade me from carrying it out.

"What am I going to do? Why, return to France, of course; but to my father's house instead of to Paris."

"That is right, my dear fellow; go home, and in time you will recover from the awful condition into which this unexpected blow has thrown you. Come, cheer up."

"I will, but I must be off at once. I could not answer for myself to-morrow."

"We can easily get you off to-night, for I have friends among the police and the postal officials. I will have your passport ready in two hours, and will get you a

---

[1] My fair comforter was of course at the bottom of all this. Her worthy mother, who was perfectly well acquainted with the true state of the case, accused me of having brought trouble into her family, and announced her daughter's marriage with M. P——.

seat in the diligence which starts five hours hence. Go
to your hotel and get ready, and I will meet you there."

Instead of following his advice, I betook myself to
one of the quays on the Arno, where I knew there was
a French *modiste*. I enter the shop, look at my watch,
and say : "It is now twelve o'clock, madame; I leave
by the mail this evening, and I want to know if you
can let me have a costume such as would be worn by
a lady's-maid, by then ? I will pay you whatever you
choose to ask."

After a moment's consideration, it is arranged that I
am to have what I want. I deposit part of the price,
and return to the Hôtel des Quatre Nations, on the
opposite bank of the Arno.

I call the head-porter.

"I am going to Paris at six o'clock this evening,
Antoine, and I cannot take my trunk, so kindly look
after it, and send it after me to my father's house, as
soon as you can. I have written down the address."

I then took the score of the *Scène du Bal*, and, as the
instrumentation of the *coda* was not quite completed, I
wrote across it : "*I have not time to finish this; but, if
the Paris Concert Society should take it into its head to
perform this work during the* ABSENCE *of the author, I
request Habeneck to double the passages for flutes in the
bass octave, with the clarinets and horns the last time
the theme is introduced, and to write the chords which
follow for full orchestra ; that will do for the ending.*"

I then seal it up, address it to Habeneck, and pack it
in a bag with some clothes. I have a double-barrelled
pistol, which I load carefully, and two little bottles of
laudanum and strychnine, which I examine and put in
my pocket. Then, my mind being at rest with regard

to my weapons, I spend the remainder of my time in wandering about the streets of Florence, with the restless, disgusting demeanour of a mad dog.

At five I adjourn to my dressmaker's, and try on my dress, which fits to perfection. In paying for it I put down twenty francs more than the price agreed, and the girl at the desk tries to point out my mistake, but is deterred by her mistress, who hastily sweeps the gold into a drawer, saying: "Leave the gentleman alone, you little stupid; don't you see that he is too busy to listen to your chatter? A thousand thanks, sir; I wish you success. You will look your part to perfection." I smiled ironically, and she bowed me gracefully out of the shop.

At last it strikes six, and I bid farewell to my friend Schlick, who looks upon me as a lost sheep returning to the fold. I stow away my feminine apparel in one of the side pockets, give a parting glance to Cellini's Perseus, with the famous inscription, *Si quis te læserit, ego tuus ultor ero*,[1] and we are off.

We leave mile after mile behind us, but not a word passes between me and my companion. I had a great lump in my throat, and sat with my teeth tightly clenched, unable either to sleep or eat. About midnight, however, the conductor said something to me about my pistols, which he prudently uncapped and hid under the cushions. He was afraid we might be attacked, and in that case, said he, it is much better to remain passive, unless you wish to be murdered.

"Just as you please," I replied. "I don't want to raise any difficulties, and I bear the brigands no grudge."

[1] "If any offend thee, I will avenge thee." This celebrated statue stands in the Grand Ducal Square, from which the mails start.

My companion did not know what to make of me, and, as I had taken nothing but a little limejuice since we started, he began to regard me as scarcely human. When we arrived at Genoa I discovered that a fresh misfortune had befallen me, and that I had lost my dress. We had changed carriages at a village called Pietra Santa, and I had left my disguise behind. "Good heavens!" I said, "it looks as if some friend were bent on hindering my purpose. But we shall see!"

I sent for a courier, who could speak both French and Genoese, and asked him to take me to a dressmaker. It was nearly twelve, and the next coach started at six. I demand a costume : impossible to produce it in so short a time. We go to another dressmaker, then to a third, and a fourth, without success. At last we find a woman who is willing to try ; she accomplishes the task, and my disaster is repaired. Unluckily, however, upon examining my passport, the Sardinian police take it into their heads that I am a *carbonaro*, a conspirator, a patriot, or Heaven knows what, refuse to *viser* my passport for Turin, and advise me to travel *viâ* Nice instead.

"Well, then, *viser* it for Nice, in Heaven's name! What do I care whether I pass through hell, so that I get on?" . . .

I don't know which of us was the greater fool, the police, who discovered a revolutionist in every Frenchman, or I, who feared to set foot in Paris except disguised as a woman, lest my purpose should reveal itself in my face ; forgetting, like an idiot, that I could have remained quietly in an hotel in Paris for a few hours, and sent for any number of disguises at my leisure.

When people are possessed with any single idea they

always fancy, in the drollest way, that everyone else is full of it too, and act upon the supposition.

I set out quite cheerfully on my way to Nice, rehearsing every point of the little comedy I intended to play in Paris by the way. I would go to my *friend's* house, about nine o'clock in the evening, when the family would be assembled for tea, and send in to say that the Countess M.'s maid is waiting with an urgent message; I am shown into the drawing-room; I hand over a letter, and, while it is being read, produce my pistol and blow out the brains, first, of number one, and then of number two; and, seizing number three by the hair, throw off my disguise, and finish her off in the same manner, regardless of her shrieks. Then, before we are interrupted, I hasten to deposit the contents of the remaining barrel in my own right temple; and if the pistol misses fire (which has happened before now), I shall at once resort to my small bottles. A charming comedy! It is really a great pity it was never put upon the stage.

And yet there were moments when, in spite of my wrath, I could not help feeling sorry that my plans involved my own suicide. It seemed hard to bid farewell to life and art, to go down to posterity as a brute who could not get on in the world; to leave my unfinished symphony, and all the other greater works which were seething in my brain. . . . Ah ! . . . it is . . . And then suddenly my fell purpose gained the upper hand once more. . . . No, no, no, no, no, they must all die, they must, and they shall ! . . . And the horses trotted on, bearing me nearer and nearer to France. It was night, and we were travelling along the Cornice road, which is cut out of the steep precipice of rocks overhanging the sea.   For more than an hour I had been indulging in bright dreams of what the future might have had in store for me when the postilions stopped the horses to put on the drag, and suddenly, through the stillness, the sound of the roaring breakers dashing against the foot of the precipice broke on my ear.   The raging fury of the waves raised a corresponding tempest in my breast, fiercer and deadlier than any I had yet experienced.   I sat like a raving lunatic, clutching the seat with both hands, ready to spring out and dash myself over the cliff, and uttered such a wild, fierce yell that the unfortunate conductor started away in horror, evidently regarding me as a devil doomed to wander on the earth with a piece of the true cross in his possession.

It must be admitted that, although I was not yet out of danger, the fever was intermittent.   When I became aware of this, I reasoned thus with myself—not altogether foolishly, considering the place and the hour : Supposing, in one of these interludes (the interludes were the moments in which life smiled to me, you see I was virtually vanquished), supposing, in one of these interludes, I said, I were to prepare myself for the next attack by binding myself in some way and having something to cling to . . . I might arrive at some . . . definite . . . conclusion.

Let me see.   We were passing through a little Sardinian village[1] on the sea-shore (the sea was much calmer), and when we stopped to change horses I told the conductor to wait while I wrote a letter; I go into a little café and write a letter on a scrap of paper to the director of the Académie de Rome, asking M. Horace Vernet *to be so good as not to strike my name off the*

____
[1] Vintimille, I think.

Academy lists, if he had not already done so, as I had not yet broken through the rules; and I gave him MY WORD OF HONOUR *that I would not cross the frontier until I had received his answer, which I would await at Nice.*

Now that I had bound myself by a promise I went on my way most peacefully, feeling that if I were expelled from the Academy and launched penniless on the world, I could still fall back upon my former plan; and then . . . I suddenly found out that . . . I was hungry, having eaten nothing since I left Florence. Oh, beneficent nature! I was evidently cured!

The struggle was not quite over, however, when I reached Nice. I waited for several days, and then M. Vernet's answer came. It was a friendly, kindly, paternal letter, and touched me deeply. He did not know the cause of my trouble, but he gave me the most kindly counsel, and pointed out to me that in work and art I should find a panacea for my sorrow. He told me my name was still on the lists, that the minister should not hear of my escapade, and that I should be received with open arms when I returned.

"Well, they are saved," I said, with a deep sigh. "And supposing now I were to lead a quiet, happy life, and give myself up entirely to music, would not that be too curious? Let us try."

And so I drink deep draughts of the sunny, balmy air of Nice, and life and joy return to me, and I dream of music and the future. I spend a whole month in Nice, wandering in groves of orange-trees, bathing in the sea, sleeping on the heather on the Villefranche hills, and looking down from those glorious heights on the silent coming and going of the distant ships. I live entirely alone. I write the overture to *King Lear*. I sing. I believe in a God. Convalescence !

These were the three happiest weeks in my life. Oh Nizza !

Once more my peace was disturbed by the King of Sardinia's police.

I had recently made the acquaintance of two officers of the Piedmontese garrison, whom I used to meet at the café ; and one day I played a game of billiards with them, which was quite enough to awaken the vigilance of the police.

"It is quite clear that that young musician has not come here to see *Matilda de Sabran* " (the only piece which was then being played), "because he never goes to the theatre. He spends his days on the Villefranche rocks . . . evidently waiting for a signal from some revolutionary ship. . . . He does not dine at the *table d'hôte* . . . that is to avoid being drawn into conversation by the secret agents. Now he is gradually making the acquaintance of our officers . . . in order to open up the negotiations with which *Young Italy* has entrusted him. The conspiracy is as clear as daylight."

Oh, great man—oh, wily diplomat—thou ravest !

I am summoned to the police-office, and formally interrogated.

" What are you doing here ? "

" Recovering from a painful illness. I compose and dream, and thank God for the sunshine, the beautiful sea, and the green hills.

" You are not a painter ? "

" No."

" Yet you are always drawing something in an album. Is it plans ? "

"Yes; plans for an overture for *King Lear*. The designs and the instrumentation are ready, and I think the beginning will be somewhat formidable."

"What do you mean by the beginning? Whom do you mean by *King Lear?*"

"He is a poor old English king."

"English !"

"Yes. Shakespeare says he lived about eighteen hundred years ago, and he foolishly divided his kingdom between his two wicked elder daughters, who turned him out of doors when he had nothing more to give them. You see there are few kings . . . ."

"Never mind the king. . . . What do you mean by instrumentation? . . . ."

"It is a musical term."

"Always the same excuse ! Now, sir, we are well aware that it is impossible to write music walking silently about the sea-shore, with nothing but an album and a pencil, and no piano. So be good enough to tell us where you want to go, and you shall have your passport. You cannot stay here any longer."

"Then I will return to Rome, and compose there without a piano, if you have no objection."

So the following day I left Nice, reluctant, but full of life and happiness. And in this way it came to pass that my loaded pistols missed fire.

All the same, I liked my little comedy; and I sometimes think it is a pity that it was never played.

CHAPTER XXXV.

ON my way through Genoa, I went to hear Paër's *Agnese*, which was regarded as a great opera during the dark ages that preceded the advent of Rossini. It was abominably performed, and perhaps that is why I was so bored by it. I noticed at once that it had been "touched up," and that one of those busybodies, who are unable to produce anything original, and therefore deem it their special province to detect flaws in the creations of others, had reinforced Paër's calm, wise instrumentation with the thunder of the big-drum; the inevitable result being that the orchestra was completely drowned. Madame Perlotti sang the part of Agnese, and carefully abstained from acting it. As she appraises the market value of her voice to a franc, she replied to her poor father's incoherent ravings with the most imperturbable coolness and self-possession; and sang her part all through as though she were at a rehearsal, anxious to save her voice as much as possible, and not do more than merely give an indication of her part.

The orchestra was tolerable; the violins played in tune; and the wind kept good time. *À propos* to violins. All Paris was raving about Paganini, while I, with my usual luck, was kicking my heels in his native town instead of listening to him. I tried to gather some information about their distinguished townsman from the Genoese, but found that, like other people engaged in commerce, they cared little for the fine arts, and spoke quite indifferently of the genius whom Germany, France, and England had received with open arms. They could not even show me his father's house. I also searched all Genoa for the temple, pyramid, or monument of some sort which I felt certain must have been raised in memory of Christopher Columbus, and I never even chanced upon so much as a bust of the great discoverer to whom the ungrateful city owes its fame.

Of all the Italian cities, Florence is the one of which I have the pleasantest recollections. Instead of being overwhelmed with spleen, as I was afterwards at Rome and Naples, I spent delightful days wandering about in solitude and freedom through the palaces and picture galleries, dreaming of Michael Angelo and Dante, reading Shakespeare, and venting my enthusiasm in the delicious silence of the woods. Although my Nice expedition had made a considerable breach in my fortune, I still possessed a few handfuls of piastres, and was therefore free from care. I knew very well that I was not likely to find in Florence what I barely hoped for even in Naples and Milan, so I never even thought of going to hear any music, until I heard casually at the *table d'hôte* that Bellini's new opera, *I Montecchi ed I Capuletti*, was going to be played. Both the music and the libretto were warmly praised, at which I was the more surprised because I knew how little the Italians usually care about the words of an opera. This must be an innovation !

At last, after so many wretched failures, I shall hear a real opera worthy of Shakespeare. Such a subject!— actually created for music!... First, there is the splendid ball at the Capulets', at which young Montague first sees the "sweet Juliet," whose love will cost her her life, in the midst of the whirling bevy of beautiful girls; then those fierce combats in the streets of Verona, over which the fiery Tybalt presides like the genius of revenge; the unutterable night scene in Juliet's balcony, in which the lovers utter their tender love, true and pure as the light of the evening star which shines smiling down upon them; then there is careless Mercutio's mirthful buffoonery, the old nurse's simple chatter, the grave hermit, with his fruitless efforts to pour oil upon the troubled waters in this conflict of hate and love which has penetrated even to his still, sequestered cell; ... then the awful catastrophe, the conflict between delirious love and despair, passion dying away into the death-sob; and finally the solemn, tardy reconciliation of the feudal families burying their hate in the graves of their dead children. I rushed off to the Pergola Theatre. The stage was crowded with the chorus; their voices were true and clear, and they seemed to me to sing fairly well; a most charming effect was produced by the contralto parts, which were sung by a dozen little boys of fourteen or fifteen years of age. The principal characters appeared in due course, and all except Juliet (who was played by a large fat woman), and Romeo (by a small thin one), sang out of tune. Why, because Zingarelli, Vaccai, and others have done so, continue to make Romeo a woman's part?... On what principle is Juliet's hero to be shorn of his manhood? What is there childlike in the *champion fencer* who slays the furious Tybalt in three passes, and who afterwards bursts the gates of Juliet's tomb, and then knocks Count Paris down with one casual blow? And his intense despair on the eve of his exile, his awful resignation when he hears of Juliet's death, his wild delirium after drinking the poison—do such fierce passions lodge in eunuchs' souls?

Is there some notion that two women's voices sound better together? . . . Then why have tenors, baritones, and basses at all? Why not confine ourselves entirely to sopranos and contraltos, and let Othello and Moses, as well as Romeo, pipe in a high key?

Well, we must not mind this; the rest of the work will compensate. . . .

What a disappointment! There is no ball at the Capulets', no Mercutio, no chattering nurse, no grave, calm hermit, no balcony scene, no sublime soliloquy when Juliet receives the phial from the hermit, no duet in the cell between banished Romeo and the disconsolate hermit; in fact, no Shakespeare, nothing but utter failure. And yet he is a great poet this Felix Romani, who was obliged to boil down Shakespeare's masterpiece into such a bald book to suit the requirements of the contemptible Italian stage!

However, the composer has done full justice to the principal situations; at the end of one act, in which the lovers are forcibly separated, they escape for a moment and rush into each other's arms,' singing, "We shall meet in heaven." The setting of these words, which is intense, passionate, and full of life and fire, is sung in unison, which, under these special circumstances, intensifies the power of the air in the most wonderful manner; whether it were owing to the setting of the musical phrase, to the manner in which it is introduced, to the unexpected effect

of the unison, or to the actual beauty of the song itself, I
do not know; but I was completely carried away, and
applauded frantically. Duets in unison have been done
to death since.

I was resolved to drink the cup to the dregs, and went
to hear Pacini's *Vestale* a few days later. From what I
knew of it already I gathered that it had nothing in
common with Spontini's work except the name; but still
I was not prepared. . . . Licinius was played by a
woman ! . . . After listening for a few moments, I cried
out like Hamlet, "Wormwood ! wormwood !" and, unable
to endure any more, I rushed out in the middle of the
second act with a fierce parting kick to the floor from
which my big toe suffered for several days. Poor Italy !
. . . I shall be told that in the churches at any rate the
music is on a par with the grandeur of the ceremonial.
Poor Italy ! . . . It will be seen what sort of music is
tolerated in Rome, the capital of the Christian world;
meanwhile this is what I myself heard while I was in
Florence.

Louis Bonaparte's two sons had taken part in the insurrection which had just been crushed at Modena and
Bologna. Queen Hortense was escaping with one, the
other died in his father's arms, and this was his funeral
service. The church was draped in black, and there was
a great paraphernalia of priests, catafalques, and torches,
which was less calculated to awaken solemn thoughts
than to evoke memories connected with the name of the
dead man . . . Bonaparte! his name; his nephew; almost
his grandson; dead at twenty; and his mother a fugitive
to England, with her only remaining son snatched from
the reactionary gibbet, not daring to return to France,
where she spent her glorious youth. . . . Glancing back

through the corridors of time, I pictured the brilliant creole child on the deck of the vessel which bore her to the shores of the old world as the daughter of plain Madame Beauharnais; then the adopted daughter of the master of Europe; the Queen of Holland; and now exiled, orphaned, a despairing mother, a crownless, realmless queen. . . . Oh Beethoven! . . . where was the great Homeric mind which conceived the *Eroica*—the *funeral march on the death of a hero*—and thus added to the grand poetry of music which elevates the soul while the heart is oppressed with grief. The organist had got out his *little flute* stops and was frolicking about on the upper manual, piping out *gay little tunes*, like a wren on a garden-wall fluttering its wings and chirruping in the pale winter sunshine . . .

The feast of the *Corpus Domini* was close at hand, and I had heard so much of the manner in which it was celebrated at Rome, that I hurried on my journey to the capital of the Papal States, in company with several Florentines who were going there for the same purpose. During our whole journey we talked of the wonders which were in store for us, and my imagination was dazzled by the visions of tiaras, mitres, chasubles, shining crosses, golden vestures, glowing through clouds of incense, which were presented to me.

"*Ma la musica?*"

"*Oh, Signore, lei sentirà un coro immenso!*" Then they relapsed into the clouds of incense, golden vestures, shining crosses, thunders of artillery, clanging of bells, etc. But "Robin always reverts to his flute."

"*La musica?*" I persisted; "*la musica di questa ceremonia?*"

"*Oh, Signore, lei sentirà un coro immenso!*"

Well, at any rate there will be this "huge chorus." I conjured up a vision of Solomon's Temple and the musical magnificence of its ceremonial; and, as my imagination became more excited, I even pictured a scene which might rival the splendours of ancient Egypt. Accursed gift, which turns life into a series of miracles! . . . But for this I might have been charmed with the *castrato's* discordant falsetto, ringing through the insipid counterpoint; but for this I should not have anticipated the pure, fresh voices, and the glowing, enthusiastic faces of a bevy of young virgins pouring forth their pious songs to heaven—the perfume, as it were, of these human flowers; but for this fatal imagination of mine I should not have been so disgusted by the impious, coarse cacophony of those two groups of *clarinettes canardes*, roaring trombones, crashing drums, and mountebank trumpets. This is what they call *military music* at Rome. Had it ushered in old Silenus, riding on his ass, and escorted by a troupe of coarse satyrs and bacchantes, it would have been highly appropriate; but the Holy Sacrament, the Pope, and the pictures of the Virgin![1]

This was, however, only one of the many marvels which awaited me. But I will not anticipate.

Here I am, back again in the Villa Medici, kindly received by the director, and feasted by my companions, whose curiosity must have been aroused by my pilgrimage, though they one and all refrained from any allusion to it. I must have had some reason for going, and I went; I returned; and all was right; no remarks were made, and no questions asked.

---

[1] Barbarous! barbarous! Like all other sovereigns, the Pope is a barbarian; and, like all other people, the Romans are barbarians.

CHAPTER XXXVI

Life at the Academy—Walks in the Abruzzi Mountains—St. Peter's
—*Le Spleen*—Excursions into the Campagna—The Carnival—
The Piazza Navone.

I was soon quite at home in the daily routine both
inside and outside the Academy. Our meals were heralded
by a bell, which was rung up and down the passages and
through the gardens; and we all rushed in just as we
were, without collars, in straw hats, blouses torn or
smeared with clay, slippers—in fact, in our studio un-
dress. After dinner we generally wasted an hour or
two in the gardens, playing quoits or tennis, pistol-
shooting, killing the unlucky blackbirds in the laurel
bushes, or training puppies. M. Horace Vernet, whose
relations with us were more those of a pleasant comrade than a stern director, often took part in our
sports. In the evening there was the inevitable visit
to the Café Greco, when the French artists who did
not belong to the Academy, and whom we called *les
hommes d'en bas* (the lower orders), smoked the pipe
of peace and shared the patriotic punch-bowl with
us. After this we all dispersed, those who virtuously
returned to the academic barrack generally gathering in the great hall, which opened on to the garden.
When I was one of the party, my wretched voice
and paltry guitar were often requisitioned; and there,

sitting round the marble basin of a little fountain, which splashed and flashed in the moonlight, we sang dreamy songs from *Oberon* and the *Freyschütz*, stirring choruses from *Euryanthe*, whole acts of *Iphigénie en Tauride*, *La Vestale*, or *Don Juan;* for I must admit, in justice to my contemporaries at the Academy, that their taste in music was anything but vulgar. True, there was another kind of concert, which followed a somewhat disorderly dinner, and was called the *English concert*, and which had a charm of its own. Each one who could sing at all had his own special song, and, to make as great a variety as possible, each man sang in a different key to his neighbours. Due, the gifted architect, sang his song of *La Colonne;* Dantan, the *Sultan Saladin;* Montfort's masterpiece was the march from *La Vestale;* Signol was always happy in his romance, *La Fleuve du Tage;* and I was effective in the tender, simple air, *Il pleut, bergère.* At a given signal, the performers started off, one after another, and this grand *ensemble* for twenty-four performers was shouted out in a continuous *crescendo*, to the accompaniment of the dismal howling of all the dogs on the Pincian, while the barbers, standing at their shop-doors in the Piazza di Spagna below, remarked to each other, with a contemptuous smile and a shrug, "*Musica francese.*" Thursday was the director's great reception-day. The most brilliant society in Rome frequented the fashionable *soirées*, at which Madame and Mademoiselle Vernet presided so gracefully; and, of course, we always attended them. But we generally spent our Sundays in long excursions in the neighbourhood of Rome; either to Ponte Molle, where you drink the cloying, oily drug called Orvieto wine, which is the Roman's favourite beverage; or the Villa Pamphili; or St. Laurent, outside the walls; or, best of all, to Cecilia Metella's splendid tomb, where it is the correct thing to awaken the echo till you are hoarse, so as to have an excuse for moistening your throat with a coarse black wine, thick with midges, in a neighbouring tavern.

With the director's permission, the students were allowed to make journeys of indefinite duration, provided they did not quit the Papal States until the conditions of their agreement enabled them to travel all over Italy. This is why the full number of students is so rarely to be found in the Academy. Two or three are always wandering about to Naples, Venice, Florence, Palermo, or Milan. The painters and sculptors, who have Raphael and Michael Angelo at Rome, usually remain there ; but the architects are always eager to explore the temples at Pæstum, Pompeii, and Sicily, while landscape-painters spend the greater part of their time in the country. As for the musicians, since the capitals of Italy are all about equally interesting to them, their only reason for leaving Rome is the desire to see, and their own restless disposition; and so their destination and the duration of their journeys depend entirely on their personal feelings.

When I was weary of Rome and felt my blood stagnating, I rushed off in adventurous excursions into the Abruzzi mountains, and but for this liberty the monotony of our existence would have been intolerable. Neither our noisy artistic gatherings, the brilliant balls at the Academy and the Embassy, nor the freedom of the café, could make me forget that I had left Paris, the centre of civilisation, and that I was suddenly deprived of music, theatres,[1] literature,[2] excitement—in fact, all that made life worth living.

Is it surprising that the shadow of Ancient Rome,

[1] The theatres at Rome are only open during four months.
[2] Most of the books I then admired were under the Papal ban.

which alone casts a glory round Modern Rome, did
not compensate me for all I had lost? It must be
remembered that the eye so soon becomes accustomed
to things on which it rests day after day that they
cease to arouse any unusual thoughts in the mind.
The only exception was the Coliseum; I never got used
to its aspect either by day or by night. And I never
saw St. Peter's, either, without a thrill. It is so grand,
so noble, so beautiful, so majestically calm! During the
fierce summer heat I used to spend whole days there,
comfortably established in a confessional, with Byron as
my companion. I sat enjoying the coolness and stillness, unbroken by any sound save the splashing of the
fountains in the square outside, which was wafted up to
me by an occasional breeze; and there, at my leisure, I
sat drinking in that burning poetry. I followed the
Corsair in his desperate adventures; I adored that in-
exorable yet tender nature — pitiless, yet generous — a
strange combination of apparently contradictory feelings:
love of woman, hatred of his kind.

Laying down my book to meditate, I would cast my
eyes around, and, attracted by the light, they would be
raised to Michael Angelo's sublime cupola. What a
sudden transition of ideas! From the cries and barbarous orgies of fierce pirates, I passed in a second
to the concerts of the seraphim, the peace of God, the
unutterable stillness of heaven; . . . then, falling to
earth again, I sought on the pavement for traces of the
noble poet's footsteps. . . .

" He must have come to see that fine group of Canova's,"
I said to myself; " he must have stood just here; his hands
must have rested on these rails; he breathed this air; the
echo repeated his words . . . words, it may be, of ten-

derness and love. . . . Ah yes! he surely must have come here with his friend the Countess Guiccioli,[1] that admirable, rare woman, who understood him so thoroughly, and loved him so completely. . . . A poet . . . beloved . . . rich. . . . *He* was all three!" . . . And I ground my teeth so that the walls of the confessional re-echoed and the souls of the damned must have quaked.

One day, when in one of these moods, as I rose to rush out, my footsteps were suddenly arrested, and I stood stock still in the middle of the church. A peasant entered, quietly went up to the statue of St. Peter and kissed his great toe !

"Happy biped!" I murmured bitterly, "what more can you desire? You believe and you hope; once upon a time, the statue you adore was called Jupiter the Thunderer, and held thunderbolts in his hand instead of the keys of paradise; you don't know this, and are not disenchanted. When you go hence, what will you seek? shade and slumber; you will find both in the shrines in the fields. What are your dreams of wealth? A handful of piastres will buy you a donkey or enable you to marry—and three years' savings will give you competence. What is a wife in your eyes? A being of another sex. What is art to you? A means of materialising the objects of your worship, and exciting you to dancing or laughter. A virgin, streaked with red and green, fulfils your ideas of painting; marionettes and Punch are your dramas; the hurdy-gurdy and the drum, your music; while I am full of despair and bitterness because I lack everything that I need, and have no hope of ever obtaining it."

[1] I saw her one evening at M. Vernet's, with her long white hair falling round her sad face like the branches of a weeping willow. Three days afterwards I saw her bust, in clay, in Dantan's studio.

After listening for some time to the raging storm within me, I discovered that it was evening. The peasant had departed; I was alone in St. Peter's. ... I went out. I met some German painters, who carried me off to a German *osteria* outside the town, where we drank countless bottles of Orvieto, talked nonsense, smoked, and ate some small birds we had bought from a sportsman—raw. The others liked this savage meal, and although I thought it disgusting at first, I soon came round to their opinion.

We returned to Rome singing Weber's choruses, which reminded us of musical treats we were not to enjoy for many months to come. At midnight I went to the ambassador's ball, and saw an English girl[1] there, as beautiful as Diana, reported to have fifty thousand a year; she had a superb voice, and played the piano beautifully, and I enjoyed it. Fortune is so just; her favours are so equally divided! I saw some hideous hags bending over the *écarté* table, their faces flushed with greed—Macbeth's witches! I saw some simpering coquettes, and two sweet young girls, who were making what their mothers call their *first appearance in the*

---

[1] Mendelssohn mentions this lady in his letters from Rome (Dec. 22, 1830). "I must tell you about a ball to which I went the other day, and where I danced even more than usual. I had given a hint to the master of the ceremonies, and he allowed the *galop* to continue for more than half an hour; so I was in my element, and quite aware that I was dancing in the Palazzo Albani at Rome, and also with the prettiest girl in the room, according to the verdict of Thorwaldsen, Vernet, and other good judges. The way in which I got to know her is now quite an anecdote of Rome. I was at Torlonia's first ball, not dancing, as I knew none of the ladies, but merely looking on. Suddenly someone tapped me on the shoulder, and said, ' So you are admiring the English beauty too? I am quite dazzled.' It was Thorwaldsen, standing in the doorway, lost in admiration. He had hardly spoken when we heard a torrent of words behind us :

world; delicate, precious flowers whom its breath will soon wither. I was delighted. Three amateurs were disputing on enthusiasm, poetry, and music. They drew comparisons between Beethoven and M. Vaccai, Shakespeare and M. Ducis; asked me if I *had read Goethe*, whether Faust had *amused* me; and a thousand other wonderful things. I was so delighted with the whole business that I left the room, wishing that a thunderbolt as big as a mountain would fall on the Palace, and bury it and all inside it.

As we ascended the steps of the Trinità del Monte, we had to draw our big Roman knives. Some wretches lurking in the shadow demanded our money or our lives; but as there were two of us and only three of them, and as they caught the gleam of our knives in the moonlight, they relapsed temporarily into the path of virtue.

I was often unable to sleep after one of these insipid parties, where hearing vapid songs vapidly sung only whetted my craving for music, and embittered my temper. So I put on my hooded cloak and went down into the garden, where I sat on a block of marble till dawn, buried in sombre misanthropic reveries, and listening to

'Mais où est-elle donc, cette petite Anglaise? Ma femme m'a envoyé pour la regarder. Per Bacco!' It was clear to me that the little thin Frenchman, with the stiff gray hair and the Legion of Honour, must be Horace Vernet. He and Thorwaldsen then set to work to discuss the young lady in the most earnest and thorough manner, and it was delightful to see the two old masters admiring her, while she was dancing away quite unconcerned. They were then presented to her parents, during which I had to stand aside. A few days afterwards, however, I visited some Venice acquaintances in order to be introduced to some of their friends, and these friends turned out to be the young lady and her parents. So your son and brother was highly delighted."

the cries of the owls. If my companions had known
of these sleepless nights, they would have accused me
of affectation (*manière*—the orthodox expression), and
perpetrated ceaseless jokes at my expense. But I never
mentioned them.

If we include some sport and riding,[1] we get a clear
idea of the agreeable routine in which my mental and
physical existence was spent during my stay in Rome. If,
on the other hand, you include the paralysing effect of the
sirocco, the ever-increasing longing for artistic pleasures,
sad recollections, the trial of finding myself exiled for
two years from the musical world, and the actual, though
perhaps inexplicable, impossibility of doing any work at
the Academy, you will have some idea of the dejection
from which I suffered.

I was as fierce as a chained dog, and the attempts
of my comrades to induce me to share in their
amusements only increased my irritation. Their enjoy-
ment of the "delights" of the Carnival exasperated
me.   I never could (and I cannot now) conceive what
pleasure there is in the amusements of what are called
both in Paris and Rome, *les jours gras.* Fat days,
indeed! Fat with grease, and ointment, and plaster,
and stale wine, and filthy jests, and coarse jokes, and
street girls, and drunken detectives; vile masks, worn-out

---

[1] It was during my rides in the neighbourhood of Rome with Felix
Mendelssohn that I told him how surprised I was that no one had
written a *scherzo* on Shakespeare's glittering little poem *Queen Mab.*
He was equally surprised, and I instantly regretted having put the
idea into his head. For several years afterwards I dreaded hearing
that he had carried it out. Had he done so he would have made my
double attempt (a vocal *scherzetto* and an instrumental *scherzo*, both
on *Queen Mab*) in the *Romeo and Juliet* Symphony impossible or at
any rate highly undesirable. Fortunately he never thought of it.

hacks, laughing fools, gaping idiots, and weary idlers. In Rome, when the good old traditions of the past still survived, a human sacrifice was offered up during *les jours gras*. I do not know whether this admirable custom, which seems to exhale the subtle perfume of the circus, still exists; in all probability it does, for great ideas linger long. In those days some poor devil under sentence of death was retained for the purpose; he, too, was fattened, so as to be worthy of the god (the Roman people) to whom he was to be offered up; and when the hour had struck, and this rabble of fools from all nations (for it is only fair to state that the strangers were as keen after these noble sports as the natives), this horde of well-dressed savages, was weary of watching the races, and pelting one another with plaster sweetmeats, and laughing at the refinement of their wit, they adjourned to see the man die; yes, the *man*! They do well, these worms, to call him such. Generally, it is some unlucky brigand, who, weakened by loss of blood, was half dead when the Pope's *brave* soldiers captured him; and he has been nursed, and cared for, and fattened and shrived for the festival; and, in my eyes at least, this wretched victim is a thousand times more worthy of the name of man than that rabble of victors whom the temporal and spiritual head of the Church (*abhorrens a sanguine*), the representative of God upon earth, is obliged occasionally to gratify by the sight of an execution.[1]

---

[1] The Parisians are worthy rivals of the Romans of 1831 in this particular. M. Léon Halévy, the brother of the worthy composer, has just published a letter full of good sense and good feeling, in the *Journal des Débats*, on the subject, demanding the suppression of the ignoble scene enacted during the Carnival round the *Fat Bull*, which is paraded about the streets for three days, and finally slain with much pomp at the shambles. I was deeply touched by this

However, the intelligent, sensitive spectators soon hasten to cleanse their clothes from the possible blood-stains in the Piazza Navone. The square is at once transformed from a vegetable-market to a reeking, filthy pond, with cabbage-stalks, lettuce-leaves, melon-rind, wisps of straw, and almond-husks floating on its surface instead of water-lilies. On a raised platform on the shores of this enchanted lake, stand fifteen musicians, with drums, large and small, a triangle, a Chinese pavilion, and two pairs of cymbals, supported, for the sake of appearance, by some horns or clarinets, and performing music of the same degree of purity as the water at their feet. Meanwhile, the most brilliant equipages pace slowly through the pool, while the air resounds with the acclamations of the *sovereign people*.

"*Mirate! mirate!* there is the Austrian ambassador!"

"No; it is the English envoy."

"Look at his arms—a kind of eagle."

"Not at all; it is some other animal; and besides, I can see *Dieu et mon droit*."

"There is the Spanish consul, with his trusty Sancho. Rosinante does not seem particularly delighted with this watery promenade."

"What! the French representative here too?"

eloquent protest, and could not help writing the following letter to the author :

"Sir,—Allow me to shake you by the hand for your admirable letter on the *Fat Bull*. Never think for a moment that you have made yourself ridiculous; and even if you had, it would be ten thousand times better to appear so in the eyes of the frivolous than to be regarded as coarse and brutal by men of feeling for remaining indifferent to the scenes you have so justly stigmatised, which transform so-called civilised men into cowardly, hateful brutes.

"7th March, 1865."

"And why not, pray? That old man with the cardinal's hat behind him is Napoleon's maternal uncle."

"And that little punchy man, with the malicious smile, trying to look serious?"

"He is a clever man,[1] who has written about art, and is consul at Civita Vecchia; he considers himself forced to come and loll in his carriage in this slum, because it is the *fashion;* he is now contriving a new chapter for his novel, *Rouge et Noir.*"

"*Mirate! mirate!* here is our great Vittoria, our small- (not so very small) footed Fornarina, reposing from her labours in the Academy studios last week, and showing herself off in her cardinal's dress. There she sits, in her chariot, like Venus risen from the waves. Listen! the tritons of the Piazza Navone, who all know her, are going to lift up their voices in a triumphal march. *Sauve qui peut!* What a hullabaloo! What has happened? A shopkeeper's carriage upset? Yes; I see it is the excellent wife of our tobacconist in the Via Condotti. Bravo! she is swimming to shore like Agrippina, in the Bay of Pozzuoli; and, while she is whipping her little boy as a compensation for his bath, the horses, not being sea-horses, are plunging about in the muddy water. Hurrah! someone is drowned! Agrippina is tearing her hair. Increasing delight on the part of the audience. They are pelting her with orange-peel. How touching are thy frolics, O gentle populace! How sweet are thy pleasures! What poetry in thy sports! What gracious dignity in thy joy! Truly the great critics are right; art is for everyone. If Raphael

---

[1] M. Beyle, who wrote Rossini's life under the pseudonym of De Stendahl, and also the most irritating lucubrations on music, for which he fancied he had some feeling.

painted his divine Madonnas, it was because he well
knew how exalted is the love of the masses for the
beautiful, the ideal, the chaste, the pure; if Michael
Angelo wrung his immortal Moses from the stubborn
marble, if his powerful hands raised a sublime temple,
it was, doubtless, that he might respond to the demand
of the masses for great emotions answering to the needs
of their souls; and it was to feed the poetic flame which
devours them that Tasso and Dante sang their immortal
strains. Yes; let all works which are not admired by
the masses be anathema! If they scorn them, it is
because they are worthless; if they despise them, it is
because they are despicable; if they reject them with
hisses, reject the author likewise, for he is lacking in
respect for the public; he has outraged its vast mind,
and jarred its deep feelings. *Carry him off the course!*

CHAPTER XXXVII.

I FOUND life in town perfectly intolerable, and spent all the time I could in the mountains. I often went as far as Subiaco, a big village some miles from Tivoli, inside the Papal States, a part of the country which is usually only visited by landscape painters.

This was a favourite remedy for one of my attacks of "spleen," and it always seemed to give me new life. I started off, in an old gray shirt, with half-a-dozen piastres in my pocket, and my gun or guitar in my hand, strolling along, shouting or singing, careless as to where I should sleep, knowing that, if other shelter failed me, I could always turn into one of the countless shrines by the wayside. Sometimes I went along at racing pace, or I might stop to examine an old tomb ; or, standing on the summit of one of the dreary hillocks which dot the Roman plain, listen meditatively to the far-off chime of the bells of St. Peter's, whose golden cross shone on the horizon ; or, halting in pursuit of a lapwing, note down an idea for a symphony which had just entered my brain ; always, however, drinking in, in deep draughts, the ceaseless delights of utter liberty.

Sometimes, when I had my guitar with me instead of my

gun, a passage from the *Æneid*, which had lain dormant in my mind from childhood, would suddenly rise to my recollection, aroused by some aspect of the surrounding scenery ; then, improvising a strange recitative to a still stranger harmony, I would sing the death of Pallas, the despair of the good Evander, of his horse Ethon, unharnessed and with flowing mane and falling tears, following the young warrior's corpse to its last resting-place ; of the terror of good king Latinus ; the siege of Latium, which had stood on the ground beneath my feet ; Amata's sad end, and the cruel death of Lavinia's noble lover. This combination of the past—the poetry and the music—used to work me into the most wonderful state of excitement ; and this intensified condition of mental intoxication generally culminated in torrents of tears. The funniest part of it all was that my grief was so real. I mourned for poor Turnus, whom the hypocrite Æneas had robbed of his state, his mistress, and his life ; I wept for the beautiful and pathetic Lavinia, forced to wed the stranger-brigand, bathed in her lover's blood.[1] I longed for the good old days when the heroes, sons of the gods, walked the earth, clad in shining armour, hurling slender javelins at targets framed in burnished gold. Then, quitting the past, I wept for my personal sorrows, my dim future, my

---

[1] [There were not many points in which Lord Macaulay could have resembled Berlioz, and yet he writes thus in 1851 : " I finished the *Iliad* to-day. I had not read it through since the end of 1837, when I was at Calcutta. . . . I never admired the old fellow so much, or was so strongly moved by him. What a privilege genius like his enjoys ! I could not tear myself away. I read the last five books at a stretch during my walk to-day, and was at last forced to turn into a by-path, lest the parties of walkers should see me blubbering for imaginary beings, the creations of a ballad-maker who has been dead two thousand seven hundred years." (Trevelyan's *Macaulay*, vol. iv. chap. xi.)]

spoiled career; and at length, overwhelmed by this chaos of poetry, would suddenly fall asleep with scraps of Shakespeare or Dante on my lips: *Nessun maggior dolor. . . . che recordarsi . . . O poor Ophelia! . . . Good-night, sweet ladies. . . . vitaque cum gemitu. . . . fugit indignata sub umbras. . . . .*

What folly! many will exclaim. Possibly; but also, what joy! *Sensible* people have no conception of the delight which the mere consciousness of living intensely can give: one's heart swells, one's imagination soars into space, life is inexpressibly quickened, and one loses all consciousness of one's bodily limitations. I did things then which would kill me now.

I left Tivoli in pouring rain, carrying a percussion gun with which I could defy the damp. I walked my ten leagues, killed fifteen head of game on the way, and arrived at Subiaco in the evening, having spent the whole day in my soaking clothes.

Now that I am back in the Parisian whirlpool, how vividly I can recall every aspect of the wild scenery of the Abruzzi mountains: the strange villages, the ragged villagers with their furtive eyes, and their old rickety guns, that carry so far and so true! How often I was struck by the mysterious solitude of their sites! and what curious forgotten memories rise up before me as I think of them! Subiaco, Alatri, Civitella, Genesano, Isola di Sora, San Germano, Arce, the poor old deserted convents, and their empty chapels. . . . The monks are gone. . . . Silence reigns alone. . . . Presently the monks and bandits will return together.

Then there are the sumptuous monasteries, inhabited by pious, kindhearted men, who welcome travellers hospitably, and surprise them with the charm of their intellectual conversation; the Benedictine palace of Monte-Cassino, with the dazzling splendour of its mosaics, its wood-carvings, and its reliquaries; the San Benedetto convent at Subiaco, with the grotto in which St. Benedict resided, and where the rose-bushes he planted may still be seen. Higher up on the same mountain, at the edge of a deep precipice, rising above the old Anio, stream beloved by Virgil and Horace, is the cell of Beato Lorenzo, bathed in sunshine, where the swallows seek shelter and warmth in winter. Vast woods of dusky-leaved chestnut-trees, with here and there an isolated ruin, on which at evening solitary forms—herdsmen or brigands—perch for a moment, and then vanish in silence. . . . Opposite, on the further bank of the Anio, on a huge hill like a hog's back, stands a little pyramid of stones, which it relieved my utter depression to pile up one bitter day, and to which the French painters who love these solitudes courteously gave my name. Below it lies a cave, the entrance to which can only be reached by dropping down from the rock above, and then crawling in on all-fours, at the risk of being crushed to death on the stones five hundred feet below.

To the right lies a field, where I was stopped by some gleaners, who, astonished at meeting me in such a place, overwhelmed me with questions, and only allowed me to proceed in my ascent on the assurance that my journey was undertaken in fulfilment of a vow to the Madonna. Far beyond, in a narrow plain, lies the solitary house of La Piagia, built on the banks of the inevitable Anio, where I used to ask for shelter and leave to dry my clothes after shooting through the rainy autumn days. The mistress of the house, a most worthy woman, had a beautiful daughter, who afterwards married our friend

Flacheron, the painter. I can still see the strange boy, Crispino, half bandit, half conscript, who used to bring us powder and cigars.

In the evening, the gleaners, returning late from their work in the plains below, pass by the rows of shrines dotted along the tops of the hills, singing soft litanies to the accompaniment of the sad tinkling of the distant convent bell; the pine-forests resound with the wild refrain of the song of the pifferari; great girls, with dark hair, dusky skins, and noisy laughter, are merciless in their demands on the aching fingers *di questo signore qui suona la chitarra francese*, as an accompaniment to their dancing; while the classical Basque tambourine beats time to my improvised *saltarelli*; the carabineers insist on joining our *osteria* balls, to the indignation of the French and Abruzzian dancers—Flacheron's prodigious fisticuffs; the shameful defeat of the *soldiers of the Pope*; threats of ambuscades and big knives! . . . Flacheron, without saying a word to anyone, betaking himself to the appointed place at midnight, with no other weapon than a stick. No carabineer to be seen; Crispino's enthusiastic delight !

*   *   *   *   *   *

And then Albano, Castelgandolpho, Tusculum, Cicero's little theatre, the frescoes on his ruined villa, the lake of Gabia, the marsh I slept in at midday, without thought of fever, the remains of the garden of Zenobia, the beautiful dethroned Queen of Palmyra, the long line of aqueducts, reaching as far as the eye could see.

Bitter memories of bygone days of freedom, when heart, mind, soul, all were free ; when I was free to idle, not even to think unless I chose; free to ignore the flight of time, to despise ambition, to laugh at glory, to discredit love, to wander north, south, east, or west, to sleep out of doors, to live naturally, to wander at will, to dream, to lie exhausted and panting whole days in the soft, hot, murmuring sirocco wind! Perfectly, utterly, illimitably free! Oh, great, strong Italy! wild Italy! unheeding of artistic Italy, thy sister!

The lovely Juliet stretched upon her bier!

CHAPTER XXXVIII.

Subiaco—The Convent of St. Benedict—A Serenade—Civitella—
My Gun—My Friend Crispino.

SUBIACO is a little town of four thousand inhabitants, quaintly built on the slopes of a sugar-loaf mountain. It owes what prosperity it possesses to the Anio, which works the machinery in some not very thriving manufactories, before it forms the celebrated Falls of Tivoli lower down.

In some places its course runs through very narrow valleys. Nero had it dammed up, by a huge wall the ruins of which are still visible, so as to form a vast, deep lake above the village; hence its name, Sub-lacu. The convent of San Benedetto is situated about a league higher up, on the edge of a great precipice, and, as it is almost the only place of interest in the neighbourhood, it has a great many visitors. The chapel altar has been built in front of the entrance to the little cave in which the founder of the Benedictines originally sought refuge.

The interior of the church is most curiously constructed, in two storeys, which are connected by a flight of ten steps.

After you have duly admired St. Benedict's *Santa Spelunca*, and the grotesque pictures on the walls, the monks lead you down into the lower storey, which is filled with rose-leaves from the convent garden. These flowers possess the miraculous power of curing convulsions, and the monks sell immense quantities of them. Three old battered carbines, bent and rusty, hang near the perfumed specifics, as irrefragable testimonies to a wonderful miracle, in which some sportsmen were saved from a gun-accident by a lucky appeal to St. Benedict, *made while the charge was exploding.* Two miles higher up lies the hermitage of Il Beato Lorenzo. The awful solitude of the bare red rocks is enhanced by its complete desertion since the death of the hermit. A huge dog was its solitary guardian, and he lay crouched in the cave, jealously watching my every movement. As I was wholly unprotected, and as he could easily have throttled me, or driven me over the precipice if I had chanced to arouse his suspicion, I did not linger long in the presence of my silent Argus.

Subiaco is not so buried in the mountains as to be removed from all civilising influences. It possesses a café for politicians, and a philharmonic society, the conductor of which is also the parish organist. But I was so depressed by his treating us to the overture to *Cenerentola* on Palm Sunday, that I stayed away from the singing academy lest I might betray my feelings, and thus wound these excellent amateurs. I confined my attentions to the peasants' music, which was at any rate spontaneous and original. One night I was awakened by the most orthodox serenade I had yet heard. A robust *ragazzo* was roaring out a love-song beneath the window of his *ragazza,* to the accompaniment of a huge mandoline, a bagpipe, and a little iron instrument of the nature of a triangle, called here a *stimbalo.* His song, or rather shriek, consisted of a progression of four or five descending notes, ending with a long sustained wail from the leading note to the tonic. The musette, the mandoline, and the stimbalo struck two chords in almost regular and uniform succession, in the intervals between each stanza ; then, when the spirit moved the singer, he started off again, quite careless as to whether his notes were in harmony with the chords of his accompanists, who were as indifferent on the point as he was. He might have been singing to the sound of the sea or a waterfall. Spite of the rusticity of the performance, it pleased me immensely. The rough tones of the mountaineer's voice were softened by distance and the intervening walls. By degrees I was lulled into a sort of dreamy reverie by the monotonous repetition of the short stanzas with their mournful termination, and the silence that followed ; and when the *ragazzo* came to the end of what he had to say to his fair one, I suddenly felt a great want. . . . I strained my ears. . . . My thoughts had flowed so gently to the sounds which awoke them, that when the one stopped the thread of the other was broken . . . and I lay till morning—wakeful, dreamless, idealess. . . .

This phrase recurs all over the Abruzzo mountains ; I have heard it sung from Subiaco to Naples, more or less modified by the sentiment of the singers and the movement they infused into it. I thought it lovely when I heard it sung slowly and softly one night at Alatri, without accompaniment ; it then seemed full of religious feeling, and very different to the sentiment I usually associated with it.

The number of bars in this sort of melodious cry is not always the same, but varies according to the words, and the accompaniment follows as it can. Such improvisation calls for no special poetical gifts in the mountain

·Orpheus; it is merely a form, in which he expresses the same things he would say in ordinary conversation.

Crispino, the lad I have mentioned, and who had the audacity to pretend he had been a brigand, because he had spent two years in the galleys, always greeted me, on my arrival at Subiaco, with the same tune, to these words of welcome, yelled out like a convict:

The doubling of the last vowel at the *sforzando* is indispensable. It is produced by a sound in the throat like a sob, which has a most curious effect.

In the villages round Subiaco, of which it is a kind of capital, I did not glean a single musical idea. Civitella, the most interesting of all, is a miserable, reeking hole, perched, like an eagle's nest, on the summit of an almost inaccessible rock. The reward for the climb is the magnificent view; but painters are also attracted by the strange aspect of the rocks, and the curious way in which they are piled on one another; and a friend of mine once stayed there for six months.

One flank of the village is built on such huge blocks that it is impossible to conceive how any human power could ever have got them in their places., This Titanesque wall stands in the same relation to "Cyclopean" architecture that that does to ordinary buildings; and yet it seems to be wholly unknown, and I never heard an architect mention its existence.

Besides this, Civitella offers a special attraction to the traveller which he will not find in any other village; namely an inn, or something approaching to it, at which you are fairly well lodged and fed. The rich man of those parts, one Signor Vincenzo, entertains strangers to the best of his ability; Frenchmen are especially welcome, but he overwhelms them with politics. Reasonable in all other respects, he is wholly insatiable in this. Wrapped in a dressing-gown, which he has worn for ten years, he sits cowering by his smoky fireside, and the moment you enter he begins his interrogations. However exhausted you may be with thirst and fatigue, you will not be allowed to drink a drop of wine till you have told him all about Lafayette, Louis Philippe, and the Garde Nationale.[1] All the other villages, Vico-Var, Olevano, Arsoli, Genesano, and twenty others whose names I have forgotten, are exactly alike. The same cluster of little gray houses, perched like swallows' nests on almost inaccessible barren rocks; the same half-naked children running after strangers and crying, " Pittore ! Pittore ! Inglese ! Mezzo baiocco !"[2] (All strangers are either Englishmen or painters in their eyes.) Such paths as there are are mere irregular ledges cut in the rocks and just discernible. You meet idle men who eye you suspiciously; women driving pigs, which, with maize, form the sole wealth of the country; and girls carrying heavy copper vessels or faggots on their heads ; but all so wretched, so miserable, so tattered, so filthily dirty, that, in spite of the beauty of the race and the picturesqueness of their costume, all other feelings are swallowed up in

---

[1] This was in 1832. By this time he has probably advanced as far as Changarnier and Napoleon III.

[2] A small Roman coin.

one of utter compassion. And yet I keenly enjoyed wandering through these dens on foot, with or without my gun.

When bent on scaling some unknown peak I was obliged to leave my weapon behind, for the Abruzzians coveted it so much that they would not have hesitated to dispose of its owner by a shot from one of their horrible carbines. By continually visiting their villages I became quite friendly with the inhabitants. Crispino in particular grew much attached to me, and was useful in many ways. He used to get me scented pipes of a most delicious flavour,[1] bullets and powder, and even percussion caps; and that too in a country devoid of all the products of arts and manufactures. Besides this, Crispino knew all the smart *ragazze* for ten miles round, and the flirtations, the relationships, the love-affairs, the hopes and fears, not only of themselves, but of their families and friends. He kept an accurate account of the temperature and virtue of each, and it was sometimes most amusing to consult this moral thermometer. I first won his affection by conducting a serenade to his mistress, and then by singing a duet with him to the young she-wolf with the accompaniment of the *chitarra francese*. I had further presented him with two shirts, a pair of trousers, and three severe kicks on an occasion when he had treated me with disrespect.[2]

Crispino had not had time to learn to read, and he never wrote to me; but when he had any interesting intelligence from beyond the mountains to give me he

---

[1] I was a smoker in those days. I had not then discovered how intensely disagreeable is the excitement caused by tobacco.

[2] This is not true, and proceeds from the tendency which artists always have to write for effect. I never kicked Crispino; and Flacheron was the only one of us who ever ventured to take such a liberty with him.

used to come to Rome.   What were thirty leagues *per un bravo* like him?   It was the fashion at the Academy not to fasten the doors of our rooms.   One January morning—I came down from the mountains in October, so that I had had three months of *ennui*—on turning round in bed I found myself confronted by a great swarthy scoundrel, with peaked hat and swathed legs, who was quietly waiting for me to wake.

"Hullo, Crispino !   What are you doing in Rome?"

"*Sono venuto—per vederlo !*"

"Well; and what then ?"

"*Crederei mancare al più preciso mio debito, se in questo occasione.*" . . .

"What occasion ?"

"*Per dire la verità . . . mi manca . . . il danaro.*"

"I thought so !   That is what I call telling the *truth*. So you have no money.   And what do you expect me to do for you, you *birbonnaccio ?*"

"*Per Bacco, non sono birbone !*"

I will finish his speech in English :

"If you call me a scoundrel because I am penniless, you are quite right; but if you do so because of my two years at Civita Vecchia, then you are wrong.   I was not sent to the galleys for stealing, but for the good honest carbine-shots and knife-thrusts I bestowed on the strangers (*forestieri*) in the mountains."

Here my friend was doubtless romancing.   He had probably not killed so much as a monk, but he evidently had a keen sense of honour, and was so indignant that, having accepted three piastres, a shirt, and a silk handkerchief, he would not wait until I had put on my boots to get . . . the rest.   The poor fellow was knocked on the head two years ago in a quarrel.

May we meet again in a better world ! . . .

CHAPTER XXXIX.

Life of a Musician in Rome—The Music in St. Peter's—The Sistine
Chapel—Prejudice against Palestrina—Modern Religious Music
in the Church of St. Louis—The Opera-houses—Mozart and
Vaccai—The *Pifferari*—Compositions at Rome.

WITH all my wanderings Rome was my head-quarters,
and I became more and more convinced that for an artist
who is really in earnest nothing can be sadder than to
have to live there. Life is a continual martyrdom, in
which one's poetical ideals are successively shattered, and
one's beautiful musical dreams dispelled by the grim and
hopeless reality; and day by day fresh experiences only
bring fresh disappointments. While the other arts[1] are
flourishing in all their vividness, grandeur, and majesty,
glowing with the splendour of genius, proudly displaying
their manifold beauties, music alone is degraded to the
level of a poor hunted slave, singing wretched verses with
a threadbare voice to earn a crust of bread. I became
aware of this state of things after a few weeks. Directly
I arrived I rushed off to St. Peter's. Immense ! sublime !
overpowering ! Michael Angelo, Raphael, Canova on this
side and that ; under foot precious marbles and exquisite

[1] [As regards the past this is no doubt true, but surely contemporary arts—painting, architecture, literature—were as badly off as
music was at the time of Berlioz's visit.]

mosaics. . . . The solemn silence, the cool, still air, the fine harmony of colour. . . . That aged pilgrim kneeling alone in that vast space. . . . Then a slight sound, rising from some dim corner of the church, comes rolling through the vast arches like the sound of distant thunder . . . I felt a sudden fear. . . . It seemed to me that this was really the temple of God, and that I had no right to be there. Then I remembered that this great, grand building had been erected by beings like myself, and I felt a sudden throb of proud joy; and as I thought of the glorious part my cherished Art must play there, my heart began to beat with excitement. These pictures and statues and columns, all this gigantic architecture, are, after all, thought I to myself, but the body of the building; Music is its soul; through her its being is made manifest, through her the other arts find expression, and her strong voice bears up their burning thoughts to the feet of the Almighty. Where is the organ? . . . The organ—a trifle larger than the one in the Opera-house at Paris—was *on wheels;* and was hidden from me by a pilaster. Perhaps, however, this wretched instrument only gives the key-note to the voices, and, as all instrumental effects are proscribed here, is enough for that purpose. How many singers are there? . . . I remembered the daily chorus of ninety singers in the little concert-room at the Conservatoire, and seeing that St. Peter's would hold at least sixty times as many, I came to the conclusion that the choir of St. Peter's must number some thousands.

There are *twenty-eight* on ordinary days and *thirty-two* on solemn festivals! I have even heard a *Miserere* in the Sistine Chapel sung by *five* voices.

A German critic has recently constituted himself the champion of the Sistine Chapel. "Travellers for the most part," he says, "expect a much more exciting— or I might even say, amusing—kind of music than that which pleases them so much in their own operas ; instead of which they hear an ancient plain-song of simple religious character and without any accompaniment. Then these disappointed musicians rail against the Sistine Chapel, and declare that the music is utterly uninteresting, and that all the glowing accounts of it are travellers' tales."

We should not go quite so far as these superficial observers. On the contrary, a musician finds the same interest in this music of the past, handed down to us unchanged in style or form, that a painter does in the frescoes at Pompeii. Far from regretting the absence of the trumpets and big-drums which have been introduced by the Italian composers of the day, to such excess that both dancers and singers think no effect can be produced without them, we must confess that the Sistine Chapel was the only place in Italy where we felt safe from that deplorable innovation, and from the artillery of the manufacturers of cavatinas. We grant that the Pope's thirty-two singers, though producing no effect and in fact wholly inaudible in the largest church in the world, suffice for the performance of Palestrina's works in the confined space of the pontifical chapel ; we grant that the pure, calm harmony tends to a certain kind of reverie which is not without charm. But the charm is due to the harmonies themselves, and is wholly independent of the so-called genius of the composers, if, indeed, you can dignify by that name musicians who spend their lives in compiling successions of chords like

those which constitute a portion of the *Improperia* of
Palestrina.

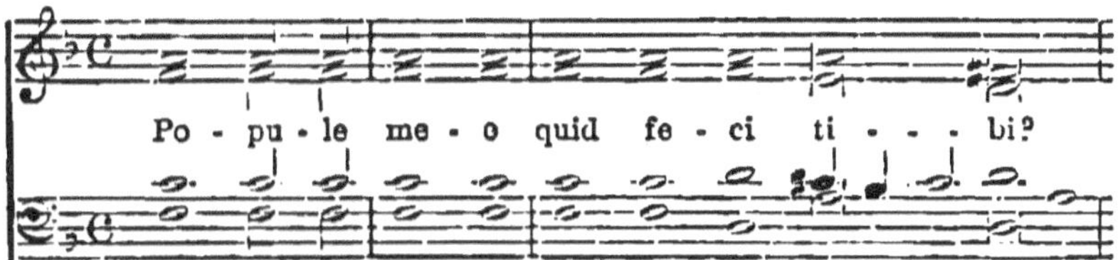

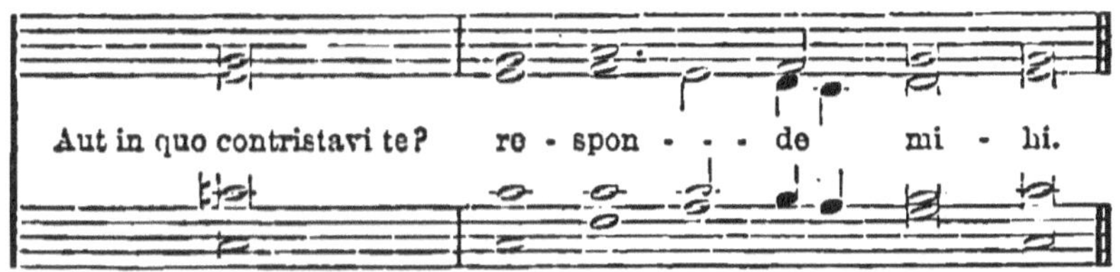

It is quite possible that the musician who wrote these
four-part psalms, in which there is neither *melody* nor
rhythm, and in which the *harmony* is confined to *perfect
chords* with a few *suspensions*, may have had some taste
and a certain amount of scientific knowledge; but genius
—the idea is too absurd.

There are, moreover, people who sincerely believe that
Palestrina wrote in this way in order that his music
might be perfectly adapted to his own ideal of the words
of the text. They would soon see their mistake if they
were to hear his madrigals, in which the most trivial
words are set to exactly the same music as those of the
Bible. For example he has set the words, "*Alla riva
del Tebro, giovinetto vidd' io vago Pastore*," etc.,[1] to a
solemn chorus, the harmony and general effect of which
is identical with that of his so-called religious compositions.
The truth is that he could not write any other kind of

---

[1] By the banks of the Tiber, a young shepherd wandered, etc.

music; and, far from carrying out any celestial ideal, his works contain a quantity of formulas adapted from the contrapuntists who preceded him, and of whom he is usually supposed to have been the inspired antagonist. If proof is wanted, look at his *Missa ad fugam*.[1]

How, then, do such works as these, clever though they may be, contribute to the expression of religious feeling? How far are such specimens of the labour of a patient chord manufacturer indicative of single-minded absorption in the true object of his work? In no way that I can see. The form of expression of a musical work is not enhanced in any way by its being embodied in a perpetual canon. Beauty and truth of expression gain nothing by the difficulties which the composer may have had to overcome in producing them, any more than his work would be increased in value from the fact that he had been suffering physical pain while he was writing it. If Palestrina had lost his hands, and been forced to write with his feet, that fact would not have enhanced the value of his works or increased their religious merit.

Nevertheless, the German critic above referred to calls Palestrina's *Improperia* sublime. "The whole ceremony," he says, "the subject in itself, the presence of the Pope and cardinals, the precision and intelligence of the singers, form one of the most imposing and touching sights of the holy week." . . . True, but that does not convert the music into a work of inspiration and genius.

Some gloomy autumn day, when the dreary north wind

---

[1] [This argument is ludicrously unfair. 'Palestrina wrote, as every musician does, in the forms of his day, and there can be no doubt that he was far in advance of his contemporaries in feeling, and in nobility and purity of expression. It is interesting to compare the above remarks with those of Mendelssohn, in his famous letter to Zelter, dated June 16, 1831.]

is howling, read *Ossian* to the accompaniment of the weird
moans of an Æolian harp hung in the leafless branches
of a tree, and you will experience a feeling of intense
sadness, an infinite yearning for another state of existence,
an intense disgust with the present; in fact, a regular
attack of "blue devils" and a longing for suicide. This
is a much more definite effect than that produced by the
music of the Sistine Chapel, and yet no one has ever
thought of ranking the makers of Æolian harps among
great composers.

It may, however, be said of the musical service at the
Sistine Chapel that it has preserved its solemnity and
dignity, whereas the other churches in Rome have in this
respect lapsed from their ancient traditions into a miserable state of degradation, I may even say demoralisation.
Several French priests have been utterly disgusted by
this disgraceful debasement of religious art.

I was present at a celebration of high mass on the King's
birthday, with full orchestra and chorus, for which our
ambassador, M. de St. Aulaire, had engaged the best
artists in Rome. The sixty performers were stationed in
a large amphitheatre in front of the organ, and began
by tuning up as noisily as if they had been in a theatre.
The diapason of the organ being much too low for the
wind instruments, it was impossible to combine it with
the orchestra. The only thing to do was to leave it out;
but of this the organist would not hear; he was resolved
to take part in the performance and earn his money,
even though the ears of the audience should bleed with
agony. And I must admit that he fairly earned his pay,
for I never laughed so heartily in my life. Like all Italian
organists he used only the high stops, and so in the *tuttis*
his piccolos were drowned by the orchestra; but when a

staccato chord was followed by a rest, the organ, which always drags a little and cannot stop short like other instruments, was heard vibrating on a quarter of a tone lower than the orchestra, and producing the most appallingly comic effect that it is possible to conceive.

In the intervals between the plain-song of the priests, the orchestra—unable, as it were, to control the demon of music which possessed it—tuned up in the coolest way; the flutes played scales in D ; the horns did the same in E flat; the violins made cadences and *gruppetti;* the bassoon rattled its keys and produced its deepest notes ; and the organ twittered over all, and completed a concert worthy of Callot. And this in the presence of a civilised audience, including the French ambassador, the director of the Academy, a large body of priests and cardinals, and artists of every nationality.

The music was worthy of the performers. Regular cavatinas, each with its *crescendo, cabaletta,* runs, and cadences ; the whole an indescribable monster, with a phrase of Vaccai's for its head, scraps of Pacini's for limbs, and a ballet of Gallemberg's for body and tail ; and, to crown all, the solos in this strange farrago were sung in a soprano voice, proceeding from a big man with a rubicund face and an immense pair of black whiskers.

"Good heavens," I said to my neighbour, who was choking with laughter, " is everything miraculous in this favoured country? Did you ever see a bearded *castrato* before ? "

" *Castrato !* " cried an Italian lady who was seated in front of us, and whose indignation was aroused by our laughter and our remarks—" *d'avvero non è castrato !* "

"Do you know him, madam ? "

" *Per Bacco ! non burlate. Imparate, pezzi d'asino, che*

quel virtuoso maraviglioso è il marito mio." They were husband and wife !

I have often heard the overtures of the *Barbiere, Cenerentola,* and *Otello* in church. They seemed to be special favourites with the organists, and formed an agreeable seasoning to the service. The music in the theatres is in much the same glorious condition, and is as *dramatic* as that of the churches is *religious.* There is the same amount of invention, the same purity of form, the same charm of style and intensity of thought. The singers I heard during the theatrical season had generally good voices, and that facility of execution which is the special characteristic of the Italians ;[1] but they were all mediocre except Madame Unger, the German prima donna,[2] who was a great favourite in Paris, and Salvator, a fair baritone. The chorus is a shade below that of the Opéra Comique as regards precision, accuracy, and warmth. The orchestra, about as imposing and formidable as the Prince of Monaco's army, has all the qualities which are generally regarded as defects. In the Valle Theatre there is *one* violoncello, a watchmaker by trade, more fortunate in this than another musician, who has to earn his bread by *mending chairs.*

The words "symphony" and "overture" are used in Rome to designate *a certain noise* which the orchestra makes before the curtain rises, and to which no one ever listens.

---

[1] Which was *then* their special characteristic.

[2] [Fräulein Unger, afterwards Madame Sabatier, of Florence, was a remarkable contralto. She sang with Sontag in the *Ninth Symphony,* at its production at Vienna in 1824, and she it was who turned Beethoven round with his face to the audience that he might *see* the applause which his deafness prevented him from hearing. She died in 1877.]

The names of Beethoven and Weber are scarcely known there. A learned abbé, belonging to the Sistine Chapel, told Mendelssohn *that he had heard someone speak of a young man of great promise called Mozart.* It is true that this worthy ecclesiastic does not often come into contact with the world, and has studied nothing but Palestrina all his life. So he may be regarded as an exceptional being, for though Mozart's music is never played in Rome, still a good many people have heard something more of him than that he was *a young man of great promise.* Some learned amateurs even knew that he was dead, and that though he cannot be classed with Donizetti, he has written some remarkable works. I knew one who had a copy of *Don Juan;* and after studying it for some time on the piano, he confided to me that he thought *that old music* was really better than the *Zadig* or *Astartea* of M. Vaccai, which had just been brought out at the Apollo Theatre. Instrumental music is a sealed book to the Romans. They have no notion of what we call a symphony.

I only noticed one popular kind of music while I was at Rome, which may be regarded as a remnant of antiquity: that of the *pifferari.* These are wandering musicians who towards Christmas come down from the mountains four or five at a time, with bagpipes and *pifferi* (a sort of haut-bois), on which they perform sacred music before the images of the Madonna. They generally wear large brown cloth cloaks and pointed brigand hats, and there is a strange, wild air about them which is quite unique. I have spent hours watching them in the streets of Rome, as they stood with heads slightly bent and eyes full of faith and devotion, gazing in rapt adoration at the statue of the Virgin. The bagpipe, accompanied by a large bass *piffero*, gives out the harmony on two or three notes, on which a shorter *piffero* plays the tune; above this there are two very small *pifferi*, much shorter than the others, and played by children of from twelve to fifteen years of age, which make shakes and trills, and surround the rustic melody with a shower of quaint ornamentation. After a long series of such phrases, repeated over and over again, comes a slow, grave prayer, of patriarchal and pious character. As the tune has been printed in various Neapolitan collections I shall not give it here. When close by the sound is overpowering, but at a little distance this curious orchestra produces an extremely impressive effect.[1] I heard the *pifferari* afterwards in their own home, and if I was struck with them in Rome it may be imagined what an impression they made on me in the wild mountains of the Abruzzi. Volcanic rocks and black pine-forests are the natural *mise-en-scène* for such primitive music; and when, in addition to this, one has before one the mysterious monuments of a lost era—cyclopean walls, and shepherds clad in sheepskins, with the wool outside (the costume of the ancient Sabine shepherds)—it is easy to imagine oneself a contemporary of the ancient people among whom the arcadian Evander, the generous host of Æneas, settled himself.

It is thus best to give up almost all hope of hearing music when you go to Rome; in fact the anti-musical atmosphere had reduced me to a state in which I found it almost impossible to compose. I only wrote three or four pieces all the time I was at the Academy: 1. An

---

[1] [The *pifferari* are imitated by Handel in the *Pastoral Symphony* in the *Messiah*, which, in the autograph score, has the word *Pif.* at the head of it.]

overture to *Rob Roy*, which was long and diffuse, and, when played in Paris a year afterwards, was so badly received by the public that I burnt it the night of the concert. 2. The *Scène aux Champs* of my *Symphonie Fantastique*, which I re-wrote almost entirely in the grounds of the Villa Borghese. 3. *Le Chant de Bonheur* of my monodrama *Lelio*,[1] which I dreamed lying on the thick clipped hedge, or rather wall, of our classic garden, lulled by the breezes of my perfidious enemy the south wind. 4. The song called *La Captive*, the success of which I little foresaw when writing it. I am wrong, however, in saying it was written at Rome, for it is dated from Subiaco. And I now remember that one day when I was watching my friend Lefebvre the architect drawing at a table in the inn at Subiaco, he pushed down a book with his elbow, which I picked up, and which happened to be Victor Hugo's *Orientales*. It opened at that delicious poem *La Captive*. I read .it, and turning to Lefebvre I said, " If I had some music paper here I would write the music to this, *for I hear it.*" " If that is all you want," he said, " I will make you some." And he thereupon ruled some paper for me, on which I jotted down the air and the bass of the little song. I then put the manuscript into my pocket-book, and thought no more about it. A fortnight afterwards, during some music at our director's, I remembered *La Captive*. " I must show you a song I composed at Subiaco," said I to Mademoiselle Vernet ; " I am curious to hear what it is like, for I have quite forgotten." ʼ

I scribbled off the pianoforte accompaniment, and we were able to give some idea of it; and it was such a

---

[1] The words, both spoken and sung, of this work, which concludes my *Symphonie Fantastique*, I had written on my way back from Nice, on foot, between Siena and Montefiascone.

success that a month afterwards M. Vernet, who had been ever since haunted by the air, said to me: "I hope when you go into the mountains again that you will not bring back any more songs with you, for your *Captive* is making life intolerable to me; wherever I go—in the garden, the wood, on the terrace, or in the corridors, one hears people singing, grunting, or growling, *Le long du mur sombre . . . le sabre du Spahis . . . je ne suis pas Tartare . . . l'eunuque noir*, etc. It is perfectly maddening. I am going to dismiss one of my servants to-morrow, and I shall engage another with the express understanding that he is not to sing *La . Captive*." I afterwards developed the song and scored it for the orchestra, and I think it is one of the most vivid I ever wrote.[1]

I must add one more to this short list of my Roman works, a *méditation religieuse*, for six voices, with orchestral accompaniment, on a prose translation of a poem of Moore's, *Ce monde entier n'est qu'une ombre fugitive* (This world is all a fleeting show), which forms the first number of my Op. 18, called *Tristia*.[2]

As for the *Resurrexit*, for full orchestra and chorus, which I sent to the academicians in Paris, in obedience to the rules, and in which those gentlemen were pleased to discover signs of remarkable *progress*, an evident *proof* of the effect of Rome on my ideas, and the decrease of my unfortunate *musical proclivities*, it is nothing but a fragment of the mass which was performed at Saint Roch and Saint Eustache, several years, as we know, before I obtained the Academy prize. So much for the opinions of the immortals !

---

[1] [It is Op. 12 in Berlioz's works, and No. 18 in the collection of his songs lately published by Richault.]

[2] [*Ce monde* is No. 20 in the collection just named.]

CHAPTER XL.

The Spleen—Its Varieties—Isolation.

It was during this period of my academic life that I once
more fell a prey to the miserable disease (mental, nervous,
imaginary, if you like), which I shall call *the bane of
isolation.* I had my first attack of it when I was sixteen,
and it came about in this wise. One beautiful May
morning, at the Côte St. André, I was sitting in a
meadow under the shade of some wide-spreading oak-
trees, reading one of Montjoie's novels called, *Manuscrit
trouvé au Mont Pausilippe.* Although absorbed in my
book, I was perfectly conscious of a soft sad kind of air
which was wafted over the plain at regular intervals.
The Rogation processions were being celebrated, and the
sound I heard arose from the chanting of the litanies by
the peasants. There is something touching and poetical
in this idea of wandering through the hills and dales in
the spring-time and invoking God's blessing on the fruits
of the earth, and I was unspeakably affected by it. The
procession halted at a wooden cross covered with creepers.
I watched the people kneeling while the priest blessed
the meadows, and then they wended their way onwards,
singing their mournful song. I could occasionally distinguish our old priest's feeble voice, and some fragments

of the words as the pious band drifted farther and farther
away :

. . . Conservare digneris.

The Peasants.   Te rogamus audi nos !

Decrescendo.   Sancte Barnaba

Ora pro nobis !

Perdendo.   Sancta Magdalena

Ora pro . . .

Sancta Maria,

Ora . . .

Sancta . . .

. . . nobis.

Silence . . . the faint rustling of the wheat, stirred by
the soft morning air . . . the loving cry of the quail to
his mate . . . the cheerful ortolan singing on the top of
the poplars . . . the utter calm . . . the slow fall of a
leaf from the oak . . . the dull throbbing of my own
heart. . . . Life was so far, far away from me. . . . On
the remote horizon the Alpine glaciers flashed like giant
gems in the light of the mounting sun . . . below me
Meylan . . . and beyond the Alps, Italy, Naples, Posilippo
. . . the beings of whom I was reading . . . burning
passions . . . an unfathomable and secret joy. . . . Oh
for wings across the space ! I want life and love and
enthusiasm and burning kisses, I want more and fuller
life ! . . . But I am only an inert frame chained to the
earth ! Those beings are either fictitious, or they are
dead. . . . What is love ? . . . what is fame ? . . . what
are hearts ? . . . Where is my star ? . . . the *Stella montis* ?
Vanished possibly for ever. . . . When shall I see
Italy ? . . .

And the paroxysm possessed me in full force. I
suffered agonies, and, casting myself down on the ground,
groaned and clutched the earth wildly, tore up the grass
and the innocent daisies, with their upturned wondering

eyes, in my passionate struggles against the horrible feeling of loneliness and sense of absence.

And yet what was this anguish, compared to the tortures I have endured since, which go on increasing day by day ? . . .

I do not know how to convey any adequate conception of this unutterable anguish. A physical experiment alone can give any idea of it. If you put a cup of water and a cup of sulphuric acid side by side, under the bell of an air-pump, and exhaust the air, you will see the water bubble, boil, and finally evaporate. The sulphuric acid absorbs the vapour as it evaporates, and, owing to the property possessed by the steam of carrying off the caloric, the water which is left in the cup freezes into a little lump of ice.

The same sort of thing happens when I become possessed by this feeling of loneliness and absence. There is a vacuum all round my beating breast, and I feel as if under the influence of some irresistible power my heart were evaporating and tending towards dissolution. My skin begins to pain and burn ; I get hot all over ; I feel an irresistible desire to call my friends and even strangers to help me, to protect me, to console me and preserve me from destruction, and to restrain the life which is being drawn out of me to the four quarters of the globe.

These crises are accompanied by no longing for death; the idea of suicide is intolerable ; it is no wish to die— far from it, it is a yearning for more life, life fuller and completer ; one feels an infinite capacity for happiness which is outraged by the want of an adequate object, and which can only be satisfied by infinite, overpowering, *furious* delights proportioned to the unutterable amount of feeling which one longs to spend upon them.

This state is not *spleen*, but precedes it. It is the ebullition and evaporation of heart, senses, brain, and nervous fluid. The spleen follows, and is the congealing of all this—the lump of ice which remains in the bell of the air-pump.

Even in my calmer moods I feel a little of this *isolation*—for instance, on Sunday evenings, when the towns are still and everyone goes away to the country—because there is *happiness in the distance* and people are *absent*. The *adagios* of Beethoven's symphonies, some of the scenes in Gluck's *Alceste* and *Armide*, a song in his opera *Telemaco*, the Elysian fields in his *Orfée*, bring on fierce fits of the same pain; but these masterpieces contribute their own antidotes; they create tears, and tears bring relief. The *adagios* of some of Beethoven's sonatas, on the other hand, and Gluck's *Iphigénie en Tauride* pertain wholly to the state of spleen, and induce it; the atmosphere is cold and dark, the sky is gray and cloudy, and the north wind whistles drearily.

There are, moreover, two kinds of spleen—one ironical, scoffing, passionate, violent, and malignant; the other taciturn, and gloomy, requiring rest, silence, solitude, and sleep. Those who are possessed by this become utterly indifferent to everything, and would look unmoved on the ruin of the world. At such times I have wished that the earth were a shell filled with gunpowder, that I might set fire to it for my amusement.

On one occasion, when a prey to this kind of spleen, I was lying asleep, rolled up like a hedgehog, on a heap of dead leaves in the laurel-wood of the Academy gardens, when I was wakened by a kick from two of my comrades —Constant Dufeu the architect, and the elder Dantan the sculptor.

"Hullo, old boy! Will you come with us to Naples?"

"Go to the devil! You know quite well that I have no money."

"You great stupid! We have got money, and we will lend you some. Now then, Dantan, help me to put him on his legs, or we shall get nothing out of him! . . . Now then, shake yourself; go and ask M. Vernet for a month's leave, and as soon as your bag is packed we will be off; it is all settled."

And so it was.

With the exception of an amusing but unrelatable scandal in the small town of Ciprano . . . after dinner, I do not remember that anything noteworthy occurred on our journey, which we performed prosaically with a *vetturino.*

But Naples! . . .

CHAPTER XLI.

NAPLES—with its vivid sky, its holiday sunshine, its fruitful soil!

Everybody has described this beautiful garden much more effectively than I can hope to do, for the scene is one which must strike every traveller. Who could help feeling the charm of that still expanse of ocean lying asleep under the rays of the midday sun, the tender tint of its azure robe, and the soft lull of its faint pulsation? Who that has seen the crater of Mount Vesuvius at midnight has not thrilled with dread at the mysterious roll of its subterranean thunder, the shrieks of fury which issue from its depths, or the awful splendour of those masses of molten rock which are hurled like glowing blasphemies towards the starlit heavens, and fall back on the broad breast of the mountain, to lie like a luminous necklace round its mighty throat? Who has not lingered sadly among the skeleton remains of desolate Pompeii, or stood waiting, a solitary spectator, on the steps of the amphitheatre, for the curtain to rise on a tragedy of Euripides or Sophocles, for which the stage seems all prepared? Who has not felt some sympathy for the lazzaroni—those

grown-up children, those merry thieves—with their quick
wit and their kindly good-nature?

I shall not, therefore, follow where so many have trod
before, but I must tell one story, because it illustrates
the character of the Neapolitan fishermen so vividly.   It
concerns a dinner which the lazzaroni gave me three days
after I arrived, and a present which I received at dessert.
It was a fine autumn day; a fresh breeze was blowing,
and the air was so clear and transparent that it seemed as
if, though standing at Naples, you had only to stretch
out your hand to pick the oranges off the trees at Capri.
I had begged my companions to leave me alone that day,
and I went for a walk in the gardens of the Villa Reale.
As I passed by a little pavilion, which I had not previously noticed, a sentry, who was posted at the entrance,
called out to me roughly in French :

"Take off your hat, sir."

"What for?"

"Look there!"

He pointed to a marble statue inside the pavilion, and
the two words, Torquato Tasso, which I saw on the pedestal
at once caused me to obey the behest of the enthusiastic
soldier.   It was right and proper; but I still wonder how
the sentinel guessed that I was a Frenchman and an
artist, and should readily follow his injunction.   He was
evidently a clever physiognomist.   But to return to my
lazzaroni.

I was wandering carelessly along the sea-shore, meditating sadly on the fate of poor Tasso, whose modest
tomb at Saint Onofrio, at Rome, I had visited with
Mendelssohn some months before, and was philosophising
to myself on the misfortunes of poets whose hearts are
too poetical, etc. etc.; and from Tasso I turned suddenly to

Cervantes, and his lovely pastoral *Galatea*, and *Galatea* recalled another delicious creation in the same story, called *Nisida*, and *Nisida* made me think of the lovely island of that name in the bay of Pozzuoli, whereupon I was at once seized with a desire to see the island.[1]

I rush off, through the tunnel of Posilippo down to the shore; I see a boat, I hire it; I demand four rowers; six present themselves; I offer them a reasonable fare, pointing out at the same time that six men are not required to row a nutshell of a boat to Nisida. They insist smiling, and demand thirty francs instead of five, which is their proper fare. Two lads were standing silently by, watching the proceedings with longing eyes. I was in a good humour, and the exorbitant demands of my boatmen struck me as rather comic than otherwise; so, pointing to the lazzaronetti, I called out, "Well, then, I will give you thirty francs, but you must all come and row furiously." Such shouts of joy and such antics! We jump into the boat and reach Nisida in a few minutes. Leaving my vessel in charge of the *crew*, I land on the island, and wander all over it; watch the sunset behind the Cape of Misena, immortalised by the author of the *Æneid;* while the sea, unmindful of Virgil, or Æneas, or Ascanius and Misena, or Palinurus, sings a brilliant song of her own in a major key. . . . .

As I was wandering aimlessly along, a soldier comes up and, in very good French, offers to show me the various places of interest and the finest views, etc.—an offer of which I gladly avail myself. When we part, I take out my purse to give him the customary *buona mano*, but he steps back, looks very much offended, and says:

---

[1] The real name of the island is Nisita, but I was not then aware of the fact.

"What is that for, sir? I want nothing from you except . . . your prayers."

"You shall certainly have them," I said to myself, as I pocketed my purse. "The idea is too comic, and may the devil take me if I fail."

And true to my word, I actually said a *pater* for my excellent sergeant that night, but when I began a second I burst out laughing; so I am afraid I did not do the poor fellow much good, and he has probably remained a sergeant to this day. . . .

I should have stayed at Nisida till the following day, if one of my sailors, deputed by the captain, had not hailed me and told me that the wind was rising and that we should find it difficult to return to shore if we did not speedily weigh anchor. I adopt his advice, we seat ourselves in the ship; the captain, like the Trojan hero:

> . . . Eripit ensem
> Fulmineum   · [*unclasps his big knife.*
>   strictoque ferit retinacula ferro.
>   [*and promptly cuts the cable.*
> Idem omnes simul ardor habet; rapiuntque ruuntque;
> Littora deseruere; latet sub classibus æquor;
> Adnixi torquent spumas, et cærula verrunt.

> Eager and somewhat afraid, we hasten from the shore;
> The spray splashes from our oars, the sea flies beneath our keel.
>   (*Free translation.*)

There really was some danger, for the nutshell of a boat was bobbing about on the white crests of the big waves in a most singular fashion; my merry men had ceased laughing, and were looking for their rosaries. This seemed to me outrageously absurd, and I said to myself: "After all, why should I drown? Because an intelligent soldier worships Tasso? Less than that even;

for a hat.   For had I been bareheaded, he would
hardly have challenged me; I should not have thought
of the *Æneid*, *Galatea*, or Nisida; should not have
started on this stupid expedition, but should at this
moment be quietly sitting in the San Carlo Theatre,
listening to Brambilla and Tamburini!" These thoughts
and the motion of the doomed boat made me very sea·
sick.   But Neptune was content to frighten us, and we
were permitted to land.   The sailors, who had sat as
mute as fish, now began to chatter like magpies, and
their joy was so great that when I paid them the thirty
francs out of which they had swindled me, conscience
smote them, and they gave me a hearty invitation to
dinner, which I accepted on the spot.   They took me
to a solitary spot, in a plantation of poplars on the
Pozzuoli road, so far off that my mind misgave me as to
their intentions.   Poor lazzaroni!   But eventually we
arrived at a cottage where they were evidently well known,
and my hosts at once issued orders for dinner.

A small mountain of smoking macaroni soon made its
appearance, into which I was invited to dive with my
fingers; a can of Posilippian wine was set on the table,
from which we all drank in turn, beginning with a
toothless old man who was allowed to take precedence of
me on account of his age, which ranks even before the
rights of hospitality in the eyes of these good children.
After a most unconscionable draught, the old man
launched out into politics, and began to maunder about
King Joachim, to whom he was devoted.   In order to
change the subject and to provide me with some enter-
tainment, the young lazzaroni persuaded him to tell me a
story—for which he was famous—of a long adventurous
voyage.

Thereupon the old lazzarone held his listeners spell-bound by the narrative of how, when twenty, he had embarked on a *speronare*, on which, after tossing about *for two days and three nights* on *unknown waters*, he had at length been cast on a *remote island*, to which, *it is said*, Napoleon was afterwards exiled, and which the inhabitants called the Island of Elba. I professed the greatest interest in the story, and congratulated the brave sailor on his escape from such dangers. The lazzaroni were delighted by my sympathy. A good deal of whispering and mystery and commotion ensued in the cottage, as if some surprise were in preparation. And so it was, for when I rise to depart, the biggest of the young lazzaroni, stepping up to me with a very embarrassed air, begs me to accept a present from the party as a *souvenir*. It is the best they have to offer, and is calculated to draw tears from any eye. A gigantic onion! which I receive with a modest gravity becoming the situation, and bear off to the summit of Mount Posilippo, after many farewells, hand-shakings, and protestations of eternal friendship.

It was almost dark when I left my kind hosts, and started off limping on my way home. I had lamed my right foot in coming down from Nisida; and so, when a fine carriage rolled past me on the Naples road, and I saw that the footboard behind was empty, I leapt up into it, hoping to be carried into the town in this unfashionable manner without fatigue. I had, however, counted without my hostess, a pretty little Parisian woman, lying back luxuriously in a cloud of muslin, who cried out sharply to her coachman, "Louis, there is someone behind!" whereupon I receive a sharp cut from the whip across my face. Thank you for the gift, my gentle country-woman! A French doll! If Crispino had been alone, you should have spent an uncomfortable ten minutes!

So, meditating on the charms of a brigand's life (which, in spite of its drawbacks, would really be the only satisfactory career for an honest man, if there were not so many stupid, stinking wretches even in the smallest bands), I limped home.

To drown my sorrows I went to the San Carlo, and there, for the first time since my arrival in Italy, listened to music. In comparison with the orchestras I had heard, this one seemed to me excellent. There is nothing to fear from the wind instruments; the violins play fairly well, and the violoncellos are harmonious, though too few. Even the kind of music which the Italian orchestras usually play does not justify their always having fewer violoncellos than double basses. I must protest against the disagreeable noise which the conductor makes by striking his desk with his bow; but I am assured that but for this some of the players would find it difficult to keep time. . . . This is unanswerable; and after all one must not expect as much from an orchestra where instrumental music is almost unknown as one would in Berlin, Dresden, or Paris. The chorus is hopelessly weak; and a composer who writes for the San Carlo says it is very difficult, indeed almost impossible, to get choruses in the ordinary four parts decently performed. The sopranos cannot sing apart from the tenors, and it is almost always necessary to write them in octaves.

At the Fondo, the opera-bouffe is played with such fire, spirit, and *brio* as to raise it above almost every theatre of its class. While I was at Naples they were performing a most amusing farce of Donizetti's, *Le Convenienzi teatrali*.

Still the attraction of the theatres in Naples was not to be compared with that of the country around, and I was oftener outside the town than in it.

One morning when I was breakfasting at Castellamare with the sea-painter Munier, whom we had nicknamed Neptune, he threw down his napkin and said:

"What shall we do? I am tired of this place; let us leave it."

"Let us go to Sicily."

"By all means. I will just finish off a sketch I have begun, and at five o'clock we will go and take our places in the steamer."

"All right. Now let us see how much money we have left."

When we had counted it over we discovered that we had enough to take us to Palermo, but must trust to Providence for the return journey; so, being Frenchmen, and therefore, like true Frenchmen, wholly devoid of the faith which removes mountains, and thinking it wiser not to tempt God, we parted—he to his sketch of the sea, I to make my way on foot to Rome.

I had made up my mind some days before to do this; and that evening, after saying good-bye to Dufeu and Dantan, I met two Swedish officers whom I knew, who told me that they intended walking to Rome.

"By Jove!" I said; "I am going to Subiaco to-morrow. I want to go straight across the mountains, over rocks and streams, like the chamois hunter; let us go together."

They accepted my proposal. We sent off our baggage by a *vetturino*, and prepared to make our way to Subiaco as the crow flies, to stay there for a day, and then proceed along the high-road to Rome. So off we started, apparelled in the inevitable gray linen costumes, B—— carrying his sketch-book and pencils, and we walking-sticks, which were our only weapons. It was the time of the vintage, and the first day we lived almost entirely on excellent grapes (not nearly so good, however, as those of Mount Vesuvius). The peasants would not always take our money, and we sometimes forgot to send for the owners of the vineyards. In the evening, at Capua, we found a good supper, good beds, and . . . an improvisatore. After a brilliant prelude on his mandoline, he asked us what countrymen we were.

"French," said K——.

I had heard the improvisations of this Campanian Tyrtæus a month before, and he then put the same question to my fellow-travellers, who answered:

"Poles."

To which he replied enthusiastically:

"I have seen the whole world—Italy, Spain, France, Germany, England, Poland, Russia; but the bravest of all are the Poles, the Poles."

Here is the song as he sang it, improvising his accompaniment, without a moment's hesitation, and addressing the so-called Frenchmen:

You can imagine how flattered I felt, and how mortified the Swedes were.

Before plunging into the intricacies of the Abruzzi mountains, we stopped for a day at San Germano, so as to see the celebrated convent of Monte Cassino.

This Benedictine monastery is built, like that at Subiaco, on the side of a mountain, but the two have no other resemblance. In place of the quaint simplicity of San Benedetto, you have here the proportions and the luxury of a palace. One's imagination recoils at the conception of the vast sums which must have been squandered on it. There is an organ with absurd figures of little angels, which blow trumpets and clash cymbals when the instrument is set in motion. The pavement is made of the rarest marbles, and the choir-stalls are covered with exquisitely-carved scenes from monastic life.

By means of a forced march we reached Isola di Sora the next day. It is a village situated on the frontier of the Kingdom of Naples, and is chiefly remarkable for a little river which, after working some mills, forms a fine cascade. Here a curious mystification awaited us. Both K—— and I had cut our feet, we were all fiercely thirsty, smothered in dust, hot and tired, and the moment we entered the town we asked for the inn.

"Inn? there isn't one," replied the peasants with a derisive assumption of pity.

"But where are we to spend the night?"

"Who are you?"

We asked permission to pass the night in a wretched coach-house; but there was not even a wisp of straw, and besides, the owner objected. We were in a state of boundless irritation, which was not diminished by the sneers and cool unconcern of the peasants. It seemed

too ridiculous to arrive in a small commercial town and
to have to sleep in the streets ; but such must have been
our fate but for a sudden and happy thought.

I had once before spent a day in Isola di Sora, and I
fortunately remembered the name of one M. Courrier,
a paper manufacturer and a Frenchman. His brother
was pointed out to me ; I explained the situation to him,
and after a moment's consideration he calmly answered
me in French, or I may say, in Dauphinois, for its accent
virtually renders it an idiom :

"*Pardi ! on vous couchera ben*" (of course you shall
have a bed).

"Hurrah ! we are saved ! M. Courrier is a Dauphinois,
I am a Dauphinois, and all Dauphinois are brothers !"

And so it turned out, for M. Courrier remembered me,
and entertained us most hospitably. After a good supper
we retired to one of those enormous beds which are found
only in Italy, and in which we all slept most comfortably, reflecting that in future it would be wise to ascertain
beforehand in what towns there are inns. Our host
comforted us the following day with the assurance that
we should reach Subiaco in two days, so that in any case
we had only one night before us. A lad showed us the
way through the vineyards and woods for a few miles,
and then left us with rather vague directions as to the
course we were to pursue.

Veroli is a large village perched on the top of a hill,
and looking in the distance like a town. We dined there
very badly on bread and raw ham, and before nightfall
reached Alatri, another inhabited rock, which was still
barer and wilder-looking. We were followed all down the
principal street by a crowd of curious women and children.
When we reached the market-place, a house, or rather a

kennel, with a shabby signboard, was pointed out to us; and in spite of our disgust we had to spend the night there. Good heavens, what a night! Sleep was impossible owing to the vermin *of all kinds*, which so tormented me as to bring on an attack of fever.

What was to be done? My companions would not leave me behind; we had to get on to Subiaco. I could not bear the idea of staying in such a hovel; but I was shivering so that it was impossible to warm me, and I felt as if I could not move a step. While I was thus trembling with cold, my friends held a consultation in Swedish, which I did not understand; but it was evident from the expression of their faces that I was causing them great inconvenience. So I determined to make a supreme effort, we started on our way, and after two hours' rapid walking the fever left me.

Before quitting Alatri we called a council of the local geographers to determine our route. There was a great diversity of opinion, but at last they decided on one leading through Arcino and Anticoli. This was the hardest day's work of all. There were no proper paths; we had to follow the course of the torrents; and so much climbing was very tiring.

At length we reached a horrible village, name unknown to me. The loathsome hovels were open but tenantless; the only inhabitants we saw were two young pigs wallowing in the black mud on the broken rocks which formed the pavement of the streets in this wretched hole. Where were the inhabitants? Well might we say, "*Chi lo sa?*"

Several times we lost our way in these rocky labyrinths, and often, after straying into a valley, had no alternative but to climb the hill we had just descended in order to hail some passer-by.

"*Ohe! la strada d'Anticoli?*"

To which he would either reply by a laugh, or else by calling out "*Via! via!*" which was anything but reassuring. At last, however, we arrived at Anticoli, and found plenty of ham and eggs, and some maize, which we roasted and rather liked. The local surgeon, a great red-faced man like a butcher, came and honoured us by a few questions about the Garde Nationale, and by the offer of a *printed book* he had for sale.

We had an immense reach of pasture land to traverse before nightfall, and a guide was necessary. The one we got did not seem very sure of the way, and often stopped in doubt. An old shepherd who was sitting by a pond, and had probably not heard the sound of a human voice for a month, all but fell into the water when we suddenly came upon him and asked him the way to Arcinasso, a pretty village (so our guide said), where we should find *all sorts of refreshments.*

Some *baiocchi* soon relieved him from his terror and proved that our intentions were friendly, but it was almost impossible to make anything of his guttural replies, which were more like *clucking* than any human sound. Arcinasso, the *pretty village*, resolved itself into a solitary tavern standing by itself in the midst of desolate steppes. An old woman sold us some wine and some fresh water. B——'s sketch-book attracted her attention, so we told her it was a Bible; thereupon she rose delighted, looked at the drawings one by one, embraced B—— cordially, and blessed us all three.

The utter silence of these great prairies is indescribable. The only inhabitants we saw were the single shepherd and his flock, and one solitary crow stalking gravely about. . . . As we approached he flew away towards the north. . . .

I watched his flight. . . . My thoughts followed him towards England, and I became absorbed in Shakespearean dreams.

But this was no time for gaping at crows and dreaming, for Subiaco had to be reached before nightfall. Our guide had left us, and it was getting dark. We were walking along in dead silence like three spectres, when I suddenly recognised a thicket in which I had killed a thrush some months before.

"Courage!" I exclaimed; "one effort more; I know where we are: and in two hours we shall be at Subiaco."

Forty minutes later we saw lights shining at a great depth below us; it was Subiaco.

I found Guibert there, and he lent me some clean linen, which I sorely needed. I wanted to go to bed, but I soon heard cries of "*Oh, Signor Sidoro.*[1] *Ecco questo signore francese chi suona la chitarra.*"[2] Flacheron came running with the beautiful Mariuccia[3] and his *tambour de basque*, and, willy-nilly, I had to dance the saltarello till midnight.

On leaving Subiaco two days later, I conceived the wonderful project which I shall now describe.

My two companions, Messrs. Bennet and Klinksporn, walked too quickly for me. As I could not induce them to go slower, or even to stop occasionally, I let them go on in front, and lay quietly down in the shade, meaning to catch them up afterwards like the hare in the fable.

They had a long start of me, and as I got up I said to myself, "I wonder if I could run all the way from here to

---

[1] Isidore Flacheron.

[2] "The French gentleman who plays the guitar"—their designation for me, as they could not pronounce my name.

[3] Now Madame Flacheron.

Tivoli?" It was about six miles. "Suppose I try." Thereupon I rushed off as if someone were carrying away my mistress. I catch up the Swedes and pass them; I run through first one village, and then another, with all the dogs in the place at my heels, scattering flocks of grunting pigs as I fly by, but sympathised with by the inhabitants, who are convinced I have *met with a misfortune.*[1]

Presently, a sharp pain in my knee-joint leads to the discovery that I cannot bend my right leg; so I have to hop along on my left, dragging the other after me. The pain was excruciating, but I would not give in, and I reached Tivoli without having stopped once in my absurd race. I deserved to die of heart disease, but nothing happened; so I suppose my heart is tough.

The Swedes reached Tivoli an hour afterwards, and found me asleep. When I awoke, and they had ascertained that I was perfectly sound in body and mind (which I forgive them for doubting), they begged me to show them the sights of the place. So we visited the pretty little temple of Vesta, which is more like a temple of Cupid; the great cascade, the small cascades; Neptune's grotto; and then the immense stalactite, a hundred feet high, under which Horace's celebrated villa, Tibur, lies buried. I left my friends to rest under the grove of olive-trees over the poet's house, and ascended a neighbouring hill in order to pluck some myrtle which grows on the top, for, like a young goat, I find a green hill irresistible. Then, descending towards the plain, we inspected the Villa of Mecænas; crossed the great arched wall through which the Arno now flows, working the machinery of the vast iron foundry, and were almost deafened by the thunder of the huge hammers.

[1] Assassinated someone.

These walls once reverberated to the sound of Horace's epicurean odes, or re-echoed the grave sweet voice of Virgil reciting some magnificent fragment of his pastoral poems at a feast presided over by the minister of Augustus.

> Hactenus arvorum cultus et sidera cœli :
> Nunc te, Bacche, canam, nec non silvestria tecum
> Virgulta, et prolem tarde crescentis olivæ.

Farther down we came upon the Villa d'Este, recalling the name of the Princess Eleonora, immortalised by Tasso, and the hopeless love with which she inspired him.

When we reached the plain again, I led my friends through the labyrinth of the Villa Adriana; we visited what remains of its vast gardens, and the valley which an imperious fancy strove to convert into a miniature copy of the Valley of Tempe; looked into the Hall of the Guards, now the haunt of swarms of birds of prey; and saw the site of the Emperor's private theatre, a field of—cabbages !

Strange transformations ! at which time and death must laugh.

CHAPTER XLII.

I now returned to the Academy barracks, and was again
a prey to *ennui*. In the town, a kind of infectious influenza was raging, and people were dying by thousands.
Clothed in a long hooded cloak of the sort in which
Petrarch is represented (a costume which afforded great
diversion to the Roman idlers), I accompanied the cart-loads of dead to the yawning vault of the Transteverine
church. A stone was removed in the inner court, and the
bodies were gently lowered by means of an iron hook into
this palace of putrefaction. Some of the skulls had been
opened by the doctors, with a view to discovering why
the sick men refused to get well, and the brains were
scattered about the bottom of the cart.

The man who in Rome replaces the gravedigger of
other nations, then gathered up these *débris* of the organ
of thought with a trowel, and shot them dexterously into
the abyss. Shakespeare's immortal gravedigger would
assuredly never have dreamt of using a trowel, nor of
employing this human mortar.

Garrez, one of the architects of the Academy, has
made a drawing of this charming scene, in which I figure
with my famous hood. The spleen increased after this.

About six months previously, I had made a rough

sketch of a new system of philosophy entitled, "System of Absolute Indifferentism in Universal Matter "—a transcendental doctrine which tended to produce in man absolute perfection and the susceptibility of a block of stone.   Three of my friends, Bézard and Gibert, painters, and Delanoie, an architect, now formed themselves with me into a society called "The Four," for the purpose of elaborating and completing my system.   But it did not take.   We were met with such objections as the existence of pain and pleasure, feelings and sensations ; and treated as if we were mad.   It was in vain that we answered with praiseworthy indifference :

"So these gentlemen think us mad, do they?   Do you mind, Bézard? . . .   What do you think of it, Gibert? . . .   And you, Delanoie?"

"It does not matter to anyone." . . .

"But I tell you that these gentlemen look upon us as lunatics."

"Let them !"

We were openly ridiculed ; but have not all great philosophers been misunderstood in like manner?

One night I went on a sporting expedition with Debay, the sculptor.   We called up the watchman at the Porta del Popolo, who, by a Papal order much to the benefit of sportsmen, had to get up and let us out by virtue of our permits.   We then walked till two in the morning.   A movement in the bushes by the road seemed to imply the presence of a hare.   We both fired, and killed . . . a friend . . . a rival sportsman . . . an unhappy cat, in the act of stalking a covey of quails, and now stretched bleeding on the ground.   At length weariness overpowered us, and we slept for hours on the turf.   After this we parted.   A drenching rain came on ; I gained a little oak wood in a ravine, but it gave me no shelter. I then killed a porcupine, and carried away more than one wound from his quills. At length I came upon a lonely village in which not a creature was to be seen but an old woman washing clothes in the tiny stream. From her I learnt that this silent spot was called Isola Farnese. It is said to be the ancient Veii, the chief town of the Volscians, Rome's formidable enemies. Here, then, Aufidius commanded, and here Coriolanus offered his aid against his own country. The old washerwoman was perhaps standing on the very spot where the sublime Volumnia, at the head of a tribe of Roman matrons, knelt to her son!

All the morning I walked over the sites of the splendid battles which Plutarch has described and Shakespeare immortalised, and which were about as important as a battle would be between Versailles and St. Cloud! I stood lost in my reverie, while the rain poured with greater vehemence than ever. My dogs were nearly blinded by it, and buried their noses in the brushwood. I then killed a stupid snake, which had no business to leave its hole in such weather. Presently Debay called me by firing shot after shot, and I rejoined him for breakfast. I took a skull out of my game-bag, which I had picked up in the cemetery at Radicoffani on my way back from Nice the year before, and now holds my writing sand. This we proceeded to fill with slices of ham, and put it into the middle of the rivulet, in order to soak the salt out of the atrocious food. Our frugal repast was seasoned with nothing but a cold rain; we had neither wine nor cigars. Debay had shot nothing, and I had only succeeded in sending one poor robin to keep company with the cat, the snake, and the porcupine. We set out for the inn at Storta, which is the only one in the whole neighbourhood. Whilst my clothes were drying I went to bed, and slept for three hours.

At last the sun shone, and the rain ceased. I dressed with great difficulty, and started off after Debay, who was too impatient to wait for me. Presently I fell in with a flight of lovely birds, which are supposed to come from the coast of Africa, but whose name I never could find out. They soar perpetually, like larks, with a little cry like a partridge's, and their plumage is variegated green and yellow. Of these I knocked down about half-a-dozen, and saved my reputation as a sportsman. I could see Debay in the distance firing ineffectually at a hare. At last we reached Rome, as muddy as Marius must have been when he came back from the Marshes of Minturnus.

After this came a stagnant week.

At last our Academy became a little more lively, thanks to the comical terror of our comrade L., who, having been caught by Vernet's Italian footman in the act of making love to his wife, lived in perpetual fear of assassination. He dared not leave his room, and when dinner was served we were obliged to go in a body, and escort him to the dining-room. He fancied he saw knives gleaming in every corner of the palace. He grew thin, pale, yellow, blue, and began to vanish into space, and at last suggested to Delanoie the following joke:

"Well, my poor L., are you still in trouble about *the servants?*"[1]

This *mot* went round the table, and received great applause.

---

[1] L. was much given to intrigues with housemaids, and he declared that a sure way of winning their affections was *to look sad and wear white trousers!*

But *ennui* possessed me more strongly than ever, and I could think of nothing but Paris. I had finished my melodrama, and touched up my *Fantastic Symphony.* I now wanted to get them both performed. Vernet gave me permission to leave Italy before my term had expired. I sat for my portrait, which, in accordance with the rules, was painted by our senior artist, and hung in the gallery of the refectory. I made a final excursion to Tivoli, Albano, and Palestrina; sold my gun, and destroyed my guitar; wrote in several albums; treated my comrades to a large bowl of punch; lavished caresses on M. Vernet's two dogs, my usual sporting companions; and had a moment's unutterable sadness at the thought that I was leaving this poetical country, perhaps for ever. My friends accompanied me as far as Ponte-Molle; there I got into a horrible vehicle, and set off.

CHAPTER XLIII.

I WAS very morose, although my ardent desire of seeing
France again was on the point of being satisfied. Such a
farewell to Italy had something solemn about it, and
without being able to account to myself for my feelings,
I was oppressed in spirit. The sight of Florence, to which
I was now returning for the fourth time, made an overwhelming impression upon me. During the two days of
my sojourn in that city, which may be called the Queen
of the Arts, I was informed that the painter, Chenavard
(whose immense head is bursting with brains), had been
looking for me everywhere without success. Twice he
had missed me in the Pitti Palace ; had asked for me at
my hotel, and was evidently most anxious to see me. I
felt much gratified at this proof of sympathy from so
distinguished an artist, and in my turn tried to find him,
but in vain. I left without making his acquaintance,
and it was not till five years later that we met in Paris,
and I was able to admire the penetration, sagacity, and
wonderful lucidity of his mind, whenever he applied it
to the vital questions of the arts themselves—even to music
and poetry—so unlike the one which he has cultivated.

One evening I had just crossed the cathedral in pursuit of him, and was sitting near a column watching the motes dancing in a splendid ray of the setting sun, as it slanted across the gathering gloom, when a troop of priests and torch-bearers entered the nave for a funeral ceremony. I drew near, and inquired of a Florentine whose funeral it was. "*E una Sposina, morta al mezzo giorno*," he answered in a gay tone.[1] The prayers were astonishingly short, and the priests had hardly begun before they seemed in haste to finish. Then the body was laid on a sort of open litter, and the *cortège* proceeded to the place where the corpse was to remain until the next day, when it would be buried. I followed. On the way the torch-bearers muttered some vague prayers between their teeth, but their principal occupation was to melt as much as possible of the wax candles with which they had been provided by the family of the deceased. This was their reason. The remnant of the candles was to go back to the church, and as they dared not steal whole pieces, they kept perpetually splitting the wicks, and then sloping them so as to pour the melting wax upon the pavement. A troop of young rascals followed them along, and, flinging themselves on the ground, eagerly stripped off the wax from the stone, and rolled it into a ball, which grew bigger and bigger as they proceeded. Thus at the end of their journey—a tolerably long one, for the dead-house was at one of the farthest extremities of the town— these miserable hornets had amassed a tolerably good provision of mortuary wax. Such was the pious occupation of the wretches by whom the poor Sposina was borne to her last resting-place.

On reaching the morgue, the same gay Florentine who

[1] A young bride, who died this afternoon.

had answered my inquiry in the cathedral, and who had been in the procession, came up and accosted me in a curious kind of patois French, seeing that I was looking on with interest.

"Would you like to go in ?"

"Yes.　How can I manage it ?"

"Give me three paoli."

I slipped the three coins into his hand ; he held a moment's parley with the doorkeeper, and I was ushered in.　The dead woman was lying upon a table.　She was almost entirely covered by a long white garment, gathered in round the neck and below the feet.　Her black hair was partially plaited, and the rest fell in masses about her shoulders ; she had large blue eyes, half closed ; a small mouth, a sad smile, a neck of alabaster, an air of nobility and candour, young—so young, and dead !　The Italian, with his everlasting simper, exclaimed : *"È bella !"* and in order to give me a better opportunity of admiring the features, he raised the beautiful young head, with his dirty hands pushed aside the hair which had seemed to insist on modestly veiling the ineffable grace of the countenance, and then roughly let it fall back upon the table.　The whole room re-echoed with the shock. . . .　I thought that my very heart would have burst at the impious and brutal noise. . . .　Unable to contain myself, I fell upon my knees, seized the hand of the desecrated beauty, and covered it with expiatory kisses, a prey to an intenser anguish than I had ever felt in my life.　The Florentine, however, continued to laugh.

But suddenly the thought occurred to me, what would the husband say if he could see that beloved cold hand warmed by the kisses of an unknown stranger?　In his indignant horror, might he not have some ground for believing that I was a secret lover of his wife, who, more ardent and faithful than himself, was giving full vent to his Shakespearean despair over her beloved form? Heaven forbid that the unfortunate man should think this, although he almost deserved the torture which such an idea would inflict on him. Oh, apathetic husband! how could you let them tear away from your living arms the dead wife whom you loved so well? *"Addio! Addio! bella sposa abbandonata! Ombra dolente! Adesso, forse, consolata! Perdona ad un straniero le pie lagrime sulla pallida mano. Almen colui non ignora l'amore ostinato ne la religione della beltà."*

I went away altogether overcome by the whole scene.

But these are very cadaverous stories. My fair readers —if, indeed, I have any—may well ask if it is in order to torment them that I insist on exhibiting such hideous images. Well, no; I cannot say that I have the smallest desire thus to distress them, nor yet to reproduce Hamlet's ironical apostrophe. I have no strong taste for death, and I love life a thousand times better. I am merely relating a few of the things which have struck me, and naturally some episodes are more sombre than others— that is all.

I may, however, forewarn those of my lady readers who do not laugh at the idea of their some day playing such a part themselves, that I shall tell them no more ugly stories. Henceforth they may peruse these pages without fear, unless, indeed, as is probable, they prefer to attend to their dress, listen to bad music, dance the polka, talk nonsense, and torment their lovers.

In passing Lodi, I took care to see the famous bridge, and could even fancy that I heard the thunder of Bonaparte's grape-shot, and the cries of the flying Austrians.

The weather was superb, but the only person on the bridge was an old man fishing from off the parapet. Ah, St. Helena !

When I reached Milan, Donizetti's *L'Elisir d'Amore* was being played at the Cannobianna, and, to satisfy my conscience, I went to see it. I found the theatre full of people talking at the top of their voices, with their backs to the stage ; the singers all the time gesticulating and shouting in eager rivalry. So at least I judged by seeing their huge open mouths, for the people made so much noise that it was impossible to hear a sound beyond the big-drum. In the boxes some were gambling, and others were having supper. I therefore retired, since it was no use hoping to hear the smallest fraction of the music, which was then quite new to me. It appears, however— so at least I am assured—that the Italians do occasion- ally listen. But, at any rate, music to the Milanese, no less than to the Neapolitans, Romans, Florentines, and Genoese, means nothing but an air, a duet, or a trio, well sung. For anything beyond this they feel simply aversion or indifference. Perhaps these antipathies are mainly due to the wretched performance of their choruses and orchestras, which effectually prevents their knowing anything good outside the beaten track they have so long followed. Possibly, too, they may to a certain extent understand the flights of men of genius, if these latter are careful not to give too rude a shock to their rooted predilections. The great success of *Guillaume Tell* at Florence supports this opinion,, and even Spontini's sublime *Vestale* obtained a series of brilliant representa- tions at Naples some twenty-five years ago. Moreover, in those towns which are under the Austrian rule, you will see the people rush after a military band, and listen with avidity to the beautiful German melodies, so unlike their usual insipid cavatinas. Nevertheless, in general it is impossible to disguise the fact that the Italians as a nation really appreciate only the material effects of music, and distinguish nothing but its exterior forms.

Indeed, I am much inclined to regard them as more inaccessible to the poetical side of art, and to any conceptions at all above the common, than any other European nation. To the Italians music is a sensual pleasure, and nothing more. For this most beautiful form of expression they have scarcely more respect than for the culinary art. In fact, they like music which they can take in at first hearing, without reflection or attention, just as they would do with a plate of macaroni.

Now, we French, mean and contemptible musicians as we are, although we are no better than the Italians when we furiously applaud a trill, or a chromatic scale by the last new singer, and miss altogether the beauty of some grand recitative or animated chorus, yet at least we can listen, and if we do not take in a composer's ideas it is not our fault. Beyond the Alps, on the contrary, people behave in a manner so humiliating both to art and to artists, whenever any representation is going on, that I confess I would as soon sell pepper and spice at a grocer's in the Rue St. Denis as write an opera for the Italians—nay, I would *sooner* do it.

Added to this, they are slaves to routine and to fanaticism to a degree one hardly sees nowadays, even at the Academy. The slightest unforeseen innovation, whether in melody, harmony, rhythm, or instrumentation, puts them into a perfect fury; so much so, that the *dilettante* of Rome, on the appearance of Rossini's *Barbiere di Siviglia* (which is Italian enough in all conscience), were

ready to kill the young maestro for having the insolence
to do anything unlike *Paisiello*.

But what renders all hope of improvement quite
chimerical, and tempts one to believe that the musical
feeling of the Italians is a mere necessary result of their
organisation—the opinion both of Gall and Spurzheim—
is their love for all that is dancing, brilliant, glittering,
and gay, to the utter neglect of the various passions by
which the characters are animated, and the confusion of
time and place—in a word, of good sense itself.   Their
music is always laughing,[1] and if by chance the composer
in the course of the drama permits himself for one moment
not to be absurd, he at once hastens back to his prescribed
style, his melodious roulades and *grupetti*, his trills and
contemptible frivolities, either for voice or orchestra, and
these, succeeding so abruptly to something true to life, have
unreal effect, and give the *opera seria* all the appearance
of a parody or caricature.

I could quote plenty of examples from famous works;
but speaking generally of these artistic questions, is it not
from Italy that we get those stereotyped conventional
forms adopted by so many French composers, resisted by
Cherubini and Spontini alone among the Italians, though
rejected entirely by the Germans?   What well-organised
person with any sense of musical expression could listen
to a quartet in which four characters, animated by totally

---

[1] A certain part of Bellini's music, and that of his followers, must,
however, be excepted.   Their style, on the contrary, is essentially
dolorous, and the tone is either groaning or howling.   These writers
return to the absurd style every now and then only in order that the
tradition of it may not be entirely lost.   Nor should I be so unjust
as to include in these falsely sentimental works many parts of
Donizetti's *Lucia di Lammermoor*.   The finale of the second act, and
the scene of Edgardo's death, have an admirable pathos about them.
Of Verdi's works I know none.

conflicting passions, should successively employ the same melodious phrase to express such different words as these: *"O toi que j'adore!"* *"Quelle terreur me glace!"* *"Mon cœur bat de plaisir."* *"La fureur me transporte!"*[1] To suppose that music is a language so vague that the natural inflections of fury will serve equally well for fear, joy, and love, only proves the absence of that sense which to others makes the varieties of expression in music as incontestable a reality as the existence of the sun. But this discussion, which has already been raised hundreds of times, would carry me too far. It is enough to say that after having given a long unbiassed study to the musical sentiment of the Italians, I regard the course taken by their composers as the inevitable result of the instincts of the public, which instincts react more or less on the composers themselves. They are apparent as early as Pergolesi, who in his famous *Stabat* sets the verse—

Et mœrebat
Et tremebat
Cum videbat
Nati pœnas inclyti—

as a sort of bravura. The learned Martini, Beccaria, Calzabigi, and many eminent writers have complained of these incongruities. In spite of his herculean genius and of the colossal success of *Orfée*, even Gluck has not been able wholly to avoid them; they are kept up by singers, and certain composers in their turn have developed them in the public. In fact they are as indestructible in the Italians as the passion for vaudeville is in the French. As for the feeling for harmony among

---

[1] "Thou whom I adore!" "What terror freezes me!" "My heart beats with pleasure." "Fury transports me!" [But Beethoven has done much the same in the Quartet in the first act of *Fidelio*.]

the Ultramontanes[1] of which people talk so much, I may safely say that the accounts of it have been immensely exaggerated. At Tivoli and Subiaco I have heard some of the common people sing second pretty fairly, but in the south of France, which has no reputation of this sort, the thing is exceedingly common. In Rome, on the contrary, I have never once caught a harmonious intonation out of the mouth of any of the people. The *peccorare* (herdsmen) of the Campagna have, indeed, a curious grunt which follows no musical scale, and is absolutely impossible to write down. It is a barbarous style of singing said to be slightly analogous to that of the Turks.

Turin was the first place at which I heard street chorus-singing. But the singers were mostly amateurs who had learned what they knew by frequenting the theatres. In this respect Paris is quite as well off as the capital of Piedmont, for often and often have I heard very decent harmonies resounding through the Rue Richelieu in the middle of the night. I ought also to say that the Piedmontese choristers mix up their harmonies with consecutive fifths which, when given in that way, are odious to all practised ears.

As for seeking for the boasted Italian harmonies in villages which have no church-organs and no relations with large towns, it is mere folly, as there is not the slightest trace of them. Even at Tivoli, where two lads struck me as having sufficient feeling for thirds and sixths to sing pretty couplets together, I was astounded a few months later by the burlesque manner in which a mass of people shouted out their litanies in unison.

Without wishing to create any reputation of this sort for the people of Dauphiné, whom, on the contrary, I

---

[1] [By Ultramontanes, Berlioz here means the Italians.]

believe to be absolutely innocent in all matters connected
with music, I cannot help saying that the melody of
their litanies is sweet, supplicating, and pathetic, and like
a prayer addressed to the Mother of God, whilst at Tivoli
they sound like a song in a guard-house. I give a specimen
of each, for the purpose of comparison.

1.—MELODY OF TIVOLI.

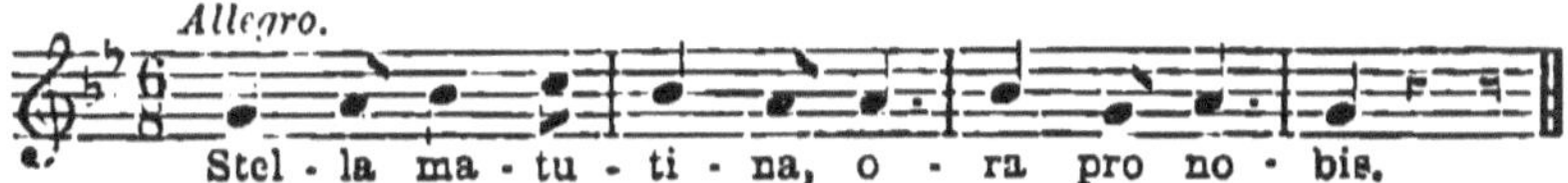

2.—MELODY OF LA CÔTE ST. ANDRÉ (Dauphiné), with the
bad Latin prosody adopted in France.

No doubt beautiful voices—not only sonorous and
clear, but agile and flexible—are more common in Italy
than elsewhere. Such voices facilitate vocalisation, and,
by pandering to that natural love of effect which I have
already mentioned, must have given birth to the mania
for *fioriture* which deforms the most beautiful melodies,
and to those convenient formulas which give all Italian
phrases so strong a family likeness. We may thank the
same causes for those final cadences which the singer may
embellish as he pleases, but which torture many a hearer
by their insipid uniformity, as well as for that incessant
tendency to buffoonery that obtrudes itself even in the
most pathetic scenes ; in fact, for all those abuses which
have rendered melody, harmony, time, rhythm, instrumentation, modulation, the drama, the *mise-en-scène*,
poetry, the poet, and the composer, all abject slaves to
the singer.

On the 12th of May, 1832, as I came down the Mont Cenis, I beheld again in its loveliest spring attire that delicious valley of Grésivaudan, through which the Isère winds, where I had passed the happiest hours of my childhood, where I had been thrilled by my first impassioned dreams—the old rock of St. Eynard, the charming spot from which had gleamed the *Stella montis;* . . . my grandfather's house smiling at me through the blue distance! How beautiful they are! the villas, the rich verdure! how fascinating! There is nothing like them in Italy. But this transport of innocent delight was suddenly stopped by a sharp pang of sorrow. . . . I seemed to hear the murmur of Paris in the distance.

CHAPTER XLIV

The Censorship—Preparations for Concerts—Return to Paris—The new English Theatre—Fétis—His Corrections of Beethoven's Symphonies—I am introduced to Miss Smithson—She is ruined—Breaks her leg—I marry her.

A SPECIAL authorisation from M. Vernet having, as I said, permitted me to leave Rome six months before the expiration of my two years' exile, I went to my father's house for the first half of the time, with the intention of employing the second in organising a few concerts in Paris before going to Germany, where the rules of the *Institut* obliged me to spend another year. I employed my leisure at the Côte St. André in copying the orchestral parts of the monodrama which I had written during my wanderings in Italy, and was anxious to produce in Paris. I had copied the chorus parts in Rome, and the number called *Les Ombres* caused me a quarrel with the Papal censorship. The text of this chorus, which I have already mentioned, was written in an unknown tongue—a dead language, incomprehensible to the living. When I applied to the censor for leave to print it, the meaning of the words sung by the ghosts puzzled the philologists a good deal.[1]

What was this language? and what was the meaning

[1] Since that time I have always adopted French words, reserving the dead language exclusively for the pandemonium in *The Damnation of Faust*.

of those strange words? They had in a German, who declared he could not understand a syllable; an Englishman had no better luck. All the interpreters—Danish, Swedish, Russian, Spanish, Irish, or Bohemian—were at their wits' end. Great perplexity in the censor's office! The printer could not proceed, and the publication remained indefinitely suspended. At last one of the censors, after profound reflection, discovered an argument the justice of which struck his colleagues. "Since neither English, Russian, Spanish, Danish, Swedish, Irish, nor Bohemian interpreters understand this mysterious language," said he, "it is very probable that the Roman people will not understand it either. It seems to me, therefore, that we may fairly authorise the publication, without any risk either to morality or religion." And the ghosts' chorus was accordingly printed. Imprudent censors! What if it had been Sanscrit?

On my arrival in Paris, one of the first visits I paid was to Cherubini. I found him much aged and enfeebled, and he received me with a kindliness which I had never observed in him before. This contrast to his former behaviour quite touched me, and I felt disarmed. "Good heavens!" I said to myself; "I find a Cherubini so unlike the one I left, that the poor man must be going to die." But it will be seen that I very soon received such tokens of his vitality as completely to reassure me on that point.

As the apartment in the Rue Richelieu which I had occupied before going to Italy was no longer vacant, a secret impulse prompted me to take one in the house opposite, where Miss Smithson had formerly lived—Rue Neuve St. Marc, No. 1, and there I established myself. Next morning I encountered the old servant, who for a long time had been housemaid to the establishment, and at once inquired if she knew anything of Miss Smithson.

"But, monsieur, don't you know? She is in Paris; she was even lodging in this very house a few days ago. She only left the apartment you are occupying the day before yesterday, for one in the Rue de Rivoli. She is the directress of an English theatre, which is to begin its representations next week."

I was struck dumb by this extraordinary concurrence of events. I saw at once that henceforth it would be impossible for me to struggle against my fate. For more than two years I had heard nothing of the fair Ophelia; whether she were in England, Scotland, or America, I knew not; and now, I had come back from Italy precisely at the same time that she returned to Paris from the north of Europe. And we had but just missed meeting each other in the same house, and I was in possession of an apartment which she had left only on the previous evening!

Now, a believer in magnetic influences, secret affinities, and mysterious promptings would certainly find in all this a powerful argument in favour of his system. Without going so far as that, I reasoned with myself after this manner: "I have come to Paris to produce my new work. If, before giving my concert, I go to the English theatre and see her again, I shall infallibly become delirious about her, lose all my liberty of mind for a second time, and be incapable of making the exertions essential to my success. Let us first of all give the concert, and after that, though Hamlet or Romeo should carry off my Ophelia or Juliet, I will see her again, if I am to die for it; and will then give myself up to the fate which seems to pursue me without further struggle."

In consequence of this determination the Shakespearean bills were placarded about the streets in vain, as far as I was concerned. I resisted their fascination and the preparations for the concert went on. The programme consisted of my *Symphonie Fantastique*, followed by *Lelio, or the Return to Life*, a monodrama which is the complement of that work, and forms the second part of the *Episode in the Life of an Artist*. The subject of this musical drama is, as everybody knows, the history of my love for Miss Smithson, my anguish and my distressing dreams. Now, wonder at the series of incredible chances about to be opened to your view!

Two days before the concert, which I looked on as a farewell to art and life, I found myself in Schlesinger's music-shop, when an Englishman entered, and went out again almost immediately.

"Who is that man?" said I to Schlesinger, with a singular curiosity which had really no motive.

"It is Mr. Schutter, one of the editors of *Galignani*. Stay, I have an idea!" exclaimed Schlesinger, tapping his forehead. "Give me a box ticket. Schutter knows Miss Smithson. I will get him to give her the ticket, and induce her to attend your concert."

This proposal made me tremble all over; but I had not the courage to reject it, and so gave him the box. Schlesinger ran after Mr. Schutter, explained to him, no doubt, the exceptional interest which the presence of the celebrated actress would give to this musical *séance*, and Schutter promised to do his best to bring her there.

You must know that during the whole of my rehearsals and preparations, the unfortunate directress of the English Theatre had been occupied in completely ruining herself. Poor innocent thing! She had been reckoning upon the

constancy of Parisian enthusiasm and the support of the
new literary school, which only three years ago had
lauded Shakespeare and Shakespeare's worthy interpreter
up to the skies. But Shakespeare was no longer a novelty
to this frivolous and fickle public ; the literary revolution
evoked by the romanticists was accomplished, and not
only had the chiefs of that school ceased to desire any
more apparitions of this giant of dramatic poetry, but,
without admitting so much themselves, they even dreaded
them on account of the numerous plagiarisms that various
persons had made from his masterpieces, with which
consequently it was to their interest not to allow the
public to become too familiar.

Hence the general indifference to the representations at
the English theatre, and the poor receipts, which fell so
far short of the expenses that the result was a yawning
gulf deep enough to swallow up everything the imprudent
directress possessed.

It was under these circumstances that Schutter went
to Miss Smithson to offer her a box for my concert, and
this is what followed. She herself gave me the details
long afterwards.

Schutter found her in a state of profound despondency,
and at first his offer was received somewhat ungraciously.
" Was it likely that she could think of music at such a
moment ?" Her sister, however, joined her entreaties to
those of Schutter that she would accept this offer of
distraction ; and there was also an English actor present,
who appeared desirous on his part of profiting by the
box. Accordingly a carriage was sent for, Miss Smithson
allowed herself to be put into it almost against her own
will, and Schutter triumphantly ordered the coachman to
drive to the Conservatoire. On the way the poor thing's

eyes fell for the first time on the programme which, till then, she had not looked at. They had not mentioned my name to her, but she now learnt that I was the director of the concert. The titles of the symphony and other pieces in the programme rather astonished her, nevertheless she was still far from guessing that she was herself the heroine of this strange and painful drama.

On entering her box in front of the stage, she found herself in the midst of an immense orchestra, and an object of interest to the whole room. So astonished was she at the unprecedented murmur of conversation of which she was plainly the object, that, without being able to account to herself for it, she was filled with a kind of instinctive terror, which moved her powerfully. Habeneck was conducting. When I came in panting and sat behind him, Miss Smithson, who till then had doubted whether she were not mistaken in the name at the head of the programme, saw and recognised me.

"It is the same," she said to herself. "Poor young man! No doubt he has forgotten me. I hope—that he has——" The symphony began, and created a tremendous effect. It was a time of great public ardour in that hall from which I am now excluded. This success, and the passionate character of the work—its burning melodies, its cries of love, its *accès* of fury, and the violent vibrations of such an orchestra, heard close by, were bound to produce, and did in fact produce, an impression as profound as it was unlooked for upon her nervous organisation and poetical imagination. , Then in her heart of hearts she said, "What if he loved me still!" In the *entr'acte* which followed the performance of the symphony—Schutter's ambiguous speeches to Schlesinger, who had not been able to resist the desire of coming into her box, and their transparent allusions to the well-known sorrows of this young composer of whom everyone was talking—all these raised a doubt in her which agitated her more and more; but when, in the mono-drama, Bocage, the actor who recited the part of Lelio[1] (in other words, my own), pronounced these words:

"*Ah, could I but find her, this Juliet, this Ophelia whom my heart is ever seeking! Could I but drink to the full of that mingled bliss and sadness which true love creates, and on an autumn evening, cradled with her by the north wind upon some wild moor, sleep my last in her beloved arms!*"

"Good God! Juliet—Ophelia—I can doubt no more!" thought Miss Smithson. "It is of me he speaks; he loves me still!" And from that moment, as she has often told me since, it seemed to her as if the room reeled. She heard no more, and went home like one walking in her sleep, almost unconscious of all that was happening around her. This was the 9th of December, 1832. Whilst this curious drama was being unfolded in one part of the room, another was preparing on the opposite side, a drama in which the wounded vanity of a musical critic was to play the principal part, and create a violent animosity against me, of which he did not fail to give me many proofs, until a sense of his injustice towards an artist and critic who, in his turn, had become dangerous, warned him to practise a prudent reserve. This person was M. Fétis, to whom, through the medium of my mono-drama, I had distinctly addressed a scathing reproach, dictated by a very natural indignation.

Before my departure for Italy, among my resources for

---

[1] *Lelio* was not performed dramatically, as was done later in Germany, but only as a concert-piece mixed up with monologues.

gaining a livelihood, I must not omit to include that of
correcting the proofs of music. Among other works,
Troupenas, the publisher, had given me the scores of
Beethoven's symphonies to correct, which M. Fétis had,
in the first instance, been employed to edit. I found
them full of the most insolent modifications of the very
conceptions of the composer, and of annotations still more
outrageous. Everything in Beethoven's harmony that did
not fit in with the theory of M. Fétis was altered with
incredible audacity. Opposite the long holding E flat
of the clarinet over the chord of the 6th $\left\{\begin{array}{l} \text{A flat} \\ \text{F} \\ \text{D flat} \end{array}\right\}$ in
the *Andante* of the Symphony in C minor, M. Fétis had
placed this naïve remark in the margin : "This E flat is
evidently an F; it is not possible that Beethoven should
have made so gross a blunder." In other words, it is
impossible that a man like Beethoven should not entirely
agree with M. Fétis in his theories about harmony.

Consequently, M. Fétis had put an F in place of the
characteristic E flat, thus destroying the evident intention
of the suspension, which does not arrive at the F till
it has passed through the E natural, thus producing a
little ascending chromatic progression, and a *crescendo* of
remarkable effect. I had already been irritated by other
corrections in the same style, which it would be useless
to cite, but by this I was simply exasperated. "What?"
said I to myself; "they are making a French edition of
the most marvellous instrumental works ever brought
forth by human genius, and because the publisher has
called in the aid of a professor who is intoxicated with
his success, and as capable of making progress within
the narrow circle of his own theories as a squirrel in his
cage, therefore these monumental works are to be muti-

lated, and Beethoven is to submit to corrections like the veriest pupil in a harmony class. No, indeed, that shall never be." I went at once to Troupenas, and said to him, "Fétis is offering insults both to Beethoven and good sense. His corrections are crimes. The E flat which he wishes to remove from the *Andante* of the Symphony in C minor is magical in its effect, and celebrated in every European orchestra; the F of M. Fétis is a platitude. I warn you that I shall denounce your edition and M. Fétis's proceedings to all the musicians of the Société des Concerts and the Opéra, and your professor shall soon be treated as he deserves by those who respect genius and distrust pretentious mediocrity." I was as good as my word. The news of these insane profanations incensed the Parisian artists, and not the least infuriated among them was Habeneck, who had indeed himself corrected Beethoven by suppressing an entire repeat of the *finale*[1] in the same Symphony, and also the double-bass parts at the opening of the *scherzo*. So great was the uproar that Troupenas was obliged to cancel the corrections and restore the original text, whilst M. Fétis thought it advisable to publish a stupendous falsehood in his *Musical Review*, denying that there was the smallest foundation for the rumour which accused him of having corrected Beethoven's symphonies. This first act of insubordination on the part of one who had been throughout his studies encouraged by M. Fétis, appeared to that gentleman all the more unpardonable, because he saw in it, not only an evident leaning towards heresy, but an act of *ingratitude*.

Many people are thus constituted. From the day that

---

[1] [Habeneck was a prophet! This repeat is now usually suppressed. It is difficult to believe that Beethoven can have intended either it or the repeat in the *finale* of the *Sonata Apassionata*.]

they have been willing to treat you as not wholly devoid
of merit, you are bound, for that reason alone, to admire
them for ever—without reserve—in all that they may
please to do, or to leave undone, on pain of being considered *ungrateful.*   On this principle many a petty
composer fancies that, because he has expressed some
interest in my works, I am therefore necessarily a bad man
if at some future time I speak with lukewarmness of the
miserable commonplaces that he has produced under
various titles—masses, or, equally comic operas.

On my departure for Italy I thus left behind me in
Paris the first really active and bitter enemy I had yet
made.   As for the others, more or less numerous, whom I
already possessed, I must say that I had done nothing to
deserve their hostility.   They sprang into being spon-
taneously, like the animalcula in stagnant water.   However, I troubled myself little about either.   Indeed, as for
Fétis, I was even more his enemy than he was mine, and I
could never think of his attempt on Beethoven without
quivering with anger.   I did not forget him in composing
the literary part of the monodrama, and this is what I put
into the mouth of Lelio in one of the monologues of that
work :

"But the worst enemies of genius are the dull
inhabitants of the Temple of Routine ; fanatical priests,
who would sacrifice their sublimest new conceptions—
supposing it were ever given them to have any—to their
stupid divinity ; young theorists of eighty, living in an
ocean of prejudices, and persuaded that the world ends
with the shores of their own island ; old libertines of all
ages, who employ music to caress and divert them, never
admitting that the chaste muse could possibly have a
nobler mission ; but, above all, the desecrators who dare

to attack original works, submitting them to horrible
mutilations which they call corrections and improvements,
and for which task, say they, 'much taste is required.'[1]
May they be accursed ! They offer a ridiculous outrage
to art. They are like the vulgar birds that swarm in
our public gardens and perch arrogantly on the most
beautiful statues; and when they have soiled the forehead of Jupiter, the arm of Hercules, or the bosom of
Venus, strut about with pride and satisfaction, as though
they had laid a golden egg."

At the last words of this tirade the bursts of laughter
and applause were all the more vehement because most of
the artists in the orchestra, and many of the audience,
understood the allusion. At the words " much taste is
required," Bocage even mimicked the affected voice of
Fétis, who was actually present in a very conspicuous
place in the gallery, and thus received my broadside full
in his face. I need not describe his fury and the deadly
hatred with which he honoured me from that day forth ;
it is easy to imagine it.

However, the acrid sweetness which I experienced in
having thus avenged Beethoven was soon forgotten. I
had obtained leave from Miss Smithson to be introduced
to her. From that day forth I had not a moment's rest.
Terrible fears were succeeded by delirious hopes. What I
went through in the way of anxieties and agitations of all
sorts during this period, which lasted for more than a
year, may be imagined but cannot be described. Her
mother and sister formally opposed our union. My
parents would not hear of it. Discontent and anger on
the part of both families, and all the scenes to which
such opposition gives birth in like cases. Meanwhile the

---

[1] An expression I had heard from Fétis himself.

English theatre in Paris was compelled to close. Miss Smithson was left absolutely without resources, her whole fortune not being sufficient to pay the debts which she had contracted through this unfortunate undertaking.

Shortly afterwards the finishing touch was put to all her misfortunes by a cruel accident. As she was getting out of a carriage before her own door, on her return from preparing for a representation which she had been getting up for her own benefit, her foot slipped on the pavement, and she broke her leg. She was with difficulty prevented from falling, and was taken in, half fainting, to her apartments. In England the story was believed to be a *ruse* of the directress of the English theatre for the purpose of softening her creditors; but the fact was only too real, at any rate it aroused the keenest sympathy in Paris. Mdlle. Mars behaved splendidly. She placed her purse, her influence, all that she had in fact, at the service of the poor Ophelia who had lost everything; but who, nevertheless, on hearing one day from her sister that I had brought her a few hundred francs, shed tears in abundance, and forced me to take back the money, threatening never to see me again if I refused.

She responded but slowly to our care; both bones had been broken just above the instep; time alone could bring about a perfect cure; indeed, it was possible that she might always be lame. Whilst the poor invalid was thus chained to her bed of suffering, I succeeded in getting up the fatal representation which had been the cause of the accident. Both Liszt and ·Chopin took part in an *entr'acte*, and the result was a tolerable sum of money, which was at once applied to the payment of the most pressing debts. At length, in the summer of 1833, though ruined and still an invalid, I married her, in spite of the violent opposition of her family. As to my own, I was forced to have recourse to the *sommations respectueuses.* On the day of our marriage she had nothing in the world but debts, and the fear of never again being able to appear to advantage on the stage. My property consisted of three hundred francs, borrowed from my friend Gounet, and a fresh quarrel with my parents. . . . But she was mine, and I defied the world.

CHAPTER XLV.

I HAD one feeble resource left in my prize pension, which
had still another year and a half to run. The Minister
had exempted me from the tour in Germany imposed on
me by the Academy. I was beginning to have some
adherents in Paris, and my faith in the future was
strong. In order to finish paying .off my wife's debts, I
resumed the painful task of taking benefits, and, after
immense exertions, succeeded in getting up a representation and a concert at the Théâtre Italien. On this
occasion, my friends again came to my assistance—among
others, Alexandre Dumas, who has shown me the greatest
kindness all his life.

The evening's programme consisted of Dumas' *Antony*,
played by Firmin and Mdme. Dorval ; the fourth act of
Hamlet, by my wife and some English amateurs ; followed
by a concert, to include my *Symphonie Fantastique*, the
overture to *Les Francs Juges*,' and *Sardanapalus*, with
Weber's *Concertstück*, played by the excellent and admirable Liszt, and one of Weber's choruses—all conducted
by myself.

It will be seen that there was far too much acting and

music, and that the concert, if it ever reached the end,
would not be over till one in the morning.

But for the sake of young artists, I must, at any cost
to myself, give the exact account of this unfortunate
performance. Being but little acquainted with the manners
of theatre musicians, I had made a bargain with the leader
of the theatre by which he engaged to give me his room
and his orchestra, to which I was to add a small number
of artists from the Opéra. This was the most dangerous
of combinations. The musicians, being obliged by their
contract to take part in all concerts given in the theatre,
look upon these exceptional *soirées* as so much extra toil,
and bring only *ennui* and ill-will to the work. If, in
addition, they have to play with other musicians, who
are paid when they are not, their ill-humour is increased,
and the giver of the concert very soon feels the benefit
of it.

My wife and I being both ignorant of such petty
stage-tricks, had neglected the precautions usually taken
in such cases to ensure the success of the heroine of the
fête; we had not given a single ticket to the *claque*.
Mdme. Dorval, on the contrary, believing that there
would be a formidable clique in my wife's favour, and
that, as usual, everything would be arranged to secure
her triumph, had not failed to provide for her own success
by filling the pit with the tickets we gave her, those
which Dumas got from us, and others which she bought.
Mdme. Dorval, who played the part of Adèle admirably,
was therefore immensely applauded, and recalled. When
the fourth act of *Hamlet* followed (a fragment altogether
incomprehensible, especially to the French, unless introduced by the preceding acts), the sublime part of Ophelia,
which had produced so deep and poetical an effect but a

few years before, lost three-fourths of its prestige, and seemed cold.

The actress was still mistress of her wonderful art, but the exertion displayed when she raised herself from the stage, at the close of the scene in which she kneels before her black veil as if it were her father's shroud, was too obvious to escape observation. For herself this was a cruel discovery. She no longer showed her lameness, but the certainty and freedom of her movements were gone; and when the curtain went down, and she found that the public, whose idol she had once been, and who had just given Mdme. Dorval so great an ovation, did not call her back . . . it was a heart-breaking disappointment! Every woman and every artist will understand it. Poor Ophelia! Thy sun was going down. . . . I was desolate.

Then the concert began. The overture to the *Francs Juges*, though most indifferently performed, was greeted with an amount of applause which fairly astonished me. Weber's *Concertstück*, played by Liszt with the overpowering vehemence which he always puts into it, obtained a splendid success. Indeed, I so far forgot myself, in my enthusiasm for Liszt, as publicly to embrace him on the stage; a stupid impropriety, which might well have covered us both with ridicule, had the spectators been disposed to laugh. In the musical introduction to *Sardanapalus*, my inexperience in conducting was the cause of the second violins beginning wrong; the whole orchestra got out, and I was obliged to beat the final chord and skip all the rest. Alexis Dupont sang the cantata pretty well; but the famous conflagration at the end was badly played and badly interpreted, and produced little effect. After that nothing went well. I heard only the dull sound of my own pulse, and felt as if I were gradually sinking into the earth.   It was getting late too, and Weber's chorus and the *Symphonie Fantastique* still remained to be done.

The rules of the Théâtre Italien do not oblige the band to play after midnight. Consequently, they, being for the reasons already given ill-disposed towards me, were impatiently awaiting the moment of escape, at any risk; and while the Weber chorus was being sung, these mean-spirited scoundrels, unworthy of the name of artists, all disappeared. It was midnight. The paid musicians alone remained at their posts, and when I turned round to begin the symphony, I found myself reduced to five violins, two tenors, four basses, and one trombone. In my consternation I really did not know what to do. The public had evidently no wish to go away, and soon began to get impatient and to demand the symphony. I was not fool enough to begin. Finally, in the midst of the tumult, a voice called out from the gallery, "The *March to Execution*!" On which I made answer, "I cannot perform the *March to Execution* with five violins! It is not my fault. The orchestra has disappeared. I hope that the public——" I was burning with shame and indignation. The audience rose up in disappointment, and the concert terminated. My enemies did not fail to turn the event into ridicule, and say that my music drove away all musicians. I do not believe that there has ever before been an occurrence inspired by such ignoble motives. Ah, cursed strummers! miserable wretches! Your names are protected by their obscurity; but I regret that I did not collect them.

That sorry *soirée*, however, brought me in about seven thousand francs, but in a few days it was all swallowed up by my wife's debts; not that it was enough to discharge them; that was a work requiring several years and many cruel privations.

I should have greatly liked to give Henrietta the opportunity of a grand revenge; but there was not a single English actor in Paris. She would have been obliged again to apply to incompetent amateurs, and to appear in mere mutilated fragments of Shakespeare. This would have been absurd, as the event just described proved; so the plan had to be given up. But I lost no time in replying to the attacks on myself by an undeniable success. By paying a good price, I engaged a first-rate orchestra of the very *élite* of Paris musicians, among whom I could reckon many friends, or at the very least impartial judges of my works; and I announced a concert at the Conservatoire. The expense was so great that it was quite possible that it might not be covered by the receipts. But my wife encouraged me to do it, and thus showed herself, what she has always been since, an enemy to all half measures or petty means; and, where the interests of art or the glory of the artist were in question, brave even to rashness.

I was afraid to compromise the performance by again conducting. Habeneck obstinately refused; but Girard, at that time one of my staunch friends, consented to accept the task, and acquitted himself well. The *Symphonie Fantastique* again figured in the programme, and took the whole room by storm, being applauded throughout. My success was complete, and the former judgment on me was reversed. My musicians—it may be imagined that I took none from the Théâtre Italien—looked radiant with delight as they left the orchestra. Lastly, my happiness was completed when the public had all gone, and a man stopped me in the passage—a man

with long hair, piercing eyes, a strange and haggard face—
a genius, a Titan among the giants, whom I had never
seen before, and at first sight of whom I was deeply
moved ; this man pressed my hand, and overwhelmed me
with burning eulogies, which literally set both my heart
and brain on fire. *It was Paganini* (22nd December,
1833). From that day date my relations with that great
artist, who exercised such a happy influence upon my
destiny, and whose noble generosity has given birth to
such absurd and malicious comments.

Some weeks after the triumphant concert which I
have just described, Paganini came to see me.

"I have a wonderful viola,"[1] said he, "an admirable
Stradivarius, and should greatly like to play it in public.
But I have no music for it. Would you write me a solo ?
I have no confidence in anyone but you for such a work."

"Certainly," I answered; "I am more flattered than
I can say; but in order to fulfil your expectation, and
make a composition sufficiently brilliant to suit such a
virtuoso as yourself, I ought to be able to play the viola,
and this I cannot do. It seems to me that you alone can
solve the problem."

"No," replied Paganini; "you will succeed. As for
me, I am too unwell at present to compose. I could not
think of such a thing."

In order to please the illustrious virtuoso, I then endeavoured to write a solo for the viola, but so combined
with the orchestra as not to diminish the importance of
the latter, feeling sure that Paganini's incomparable
execution would enable him to give the solo instrument

---

[1] [The "viola," "alto," or "tenor," is the second member of the violin
family, tuned a fifth lower than the violin itself. The solo part in
Berlioz's *Harold* is written for it.]

all its due prominence. The proposition was a new one. A happy idea soon occurred to me, and I became intensely eager to carry it out.

No sooner was the first movement written than Paganini wished to see it. At sight of the pauses, however, which the viola has to make in the *allegro*, "That is not at all what I want," cried he. "I have to wait a great deal too long. I must be playing the whole time."

"That is exactly what I said," I answered. "What you really want is a *concerto* for the tenor, and you are the only man who can write it."

To this he made no reply, but seemed disappointed, and left me without any further remarks. A few days afterwards, being already a sufferer from that throat affection which was ultimately to prove fatal to him, he went to Nice, and did not return till three years later.

Finding that my plan of composition did not suit him, I applied myself to carrying it out in another way, and without troubling myself any further as to how the solo part should be brought into brilliant relief, I conceived the idea of writing a series of scenes for the orchestra, in which the viola should find itself mixed up, like a person more or less in action, always preserving his own individuality. The background I formed from my recollections of my wanderings in the Abruzzi, introducing the viola as a sort of melancholy dreamer, in the style of Byron's *Childe Harold*. Hence the title of the symphony, *Harold in Italy*. As in the *Symphonie Fantastique*, one principal theme (the first strain of the viola) is reproduced throughout the work, but with this difference, that in the *Symphonie Fantastique* the theme—the *idée fixe*—is obstinately introduced amid scenes wholly foreign to it, like a passionately episodic subject, whilst Harold's strain is superadded to the other orchestral strains, with which it contrasts both in movement and character, without hindering their development. Notwithstanding its complicated structure, I took as little time to compose this symphony as I usually did to write my other works, though I employed considerable labour in retouching it. In the *Pilgrims' March*, which I improvised in a couple of hours one evening over my fire, I have for more than six years past been modifying the details, and think that I have much improved it. Even in its first form it was always completely successful from the moment of its first performance at my concert in the Conservatoire, on November 23rd, 1834.

The first movement alone was feebly applauded, but this was the fault of Girard, who conducted the orchestra, and could not succeed in working it up enough in the *coda*, where the pace ought gradually to be doubled. Without this progressive animation, the end of the *allegro* is cold and languid. I suffered simple martyrdom in hearing it thus dragged. The *Pilgrims' March* was encored. At its second performance, and towards the middle of the second part—at the place where the convent-bell (given by two harps and doubled by the flutes, hautboys, and horns) is heard afresh after a brief interruption—at this point the harpist miscounted his bars, and lost his place. Girard, instead of setting him right, as I have done a dozen times in the same circumstances (the same mistake is constantly made), called out, "The last chord," which the band accordingly gave, thus skipping some fifty bars. This was a complete slaughter. Fortunately, however, the march had been well played the first time, and the public were under no misapprehension about the cause of the disaster at the encore. Had it happened at first, they would have been sure to attribute the *fiasco* to the composer. Still, since my defeat at the Théâtre Italien, I had such mistrust of my own skill as a conductor that I allowed Girard to direct my concerts for some time longer; but, at the fourth performance of *Harold*, he made so serious a mistake at the end of the serenade (where, if one part of the orchestra does not double its speed, the other part cannot go on, because the whole bar of the former corresponds to the half bar of the latter) that, seeing at last that there was no hope of working up the end of the *allegro* properly, I resolved in future to conduct myself, and not allow anyone else to communicate my ideas to the performers. From this resolution I only once departed, and my readers will see how nearly fatal was the result.

After the first hearing of this symphony, an article appeared in a Paris musical paper which overwhelmed me with invectives, beginning in this witty style: " Ha, ha, ha! haro! haro! *Harold*!" On the morning after the appearance of this article I received an anonymous letter, in which, after a deluge of even coarser insults, I was reproached with *not being brave enough to blow out my brains*!

CHAPTER XLVI.

In 1836 M. de Gasparin was Minister of the Interior. He belonged to that small section of our statesmen who are interested in music, and to the still more limited number who really have a feeling for it. With the view of restoring sacred music to a position which it had not enjoyed in France for long, he proposed that the Fine Art Department should give three thousand francs per annum to a French composer who should be appointed by the Minister to write either a mass or an oratorio on a large scale. He proposed also that the Minister should, in addition, charge himself with having the new work performed at the expense of the Government. "I shall begin with Berlioz," said he; "he must write a Requiem. I am sure he will succeed." My surprise was equal to my joy when these details were given me by a friend of M. de Gasparin's son, with whom I was acquainted. In order to be sure, I requested an audience of the Minister, who confirmed the correctness of all that I had heard. "I am about to leave my post," added he, "and this will be my musical legacy. You have received the official order for the Requiem?" "No, sir; and it is only by accident that I have heard of your kind intentions." "How is that? I desired the order to be sent to you a week ago. The delay is due to the carelessness of the office, and I will see to it."

Several days, however, passed without the order arriving. In great uneasiness I then addressed myself to M. de Gasparin's son, who put me up to an intrigue of which I had not the faintest suspicion.

The Director of the Fine Arts[1] did not at all approve of the Minister's project, and still less of his choice of me to open the procession of composers. He knew that in a few days M. de Gasparin would leave the Ministry. Now by delaying till then the preparation of the order for founding the institution and calling upon me to compose the Requiem, it would be easy afterwards to defeat the project by dissuading his successor from carrying it out. This is what M. le Directeur had in his head. But M. de Gasparin did not at all understand such tricks, and on learning from his son that nothing had been done, on the very eve of his leaving the Ministry he sent a most peremptory command to the Director to draw up the order immediately and send it to me, which was accordingly done.

Such a check could hardly fail to intensify the ill-feeling of the Director towards myself; it did, in fact, increase it.

This arbiter of the destinies of art and artists did not condescend to recognise real worth in any music but that of Rossini. One day, however, having in my presence reviewed, with condescending appreciation, all the ancient and modern masters, with the exception of

---

[1] He has been dead ten or twelve years, but it is as well not to give his name.

Beethoven, whom he *forgot for the moment*, he suddenly stopped and said : "But surely there must be another— what is his name ? A German, whose symphonies they play at the Conservatoire. You must know *him*, M. Berlioz." "Beethoven ?" "Ah, Beethoven. Well, *he* was not devoid of talent." I myself heard the Director of the Fine Arts express himself thus, and admit that Beethoven *was not devoid of talent.*

In this he was only the leading representative of musical opinion in the then French official world. Hundreds of connoisseurs of this sort choked up the avenues through which artists had to pass, and set in motion the wheels of the Government machine by which our musical institutions were kept going. In the present day. . . . .

Once armed with my order, I set to work. For a long time the text of the Requiem had been to me an object of envy, on which I flung myself with a kind of fury when it was put within my grasp. My head seemed ready to burst with the pressure of my seething thoughts. No sooner was one piece sketched than another presented itself. Finding it impossible to write fast enough, I adopted a sort of shorthand, which helped me greatly, especially in the *Lacrymosa.* Every composer knows the anguish and despair occasioned by forgetting ideas which one has not time to write down, and which thus escape for ever.

I consequently wrote this work with great rapidity, and it was not till long afterwards that I made the slight changes which are to be found in the second edition of the work, published by Ricordi, at Milan.[1]

[1] Strange that just at this time, whilst I was writing this great work, and after my marriage to Miss Smithson, I should twice

The official order guaranteed that my Requiem should
be performed at the Government expense on the day of
the service annually celebrated for the victims of the
Revolution of 1830.

As the day appointed for the ceremony approached, I
had the parts of my work copied, and acting on the advice
of the Director of the Fine Arts, began my rehearsals.

Almost immediately afterwards, however, I received an
official letter from the Department to the effect that the
ceremony was to take place without music, and requesting
me to suspend all my preparations. The Minister was
none the less indebted for a considerable sum to the
copyist and the two hundred choristers who, on the faith of
their agreements, had been working at my rehearsals. For
five months I in vain solicited the payment of these
debts. As for what was owing to myself, I did not
venture even to speak of it, so far did they seem from
remembering it. I began to lose patience, when one day,
on leaving the Director after an exceedingly animated
discussion with him on the subject, the cannon of
the Invalides announced the capture of Constantine.[1]
Two hours later I was hastily summoned back to the
Minister's office.

The Director had found out a way of getting rid of me;
at least, so he believed. General Damrémont having
perished beneath the walls of Constantine, a solemn

_____

have had the same dream.   I was in Mdme. Gautier's little garden
at Milan, seated at the foot of a delightful weeping acacia, but
alone. Mademoiselle Estelle was not there, and I was saying to
myself, "Where is she—where is she?" Who will explain that?
Perhaps sailors may, or learned men who have studied the movements of the magnetic needle, and know that those of the human
heart are much the same.

[1] [A city in Algeria taken by General Damrémont, Oct. 13, 1837.]

service for him and the other soldiers who had fallen
during the siege was to be held in the Church of the
Invalides. This ceremony was the concern of the Minister
of War, and General Bernard, who occupied that post,
consented to have my Requiem performed. Such was the
unexpected news which greeted me on my arrival.

The plot now thickens, and the most important events
rapidly follow each other. I recommend all poor artists
who read me to profit by my experience, and meditate
on what happened; they will gain from it the doubtful
advantage of mistrusting everything and everybody, whenever they shall find themselves in a like position; of putting
no more faith in written words than in spoken ones, and
of taking precautions alike against heaven and hell. The
news that my Requiem was to be performed in a grand
official ceremony was no sooner brought to Cherubini
than it put him into a perfect fever. It had long been
the custom to perform one of his two Requiems under
like circumstances, and such an attack, directed against
what he considered as his rights, his dignity, his just
celebrity, his unquestionable worth, and in favour of a
young man, just starting in life, with the reputation of
having introduced heresy into the school, annoyed him
extremely. His friends and pupils, with Halévy at their
head, sharing in his annoyance, combined to turn the
storm on me, that is to say to ensure the dispossession of
the young man in favour of the old one. One evening I
happened to be at the office of the *Journal des Débats*, to
the staff of which I had recently become attached, and
whose chief, M. Bertin, had always shown me the greatest
kindness, when Halévy presented himself. I at once
guessed the object of his visit. He was going to invoke
the powerful influence of M. Bertin on Cherubini's side.

Slightly disconcerted at finding me there, and still more
by the coldness with which he was received by the
Bertins—father and son—he instantly changed his tactics.
The door of the room into which he followed the elder
Bertin remained ajar, and I overheard him saying that
the shock had been so great as to make Cherubini take to
his bed, and that he had, therefore, come to beg M. Bertin
to use his influence in obtaining the Cross of the Legion
of Honour for the illustrious master as some consolation.
M. Bertin's severe voice here interrupted him with these
words : " Yes, my dear Halévy, we will do what you wish
to get Cherubini the distinction he so well merits ; but if
it is a question about the Requiem, if they are going to
propose any compromise to Berlioz, and if he has the
weakness to give in by one hair's breadth, I will never
speak to him again as long as I live." Halévy must have
felt considerably embarrassed as he retired after receiving
this answer.

Thus the excellent Cherubini, who had already sought
to make me swallow so many mortifications, was in his
turn compelled to receive a far bigger one from my hands
which he will assuredly never digest.

Now for another intrigue, still more cleverly contrived,
the black depths of which I hardly dare fathom. I
incriminate no one ; I simply give the naked facts, without the smallest commentary, but with scrupulous exact-
ness. General Bernard having himself informed me that
my Requiem was to be performed on certain conditions
which I shall presently state, I was about to begin my
rehearsals when I was sent for by the Director of the
Beaux Arts.

" You know," said he, " that Habeneck has been commissioned to conduct all the great official musical fes-

tivals?" ("Come. Good!" thought I, "here is another tile for my devoted head.") "It is true that you are now in the habit of conducting the performance of your works yourself; but Habeneck is an old man" (another tile), "and I happen to know that he will be deeply hurt if he does not preside at your Requiem. What terms are you on with him?"

"What terms? We have quarrelled. I hardly know why. For three years he has not spoken to me. I am not aware of his motives, and, indeed, have not cared to ask. He began by rudely refusing to conduct one of my concerts. His behaviour towards me has been as inexplicable as it is uncivil. However, as I see plainly that he wishes on the present occasion to figure at Marshal Damrémont's ceremony, and as it would evidently be agreeable to you, I consent to give up the baton to him, on condition that I have at least one full rehearsal."

"Agreed," replied the Director; "I will let him know about it."

The rehearsals were accordingly conducted with great care. Habeneck spoke to me as if our relations with each other had never been interrupted, and all seemed likely to go well.

The day of the performance arrived, in the Church of the Invalides, before all the princes, peers, and deputies, the French press, the correspondents of foreign papers, and an immense crowd. It was absolutely essential for me to have a great success; a moderate one would have been fatal, and a failure would have annihilated me altogether.

Now, listen attentively.

The various groups of instruments in the orchestra were tolerably widely separated, especially the four brass bands introduced in the *Tuba mirum*, each of which occupied a corner of the entire orchestra. There is no pause between the *Dies Iræ* and the *Tuba mirum*, but the pace of the latter movement is reduced to half what it was before. At this point the whole of the brass enters, first all together, and then in passages, answering and interrupting, each a third higher than the last. It is obvious that it is of the greatest importance that the four beats of the new *tempo* should be distinctly marked, or else the terrible explosion, which I had so carefully prepared with combinations and proportions never attempted before or since, and which, rightly performed, gives such a picture of the Last Judgment as I believe is destined to live, would be a mere enormous and hideous confusion.

With my habitual mistrust, I had stationed myself behind Habeneck, and, turning my back on him, overlooked the group of kettledrums, which he could not see, when the moment approached for them to take part in the general mêlée. There are, perhaps, one thousand bars in my Requiem. Precisely in that of which I have just been speaking, when the movement is retarded, and the wind instruments burst in with their terrible flourish of trumpets; in fact, just in *the* one bar where the conductor's motion is absolutely indispensable, Habeneck *puts down his baton, quietly takes out his snuffbox, and* proceeds to take a pinch of snuff. I always had my eye in his direction, and instantly turned rapidly on one heel, and, springing forward before him, I stretched out my arm and marked the four great beats of the new movement. The orchestras followed me, each in order. I conducted the piece to the end, and the effect which I had longed for was produced. When, at the last words of the chorus, Habeneck saw that the *Tuba mirum* was saved, he said: "What a cold perspiration I have been in! Without you we should have been lost." "Yes, I know," I answered, looking fixedly at him. I did not add another word. . . . Had he done it on purpose? . . . Could it be possible that this man had dared to join my enemy, the Director, and Cherubini's friends, in plotting and attempting such rascality? I don't wish to believe it . . . but I cannot doubt it. God forgive me if I am doing the man injustice!

The success of the Requiem was complete, in spite of all the conspiracies—cowardly, atrocious, officious, and official—which would fain have hindered it.

I alluded to the conditions which the Minister of War had attached to its performance. Here they are : " I will give you," said the honourable General Bernard, " ten thousand francs for the performance of your work, but this sum will only be given on your presenting a letter from my colleague the Minister of the Interior, by which he shall engage to pay what is due to you for the composition of the Requiem, according to M. de Gasparin's order, and afterwards what is owing to the copyist and to the choristers for their rehearsals last July."

The Minister had given his word to General Bernard to discharge this triple debt. The letter was drawn up, and wanted nothing but his signature. To obtain this I remained in his ante-room with one of his secretaries, armed with the letter and a pen, from ten in the morning till four in the afternoon. Not till then did the Minister come out, and the secretary, catching him in the passage, made him affix his precious signature to the letter. Without losing a minute, I ran off to General Bernard, who, after having carefully read his colleague's letter, paid me the ten thousand francs. I applied the whole of this sum to the payment of my performers. I gave three hundred francs to Duprez, who had sung the solo in the *Sanctus*, and three hundred more to Habeneck, that peerless snuff-taker who had made such an opportune use of his snuff-box. Absolutely nothing remained for myself. I imagined that I should ultimately be paid by the Minister of the Interior, who would feel himself doubly bound to pay off this debt, both by the decree of his predecessor and by the engagement he had contracted in his own person with the Minister of War. *Sancta simplicitas*! says Mephistopheles. One month, two months, three, four, eight months passed by without my being able to touch a halfpenny. By dint of petitions, recommendatory letters from friends of the Minister, constant visits, and written and verbal complaints, the practices of the choristers and the expenses of the copying were finally paid, and I was at length rid of the intolerable persecution I had so long endured from those poor people, who were weary of waiting for their due, and probably had their suspicions of my honesty, the bare idea of which still makes me blush with indignation.

But that the author of the Requiem should be supposed to attach any value to filthy lucre! That would indeed have been a calumny, and, in consequence, good care was taken not to pay me. I nevertheless took the liberty to claim the entire fulfilment of the Minister's promises. My need of money was so pressing that I was forced to make a fresh attack on the office of the Fine Arts Director. Several weeks more passed by in useless demands. My anger increased; I grew thin; I lost my sleep. Finally, I went one morning to the office, blue and pale with fury, resolved to make a scene; resolved on any and every extremity. On entering I at once attacked the Director: "Well, it is plain that they are not going to pay me." "My dear Berlioz," replied he, "you know it is not my fault. I have made stringent inquiries, and have found out everything about the affair. The money intended for you has disappeared; it has been put to some other use. I really don't know in what office. If such things took place in mine——" "Oh, then the money intended for the Fine Arts can be spent out of your department, and without your knowledge? Is your budget, then, at the disposal of the first comer? But this is nothing to me. Such questions are no concern of mine. A Requiem was ordered from me by the Minister of the Interior for the agreed sum of three thousand francs. I want my three thousand francs!" "Good heavens! have a little patience! It shall be considered. Besides, there is an idea of giving you the cross." "A fig for the cross! Give me my money!" "But——" "I'll have no buts," cried I, throwing down an arm-chair. "I will give you till twelve o'clock to-morrow; and if at twelve o'clock precisely I have not received the money, I will raise a scandal about you and the Minister the like of which has never been seen before! And you know that it is in my power to raise it." Whereat the Director is quite upset, and, forgetting his hat, rushes down the stairs leading to the Minister's rooms, I behind him, calling out, "Mind you tell him that I should be ashamed to treat my shoemaker as he treats me, and that his behaviour to me shall soon enjoy a rare notoriety."[1] This time I had hit the weak place in the Minister's armour. Ten minutes afterwards the Director returned with a cheque for three thousand francs on the Fine Art Department. The money

[1] And yet he was an excellent and well-intentioned man.

had been found.   That is how artists ought occasionally to get justice done to them in Paris.   There are other ways, still more violent, which I advise them not to overlook.

At a later date, the excellent M. de Gasparin having regained possession of the portfolio of the Interior, seemed to wish to make some amends for the intolerable injustice I had endured about the Requiem, by giving me the cross of the Legion of Honour, which they had previously tried to sell me for three thousand francs; though when offered in that way I would not have given thirty *sous* for it.   This commonplace distinction was bestowed upon me at the same time with the great Duponchel, Director of the Opéra, and Bordogni, the best singing-master of that period.

When the Requiem was afterwards printed I dedicated it to M. de Gasparin, all the more willingly that he was then no longer in power.   .

What made the behaviour of the Minister so peculiarly galling was that, after the performance of the Requiem, after having paid the musicians and choristers, the carpenters who constructed the orchestra, Habeneck, Duprez, and everyone else, and whilst I had only begun to demand my three thousand francs, the opposition newspapers pointed me out as a favourite of the Government, as a silkworm feeding on the revenue, and gravely stated that I had had thirty thousand francs for the Requiem!   In saying this they merely added a cypher to the sum which I had not received.   That is the way in which history is written.

CHAPTER XLVII.

SOME years after the ceremony, the events of which I
have just narrated, the town of Lille organised its first
festival, and Habeneck was engaged to direct the musical
part of it. Actuated by one of those kindly impulses
which were, after all, not infrequent with him, and
wishing perhaps to make me forget, if possible, his famous
pinch of snuff, he took it into his head to propose to the
committee, among other pieces, the *Lacrymosa* from my
Requiem. A *Credo* of Cherubini's was also included in the
programme. Habeneck rehearsed my piece with extraordinary care, and the performance appeared to leave
nothing to be desired. Its effect, also, was said to be very
fine; and, in spite of its great length, the piece was
loudly encored by the public. Some of the audience were
even moved to tears. As the Lille committee had not
done me the honour to invite me, I stayed in Paris; but
after the concert, Habeneck, in great delight at such a
success with so difficult a work, wrote me a short letter
something in this style, which was published in Paris by
the *Gazette Musicale:*

"MY DEAR BERLIOZ,

"I cannot resist the pleasure of telling you that your *Lacrymosa* was beautifully performed and produced an immense sensation.—Yours ever,

"HABENECK."

On his return, Habeneck called on Cherubini to assure him that his *Credo* had been very well done. "Yes," replied Cherubini in a dry tone, "but you did not write to *me*." [1]

Here was again a bitter little pill that he was obliged to swallow about that d———d Requiem, and he kindly offered me the fellow to it under the following circumstances.

The place of Professor of Harmony having fallen vacant at the Conservatoire, I was advised by one of my friends to become a candidate for it. Without deluding myself with any hope of success, I nevertheless wrote to our excellent Director, Cherubini, on the subject. On the receipt of my letter he sent for me.

"You propose yourself for the harmony class?" said he, with his most amiable manner and sweetest voice.

"Yes, sir."

"Ah, well,[2] you will get it. Your present reputation, your references———"

"So much the better, sir; I asked for it in order to get it."

"Yes, but—but that is just what is troubling me. The fact is, I wanted to give it to somebody else."

"In that case, sir, I will withdraw my application."

"No, no; I don't want that, because, you see, people would say that I was the cause of your withdrawal."

---

[1] I had told him that he would *know my name some day.*

[2] [Here again, to get an idea of Cherubini's odd pronunciation, the reader must see the original.]

" Well, then, I shall remain a candidate."

" But I tell you you will get the place if you insist on it, and—— But I did not mean it for you."

" What would you have me do, then ? "

" You know that—that—that it is necessary to be a pianist to teach harmony at the Conservatoire ; you know that, don't you ?"

" It is necessary to be a pianist, is it ? Ah, I should hardly have guessed that. Very well, that is an excellent reason. I will write to you that, not being a pianist, I cannot aspire to the professorship of harmony at the Conservatoire, and that I withdraw my application."

" Yes ; but—but—but I am not the cause of your——"

" No ; far from it. I ought to withdraw as a matter of course, after having been so stupid as to forget that it was necessary to be a pianist to teach harmony."

" Yes. Come, embrace me. You know how fond I am of you."

" Oh yes, sir ; I know it well." And he did, as a matter of fact, embrace me with really paternal tenderness. I went away, wrote to him to withdraw my application, and eight days later he had the place given to a man of the name of Bienaimé, who was no more a pianist than I was. That was what might be called a well-played trick, and I myself was the first to laugh heartily at it.

The reader will admire my self-control in not replying to Cherubini : " Then you yourself, sir, would not be able to teach harmony either?" For the great master himself was also no pianist.

I regret that soon afterwards, though quite involuntarily, I wounded my illustrious friend in the most cruel manner. I was in the pit of the Opera-house at the first representation of his *Ali Baba.* This work, as everyone agreed at the time, is one of Cherubini's feeblest and most insignificant. Towards the end of the first act, tired of hearing nothing striking, I could not help saying, loudly enough to be heard by my neighbours: "Twenty francs for an idea!" In the middle of the second act, still deceived by the same musical mirage, I added to my bid, saying: "Forty francs for an idea!" The *finale* began: "Eighty francs for an idea!" When the *finale* was ended I got up, exclaimed: "Upon my word, I am not rich enough. I give it up," and thereupon left.

Two or three young men on the same bench with myself looked at me indignantly. They were pupils at the Conservatoire, who had been placed there that they might admire their Director *to some purpose.* They did not fail, as I heard afterwards, to go next day and tell the Director of my insolent bids and still more insolent criticism. Cherubini was all the more outraged by it because, after having said to me : " You know how fond I am of you," he must doubtless have thought me, as usual, horribly ungrateful. If my former tricks might be called *adders*, this was really one of those venomous *asps* whose bite is so deadly to one's self-love. It somehow escaped me.

I ought now to say how I became attached to the staff of the *Journal des Débats.* Since my return from Italy I had published a good many articles in the *Revue Européenne, L'Europe Littéraire,* and *Le Monde Dramatique* (magazines whose existence was of short duration), in the *Gazette Musicale,* the *Correspondant,* and some other papers that are now forgotten. But these various works of small compass and importance brought me in very little, and did not much improve the state of discomfort in which I was living.

One day, not knowing which way to turn, and anxious to gain a few francs, I wrote a sort of novel called *Rubini à Calais*, which appeared in the *Gazette Musicale*. I was desperately sad when I wrote it, but the story was full of fun; a contrast which is known to occur often enough. The sketch was reproduced in the *Journal des Débats* some days later, with a few words from the editor, full of kindly feeling for the author. I went at once to thank M. Bertin, who proposed that I should edit the musical *feuilleton* of the *Débats* itself, a much-coveted throne of criticism, which was then vacant through the retirement of Castil-Blaze. At first I was not its sole occupant, and for some time had only to write the critiques on concerts and new compositions. Later on those on the lyrical theatres devolved upon me, and the Théâtre Italien remained under the protection of M. Delécluse, who has it to this day, Jules Janin preserving his rights over the Opéra ballets. I then gave up the *feuilleton* of the *Correspondant*, and limited my critical labours to such as could find a place in the *Débats* and the *Gazette Musicale*.

At present I have almost renounced all work in the last-named paper, notwithstanding its high pay,[1] and write only in the *Débats* when absolutely obliged to do so by the fluctuations of the musical world.

Such is my aversion to work of this nature, that I cannot hear a first representation without an uneasiness which goes on increasing until my *feuilleton* is finished.

This never-ending still-beginning task poisons my life.

---

[1] They give me 100 francs per *feuilleton*, that is to say about 1,400 francs in the year.

And yet, independently of the income it gives me, with which I cannot dispense, I find it almost impossible to give it up on pain of remaining defenceless in the face of the furious and almost innumerable animosities which it has stirred up against me. For the press is, in a certain way, more precious than the spear of Achilles ; not only does it occasionally heal the wounds which it has inflicted, but it also serves as a weapon to the person who makes use of it.

And yet what wretched circumspection am I not forced to use ! what circumlocution to evade the expression of the truth ! What concessions to social relations and even to public opinion ! what suppressed rage, what gulps of shame ! And yet I am considered passionate, ill-natured, and contemptuous ! The ill-bred fellows who treat me thus ! If I spoke my mind they would soon see that the bed of thorns on which they believe themselves to have been laid by me is a bed of roses compared with the gridiron on which I long to roast them !

I ought in justice to myself to say that never for any consideration has it ever happened to me to suppress the most unrestrained expressions of esteem, admiration, or enthusiasm for any works or any men who inspired me with those sentiments. I have warmly praised writers who have done me much harm, and with whom I have ceased to have any relations. Indeed the only compensation which the press offers me for so many torments, is the range it gives to my aspirations towards the great, the true, and the beautiful, wherever they exist. It is sweet to praise an enemy when that enemy has merit, indeed it is the proud duty of an honest man; while every untrue word written in favour of an undeserving friend causes me heart-breaking anguish. In both cases, however, as critics well know, the man who hates you is so furious at the praise you are likely to obtain by heartily doing him justice in public, that he detests you all the more, while the man who likes you, not being satisfied with the laboured eulogies you bestow on him, likes you all the less. Nor should it be forgotten how sick it makes those who have the misfortune, as I have, to be at once critic and artist, to be obliged to occupy themselves with a thousand Lilliputian trifles, and to put up with the fawning compliments, meanness, and cringing of people who have, or are likely to have need of you. I often amuse myself by following the subterranean operations of certain individuals as they scoop out a tunnel twenty miles long in order to get what they call a "good" *feuilleton* upon a forthcoming work. Nothing is more laughable than to hear them laboriously digging away, unless it be the patience with which they clear the passage and construct the arch, until the moment when the critic, waxing impatient at all their contrivances, suddenly opens a tap which floods the mine and sometimes drowns the miner.

When, therefore, the appreciation of my works is in question, I do not attach much value to the opinion of any persons who are not beyond the influence of the *feuilleton*. Among musicians, those only whose approbation flatters me are the members of the orchestra and the chorus, because their individual talent rarely meets the critic's approval, and so I know that they have no reason for paying court to him. For the rest, the praises dragged out of me from time to time ought not to gratify those who are the objects of them. The violence which I do to myself in commending certain works is such that the truth betrays itself in my sentences, as in a hydraulic press the water oozes out through the pores of the metal.

Balzac in various parts of his admirable *Comédie Humaine* has said many excellent things upon contemporary criticism, but in showing up the mistakes and injuries of those who carry on the business, he has not, as it seems to me, sufficiently brought out the merit of those who preserve their integrity. Nor does he appreciate their secret miseries. Even in his *Monographie de la Presse*, notwithstanding the help he got from his friend Laurent-Jan (also a friend of mine, and one of the most penetrating minds I know), Balzac has not thrown light on all the bearings of the question. Laurent-Jan has written in several newspapers, but not regularly, and more as a humorist than a critic, and neither he nor Balzac could know or see everything.

*   *   *   *   *   *

One day M. Armand Bertin, who was much concerned at my embarrassed circumstances, greeted me with these words, which pleased me all the more for being totally unexpected:

"My dear friend, your position is now made. I have spoken to the Minister of the Interior, and he has decided that in spite of Cherubini's opposition, you shall have a professorship of composition at the Conservatoire, with a salary of one thousand five hundred francs, and a pension of four thousand five hundred francs from the fund at his disposal for the encouragement of the Fine Arts. With six thousand francs a year you will be free from all anxiety, and able to devote yourself without restraint to composition."

The next evening I happened to be in the lobby at the Opéra, when M. X——, whose feeling towards me

is no secret, and who was head of the Fine Arts
Department at the Ministry, caught sight of me, and,
coming forward with studied cordiality, repeated what
M. Armand Bertin had said in much the same words.
I thanked him, and begged him to bear witness to the
Minister of my intense gratitude.   This spontaneous
promise to one who had asked for nothing was no better
kept than all the others, *and from that time forth I
never heard a word more about it.*

CHAPTER XLVIII.

THE only good I did obtain, and that always in spite of
Cherubini, was the place of librarian at the Conservatoire,
which I have still, and the salary of which is one hundred
and eighteen francs a month. Afterwards, when I was in
England, after the proclamation of the Republic, certain
worthy patriots whom the place suited thought fit to ask
for it, on the ground that it was not proper to leave it with
a man who was so often absent. On my return from
London accordingly I heard that I was to be deprived of
it. Fortunately, Victor Hugo, at that time a representative
of the people, enjoyed a certain amount of authority in
the Chamber, in spite of his genius; and he interfered to
preserve me my modest situation.

It was about the same time that M. Charles Blanc
occupied the post of Director of the Fine Arts—a sincere
and learned friend to art, and brother to the celebrated
Socialist. On several occasions he rendered me services,
with a warmth and eagerness I shall not forget.

Here is an example of the pitiless hatred that always
besets men of the press, whether literary or political,
the effects of which they are sure to feel from the
moment they happen to give the least handle to it.

Mademoiselle Louise Bertin, the daughter of the proprietor of the *Journal des Débats*, and sister of its chief editor, was remarkably successful both in literature and music. She is one of the ablest women of our time. Her musical talent, to my mind, is rather rational than emotional; but it is a real talent notwithstanding, and, in spite of a certain want of decision, and of the occasionally childish form of her melodies, her opera of *Esmeralda*, to Victor Hugo's words, is of great interest, and certainly contains very fine passages. As Mdlle. Bertin could not herself direct the study of her opera at the theatre, her father commissioned me to do so, and very generously indemnified me for my loss of time. The principal parts—Phœbus, Frollo, Esmeralda, and Quasimodo—were taken by Nourrit, Levasseur, Mdlle. Falcon, and Massol—in other words, by the best singers and actors at the Opéra.

Several pieces—among others the great duet between the Priest and the Gipsy in the second act, a romance, and Quasimodo's air—were very much applauded at the general rehearsal. Nevertheless, this work, by a woman who never wrote one word of criticism on any human being, good, bad, or indifferent, and whose sole crime consisted in her belonging to a family whose political views were detested by a certain section of the community—this work, I say, so far superior to many that succeed daily, or are at any rate accepted—broke down utterly. It was received at the Opéra with unexampled hisses, groans, and cries. At the second trial, indeed, they were obliged to drop the curtain in the middle of an act, and stop the performance.

Quasimodo's air, known as the *Air des Cloches*, was, however, applauded and encored by the whole room, and as its effect could neither be ignored nor disputed, some of the audience, more hostile than the rest against the Bertins, were not ashamed to call out, "It is not by Mdlle. Bertin ; it is by Berlioz."

I knew just as much of it as I did of the rest of the score, and I swear upon my honour that not a note of it is mine. But the cabal against the author was too furious not to take every possible advantage of the pretext offered by my share in the rehearsal of the work, and the *Air des Cloches* continued to be ascribed to me.

This incident showed me what I might expect from such personal enemies as I had made by my criticisms in the *Journal des Débats* and elsewhere, if I should ever appear myself on the boards of the Opéra, where so many acts of cowardly revenge are perpetrated with impunity. My own failure came at last. I had been greatly struck with certain episodes in the life of Benvenuto Cellini, and was so unlucky as to think they offered an interesting and dramatic subject for an opera. So I begged Léon de Wailly and Auguste Barbier—the terrible poet of the *Iambes*—to make me a libretto on the subject.

To believe even our friends, their libretto did not contain the elements essential to what is called a good play. I liked it, however, and I still do not see that it is inferior to many that are performed every day. Duponchel was then Director of the Opéra. He looked upon me as a kind of lunatic, whose music could be nothing but a tissue of extravagances. Still, in order to *please the Journal des Débats*, he consented to hear the libretto of *Benvenuto*, and appeared to like it. He afterwards went about everywhere, saying that he was getting up this opera, not for the sake of the music, which he knew must be absurd, but because of the play, which he thought charming.

It was rehearsed accordingly; and never shall I forget the tortures I endured for the three months devoted to it. The indifference and obvious distaste with which most of the actors attended the rehearsals, as if convinced beforehand that it would be a failure, Habeneck's ill-temper, the under-hand rumours circulated in the theatre, the stupid remarks of these illiterate people about a libretto differing so much in style from the dull rhyming prose of Scribe's school—all this revealed to me a universal hostility, against which I was powerless, and which I had to ignore.

Auguste Barbier might perhaps here and there, in the recitatives, have let slip an abusive term belonging to a vocabulary inconsistent with our present prudishness; but it will hardly be believed that the following words, in a duet written by L. de Wailly, were thought coarse by most of the singers :

> Quand je repris l'usage de mes sens,
> Ses toits luisaient aux blancheurs de l'aurore,
> Ses coqs chantaient, etc., etc.

"Oh, the cocks!" said they; "oh, oh, the cocks! Why not the hens?" etc. etc.

What could be said in reply to such foolery? When we came to the orchestral rehearsals, the musicians, seeing Habeneck's sulky air, treated me with the most distant reserve. They did their duty, however, but Habeneck did not do his. He never could catch the lively turn of the saltarello in the second act. The dancers, not being able to adapt themselves to his dragging time, complained to me, and I kept on repeating, "Faster, faster! Stir them up!" Habeneck struck the desk in irritation, and broke his violin bow. Having witnessed four or five of such outbursts, I ended at last by saying, with a coolness that exasperated him :

"Good heavens ! if you were to break fifty bows, that would not prevent your time from being too slow by half. It is a saltarello that you are conducting !"

At that Habeneck stopped, and, turning to the orchestra, said :

"Since I am not fortunate enough to please M. Berlioz, we will leave off for to-day. You can go."

And there the rehearsal ended.[1]

Some years afterwards, when I had written the overture of the *Carnaval Romain*, in which the theme of the *allegro* is this same saltarello, Habeneck happened to be in the green-room of the Herz concert-hall the evening that this overture was to be played for the first time. He had heard that we had rehearsed it in the morning without the wind instruments, part of the band having been called off for the National Guard. "Good !" said he to himself. "There will certainly be a catastrophe at his concert this evening. I must be there." On my arrival, indeed, I was surrounded on the orchestra by all the artists of the wind instruments, who were in terror at the idea of having to play an overture of which they did not know a note.

"Don't be afraid," I said. "The parts are correct ; you are all clever enough ; watch my baton as often as you can, count your bars, and it will be all right."

Not a single mistake occurred. I started the *allegro*

---

[1] In France, authors *are not allowed* to direct their own works in the theatres, and therefore I could not conduct the rehearsals of *Cellini* myself.

in the whirlwind time of the Transtéverine dancers. The public cried *"Bis!"* We played the overture over again ; it was even better done the second time. And as I passed back through the green-room, where Habeneck stood looking a little disappointed, I just flung these few words at him : "That is how it *ought* to go!" to which he took care to make no reply.

Never did I feel more keenly the delight of being able to direct the performance of my music myself; and the thought of what Habeneck had made me endure only enhanced my pleasure.[1] Unhappy composers! know how to conduct, and how to conduct yourselves well (with or without a pun), for do not forget that the most dangerous of your interpreters is the conductor himself.

To return to *Benvenuto.*

In spite of the prudent reserve maintained by the orchestra in accordance with their conductor's secret hostility towards me, the musicians at the close of the last rehearsals applauded several of the pieces, and some even declared my work to be one of the most original they had ever heard. This came to the ears of Duponchel; and one evening I heard him say : "Did anyone ever know such a sudden change of opinion? They now think Berlioz's music delightful, and these fools of musicians are lauding it up to the skies." Several of them, however, were far from such partisanship. One evening, in the *finale* of the second act, two were detected playing the air, *J'ai du bon tabac*, instead of their own part, in hopes of flattering Habeneck. These black-guardly tricks were matched on the stage. In this same *finale*, where the scene is darkened and represents

---

[1] [See this enlarged upon in the letter to Liszt, which forms **chapter liv.**]

a masked crowd at night in the Piazza Colonna, the dancers amused themselves by pinching their partners, making them shriek and shrieking themselves, to the great disturbance of the singers. And when I sent for the manager to put an end to the scandal, Duponchel was not to be found, never condescending to attend a rehearsal !

The opera at last arrived at performance. The overture received exaggerated applause, and the rest was hissed with admirable energy and unanimity. It was given three times, however, after which Duprez threw up the part of Benvenuto, and the work disappeared from the bills, not to reappear till long afterwards, when A. Dupond spent *five whole months* in studying the part, which he was frantic at not having taken in the first instance.

Duprez was very good in any violent scene, such as the one in the sextett, when he threatens to break up his statue ; but his voice had already ceased to lend itself to soft airs, long-drawn notes, or calm, dreamy music. For instance, in the air, *Sur les monts les plus sauvages*, he could not sustain the high G at the end of the phrase, *Je chanterais gaîment;* and, instead of holding the note for three bars as he should have done, only held it for one, and thus destroyed the effect. Madame Gras-Dorus and Madame Stoltz were both charming as Teresa and Ascanio, which they had learnt carefully and with a very good grace. Madame Stoltz, indeed, was so much noticed in her rondo in the second act, *Mais qu'ai-je donc?* that that part may be considered as the starting-point for her ultimate high position, from which she was so rudely degraded.

It is fourteen years[1] since I was thus dragged to

---

[1] It must not be forgotten that this was written in 1850. Since then the opera of *Benvenuto Cellini*, slightly modified in the poem,

execution at the Opéra; and on re-reading my poor score with strict impartiality, I cannot help recognising a great variety of ideas, an impetuous *verve*, and a brilliancy of musical colouring which I shall probably never again reach, and which deserved a better fate.

Benvenuto took me a long time to write, and but for the help of a friend I should never have been able to finish it in time. In order to write an opera, one must be free from all other work, that is to say, one must have a fixed livelihood for some time, more or less. Well, I was very far indeed from being thus circumstanced. I was living from hand to mouth by the articles I wrote for the newspapers, and which took up nearly all my time. I did, indeed, try to devote two months to my score in the first *accès* of the fever into which it put me; but stern necessity soon tore the composer's pen from my hand, to replace it by that of the critic. It was an indescribable disappointment. But hesitation was out of the question. Could I leave my wife and child in want of the necessaries of life? In the profound state of melancholy into which I had fallen, torn asunder by want, and the musical ideas I was compelled to forego, I had not courage even to fulfil my usual hated task of scribbling.

I was in the deepest depression when I received a visit from Ernest Legouvé. " Whereabouts are you in your opera ?" said he.

has been successfully put on the stage at Weimar, where it is often given under Liszt's direction. The score for voice and piano was also published with German and French words by Mayer at Brunswick in 1858. It was even published in Paris, by Choudens, in 1865.

[*Benvenuto* was performed at Hanover under the direction of Herr von Bülow in 1879, with the greatest care and finish, and with brilliant success.]

"I have not finished the first act yet.   I cannot find time to work at it."

"But if you had the time?"

"Then, by Jove, I should work from morning till night."

"What do you require to be free?"

"Two thousand francs—which I have not got."

"And if somebody?—if they were?—Come, help me out!"

"With what?   What do you mean?"

"Well, if one of your friends were to lend them to you?"

"From what friend could I borrow such a sum?"

"You need not borrow.   I offer it to you."

My joy may be imagined.   Legouvé did, in fact, lend me the two thousand francs next day, and, thanks to that, I was able to finish *Benvenuto*.   Noble heart! dear, good fellow!   Himself a distinguished writer and artist, he had divined my misery, and, with exquisite delicacy, feared to wound me by proposing to put an end to it.   Artists alone can thus understand each other. And I have been happy enough to meet several who have come to my aid in like manner.

CHAPTER XLIX

Concert of December 16, 1838—Paganini's Letter and Present—My Wife's religious fervour—Fury, Congratulations, and Scandals—My visit to Paganini—His departure—I write *Romeo and Juliet*—Criticisms on the Work.

PAGANINI had returned from Sardinia when *Benvenuto* was massacred at the Opéra. He was present at that horrible performance, and indeed went away heart-broken, saying, "If I were manager of the Opéra, I would at once engage that young man to write me three such operas; I would pay him in advance, and should make a capital bargain by it."

The failure of the work, and the effort of restraining my rage during the interminable rehearsals, brought on an attack of bronchitis that reduced me to keep my bed and do nothing. Still, we had to live; and, making up my mind to an indispensable effort, I gave two concerts at the Conservatoire. The first barely paid its expenses. To increase the receipts of the second I announced both my symphonies, *La Fantastique* and[1] *Harold*, in the programme, and in spite of my bad health and obstinate bronchitis, I was able to conduct them on the 16th of December, 1838.

[1] [Berlioz here unconsciously took a leaf out of Beethoven's book, who when he brought out his fourth Symphony (in B flat) included its three predecessors in the programme!]

Paganini was present; and I will now give the history of the famous occurrence of which so many contradictory versions exist, and so many unkind stories have been circulated.

As I have already said, I composed *Harold* at the instigation of Paganini. Though performed several times during his absence, it had not figured at any of my concerts since his return; he therefore was not acquainted with it, and heard it that day for the first time.

The concert was just over; I was in a profuse perspiration, and trembling with exhaustion, when Paganini, followed by his son Achilles, came up to me at the orchestra door, gesticulating violently. Owing to the throat affection of which he ultimately died, he had already completely lost his voice, and unless everything was perfectly quiet, no one but his son could hear or even guess what he was saying. He made a sign to the child, who got up on a chair, put his ear close to his father's mouth, and listened attentively.

Achilles then got down, and turning to me, said, "My father desires me to assure you, sir, that he has never in his life been so powerfully impressed at a concert; that your music has quite upset him, and that if he did not restrain himself he should go down on his knees to thank you for it." I made a movement of incredulous embarrassment at these strange words, but Paganini, seizing my arm, and rattling out, "Yes, yes!" with the little voice he had left, dragged me up on the stage, where there were still a good many of the performers, knelt down, and kissed my hand. I need not describe my stupefaction; I relate the facts, that is all.

On going out into the bitter cold in this state of white heat, I met M. Armand Bertin on the boulevard. There

I remained for some time, describing the scene that had just occurred, caught a chill, went home, and took to my bed, more ill than before.

The next day[1] I was alone in my room, when little Achilles entered, and said, "My father will be very sorry to hear that you are still ill; and if he were not so unwell himself, he would have come to see you. Here is a letter he desired me to give you." I would have broken the seal, but the child stopped me, and saying, "There is no answer; my father said you would read it when you were alone," hastily left the room.

I supposed it to be a letter full of congratulations and compliments, and, opening it, read as follows :

"Mio caro Amico,

"Beethoven spento non c'era che Berlioz che potesse farlo rivivere; ed io che ho gustato le vostre divine composizioni degne d'un genio qual siete, credo mio dovere di pregarvi à voler accettare, in segno del mio omaggio, venti mila franchi, i quali vi saranno rimessi dal Signor Baron de Rothschild dopo che gli avrete presentato l'acclusa. Credete mi sempre il vostro affezionatissimo amico,

"Nicolò Paganini.[2]

"Parigi, 18 Dicembre, 1838."

---

[1] [This should be two days afterwards, as is evident from the date of Paganini's letter.]

[2] [My dear Friend,—Beethoven is dead, and Berlioz alone can revive him. I have heard your divine composition, so worthy of your genius, and beg you to accept, in token of my homage, twenty thousand francs, which will be handed to you by the Baron de Rothschild on presentation of the enclosed.—Your most affectionate friend, Nicolo Paganini.—Paris, December 18, 1838.

It appears from the explicit statement of Ferdinand Hiller, grounded on information given him by Rossini, that Paganini was

I know enough of Italian to understand a letter like
this. The unexpected nature of its contents, however,
surprised me so much that I became quite confused in
my ideas, and forgot what I was doing. But a note
addressed to M. de Rothschild was enclosed, and, without
a thought that I was committing an indiscretion, I
quickly opened it, and read these few words in French :

" Sir,
    " Be so good as to remit to M. Berlioz the sum of
twenty thousand francs, which I left with you yesterday.
                        " Yours, etc., Paganini."

Then only did the truth dawn on me, and I must
evidently have grown quite pale, for my wife coming in
at that moment, and finding me with a letter in my
hand and a discomposed face, exclaimed, " What's the
matter now ? Some new misfortune ? Courage ! we have
endured as much before."
    " No, no ; quite the contrary."
    " What, then ? "
    " Paganini."
    " Well, what of him ? "
    " He has sent me—twenty thousand francs."
    " Louis ! Louis ! " cried Henrietta, rushing distractedly

merely the channel for this splendid gift, and that the real donor
was Berlioz's warm and powerful friend Armand Bertin, proprietor
of the *Journal des Débats*, whose name has so often occurred in the
above pages. " 'Are you sure and certain that this was the case?'
said I to Rossini. 'I *know* it,' replied he, with that solemn
earnestness which was as characteristic as his usual joking vein.
Some may believe this; some may doubt. I am convinced of its
truth." (*Künstlerleben*, 1880, p. 89.) This, from a man of Hiller's
known integrity and good sense, and one of Berlioz's most intimate
friends, is a strong expression.]

in search of my son, who was playing in the next room.
"Come here! come with your mother; come and thank
God for what He has done for your father." And my
wife and child ran back together, and fell on their knees
beside my bed, the mother praying, the child in astonishment joining his little hands beside her. O Paganini!
what a sight! . . . Would that he could have seen it! . . .

My first impulse, as may well be imagined, was to
answer his letter, since it was impossible for me to leave
the house. My reply has always seemed to me so
inadequate and so far from what I really felt, that I
dare not reproduce it. Some situations and feelings are
quite overwhelming!

Paganini's noble action soon became known in Paris,
and for the next two days my room was the rendezvous of
numerous artists, all eager to see the famous letter, and
learn the particulars of so strange an event. All congratulated me; one, indeed, showed a certain jealousy,
not of me, but of Paganini. "I am not rich," he said,
"or I would willingly have done as much." He was
a violinist; and it is the only example I know of a
spirit of honourable envy. Afterwards came out all the
remarks, detractions, anger, and falsehoods of my enemies,
the transports of delight and triumph of my friends, the
letter I received from Jules Janin, his splendid article in
the *Journal des Débats*, the abusive language with which
I was honoured by certain low wretches, the scandalous
insinuations against Paganini, the letting loose and the
clashing of a score of good and evil passions.

In the midst of all this agitation and impetuous
feeling, I was boiling over with impatience at not being
able to leave my bed. At last, at the end of the sixth
day, I felt a little better, and, unable longer to contain

myself, I dressed, and ran off to the Néothermes, Rue de la Victoire, where Paganini was then living. They told me he was alone in the billiard-room. I went in, and we embraced without a word. After some minutes, as I was stammering out I know not what in the way of thanks, Paganini—whom I was able to understand in the empty room—cut me short with these words :

"Don't speak of that. No, not another word. It is the greatest pleasure I have ever felt in my life. You will never know how your music affected me; it is many years since I had felt anything like it. . . . Ah! now," added he, as he brought down his fist on the billiard-table with a violent blow, "none of the people who cabal against you will dare to say another word, for they know that I am a good judge, and that *I am not easy*" (*Je ne suis pas aisé*).

What did he mean by that? Did he mean, "I am not easily moved by music," or " I don't give my money easily," or " I am not in easy circumstances "?

The sardonic tone in which he uttered the expression makes the last interpretation unacceptable to my mind. Be that as it might, however, the great artist was mistaken. His authority, powerful as it was, could not silence the ignorant and ill-natured. He did not know the Parisian rabble, which only bayed at my heels all the more soon after. A naturalist has said that certain dogs aspire to be men : I think far more men aspire to be dogs !

Having discharged my debts, 'and finding myself still in possession of a considerable sum, my one idea was to spend it in the way of music. "I must," I said to myself, "leave off all other work, and write a masterpiece, on a grand new plan, a splendid work, full of passion and imagination, and worthy to be dedicated to the illustrious artist to whom I owe so much."

Whilst I was meditating this plan, Paganini's health became so much worse that he was again obliged to go off to Marseilles and Nice, from whence, alas! he never returned. I wrote him several times about subjects for the grand composition I was meditating, of which I had spoken to him; but his answer was, "I can give you no advice about it. You know what will suit you better than anyone else."

At last, after much indecision, I hit upon the idea of a symphony, with choruses, vocal solos, and choral recitatives, on the sublime and ever-novel theme of Shakespeare's *Romeo and Juliet*. I wrote in prose all the text intended for the vocal pieces which come between the instrumental sections. Émile Deschamps, with his usual delightful good-nature and marvellous facility, set it to verse for me, and I began.

No more *feuilletons* now! or at least, hardly any. Paganini had given me money that I might write music, and write it I did. I worked for seven months, not leaving off for more than three or four days out of every thirty on any pretence whatsoever.

And during all that time how ardently did I live! How vigorously I struck out in that grand sea of poetry caressed by the playful breeze of fancy, beneath the hot rays of that sun of love which Shakespeare kindled, always confident of my power to reach the marvellous island where stands the temple of true art. Whether I succeeded or not it is not for me to decide.

The work, such as it then was, was performed three times running at the Conservatoire under my own direction, apparently with great success. I felt at once, however,

that I should have to improve it a great deal, and set
myself to study it seriously under all its aspects. To my
keen regret, Paganini never either heard or read it. I
was always hoping for his return to Paris; and, besides,
was waiting to send him the symphony until it was
entirely finished off and printed. In the meantime he
died at Nice, and to the grief I felt at his death was
added that of not knowing whether he would have
approved the work undertaken chiefly to please him,
and justify him to himself for what he had done to its
author. He also seemed much to regret not having
heard the work, as he told me in his letter from Nice,
dated January 7, 1840, in which he says, "*Now that all
is done, envy cannot but be silent.*"

Poor dear friend! Happily for him, he never read
the horrible nonsense in many of the Paris newspapers
about the plan of the work, the introduction, the *adagio*,
Queen Mab, and the story of Father Laurence. One
reproached me with the extravagance of having attempted
a new form of symphony; another could find nothing in
the *scherzo* of Queen Mab but a little grotesque noise
like that of *an ill-greased syringe*. A third, speaking of
the love-scene—the *adagio*, the part that three-fourths of
the European musicians who know it now rank above all
I have written—asserted that *I had not understood
Shakespeare*! Toad, swelling with folly! if you could
prove that to me!

No unlooked-for criticisms ever wounded me more
cruelly; and, as usual, none of these aristarchs writing
in praise or blame of my work pointed out one of its
real defects. They left me to discover them in succession,
and correct them for myself. M. Frankoski, Ernst's
secretary at Vienna, remarked on the abrupt ending to

the Queen Mab *scherzo*, and I therefore wrote its present *coda*, and destroyed the former one. I think it was by the advice of M. d'Ortigue that an important erasure was made in the recitative of Father Laurence, which suffered from the exaggerated length of the verses supplied by the poet. All the other modifications, additions, and suppressions I made of my own accord, by dint of studying the work, both as a whole and in detail, as I heard it in Paris, Berlin, Vienna, and Prague. If I have struck out no more blemishes, at least I have looked for them in all good faith, and applied such sagacity as I possess to their discovery.

After that, what is left to an author but to avow frankly that he cannot do better, and resign himself to the imperfection of his work? When I had come to that, and not till then, was the symphony of *Romeo and Juliet* published.

As regards execution, it presents immense difficulties of all sorts inherent to its form and style, and only to be overcome by long, patient, and *well-directed* study. To interpret it properly first-rate conductors and artists, instrumentalists and singers are wanted, prepared to study it as a new opera is studied in good lyrical theatres, that is to say, very nearly as though it were to be played by heart.

It will never, therefore, be played in London, where the necessary rehearsals are not to be had. In that country, musicians have no time to make music.[1]

---

[1] Since the above was written, the first four parts of *Romeo and Juliet* were played under my direction in London, and never received a more brilliant ovation from any public. [They have since been played at the Philharmonic, Crystal Palace, Mr. Ganz's Concerts, and elsewhere.]

CHAPTER L.

In 1840, as the month of July drew near, the French Government was desirous of celebrating the tenth anniversary of the Revolution of 1830 by a grand ceremonial, and by the translation of the more or less heroic relics of the Three Days to the monument lately erected to their memory in the Place de la Bastille. M. de Rémusat, at that time Minister of the Interior, was, most fortunately, like M. de Gasparin, a friend to music. It was his idea that I should write a symphony for the ceremonial, the form and mode of performance being left entirely to my own choice. For this work the sum of ten thousand francs was guaranteed me, out of which I was to pay the expenses of copying and performance.

I thought that the simplest plan would be best for such a work, and that a large body of wind instruments would alone be suitable for a symphony which was—at least on the first occasion—to be heard in the open air. I wished in the first place to recall the famous Three Days' conflict amid the mournful accents of a solemn march accompanying the procession; to follow this by a sort of funeral oration, or farewell address to the illustrious dead, while the bodies were being lowered into the tomb and finally to sing a hymn of praise as an apotheosis, when, after the sealing of the tomb, the attention should be concentrated on the column alone, surmounted by the figure of Liberty, with her wings outstretched to heaven, like the souls of those who had died for her.

Scarcely had I finished the funeral march when it was rumoured that the July ceremonies were not to take place. "Good!" said I to myself; "here is the counter-part of the Requiem business. I know the people I have to deal with, and will go no further." And I stopped short accordingly. But a few days after, as I was strolling about Paris, I came across M. de Rémusat. On catching sight of me he stopped his carriage, and made me a sign to speak to him. He wanted to know how far I had proceeded with the symphony. I bluntly told him my reason for having suspended my work, adding that I well remembered my torments over Marshal Damrémont's ceremony and the Requiem.

"But the rumour that has alarmed you is entirely false," he answered. "Nothing has been changed; the inauguration of the column and the translation of the relics are all to take place; and I reckon upon you. Finish your work as quickly as possible."

This assertion relieved my anxiety, although my mistrust had been but too well founded, and I at once set to work again. When I had finished the march and funeral oration, and found a theme for the apotheosis, I was delayed for some time by the fanfare of trumpets. I wished to bring this up by degrees from the bass to the high note where the apotheosis breaks in. I don't know how many I wrote, but I liked none of them. Either they were too common, or too narrow in form, or

not sufficiently solemn, or wanting in sonority, or ill-
modulated. What I imagined was a sound like the trump
of an archangel, simple but noble, ascending radiant and
triumphant and grandly resonant, as it announced to earth
and heaven the opening of the empyrean gates. Finally, I
decided, not without some trepidation, on the one now in
the score ; and the rest was soon written. Later on, after

my usual corrections and alterations, I added a stringed
orchestra to the symphony, and a chorus, which greatly
improves the effect, though neither of them is indispensable. I engaged a military band of two hundred for
the ceremony. Habeneck would willingly have conducted
again, but I had not forgotten the snuffbox trick, and
wisely reserved that task to myself.

I had the happy idea of inviting a large audience to the
general rehearsal of the symphony, for no one could have
judged of it on the day of the ceremony. Notwithstanding the power of the orchestra, it was scarcely heard
at all during the procession. With the exception of what

was played as we went along the Boulevard Poissonnière, where the big trees—still standing—served as a kind of reflector for the sound, all the rest was lost. On the Place de la Bastille it was still worse; scarcely anything could be distinguished even ten paces off.

As a finishing stroke, the National Guard, impatient at having to stand so long under arms in the burning sun, began to march off to the sound of fifty drums, which continued to beat relentlessly throughout the whole of the apotheosis, so that not one note of it could be heard. Music is always thus respected in France at all *fêtes* or public rejoicings, where they think it ought to figure . . . to the eye.

But I know this, and the general rehearsal in the Salle Vivienne was my real performance. Such was its effect that the man who managed the concerts there engaged me for four evenings; the new symphony had the place of honour each time, and the receipts were considerable.

On coming out from one of these performances, Habeneck—with whom for some reason or other I had had a fresh quarrel—was heard to say, "Decidedly that beast of a fellow has some grand ideas." A week later he probably said just the contrary.

This time I had no crow to pluck with the Ministry. M. de Rémusat behaved like a gentleman, and promptly sent me the ten thousand francs. When the expenses of the orchestra and copyists were paid, I had two thousand eight hundred francs[1] left for myself. Little enough certainly, but the Minister was pleased; and at each performance of my new work the public seemed to appreciate it beyond any of its predecessors, and indeed praised it extravagantly. One evening, at the Salle

---

[1] [Just over a hundred pounds.]

Vivienne, some young fellows took it into their heads to smash the chairs against the floor, with shouts of applause. The proprietor immediately gave orders that for the future this novel method of applauding was to be checked. Spontini wrote me a long and curious letter on the subject of this symphony, when it was performed some time afterwards at the Conservatoire with the two orchestras, but without the chorus. I was stupid enough to give it to a collector of autographs, and much regret that I cannot produce a copy here. I only know that it began somewhat as follows : " *Whilst still under the impression of your thrilling music*," etc. etc.

Notwithstanding our friendship, this was the only time he ever praised any of my compositions. He always came to hear them, but never spoke of them to me. I am wrong ! He did so once more, after a great performance of my Requiem at St. Eustache. He said to me that day : " You were wrong to blame the Institute for sending its prizemen to Rome ; you never could have composed that Requiem unless you had seen Michael Angelo's *Last Judgment*." [1]

In this he was strangely mistaken, for the only effect produced on me by that celebrated fresco in the Sistine Chapel was that of utter disappointment. To me it is a scene of infernal tortures rather than the last great gathering of all mankind. But I know nothing of painting, and am not susceptible to conventional beauty.

[1] [A most characteristic utterance of this master of bombast. It forms a good companion to the words which he addressed to Felix Mendelssohn during the rehearsals of his *Wedding of Camacho*. Spontini led the lad to the window of his library, and, pointing to a neighbouring dome, delivered himself of this oracular sentence : " Mon ami, il vous faut des idées grandes—grandes comme cette coupole ! "]

CHAPTER LI.

IT was towards the end of this year (1840) that I made
my first musical excursion out of France; in other words,
began giving concerts in foreign parts. M. Snel, of
Brussels, having proposed to perform some of my works
in the concert-room of the Society of La Grande Harmonie,
of which he was the head, I determined to make the
experiment.

But in order to manage this, I had to have recourse to
a regular *coup d'état* in my own home. On one pretext
or another, my wife had always been opposed to my
travelling, and had I listened to her I should never
have left Paris to this hour. A mad, and for some time
an absolutely groundless, jealousy was at the bottom of
her opposition. In order, therefore, to carry out my
plan, I was obliged to keep it secret, have my port-
manteau and packages of music cunningly conveyed out
of the house, and go off suddenly, leaving a letter to
explain my departure. But I did not go alone. I had
a travelling companion, who always accompanied me
from that time forth on my various expeditions. By
dint of having been unjustly accused and tortured in a

thousand ways, and finding neither peace nor repose at home, I luckily ended by reaping the benefits of a position of which I had hitherto had only the burden, and my life was completely changed.

To cut short the story of this part of my life, and not to enter upon very sad details, I will only say that from that day forth, and after many heart-rending scenes, my wife and I were amicably separated. I often see her; my affection for her has been in no way diminished; her bad health only endears her to me. This must suffice to explain my subsequent conduct to such persons as have only known me since then, for, I repeat, I am not writing confessions.

I gave two concerts at Brussels, one in the concert-room of the Grande Harmonie, the other in the Church of the Augustines, where Catholic worship has long been abandoned. There is an extraordinary echo in both of them, so much so that, even when but slightly animated, instrumental music becomes necessarily confused in sound. Only slow and soft pieces, especially in the former room, are unaffected by the echo of the place, and preserve their original effect.

Opinion differed as widely about my music in Brussels as in Paris. A curious discussion took place between M. Fétis (always hostile to me) and another critic, M. Zani de Ferranti, an artist and a remarkable writer, who had declared himself my champion. The latter cited the *Pilgrims' March* in *Harold* as one of the most interesting things he had ever heard. To this Fétis replied, "How can I be expected to approve of a piece in which you constantly hear *two notes out of harmony?*" (He meant the two notes C and B, recurring at the end of each strophe, and imitating bells.)

"Upon my word," answered de Ferranti, "I don't believe in such an anomaly. But if a musician is capable of composing a piece like that, and of charming me throughout by two notes out of harmony, I say that he is not a man, but a god."

"Alas!" I might have answered the enthusiastic Italian, "I am but a simple man, and M. Fétis is but a poor musician, for the two famous notes are really always in harmony. M. Fétis has not noticed that, thanks to their intervening in the chord, the various keys terminating the different sections of the march are resolved back into the principal key, and that from a purely musical point of view this very fact constitutes the novelty of the march, about which no true musician could be mistaken for a moment.

When I heard of this curious misunderstanding I was tempted to point out Fétis's blunder in some newspaper; then I thought better of it, and followed my own system— a good one, I believe—of never answering any criticism,[1] no matter how absurd. When the score of *Harold* was published, some years later, M. Fétis could see for himself that the two notes were always in harmony.

This journey was only an experiment. I was planning a visit to Germany, to last five or six months. I therefore returned to Paris to make preparations, and give a colossal farewell concert to the Parisians that I had long been meditating.

M. Pillet, then manager of the Opéra, warmly welcomed my proposal of organising a festival[2] in the theatre. I

---

[1] [This was Mendelssohn's unalterable determination also.]

[2] This word, which I employed on the handbills for the first time in Paris, has become the commonplace title of the most grotesque exhibitions. We now have dancing or musical "festivals" in the smallest music-halls, with three violins, a drum, and a cornet-à-piston.

accordingly applied myself to the work, but allowed none of our plans to transpire. The difficulty consisted in forestalling Habeneck's hostilities.

He could not fail to object to my directing such a musical solemnity—the greatest yet seen in Paris—in a theatre where he was conductor. I therefore prepared all the music for the programme I had selected, secretly, engaged musicians without telling them where the concert was to take place; and when nothing was left but to unmask my batteries, I went to M. Pillet, and begged him to tell Habeneck that I was entrusted with the management of the festival. He could not, however, make up his mind to the annoyance of this step, and left it to me, so great was his terror of Habeneck. I wrote myself, therefore, to the awful conductor, informed him of the arrangements I had made with M. Pillet, and added that, being in the habit of conducting my own concerts, I trusted not to annoy him by doing so on this occasion.

He received my letter at the Opéra in the middle of a rehearsal, read and re-read it, walked gloomily about the stage for some time; then, making up his mind abruptly, went down to the manager's office, and declared that the arrangement suited him very well, as he was desirous of spending the day named for the concert in the country. His vexation, however, was visible, and many of his orchestra soon sympathised with it, hoping by this means to curry favour with him. I had arranged with M. Pillet that this orchestra should work under me, together with the extra musicians I had engaged.

The *soirée* was to be for the benefit of the manager of the Opéra, who only guaranteed me the sum of five hundred francs for my trouble, and gave me *carte blanche* about the organisation. Habeneck's musicians were bound in consequence to take part in this performance without remuneration. But I recollected the rascals at the Théâtre Italien, and the trick they had then played me ; indeed, my position with regard to the Opéra artists was at this time still more critical. Every evening I witnessed the cabals in the orchestra during the *entr'actes*, the universal agitation, the cold impassibility of Habeneck and his incensed body-guard, the furious glances cast at me, and the distribution of certain numbers of *Le Charivari*, in which I was well cut up. Accordingly, when the grand rehearsals were to begin, seeing the storm increasing, and hearing that some of Habeneck's fanatics had declared they would not march *without their old general*, I tried to induce M. Pillet to pay the Opéra musicians with the others. On his refusal I said to him, " I understand and approve of your motives for refusing; but in this case you are spoiling the performance of the concert. Consequently, I shall apply the five hundred francs you allot me to the payment of those Opéra musicians who do not refuse to help us."

" What ! " said M. Pillet ; " you will have nothing for yourself, after wearing yourself out with the work."

" That matters little ; the chief thing is that it should go off properly. My five hundred francs will quiet the least mutinous ; as for the others, pray do not force them into doing their duty, but let us leave them to *their old general*."

So it was arranged. I had a *personnel* of six hundred performers, choral and instrumental. The programme consisted of the first act of Gluck's *Iphigénie en Tauride*, a scene out of Handel's *Athalie*, the *Dies Iræ* and the *Lacrymosa* from my Requiem, the apotheosis out

of my *Symphonie Funèbre et Triomphale*, the *adagio,
scherzo,* and *finale* in *Romeo and Juliet* and an unaccompanied chorus of Palestrina's. I cannot imagine now
how I succeeded in having such a difficult programme
learnt so quickly (in one week only) by such a scratch
pack of musicians. And yet I did manage it. I ran
from the Opera-house to the Théâtre Italien, where I
had engaged the chorus only, from the Théâtre Italien
to the Opéra Comique and Conservatoire; here directing
a choral practice, and there drilling part of the orchestra;
seeing to everything myself, and trusting to no one else.
In the lobby at the Opera-house I finally took both my
instrumental bodies by turns, the strings rehearsing from
eight in the morning till noon, and the wind instruments from noon till four o'clock. In this manner
I was on my feet, baton in hand, the whole day. My
throat was on fire, my voice nearly extinct, my right arm
almost broken. I was ready to faint from thirst and
weariness, when one of the chorus was kind enough to
bring me a large tumbler of hot wine, and this enabled
me to finish this awful rehearsal.

It had been rendered still harder, moreover, by fresh
demands on the part of the Opéra musicians. Those
gentlemen, hearing that I was giving twenty francs to
certain extra players, thought themselves entitled to
interrupt me, one after the other, with a demand for
a similar payment.

"It is not the money," said they; "but the Opéra
artists ought not to get less than those at the second-rate
theatres."

"Well, well, you shall have your twenty francs," I
answered. "I guarantee them; but for God's sake do
your work, and leave me alone."

The next day was the general rehearsal on the stage —pretty satisfactory. All went fairly well, with the exception of the Queen Mab *scherzo*, which I had imprudently included in the programme. This piece is too rapid and delicate to be played by a large orchestra. In such a case, and with so short a bar, it is nearly impossible to keep all the instruments together. They occupy too large a space; and those who are farthest from the conductor soon lag behind, since they are unable exactly to follow his rapid rhythm. Fretted as I was, it never entered my head to form a little picked orchestra, which I could have grouped round me in the middle of the stage, and so have easily carried out my purpose. Accordingly, after incredible trouble, we had to give up the *scherzo*, and strike it out of the programme. It was on this occasion that I remarked how impossible it was to prevent the little cymbals in B flat and F from dragging, when placed too far away from the conductor. I had stupidly put them at the end of the stage, beside the kettle-drums; and in spite of all my efforts they were sometimes a whole bar behindhand. Since then I have always taken care to have them beside me, and the difficulty has vanished.

The next day I was counting on a little rest, at least until the evening, when a friend[1] forewarned me of certain plots on the part of Habeneck's partisans for ruining my enterprise either wholly or partially. He wrote me word that they intended to slit the kettle-drums, grease the double-bass bows, and call for the *Marseillaise* in the middle of the concert.

This warning, as may be imagined, troubled my much needed repose. Instead of spending the day in bed, I

[1] Leon Gatayes.

began to wander about the approaches to the Opéra in a perfect fever of agitation. As I was thus panting up and down the boulevard, by good luck I came across Habeneck himself in person. I ran up, and took him by the arm. " I have been warned," I said, " that your musicians are engaged in plots to ruin me this evening; but I have my eye on them."

" Oh," replied the good saint, " there is nothing to be afraid of. They won't do anything. I have made them listen to reason."

" Zounds! it is not I that need to be reassured, but rather you, for if anything were to happen, it would rebound pretty heavily upon you. But never mind; as you say, they won't do anything."

Still I was very anxious as the hour for the concert drew near. I had placed my copyist in the orchestra during the day to guard the kettle-drums and double-basses. Those instruments were intact. But this is what I feared. In the great pieces of the Requiem, the four little brass orchestras contained trumpets and cornets in different keys (in B flat, in F, and E flat). Well, it must be understood ·that the crook of a trumpet in F, for example, differs but slightly from that of a trumpet in E flat, and it is very easy to confound them. Some treacherous brother might therefore hurl a trumpet-note in F into the *Tuba mirum* for me, instead of one in E flat, counting on excusing himself, after having produced an atrocious cacophony, by saying that he had mistaken his key.

Just before beginning the *Dies Iræ* I left my desk, and, going all round the orchestra, requested each trumpet and cornet player to show me his instrument. I thus reviewed them all, closely examining the inscriptions of the various keys, F, E flat, and B. When I came to the brothers Dauverné, Opéra musicians both of them, the elder made me blush by saying: "Oh, Berlioz, you don't trust us; that is not nice. We are honest men, and we are your friends." This reproach embarrassed me, though I might well be excused for having incurred it; and I pushed my inquiries no farther.

My brave trumpeters made no mistakes, nothing was wanting in the performance, and the Requiem pieces had their proper effect.

Immediately after this part of the concert came an interval. It was during that moment's breathing space that Habeneck's followers thought to strike their blow in the easiest and least dangerous manner. Several voices were heard crying, "*The Marseillaise! the Marseillaise!*" hoping thus to carry away the public, and disturb the whole arrangement of the evening. A certain number of the spectators, charmed at the idea of hearing this celebrated air performed by such an orchestra and chorus, were already joining in the cry, when I went forward to the front of the stage, and said at the very top of my voice: "We will not play the *Marseillaise.* We are not here for that!" At which peace was at once restored.

It was not, however, to be of long duration. Another incident, of which I had had no warning, occurred almost immediately after, and still further excited the house. Cries of "Murder! Shame! shame! Police!" proceeded from the first gallery, and created a perfect tumult among everyone present. Madame de Girardin, all dishevelled and agitated, was calling for help from her box. Her husband had just been struck at her side by Bergeron, one of the editors of the *Charivari*, who was reputed to be the first assassin of Louis Philippe—the same man whom public opinion had accused of having fired a pistol at the King some years before, on the Pont

Royal. This *esclandre* could not but spoil the rest of the concert, which, however, passed off without further interruption, though amidst a universal preoccupation.

But, be that as it may, I had solved the problem, and checkmated my enemies. The receipts amounted to eight thousand five hundred francs. As the sum I had devoted to pay the Opéra musicians was not sufficient, owing to my having promised them each twenty francs, I was obliged to give the cashier of the theatre three hundred and sixty francs, which he entered in his book with these words in red ink, " *Surplus given by M. Berlioz.*"

Thus, entirely unassisted, I succeeded in organising the greatest concert yet given in Paris—Habeneck and his people notwithstanding—by sacrificing the moderate sum allotted to me. The receipts, as I said, came to eight thousand five hundred francs, and my trouble cost me three hundred and sixty. Thus are fortunes made! I have often done the same in my life, and so I have made mine! . . . I never could comprehend how a gentleman like M. Pillet could have suffered it! Perhaps the cashier did not tell him of the circumstance.

A few days later I went off to Germany. In the letters which I addressed on my return to several of my friends (and even to two [1] who cannot claim that title), my adventures and observations on this first journey may be read. True, it was a laborious expedition, but, at any rate, it was a musical one, tolerably advantageous from a pecuniary point of view, and I enjoyed the pleasure of living in a sympathetic atmosphere, out of reach of the intrigue, the meanness, and the insipidity of Paris.

[1] Habeneck and Girard.

END OF VOL. I.

CHARLES DICKENS AND EVANS CRYSTAL PALACE PRESS.